A BRIDE'S STORY

1

Kaoru Mori

TABLE OF
CONTENTS

✦ Chapter One ✦

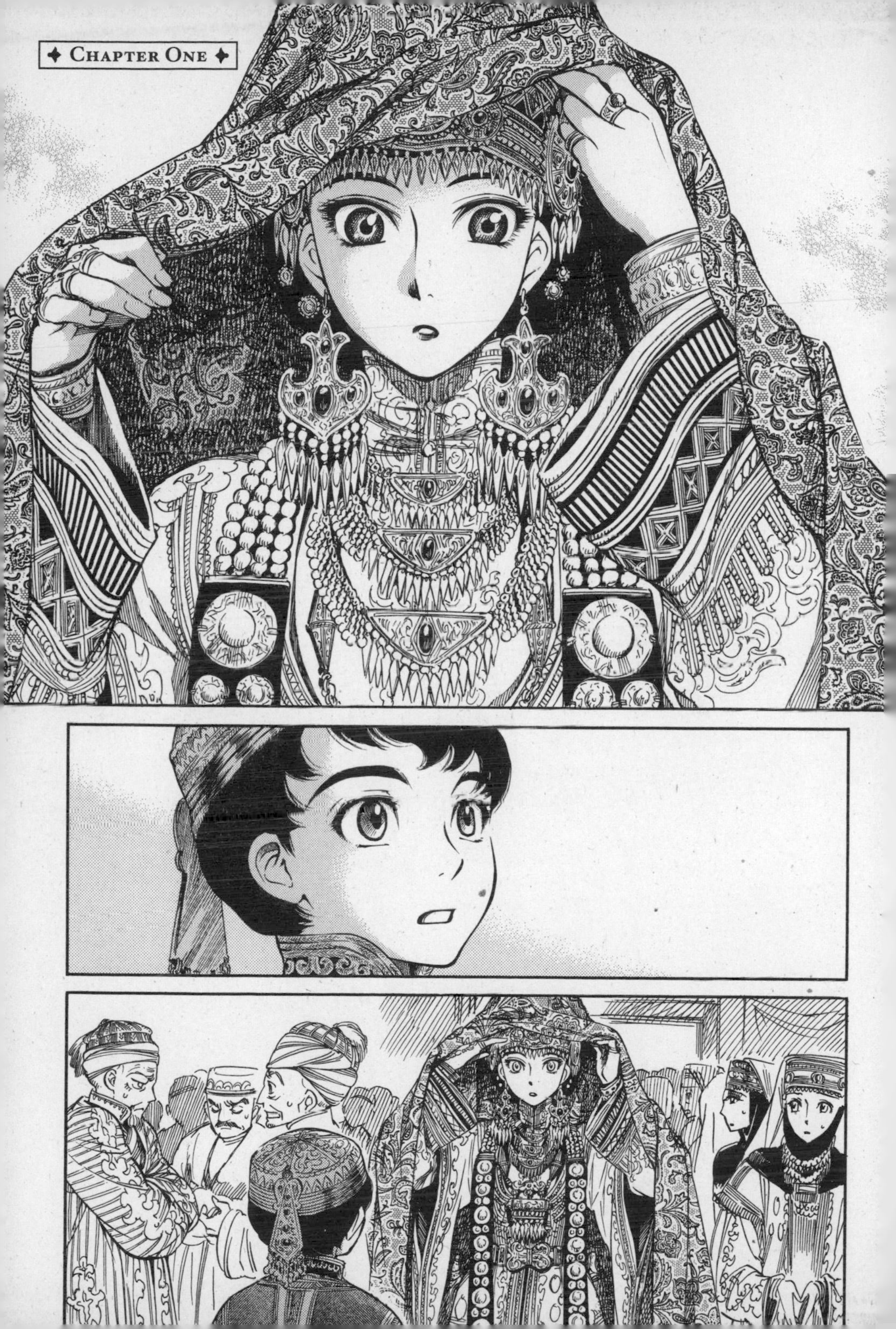

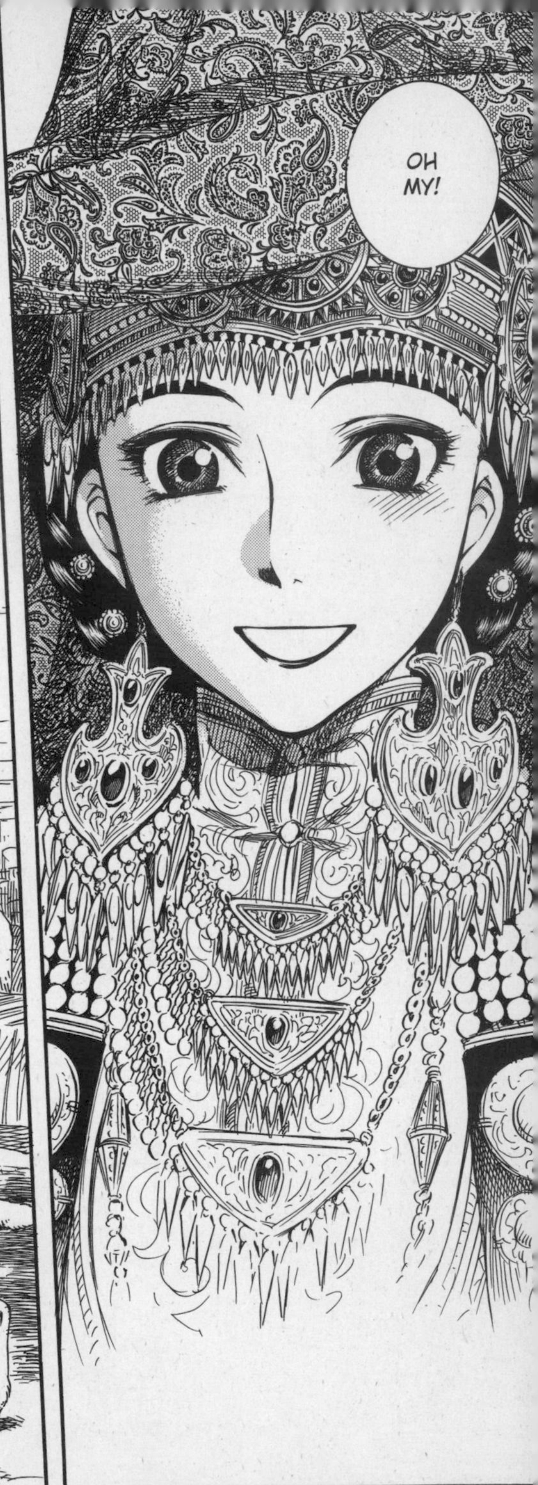
OH MY!
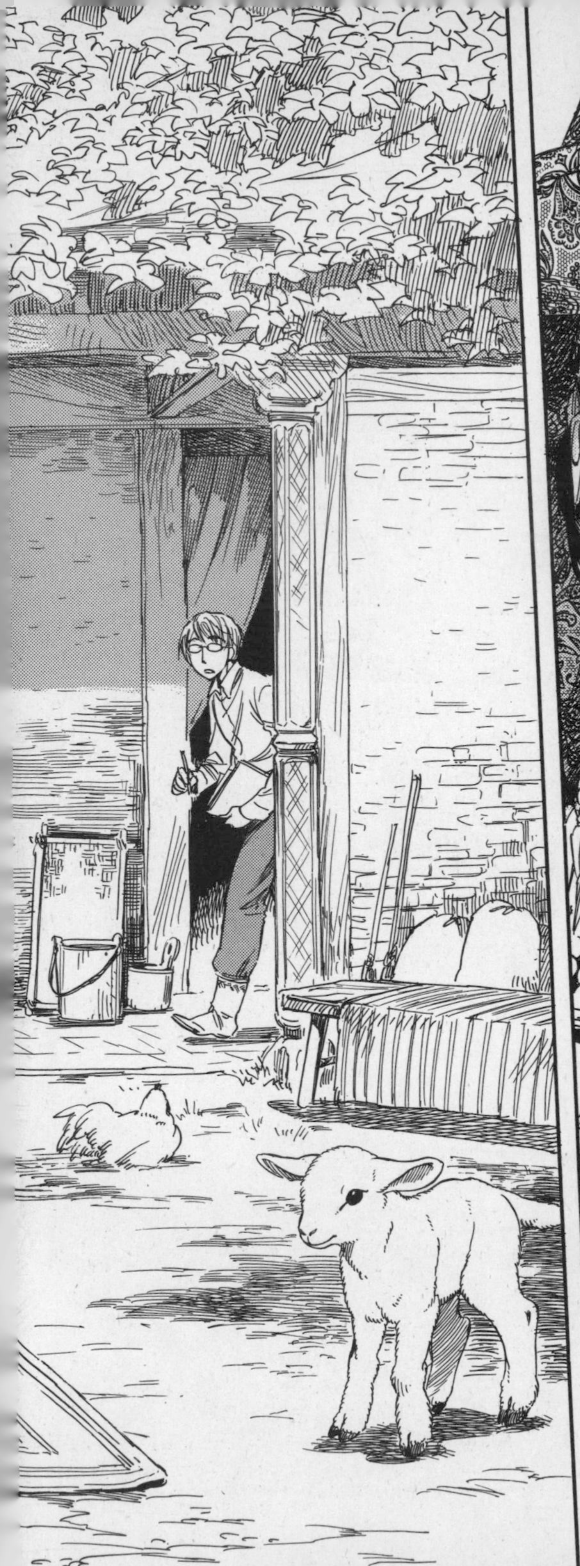

Chapter One
The Bride and Her Young Groom

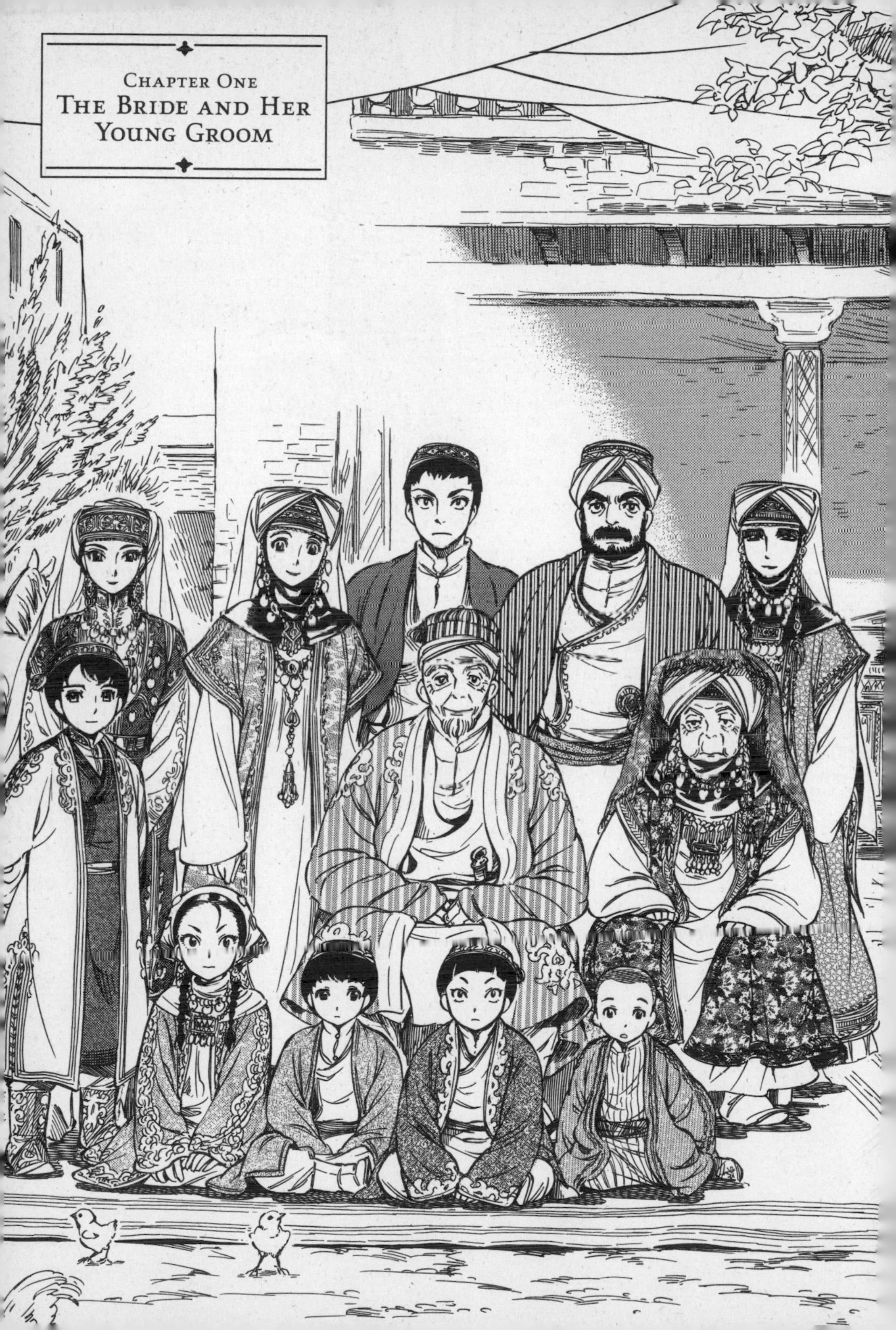

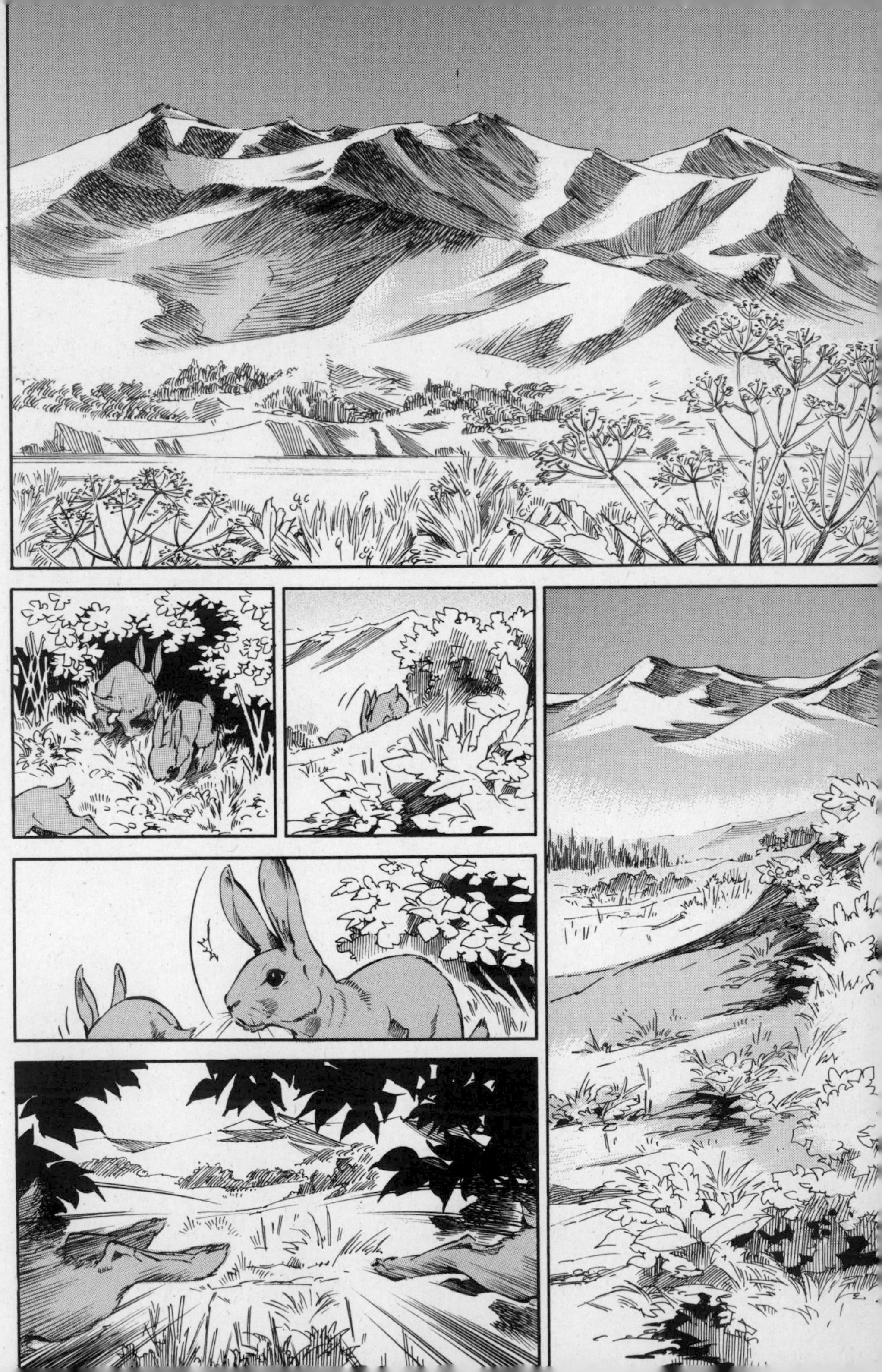

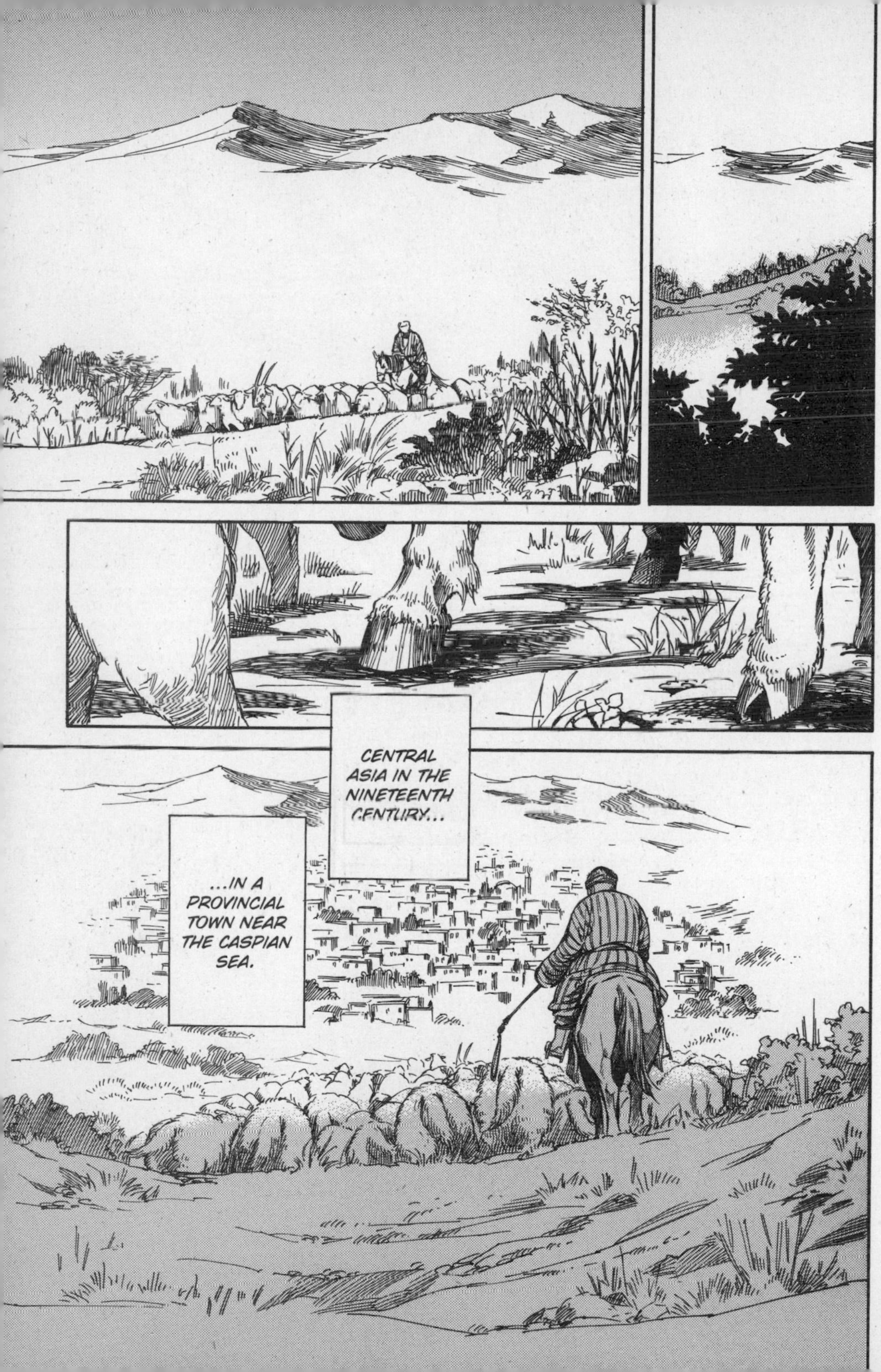
CENTRAL ASIA IN THE NINETEENTH CENTURY...
...IN A PROVINCIAL TOWN NEAR THE CASPIAN SEA.

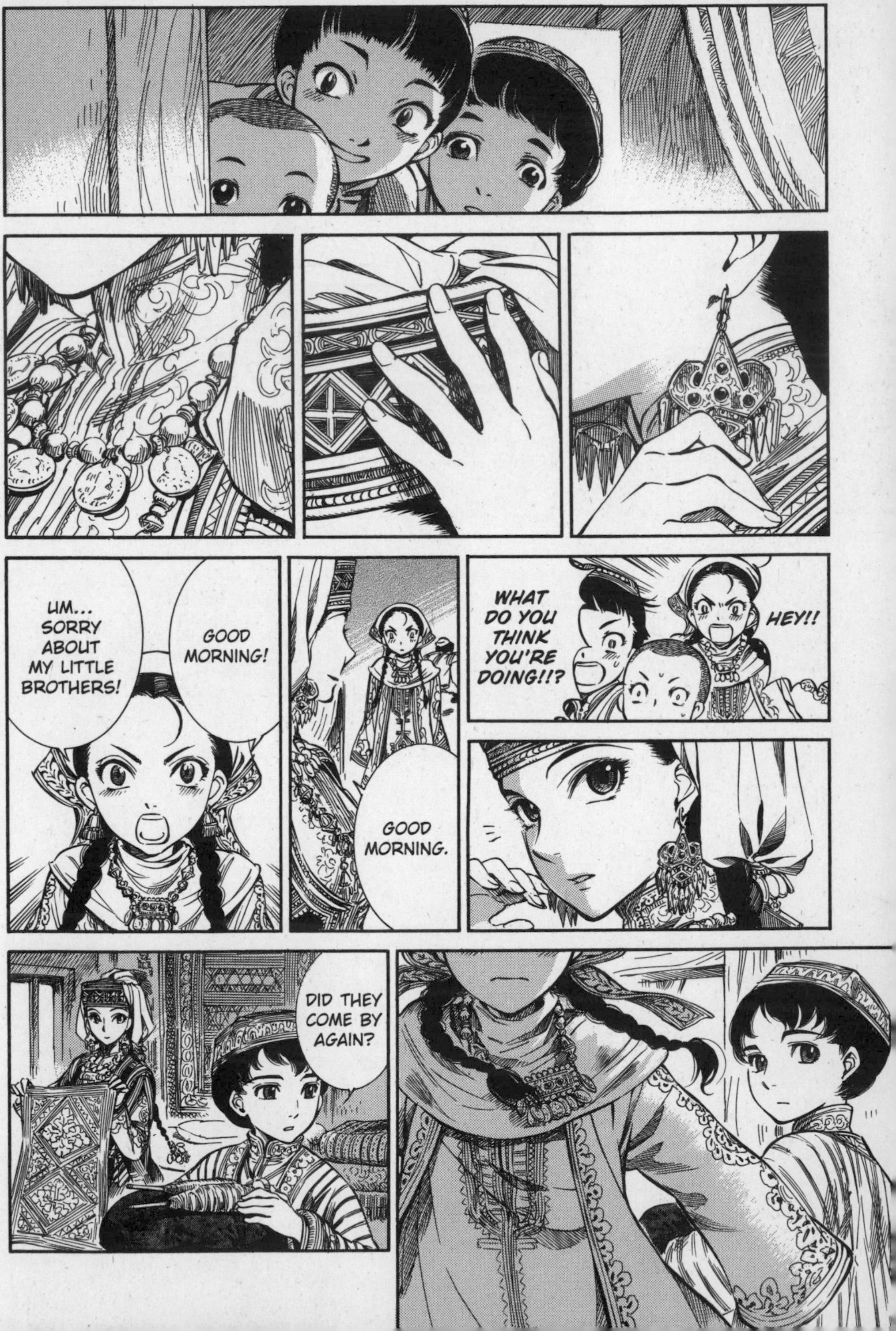
HEY!!
WHAT DO YOU THINK YOU'RE DOING!!?
GOOD MORNING.
GOOD MORNING!
UM... SORRY ABOUT MY LITTLE BROTHERS!
DID THEY COME BY AGAIN?

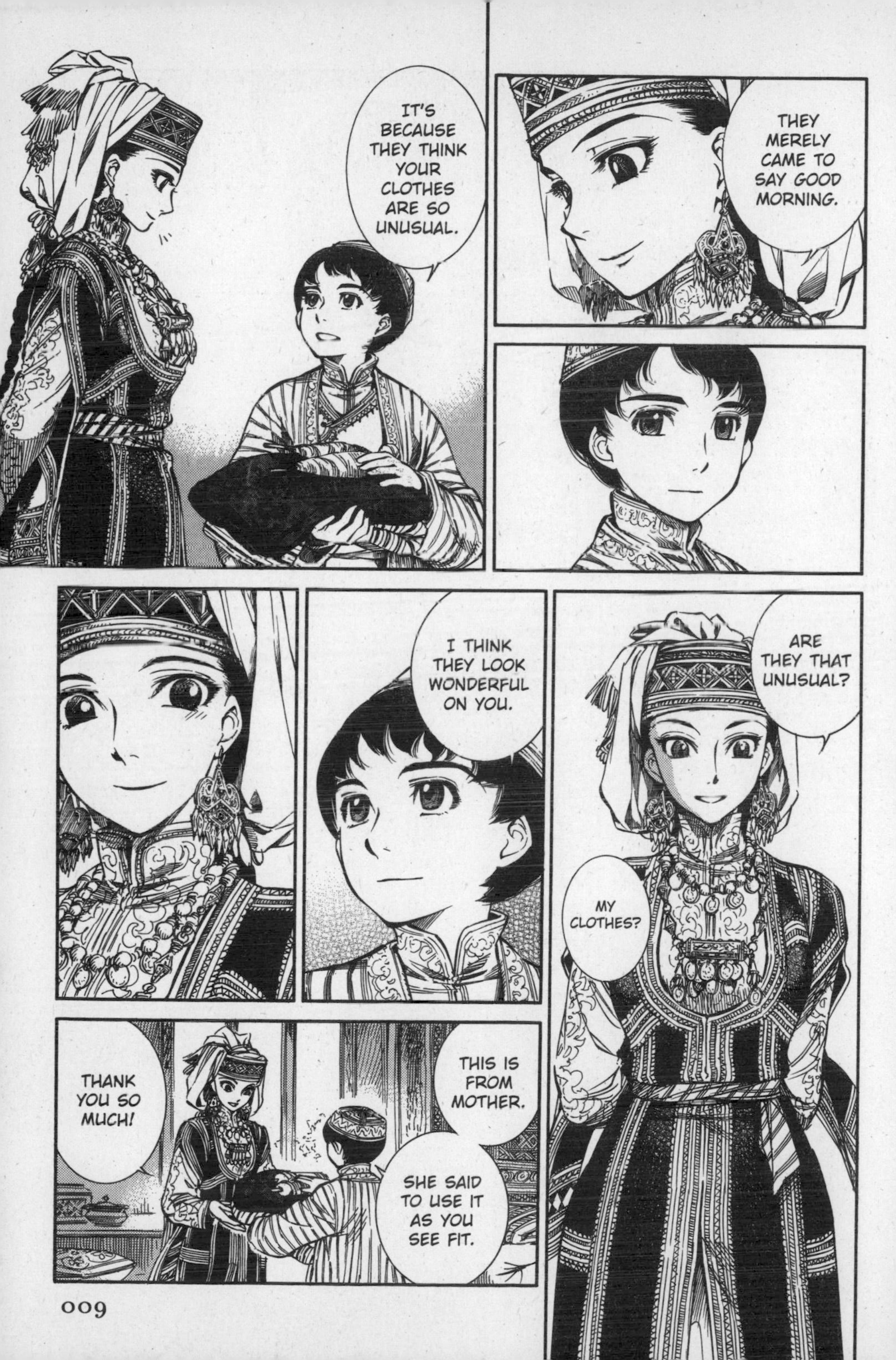
THEY MERELY CAME TO SAY GOOD MORNING.
IT'S BECAUSE THEY THINK YOUR CLOTHES ARE SO UNUSUAL.
ARE THEY THAT UNUSUAL?
MY CLOTHES?
I THINK THEY LOOK WONDERFUL ON YOU.
THIS IS FROM MOTHER.
SHE SAID TO USE IT AS YOU SEE FIT.
THANK YOU SO MUCH!

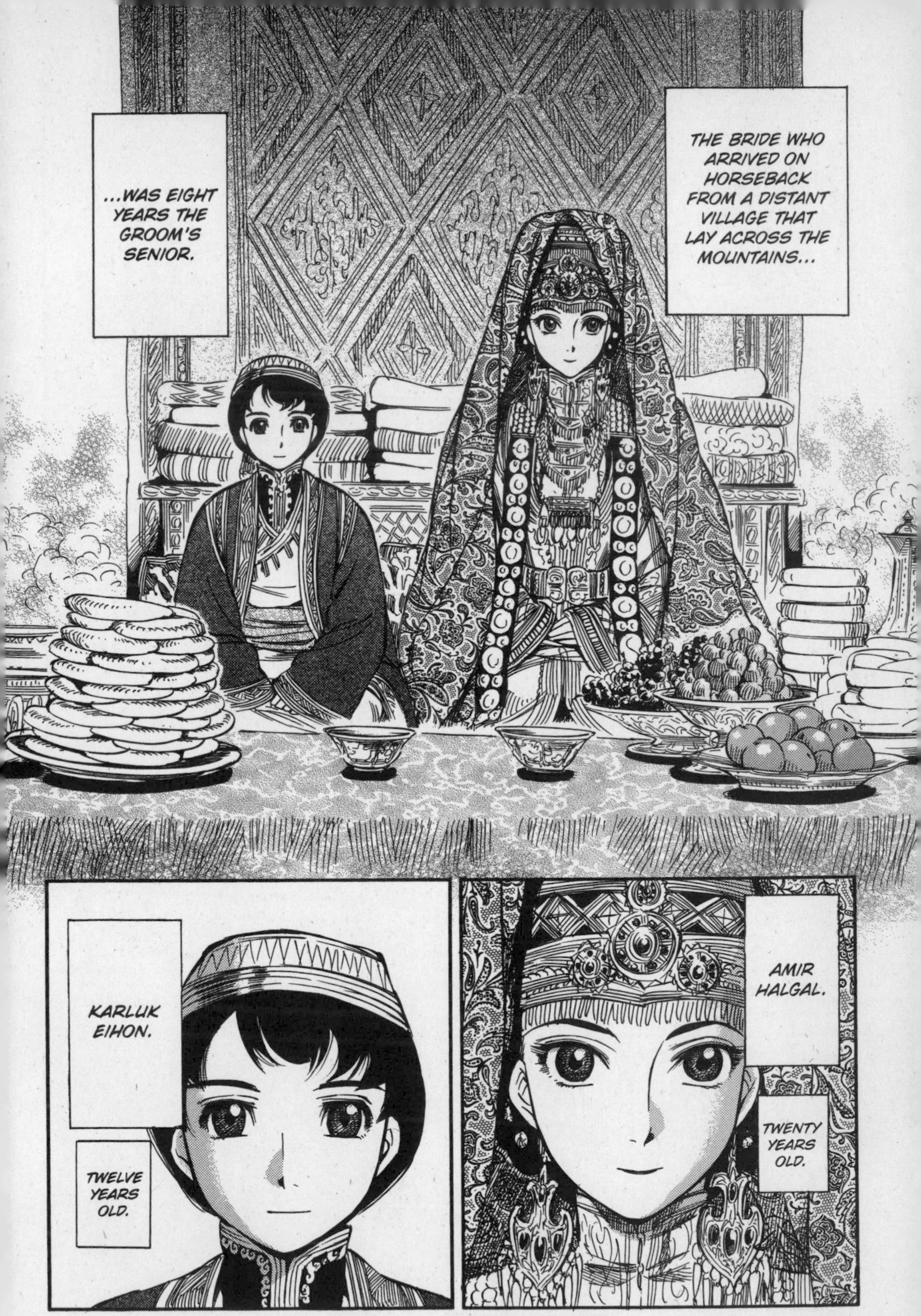
THE BRIDE WHO ARRIVED ON HORSEBACK FROM A DISTANT VILLAGE THAT LAY ACROSS THE MOUNTAINS...
...WAS EIGHT YEARS THE GROOM'S SENIOR.
AMIR HALGAL.
TWENTY YEARS OLD.
KARLUK EIHON.
TWELVE YEARS OLD.

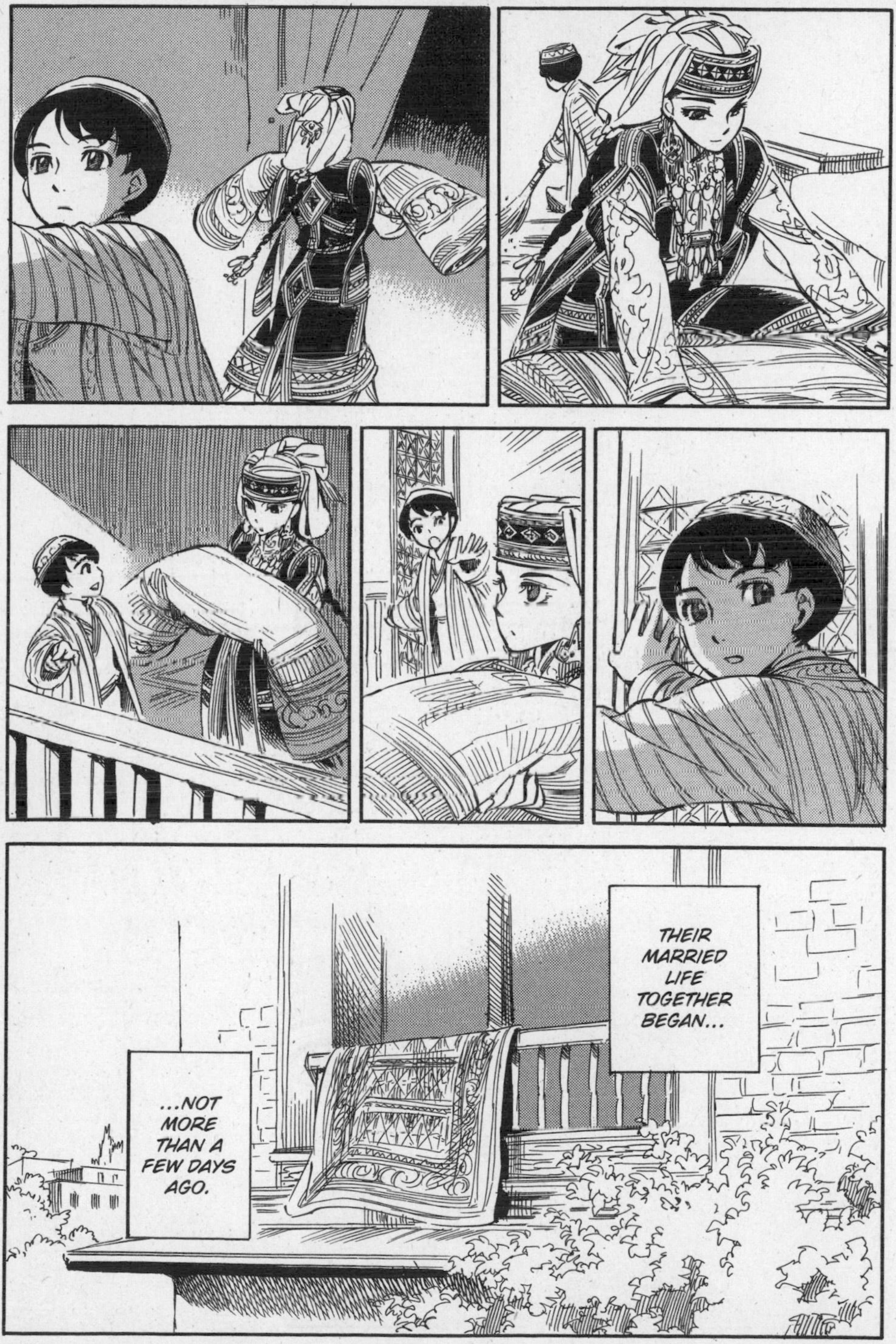
THEIR MARRIED LIFE TOGETHER BEGAN...
...NOT MORE THAN A FEW DAYS AGO.

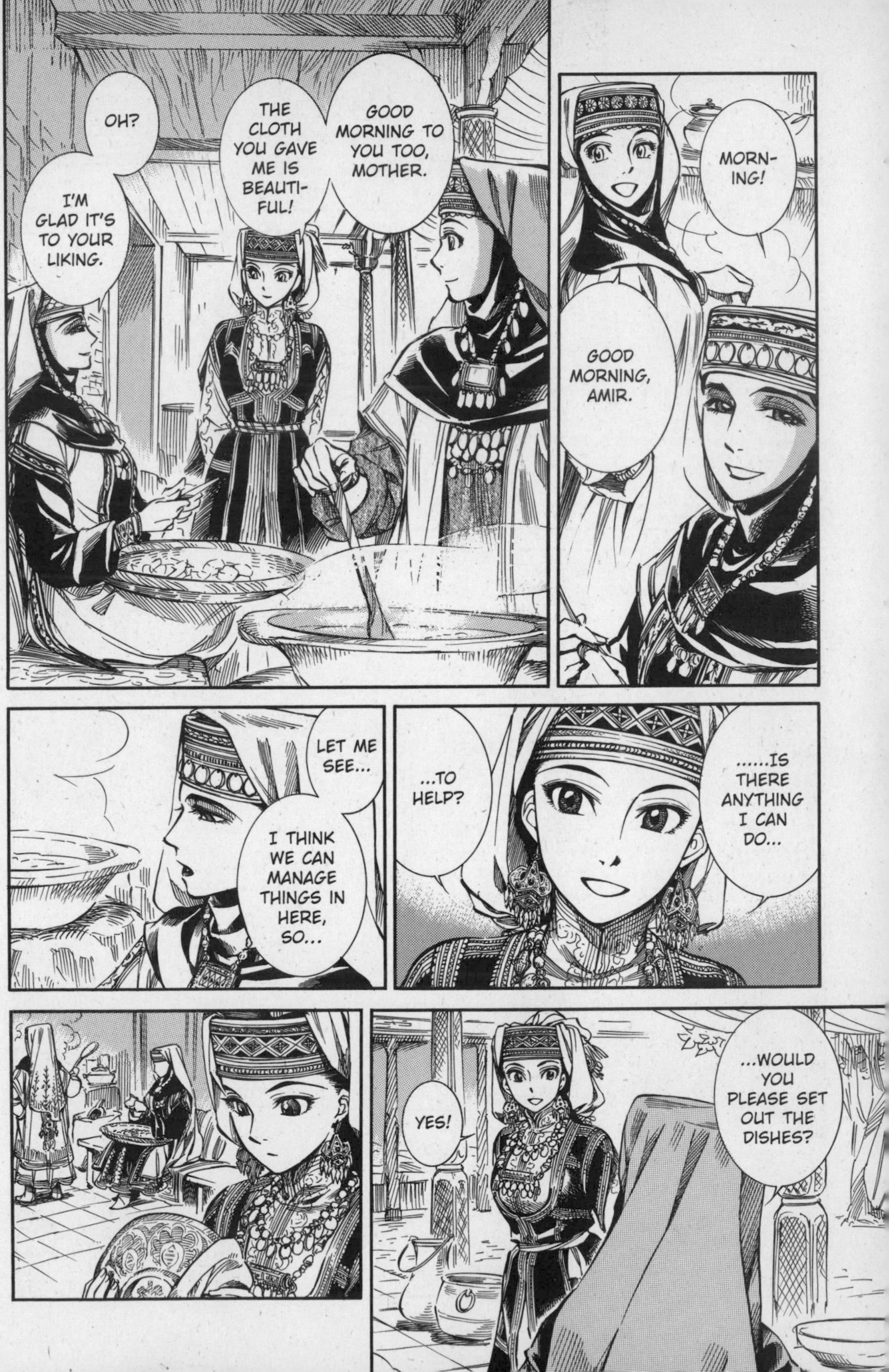
MORNING!
GOOD MORNING, AMIR.
GOOD MORNING TO YOU TOO, MOTHER.
THE CLOTH YOU GAVE ME IS BEAUTIFUL!
OH?
I'M GLAD IT'S TO YOUR LIKING.
......IS THERE ANYTHING I CAN DO...
...TO HELP?
LET ME SEE...
I THINK WE CAN MANAGE THINGS IN HERE, SO...
...WOULD YOU PLEASE SET OUT THE DISHES?
YES!

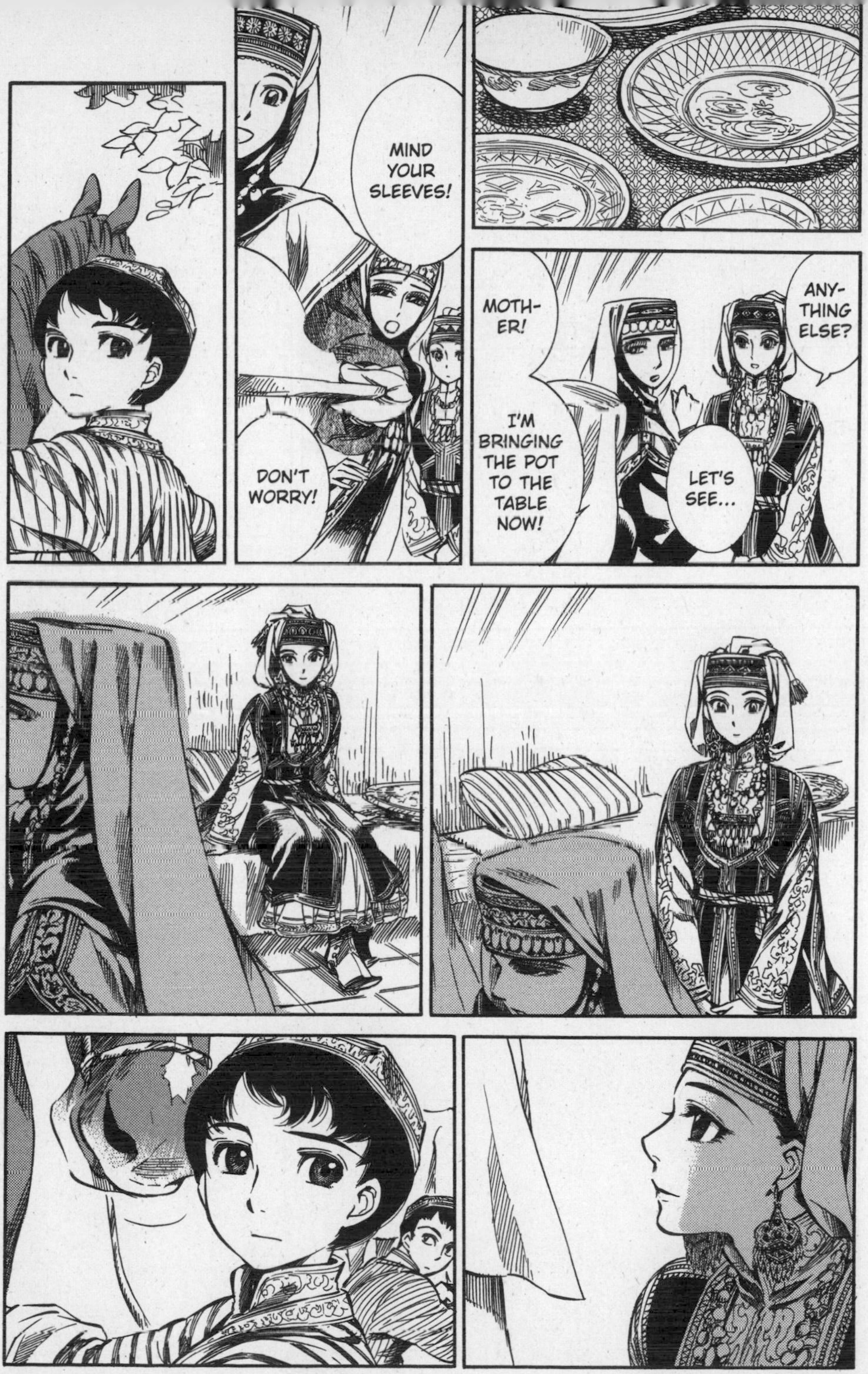
ANY-
THING
ELSE?
MOTH-
ER!
LET'S
SEE...
I'M
BRINGING
THE POT
TO THE
TABLE
NOW!
MIND
YOUR
SLEEVES!
DON'T
WORRY!

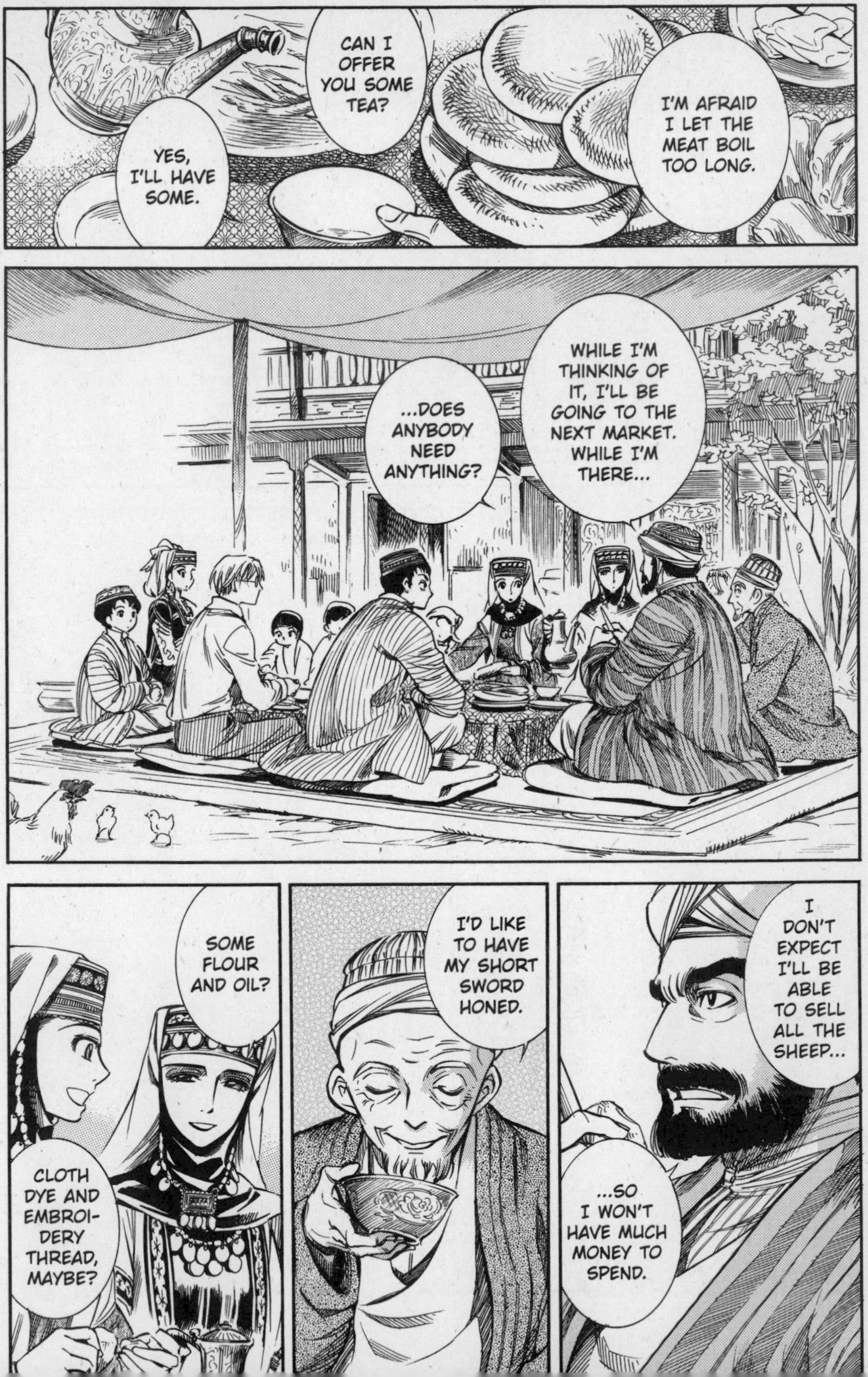
I'M AFRAID I LET THE MEAT BOIL TOO LONG.
CAN I OFFER YOU SOME TEA?
YES, I'LL HAVE SOME.
WHILE I'M THINKING OF IT, I'LL BE GOING TO THE NEXT MARKET. WHILE I'M THERE...
...DOES ANYBODY NEED ANYTHING?
I DON'T EXPECT I'LL BE ABLE TO SELL ALL THE SHEEP...
...SO I WON'T HAVE MUCH MONEY TO SPEND.
I'D LIKE TO HAVE MY SHORT SWORD HONED.
SOME FLOUR AND OIL?
CLOTH DYE AND EMBROIDERY THREAD, MAYBE?

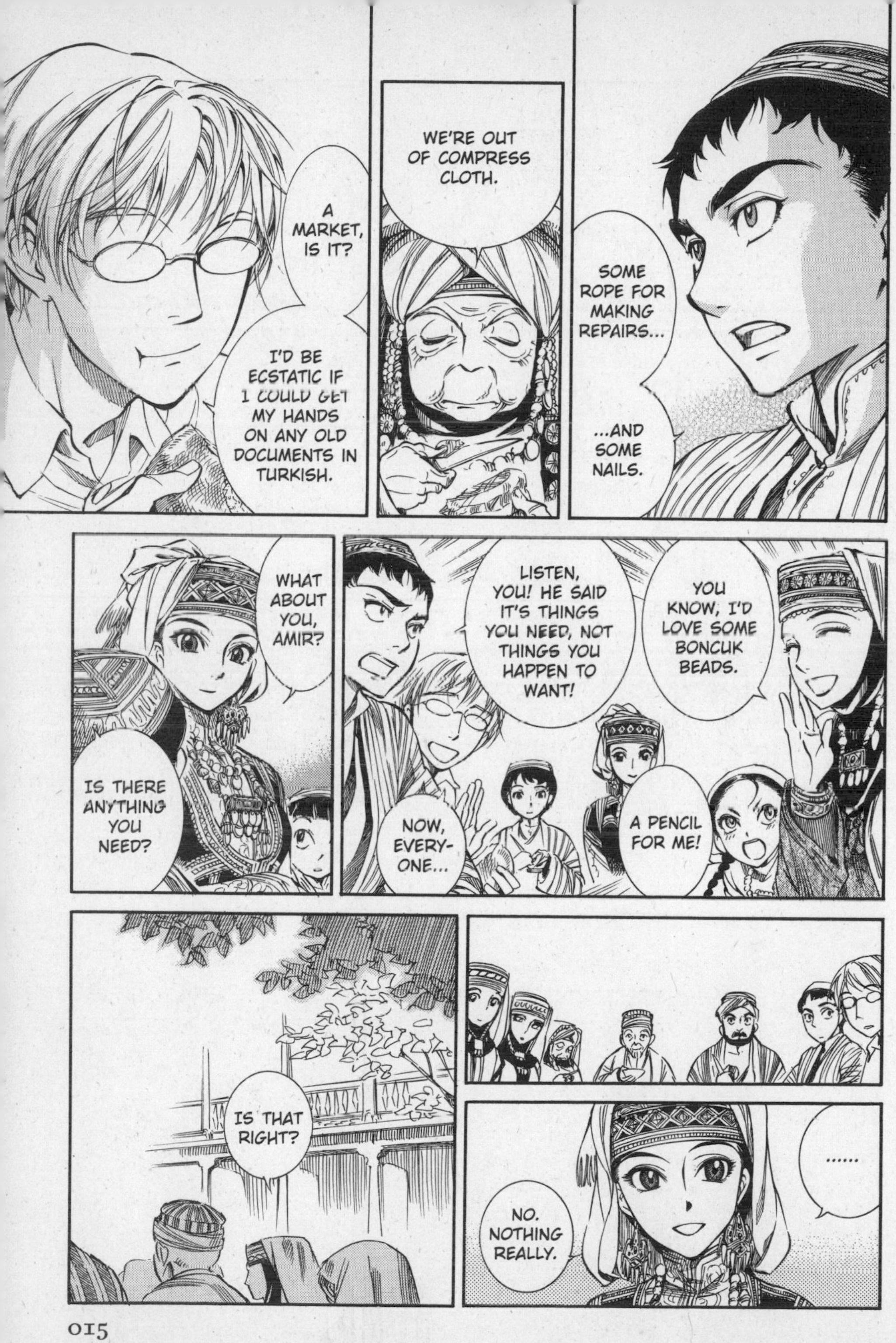
SOME ROPE FOR MAKING REPAIRS...
...AND SOME NAILS.
WE'RE OUT OF COMPRESS CLOTH.
A MARKET, IS IT?
I'D BE ECSTATIC IF I COULD GET MY HANDS ON ANY OLD DOCUMENTS IN TURKISH.
YOU KNOW, I'D LOVE SOME BONCUK BEADS.
LISTEN, YOU! HE SAID IT'S THINGS YOU NEED, NOT THINGS YOU HAPPEN TO WANT!
A PENCIL FOR ME!
NOW, EVERY-ONE...
WHAT ABOUT YOU, AMIR?
IS THERE ANYTHING YOU NEED?
......
NO. NOTHING REALLY.
IS THAT RIGHT?

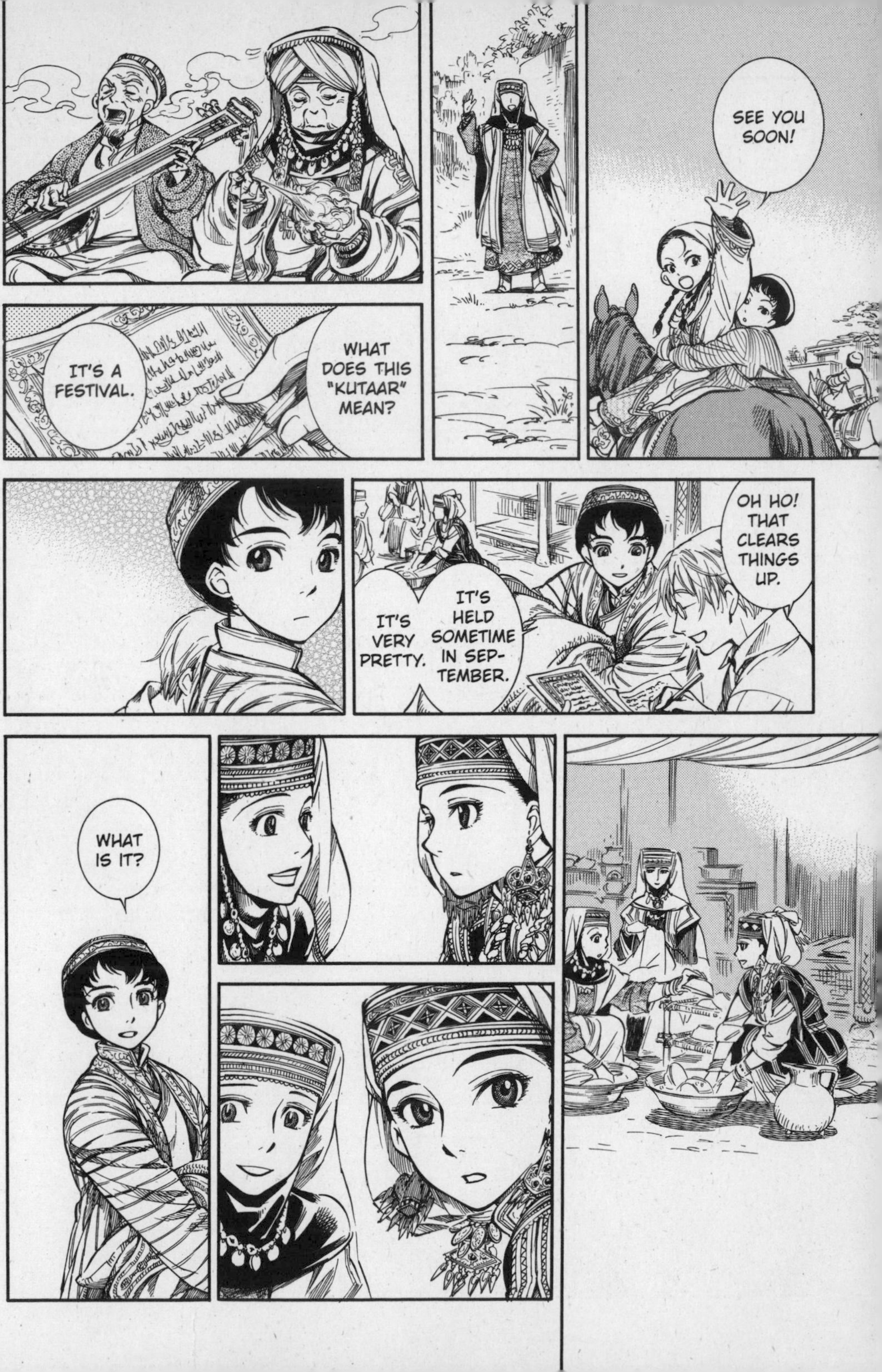
SEE YOU SOON!
WHAT DOES THIS "KUTAAR" MEAN?
IT'S A FESTIVAL.
OH HO! THAT CLEARS THINGS UP.
IT'S HELD SOMETIME IN SEP-TEMBER.
IT'S VERY PRETTY.
WHAT IS IT?

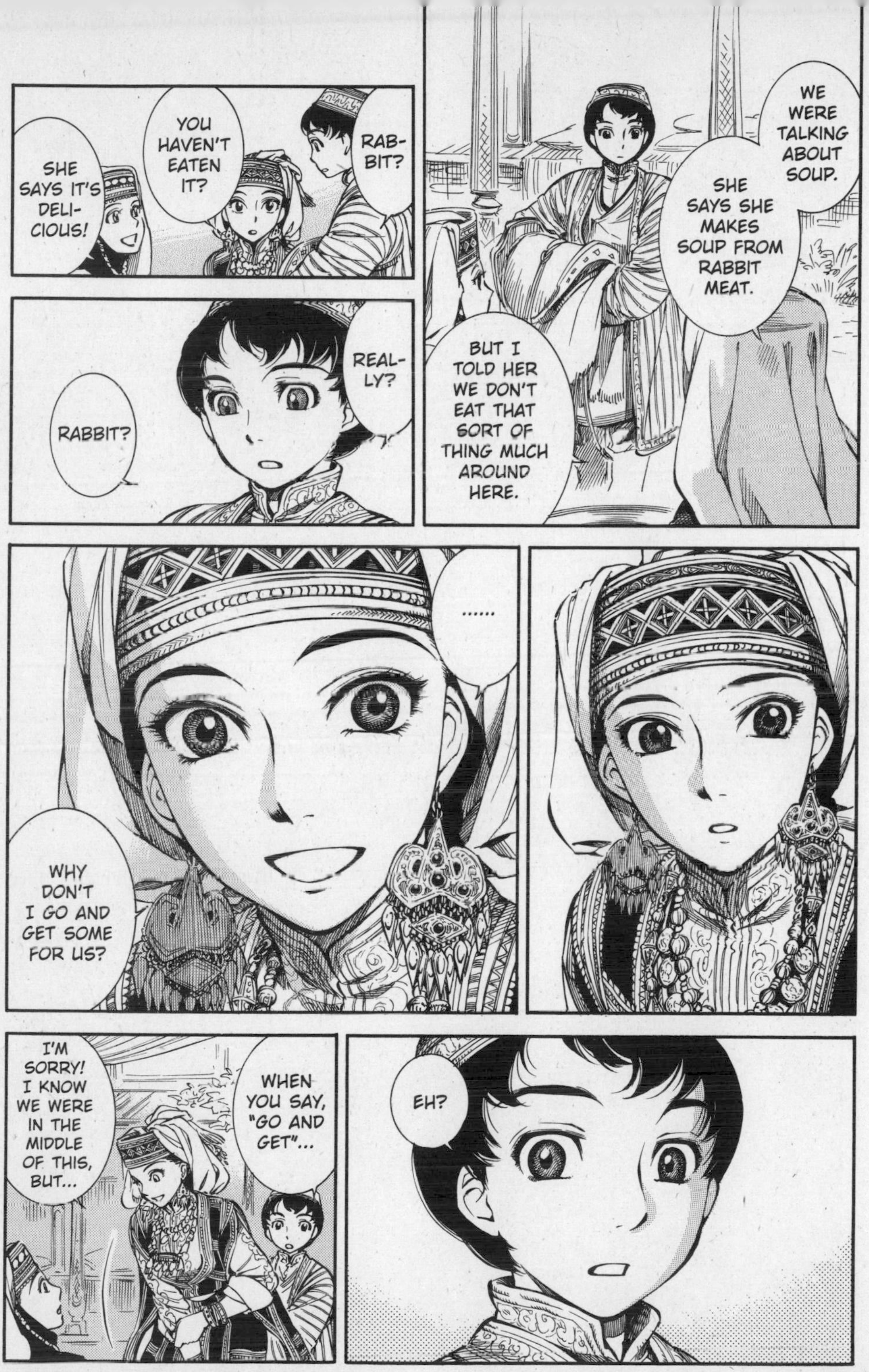
WE WERE TALKING ABOUT SOUP.
SHE SAYS SHE MAKES SOUP FROM RABBIT MEAT.
BUT I TOLD HER WE DON'T EAT THAT SORT OF THING MUCH AROUND HERE.
RABBIT?
YOU HAVEN'T EATEN IT?
SHE SAYS IT'S DELICIOUS!
REALLY?
RABBIT?
......
WHY DON'T I GO AND GET SOME FOR US?
EH?
WHEN YOU SAY, "GO AND GET"...
I'M SORRY! I KNOW WE WERE IN THE MIDDLE OF THIS, BUT...

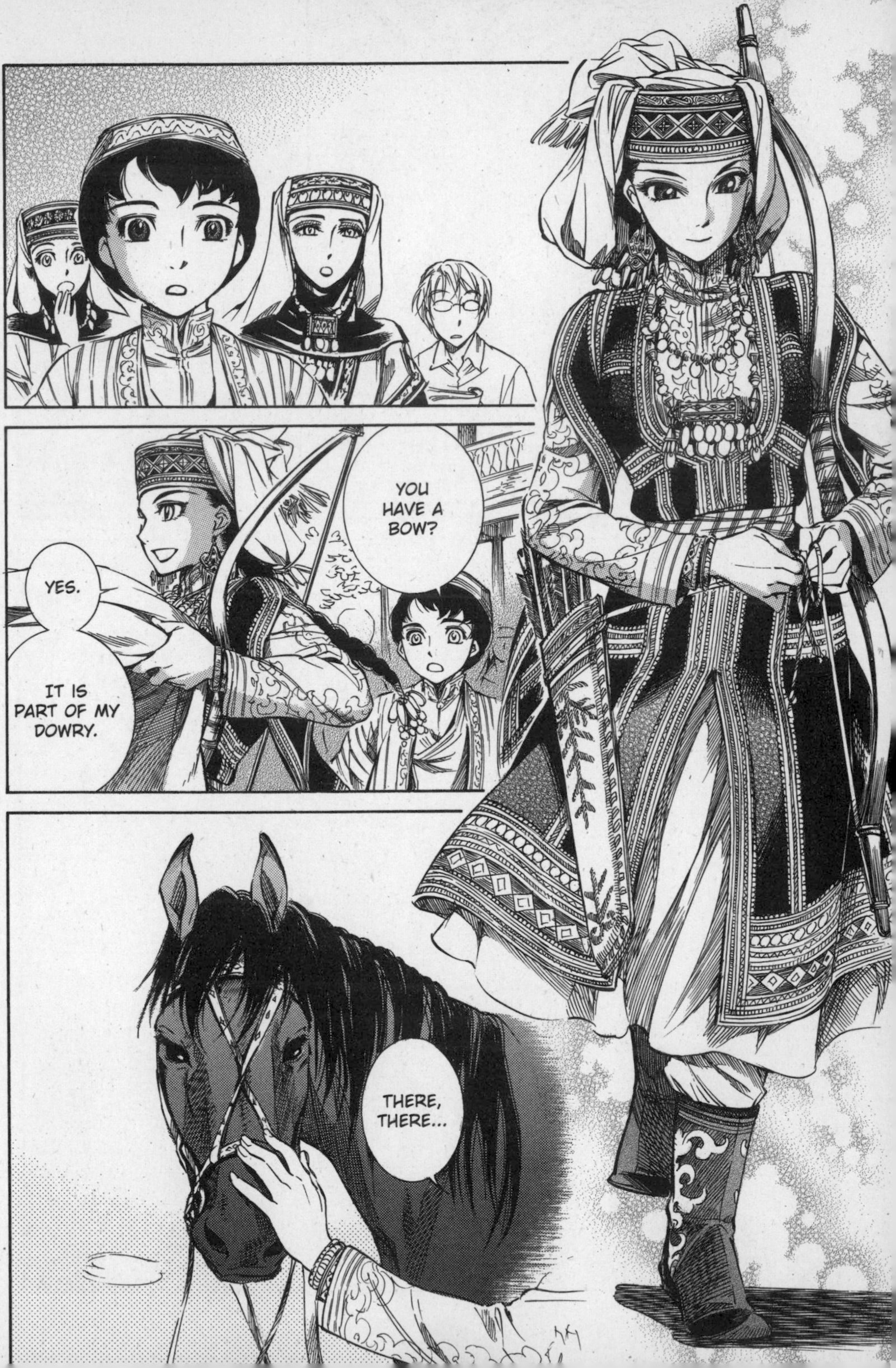
YOU HAVE A BOW?
YES.
IT IS PART OF MY DOWRY.
THERE, THERE...

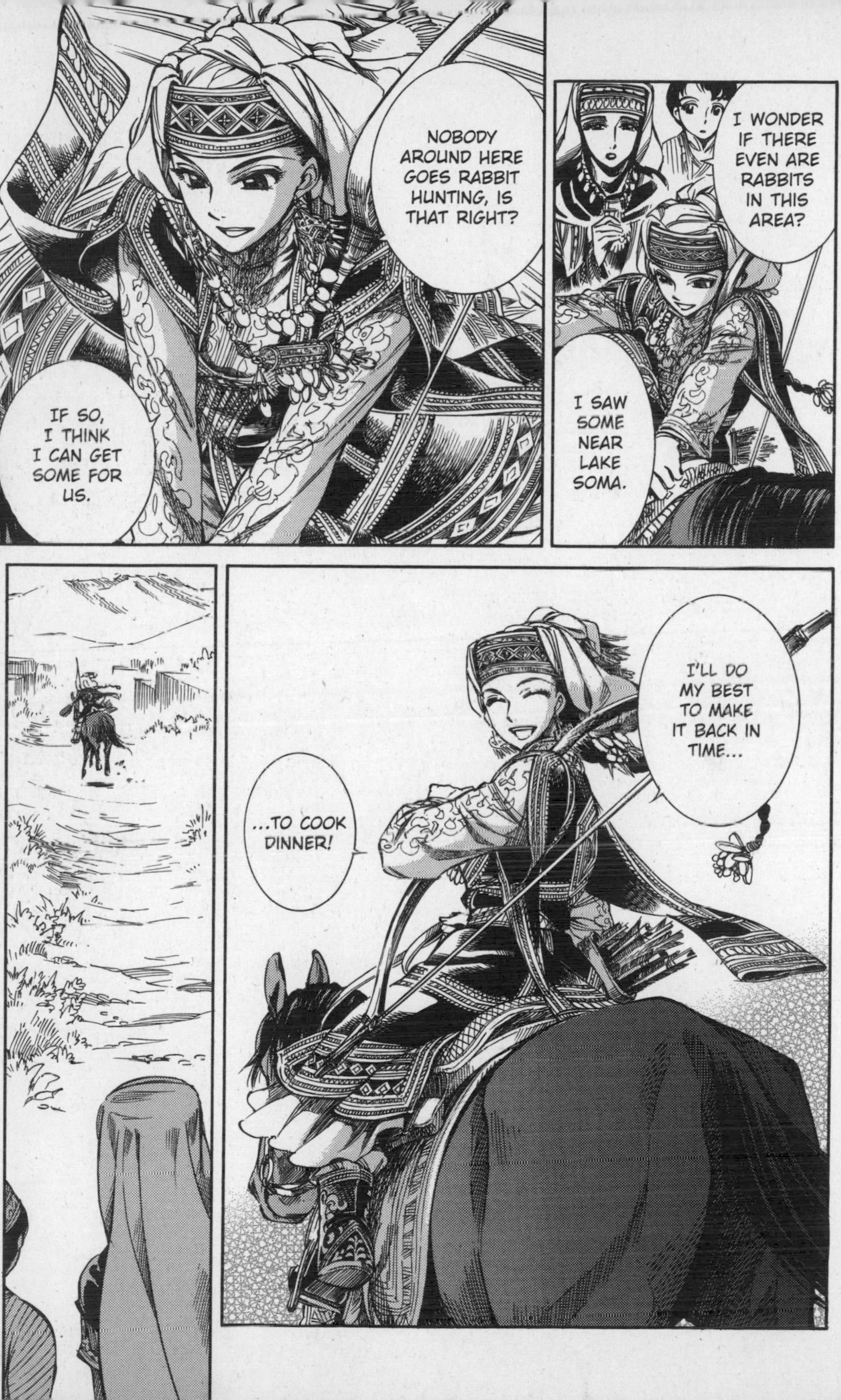
I WONDER IF THERE EVEN ARE RABBITS IN THIS AREA?
I SAW SOME NEAR LAKE SOMA.
NOBODY AROUND HERE GOES RABBIT HUNTING, IS THAT RIGHT?
IF SO, I THINK I CAN GET SOME FOR US.
I'LL DO MY BEST TO MAKE IT BACK IN TIME...
...TO COOK DINNER!

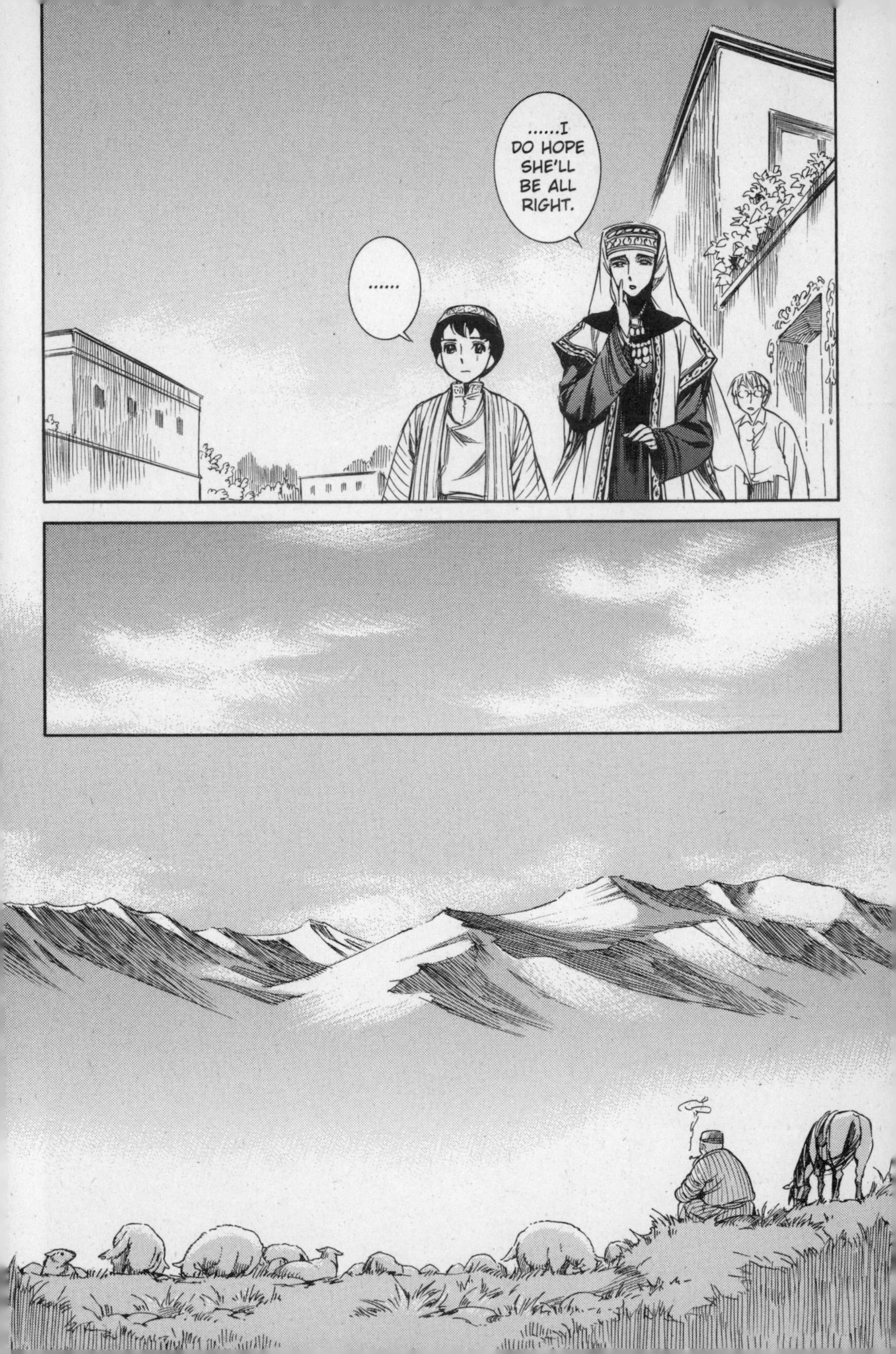
......I DO HOPE SHE'LL BE ALL RIGHT.
......

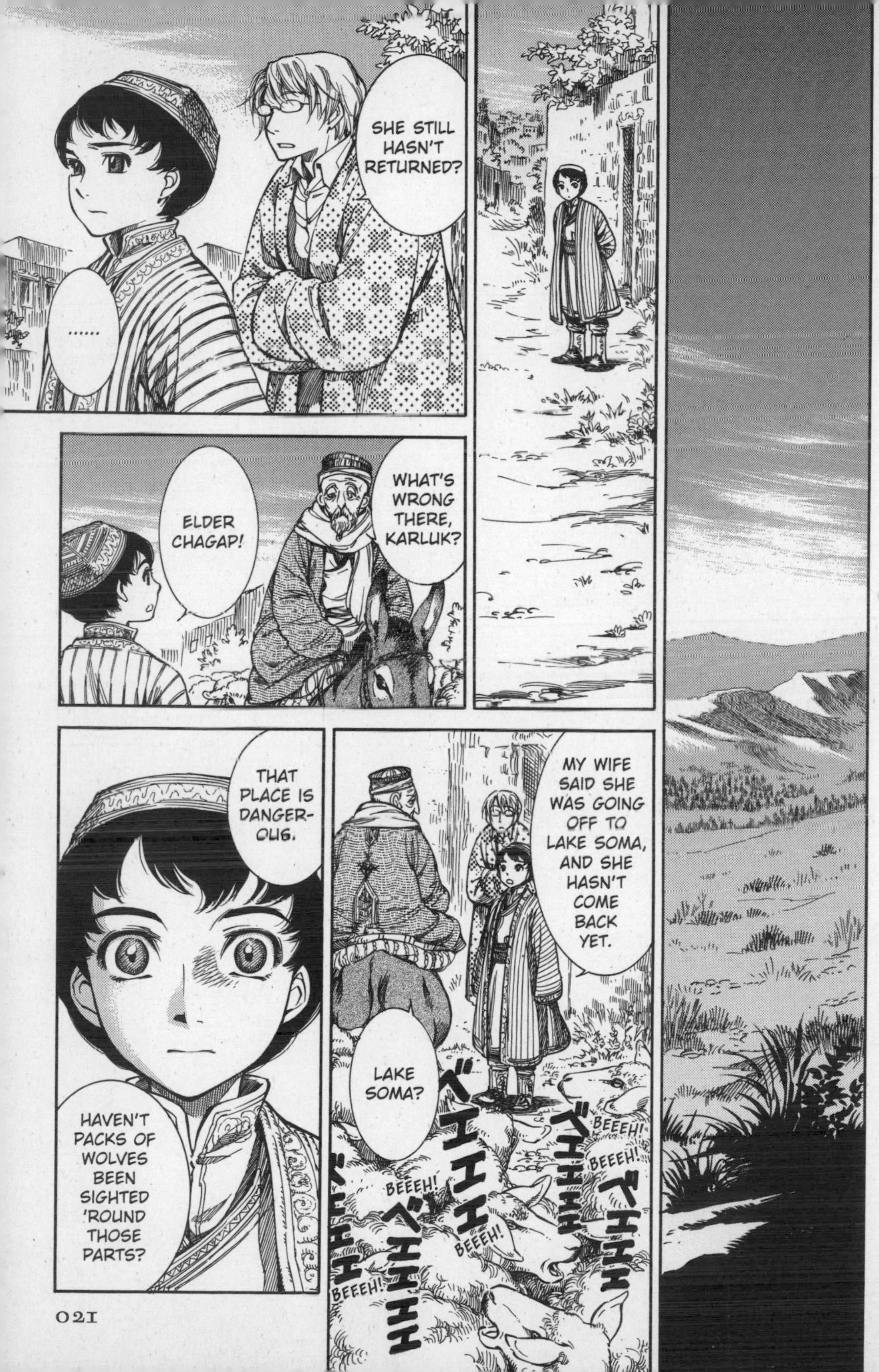
SHE STILL HASN'T RETURNED?
......
WHAT'S WRONG THERE, KARLUK?
ELDER CHAGAP!
MY WIFE SAID SHE WAS GOING OFF TO LAKE SOMA, AND SHE HASN'T COME BACK YET.
LAKE SOMA?
ベエエエエ
BEEEH!
BEEEH!
ベエエエエ
BEEEH!
BEEEH!
ベエエエ
BEEEH!
ベエエエエ
BEEEH!
THAT PLACE IS DANGER-OUS.
HAVEN'T PACKS OF WOLVES BEEN SIGHTED 'ROUND THOSE PARTS?

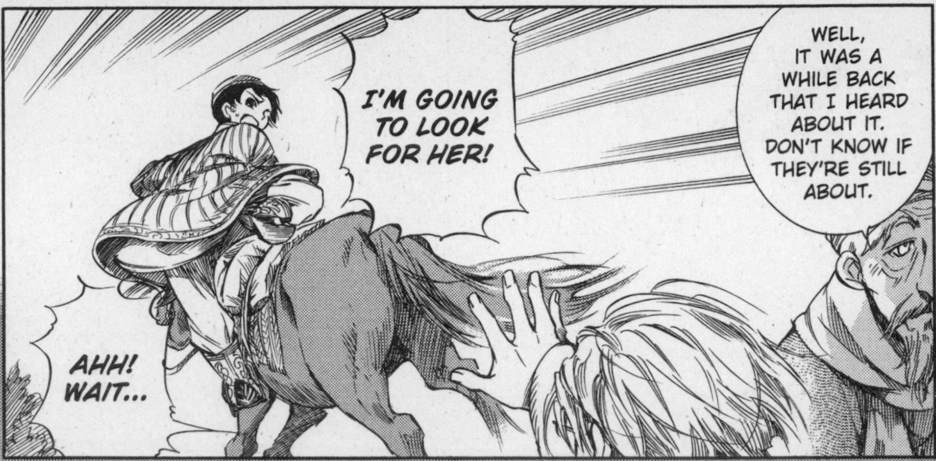
WELL, IT WAS A WHILE BACK THAT I HEARD ABOUT IT. DON'T KNOW IF THEY'RE STILL ABOUT.
I'M GOING TO LOOK FOR HER!
AHH! WAIT...

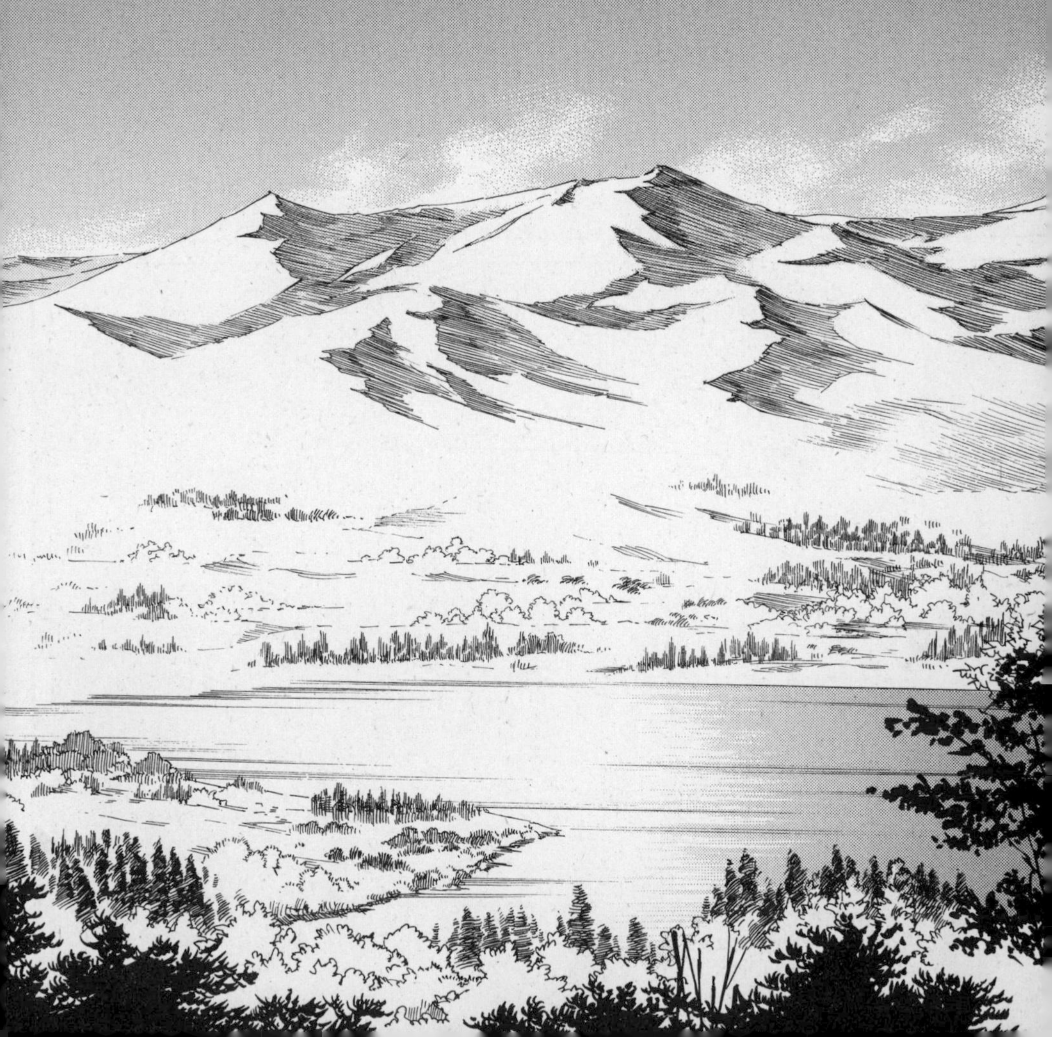

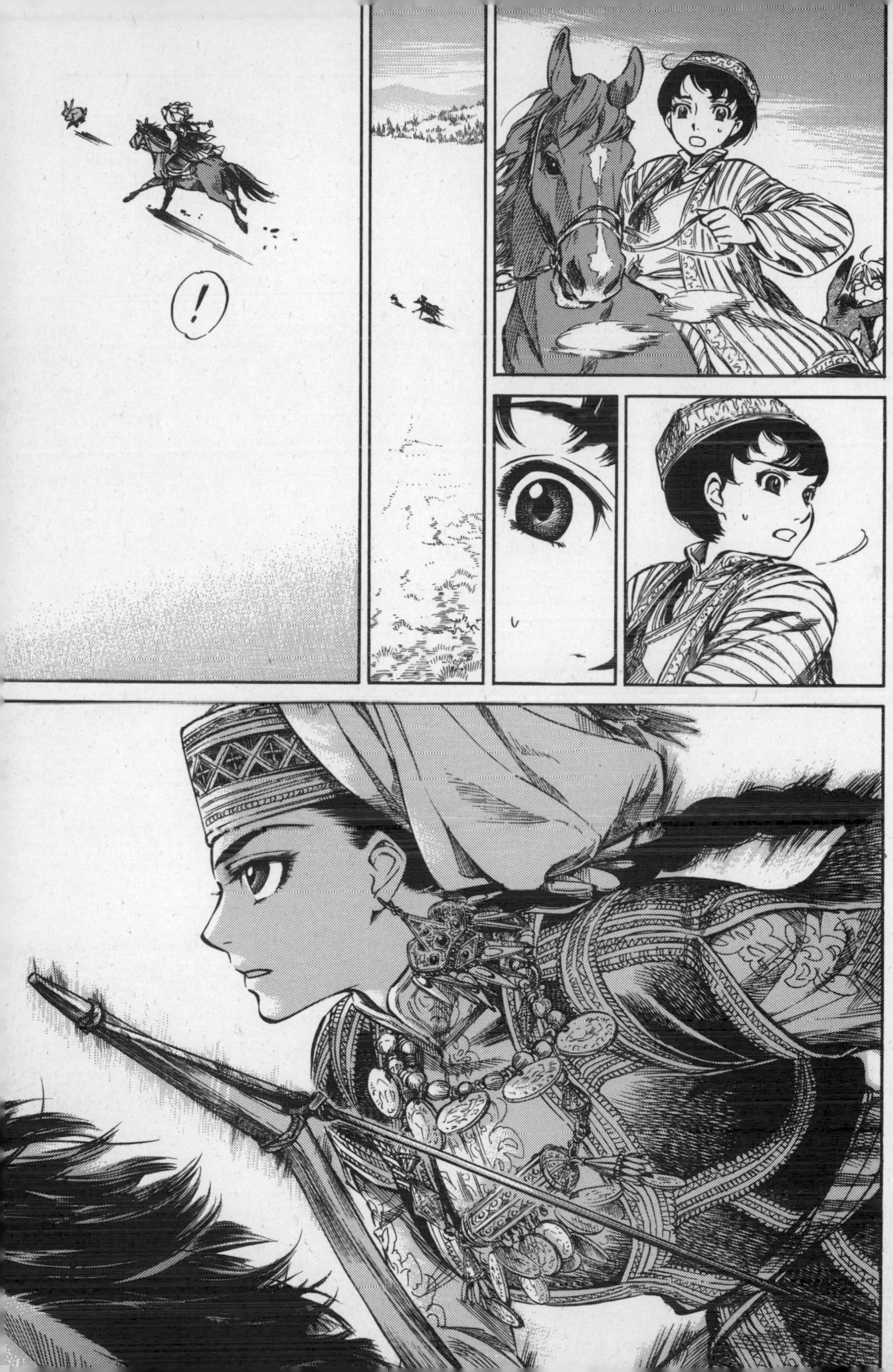
!

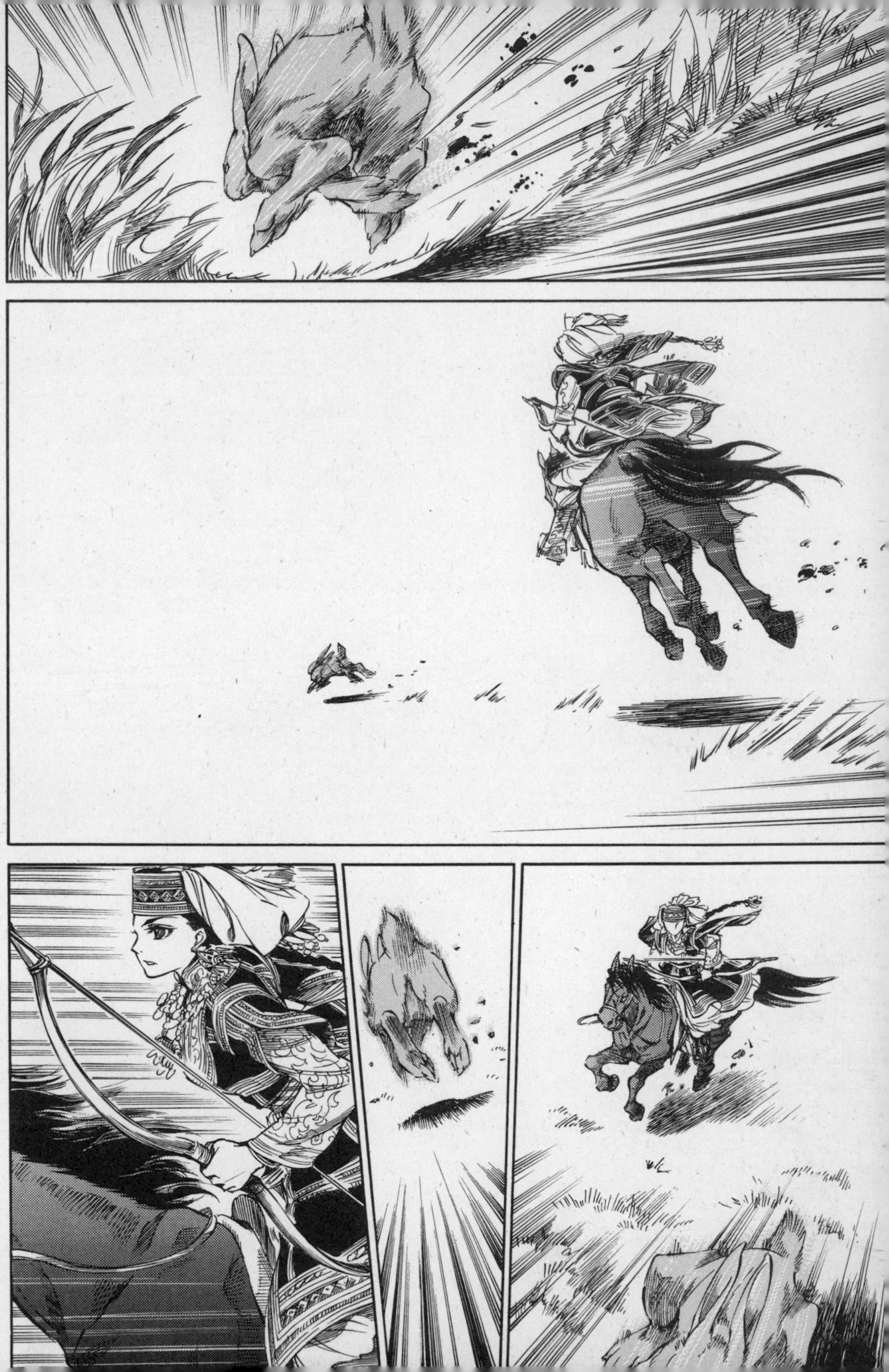

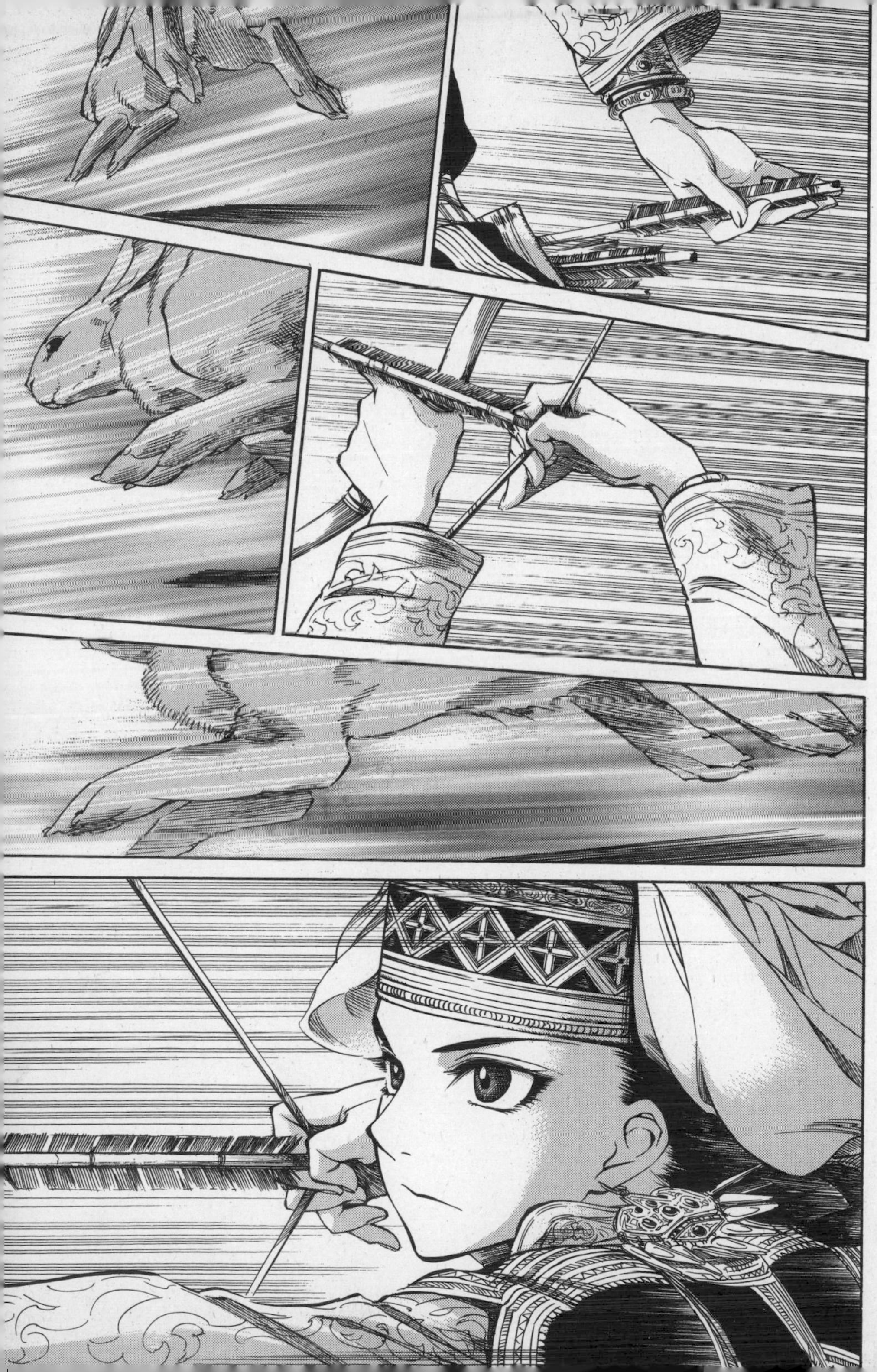

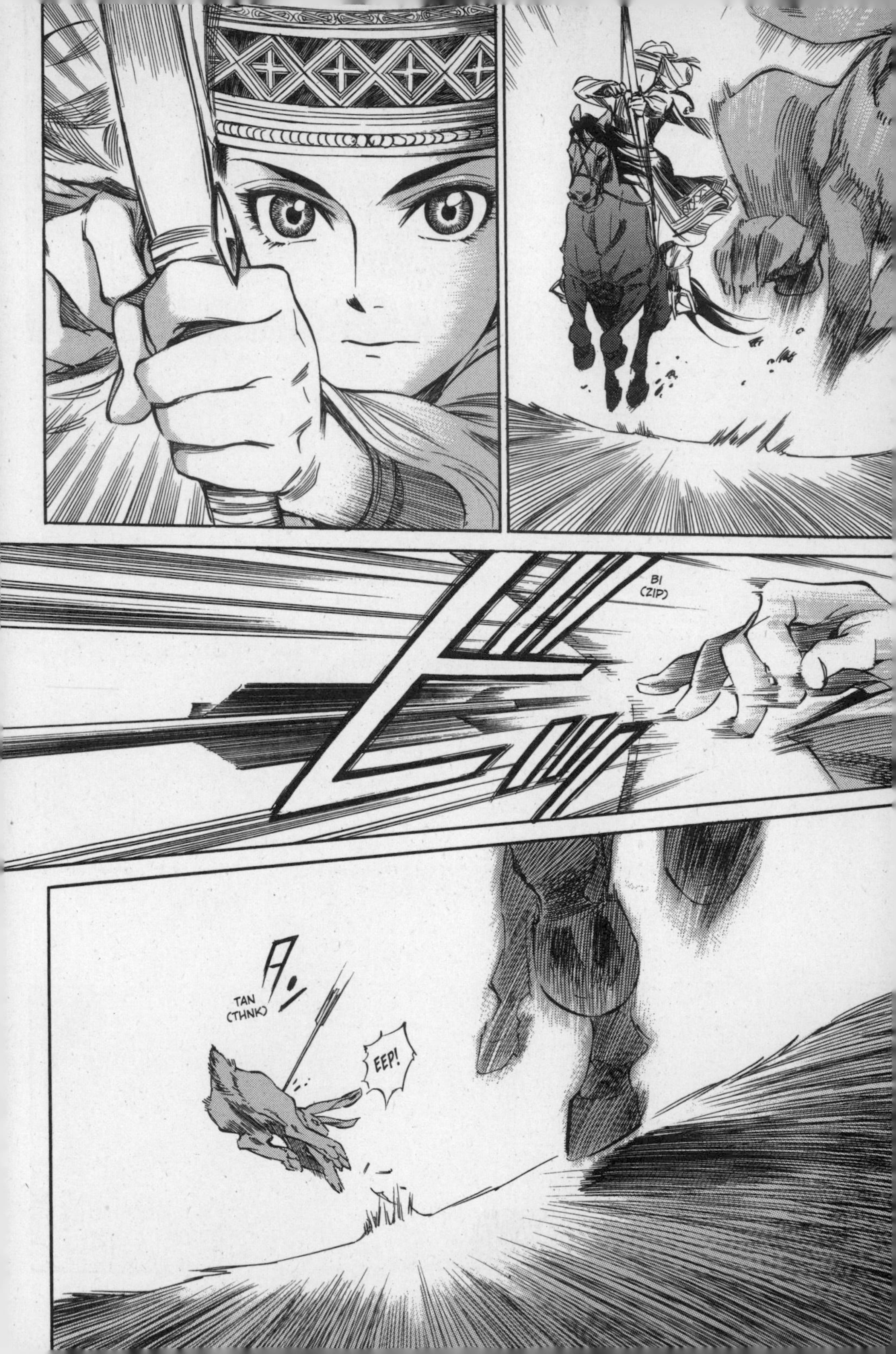
BI
(ZIP)
TAN
(THNK)
EEP!

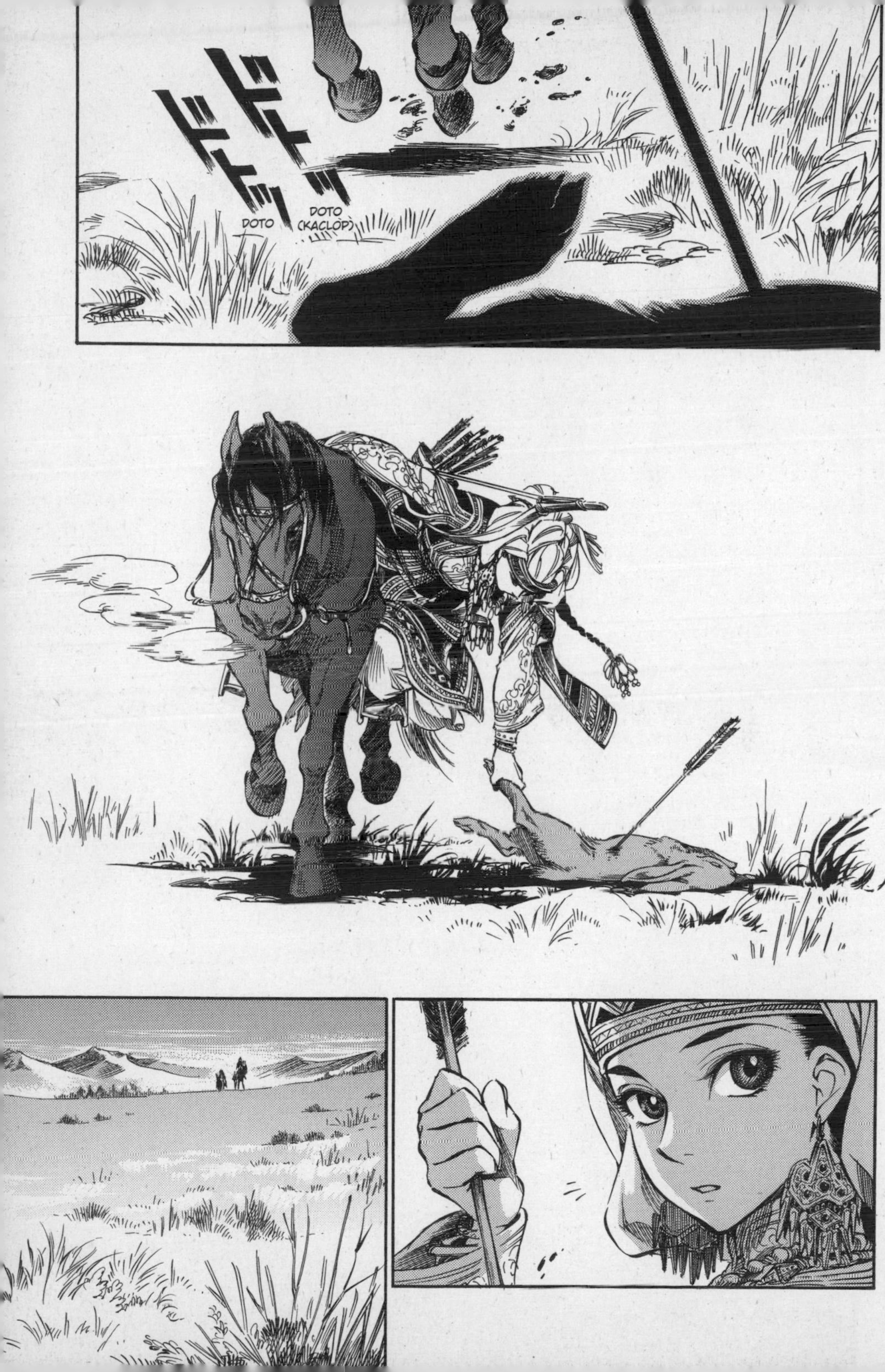
DOTO
DOTO (KACLOP)

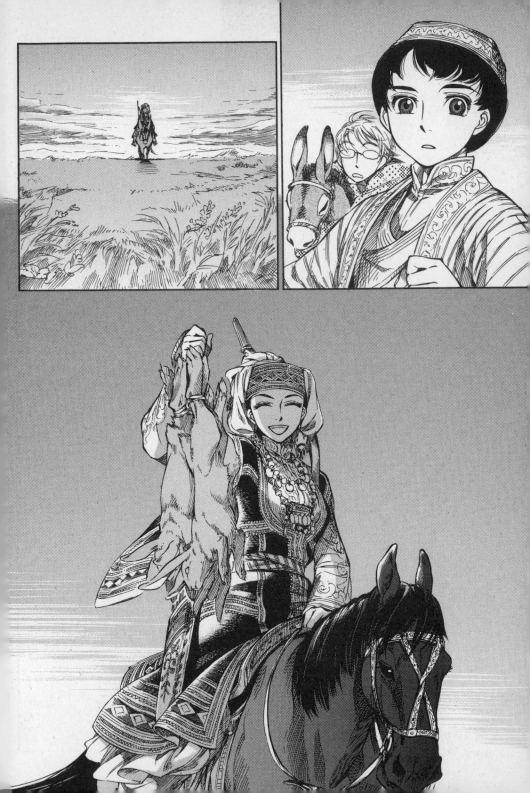

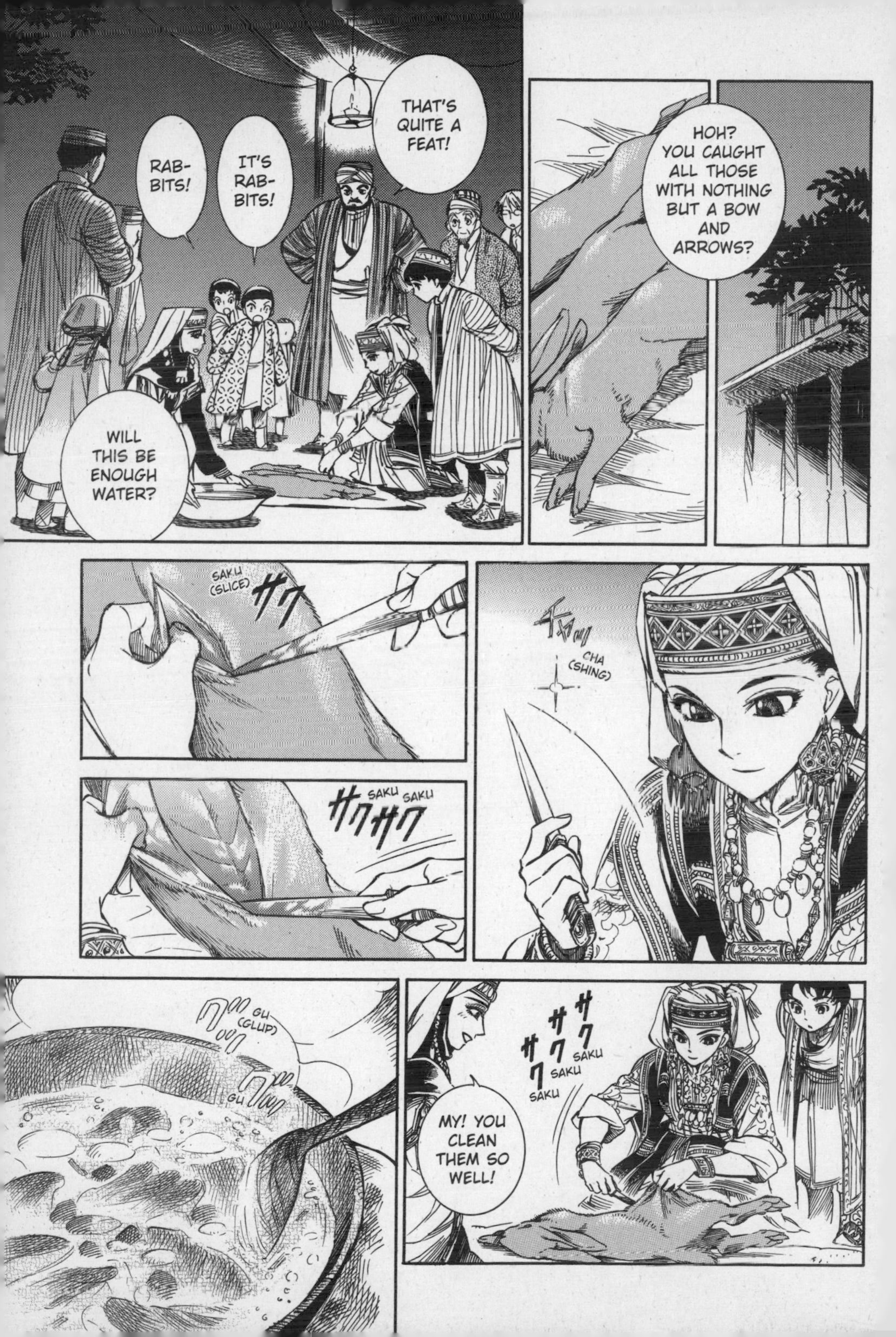
HOH? YOU CAUGHT ALL THOSE WITH NOTHING BUT A BOW AND ARROWS?
THAT'S QUITE A FEAT!
IT'S RAB-BITS!
RAB-BITS!
WILL THIS BE ENOUGH WATER?
CHA (SHING)
SAKU (SLICE)
サク
SAKU SAKU
サクサク
サク サク サク
SAKU SAKU SAKU
MY! YOU CLEAN THEM SO WELL!
GU (GLUP)
GU

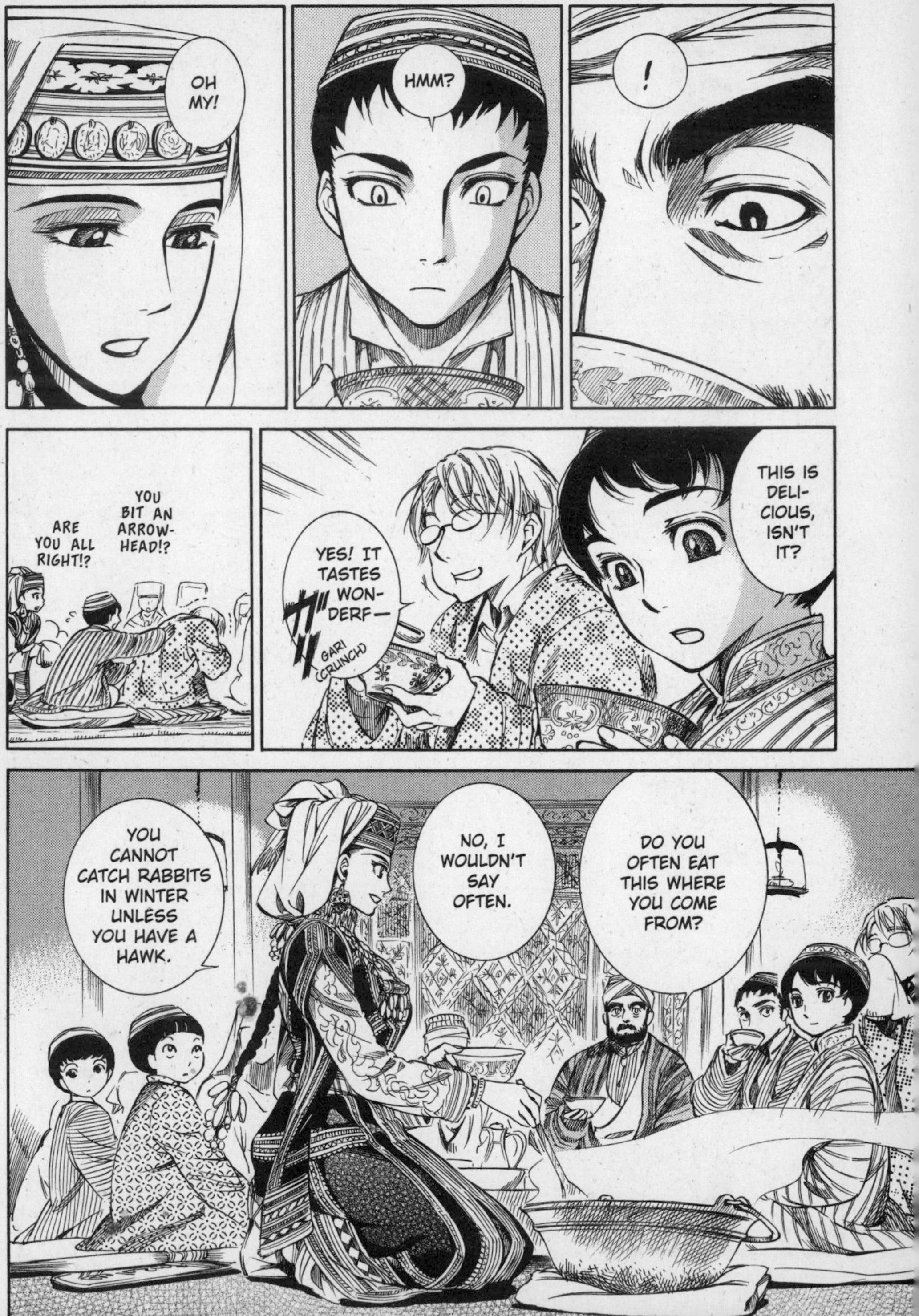
!
HMM?
OH MY!
THIS IS DELICIOUS, ISN'T IT?
YES! IT TASTES WONDERF—
GARI (CRUNCH)
YOU BIT AN ARROWHEAD!?
ARE YOU ALL RIGHT!?
DO YOU OFTEN EAT THIS WHERE YOU COME FROM?
NO, I WOULDN'T SAY OFTEN.
YOU CANNOT CATCH RABBITS IN WINTER UNLESS YOU HAVE A HAWK.

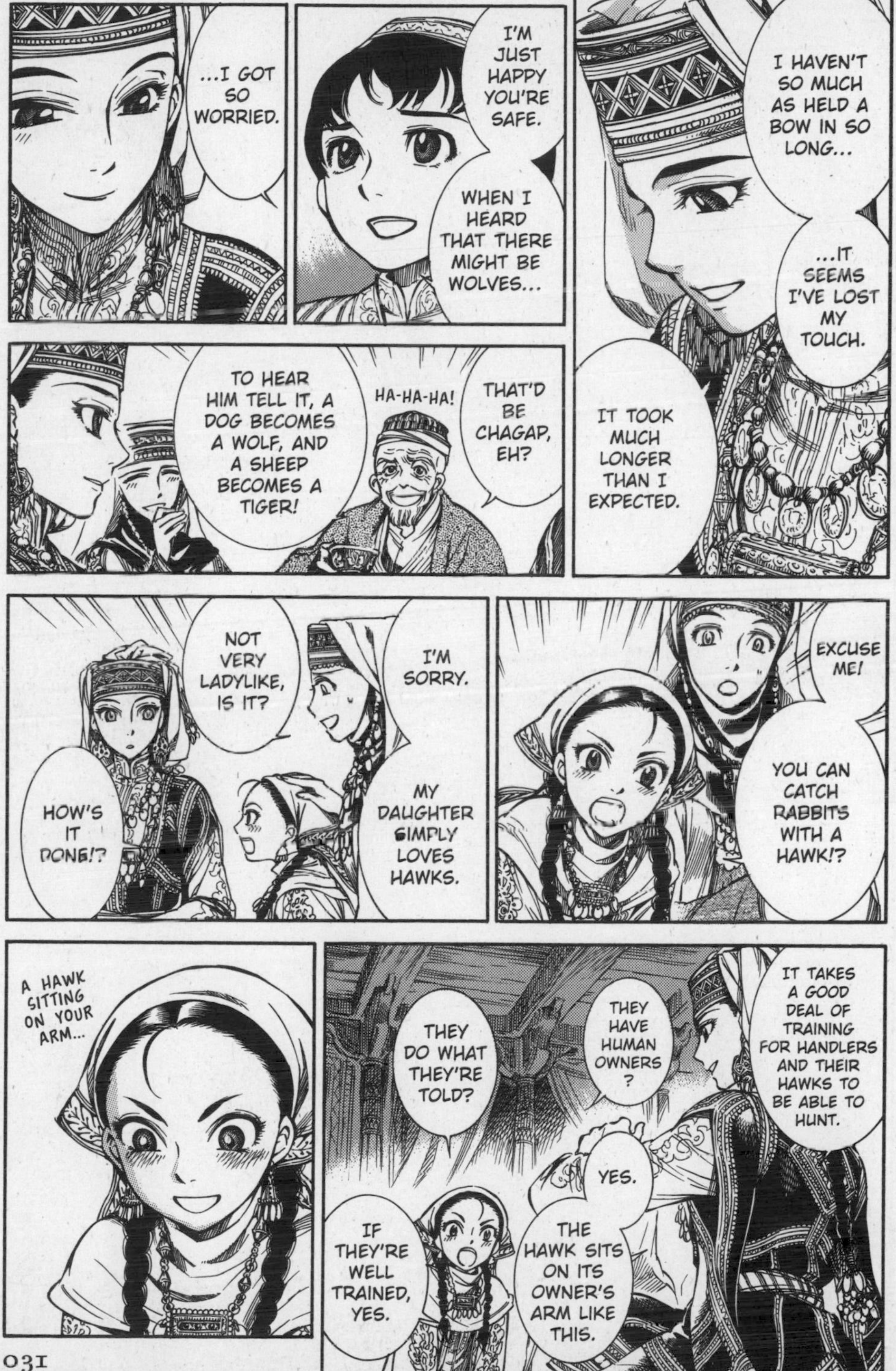
I HAVEN'T SO MUCH AS HELD A BOW IN SO LONG...
...IT SEEMS I'VE LOST MY TOUCH.
IT TOOK MUCH LONGER THAN I EXPECTED.
I'M JUST HAPPY YOU'RE SAFE.
WHEN I HEARD THAT THERE MIGHT BE WOLVES...
...I GOT SO WORRIED.
THAT'D BE CHAGAP, EH?
HA-HA-HA!
TO HEAR HIM TELL IT, A DOG BECOMES A WOLF, AND A SHEEP BECOMES A TIGER!
EXCUSE ME!
YOU CAN CATCH RABBITS WITH A HAWK!?
I'M SORRY.
MY DAUGHTER SIMPLY LOVES HAWKS.
NOT VERY LADYLIKE, IS IT?
HOW'S IT DONE!?
IT TAKES A GOOD DEAL OF TRAINING FOR HANDLERS AND THEIR HAWKS TO BE ABLE TO HUNT.
THEY HAVE HUMAN OWNERS?
THEY DO WHAT THEY'RE TOLD?
YES.
THE HAWK SITS ON ITS OWNER'S ARM LIKE THIS.
IF THEY'RE WELL TRAINED, YES.
A HAWK SITTING ON YOUR ARM...

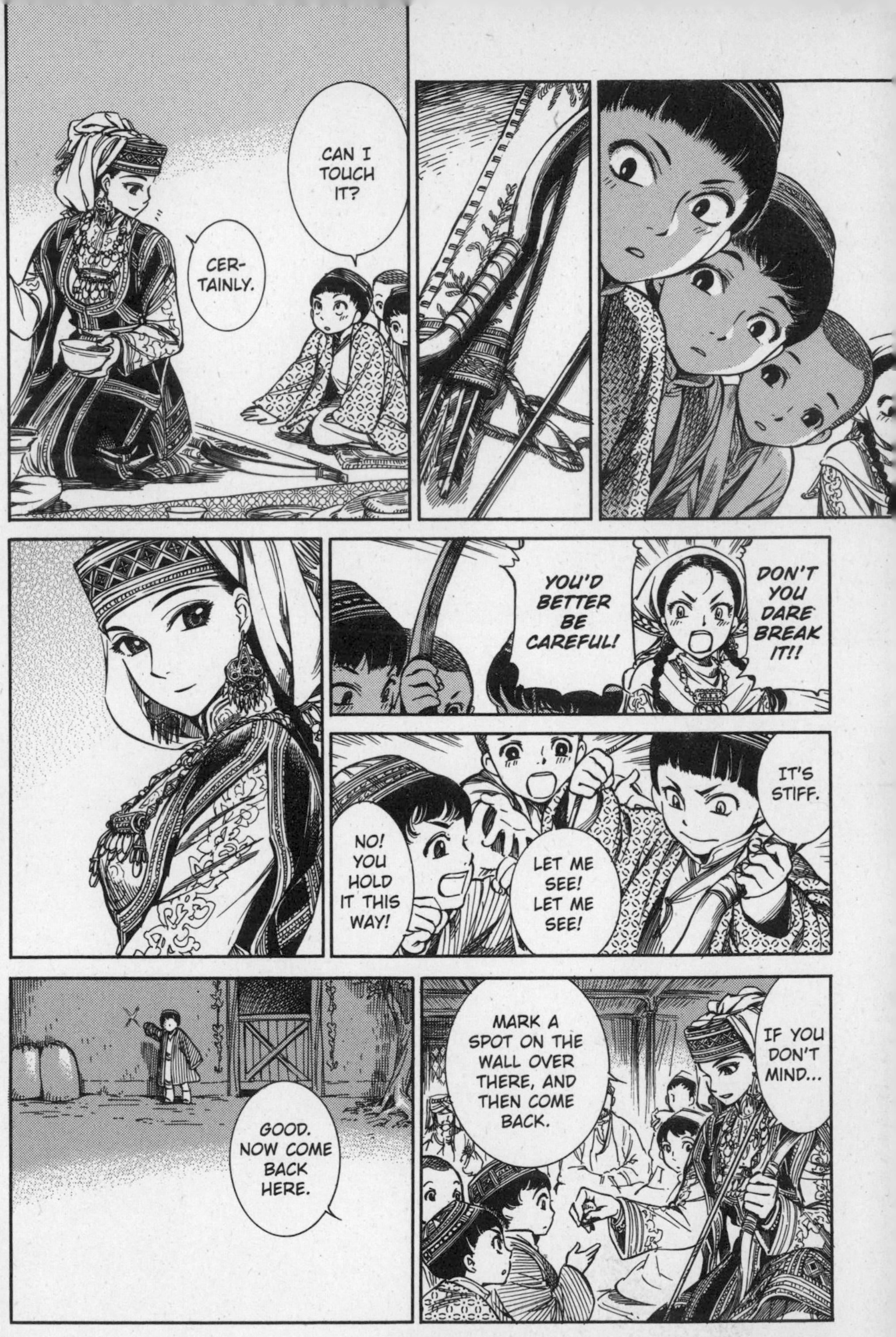
CAN I TOUCH IT?
CER-TAINLY.
DON'T YOU DARE BREAK IT!!
YOU'D BETTER BE CAREFUL!
IT'S STIFF.
LET ME SEE! LET ME SEE!
NO! YOU HOLD IT THIS WAY!
IF YOU DON'T MIND...
MARK A SPOT ON THE WALL OVER THERE, AND THEN COME BACK.
GOOD. NOW COME BACK HERE.

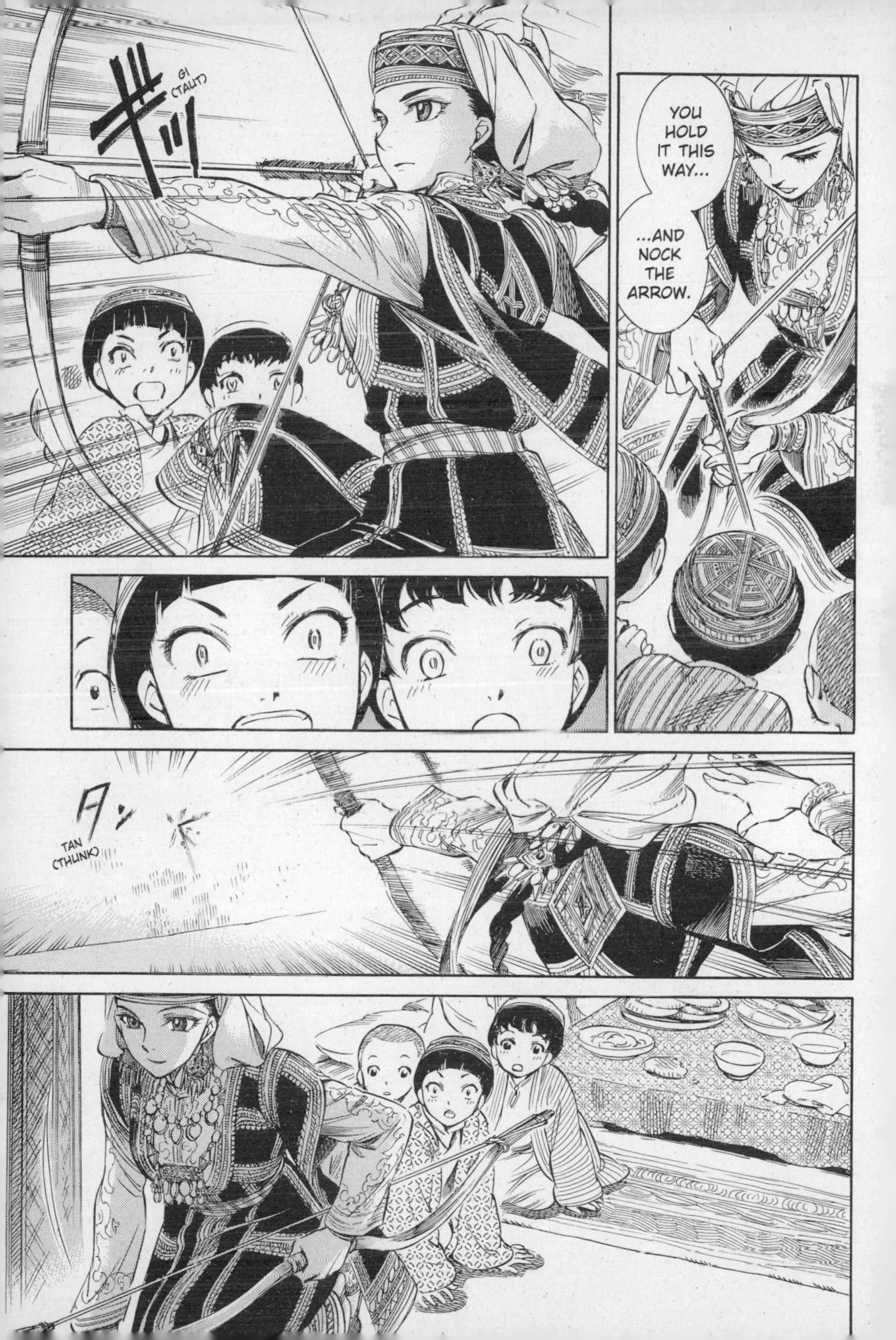
YOU HOLD IT THIS WAY...
...AND NOCK THE ARROW.
GI (TAUT)
TAN (THUNK)

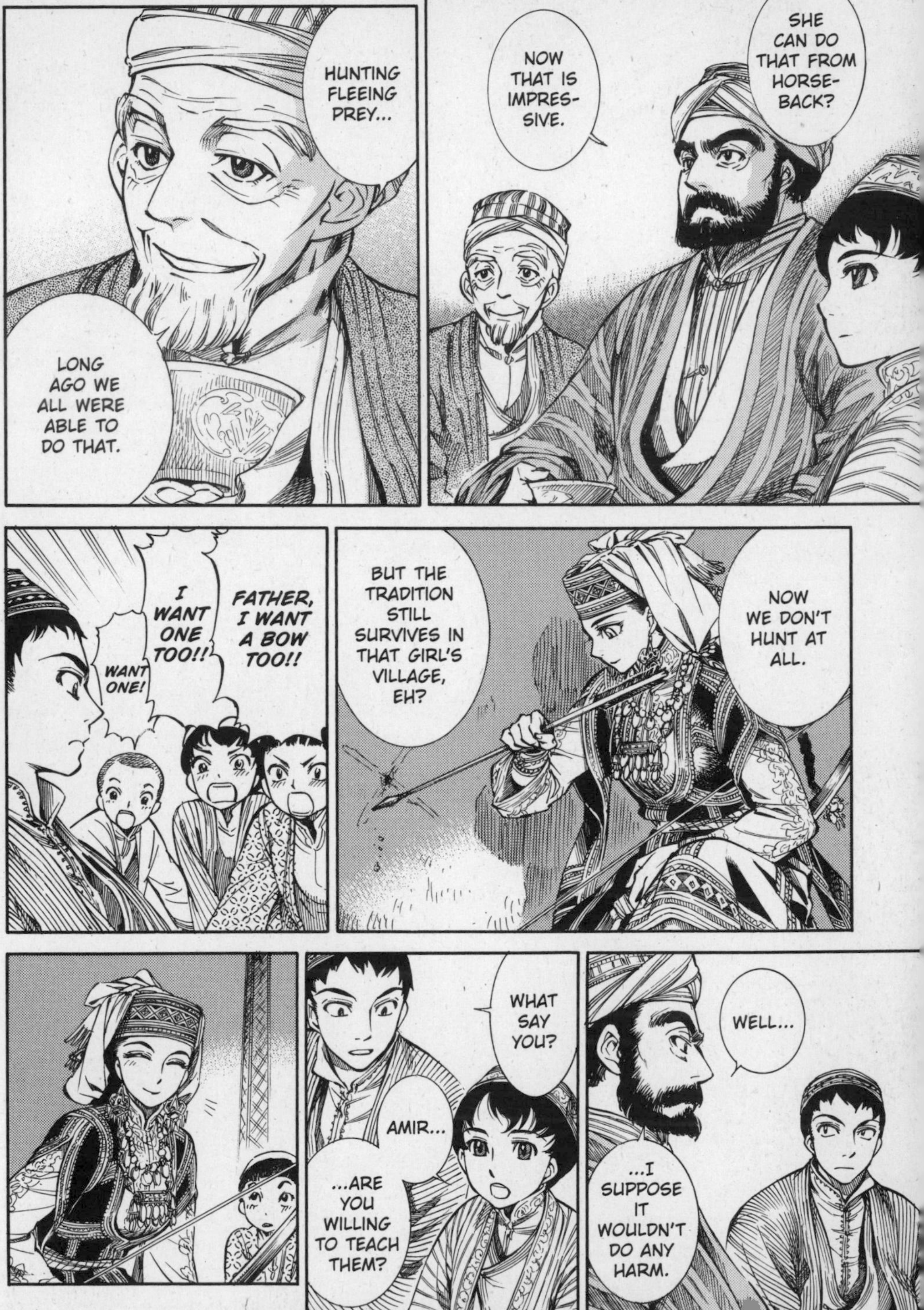
SHE CAN DO THAT FROM HORSE-BACK?
NOW THAT IS IMPRES-SIVE.
HUNTING FLEEING PREY...
LONG AGO WE ALL WERE ABLE TO DO THAT.
NOW WE DON'T HUNT AT ALL.
BUT THE TRADITION STILL SURVIVES IN THAT GIRL'S VILLAGE, EH?
FATHER, I WANT A BOW TOO!!
I WANT ONE TOO!!
WANT ONE!
WELL...
...I SUPPOSE IT WOULDN'T DO ANY HARM.
WHAT SAY YOU?
AMIR...
...ARE YOU WILLING TO TEACH THEM?

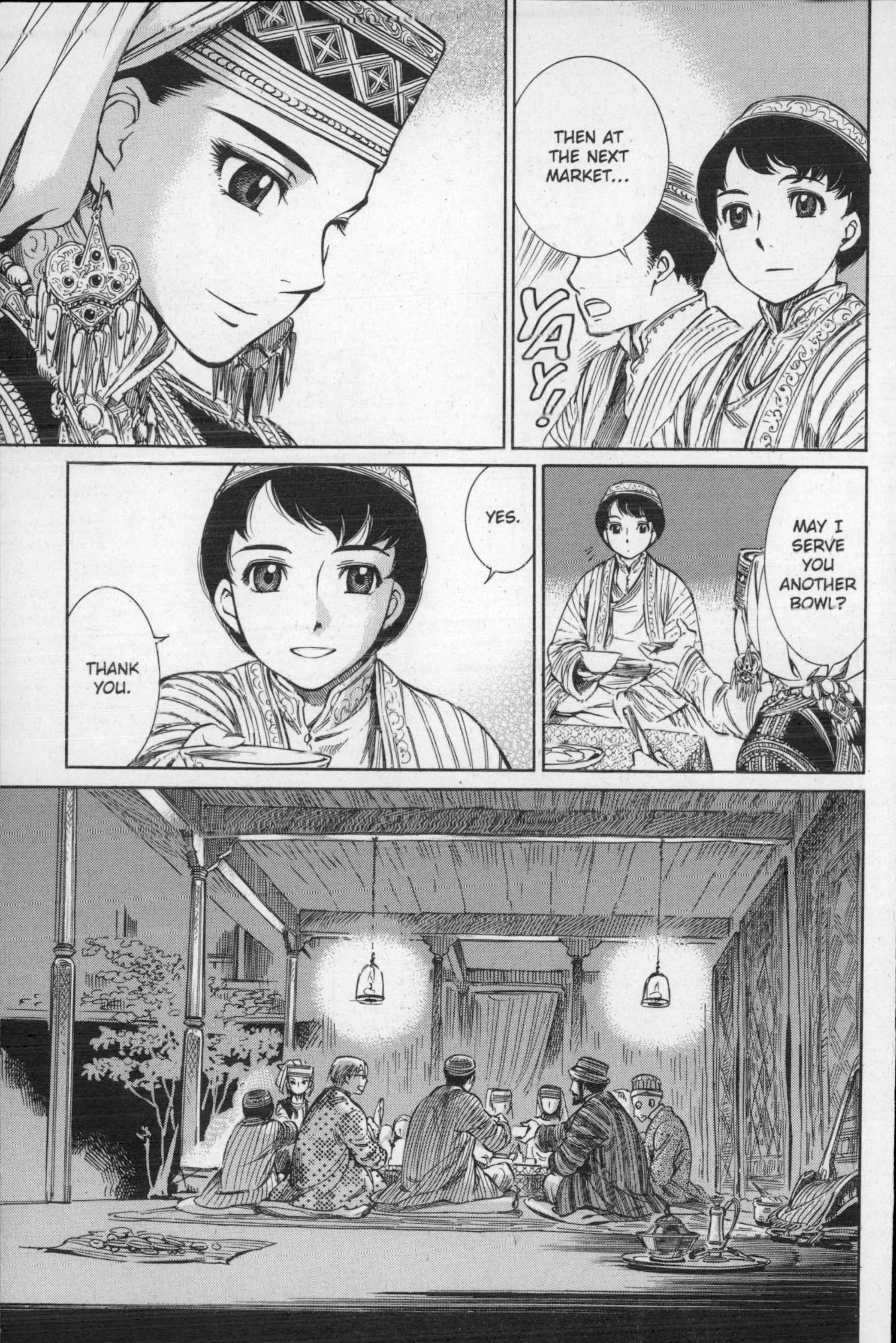
THEN AT THE NEXT MARKET...
YAY!
MAY I SERVE YOU ANOTHER BOWL?
YES.
THANK YOU.

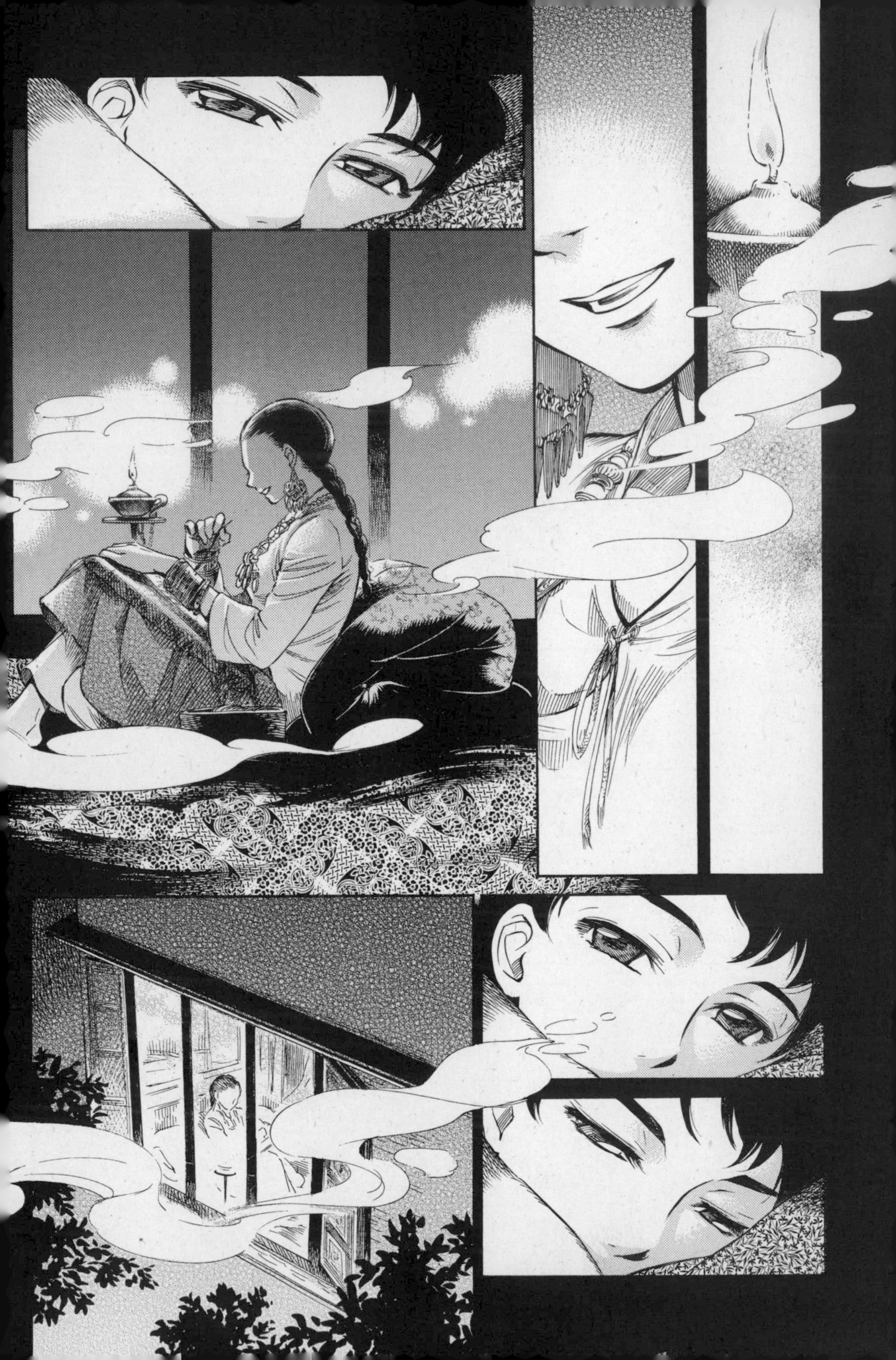

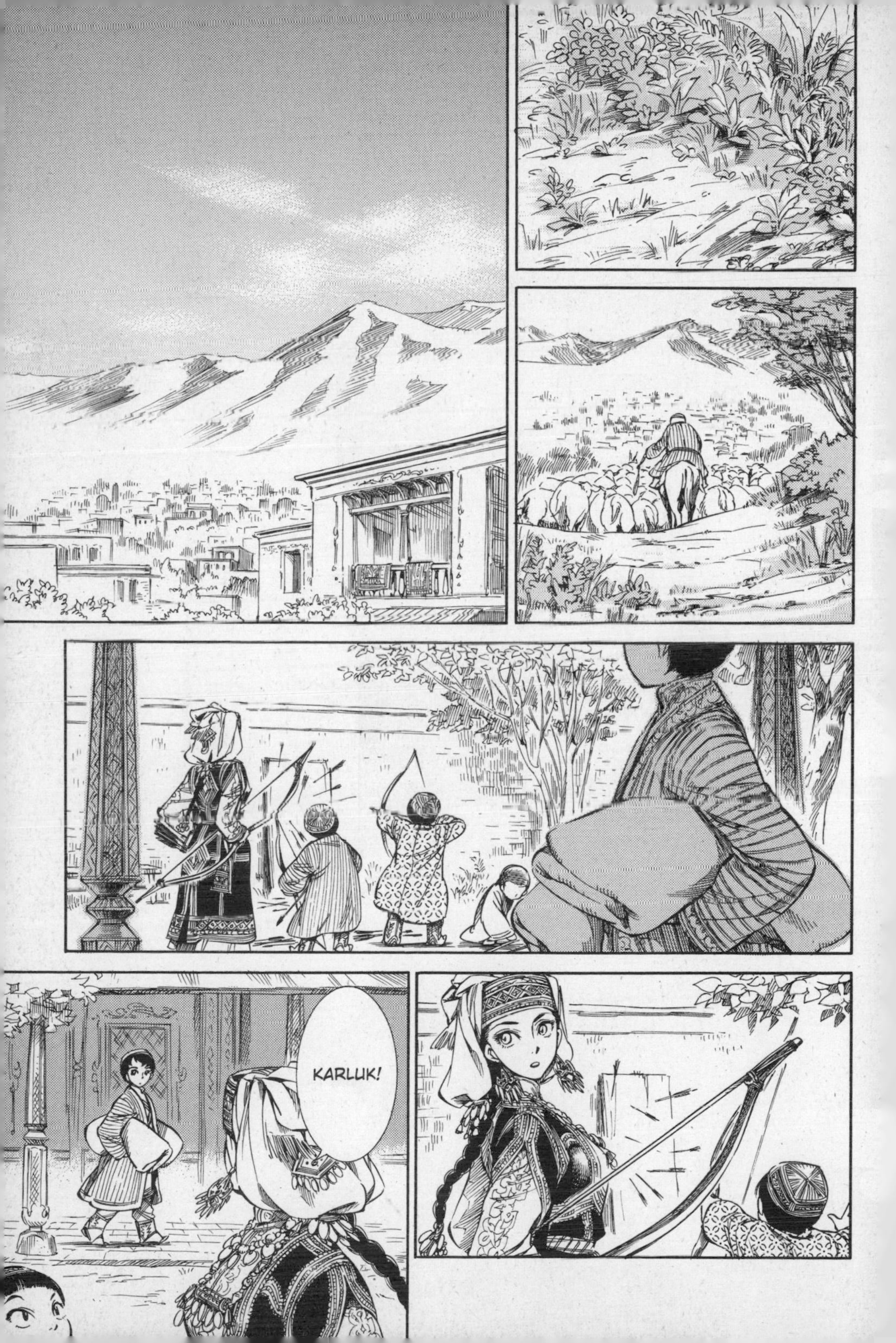
KARLUK!

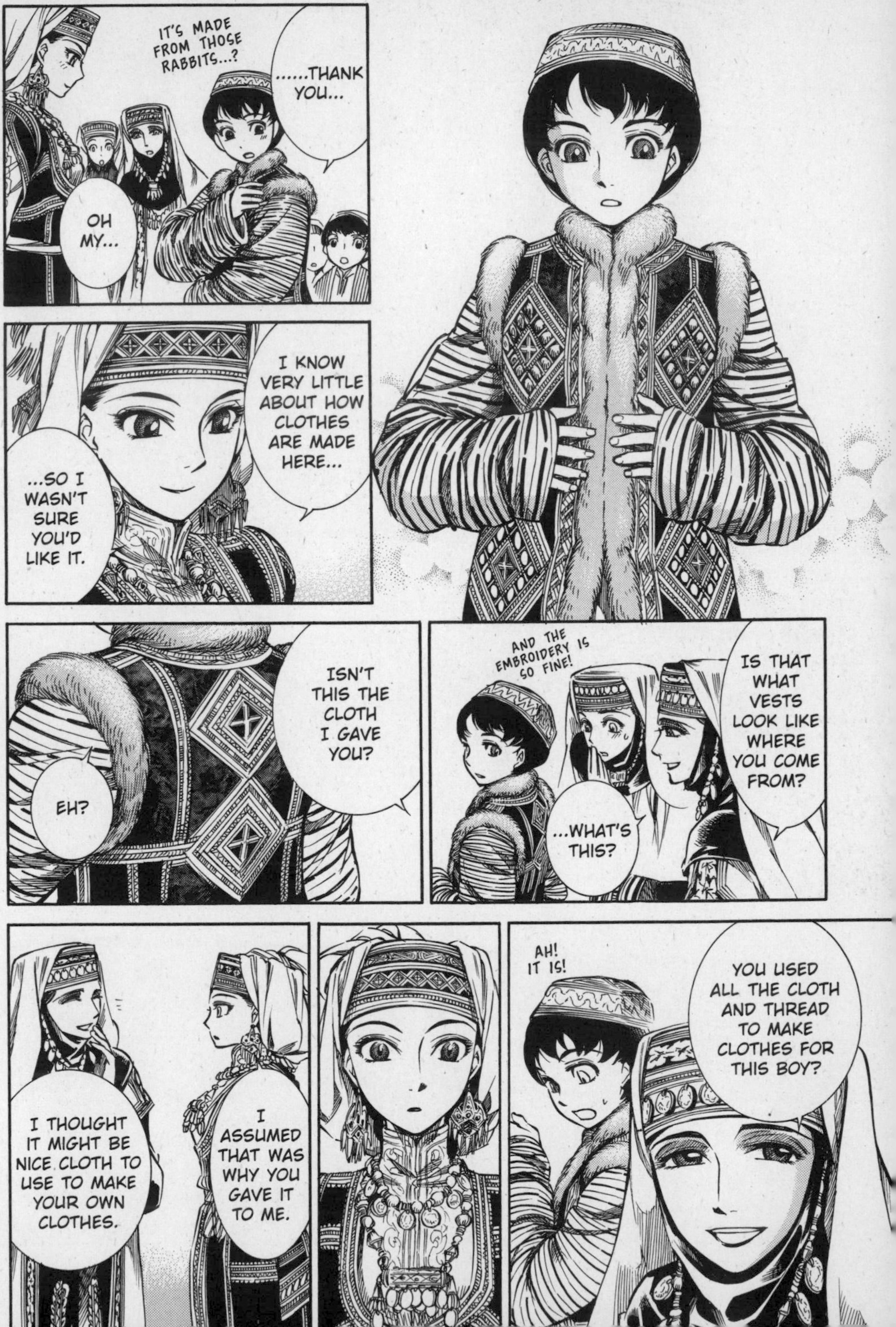
......THANK YOU...
IT'S MADE FROM THOSE RABBITS...?
OH MY...
I KNOW VERY LITTLE ABOUT HOW CLOTHES ARE MADE HERE...
...SO I WASN'T SURE YOU'D LIKE IT.
IS THAT WHAT VESTS LOOK LIKE WHERE YOU COME FROM?
AND THE EMBROIDERY IS SO FINE!
...WHAT'S THIS?
ISN'T THIS THE CLOTH I GAVE YOU?
EH?
YOU USED ALL THE CLOTH AND THREAD TO MAKE CLOTHES FOR THIS BOY?
AH! IT IS!
I ASSUMED THAT WAS WHY YOU GAVE IT TO ME.
I THOUGHT IT MIGHT BE NICE CLOTH TO USE TO MAKE YOUR OWN CLOTHES.

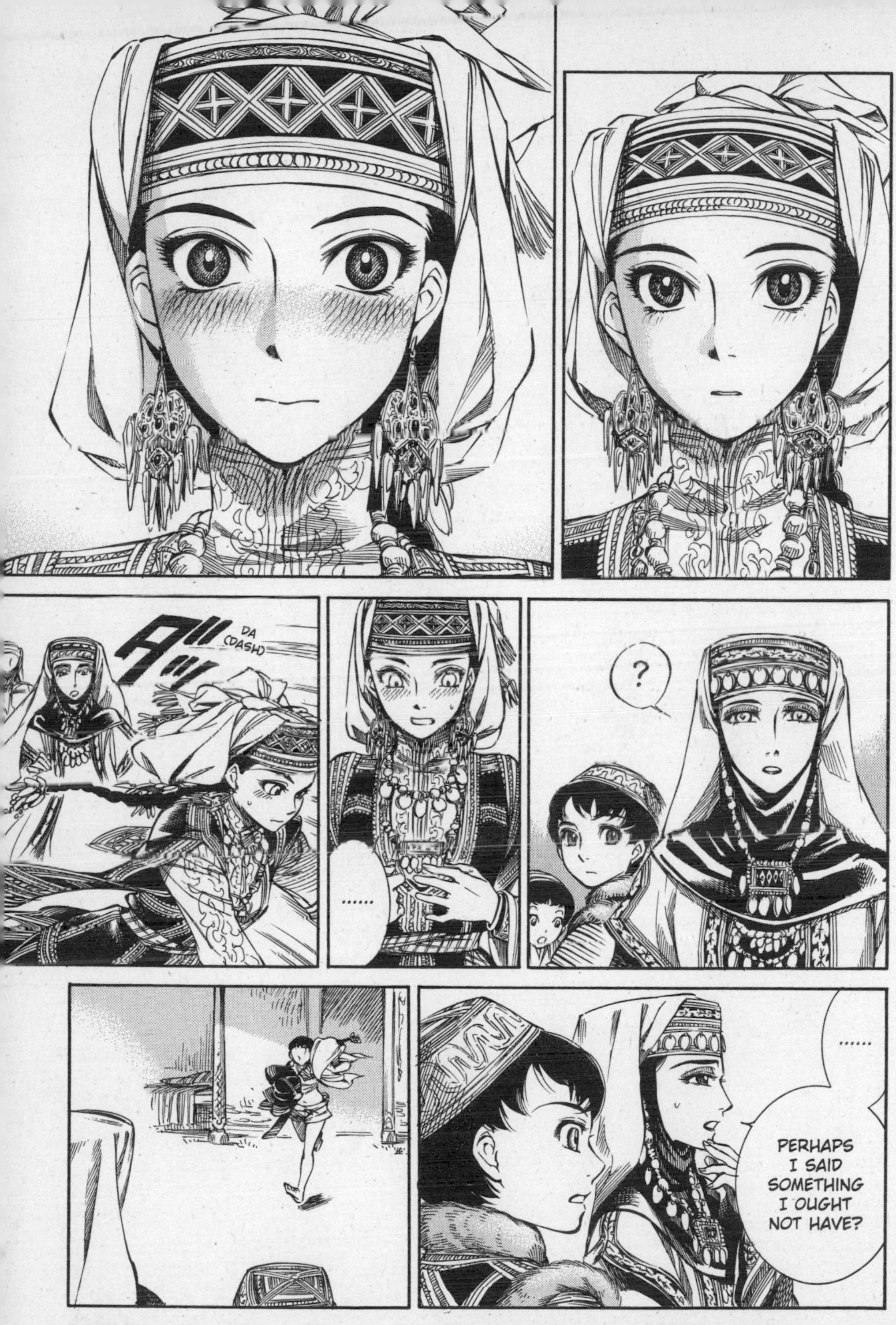
?
......
DA (DASH)
......
PERHAPS I SAID SOMETHING I OUGHT NOT HAVE?

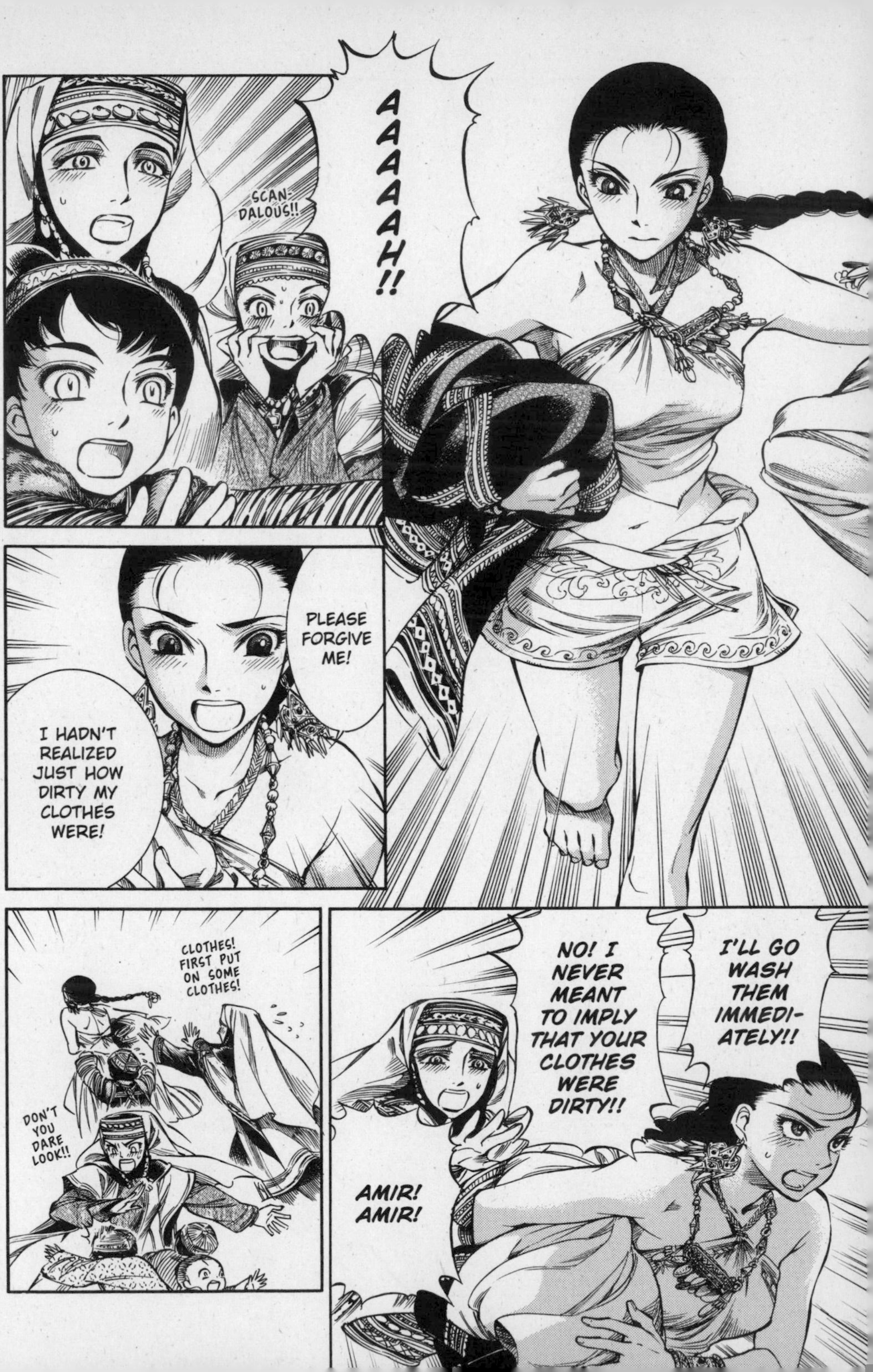
AAAAAH!!
SCAN-DALOUS!!
PLEASE FORGIVE ME!
I HADN'T REALIZED JUST HOW DIRTY MY CLOTHES WERE!
I'LL GO WASH THEM IMMEDI-ATELY!!
NO! I NEVER MEANT TO IMPLY THAT YOUR CLOTHES WERE DIRTY!!
AMIR! AMIR!
CLOTHES! FIRST PUT ON SOME CLOTHES!
DON'T YOU DARE LOOK!!

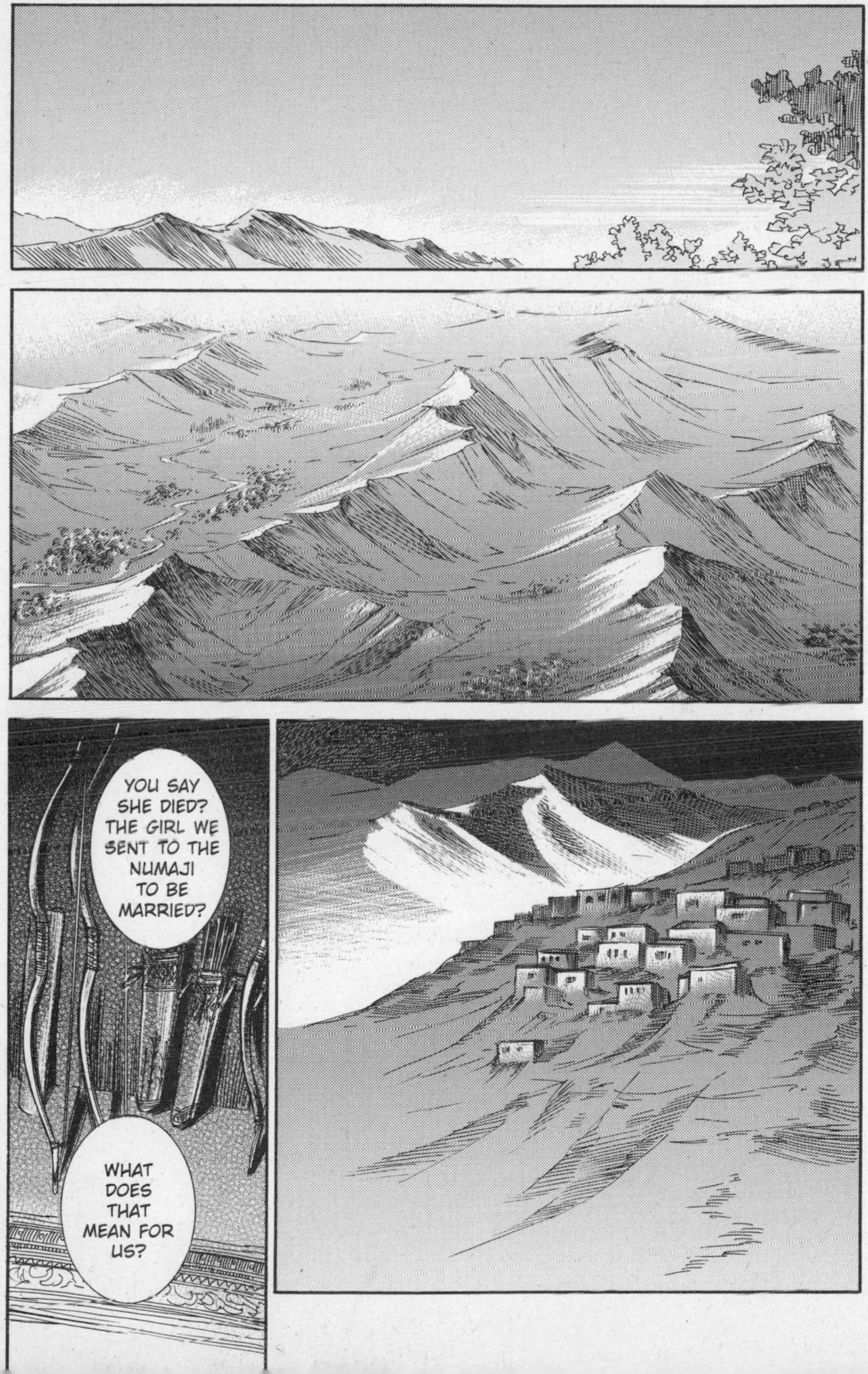
YOU SAY SHE DIED? THE GIRL WE SENT TO THE NUMAJI TO BE MARRIED?
WHAT DOES THAT MEAN FOR US?

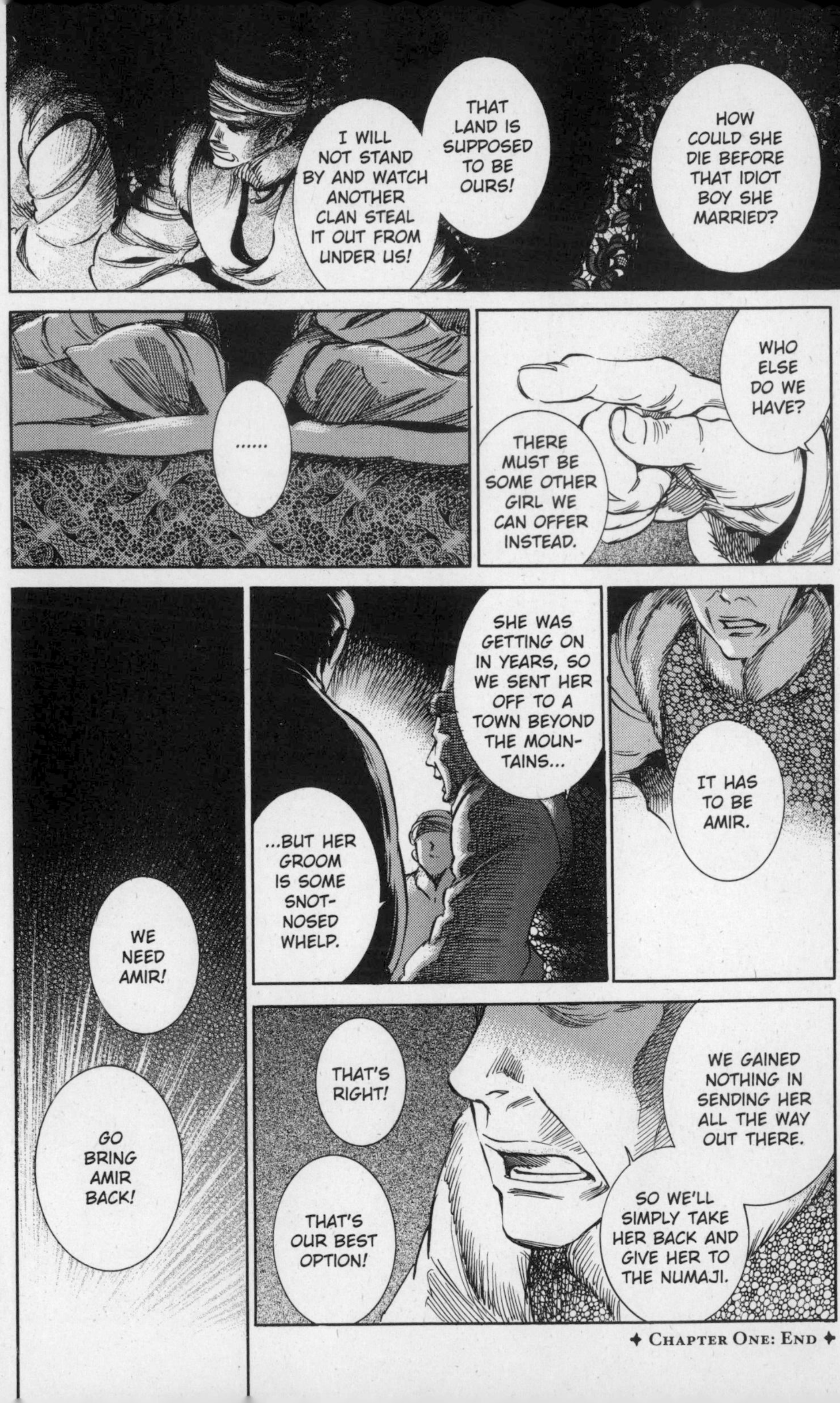
HOW COULD SHE DIE BEFORE THAT IDIOT BOY SHE MARRIED?
THAT LAND IS SUPPOSED TO BE OURS!
I WILL NOT STAND BY AND WATCH ANOTHER CLAN STEAL IT OUT FROM UNDER US!
WHO ELSE DO WE HAVE?
THERE MUST BE SOME OTHER GIRL WE CAN OFFER INSTEAD.
......
IT HAS TO BE AMIR.
SHE WAS GETTING ON IN YEARS, SO WE SENT HER OFF TO A TOWN BEYOND THE MOUN-TAINS...
...BUT HER GROOM IS SOME SNOT-NOSED WHELP.
WE GAINED NOTHING IN SENDING HER ALL THE WAY OUT THERE.
SO WE'LL SIMPLY TAKE HER BACK AND GIVE HER TO THE NUMAJI.
THAT'S RIGHT!
THAT'S OUR BEST OPTION!
WE NEED AMIR!
GO BRING AMIR BACK!

✦ Chapter One: End ✦

HEY, MISTER!

✦ CHAPTER TWO ✦

KA
(TAK)

KA
(TAK)

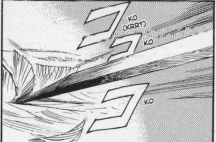

KO
(KRRT)

KO

KO

OH, IT'S YOU, KID.

BACK AGAIN, HUH?

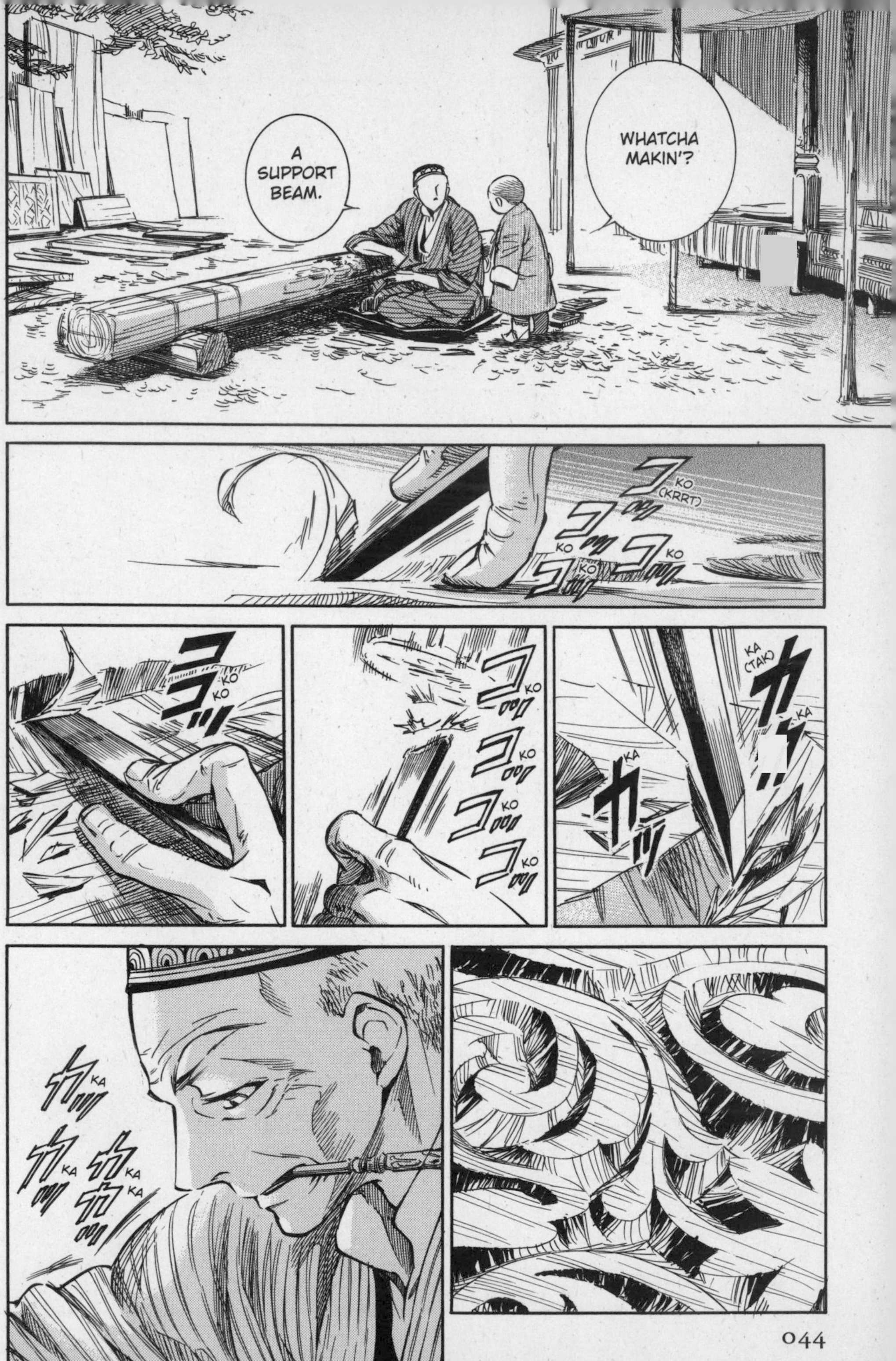
WHATCHA MAKIN'?
A SUPPORT BEAM.
KO (KRRT)
KO
KO
KO
KA (TAK)
KA
KA
KO
KO
KO
KO
KO
KO
KA
KA
KA
KA

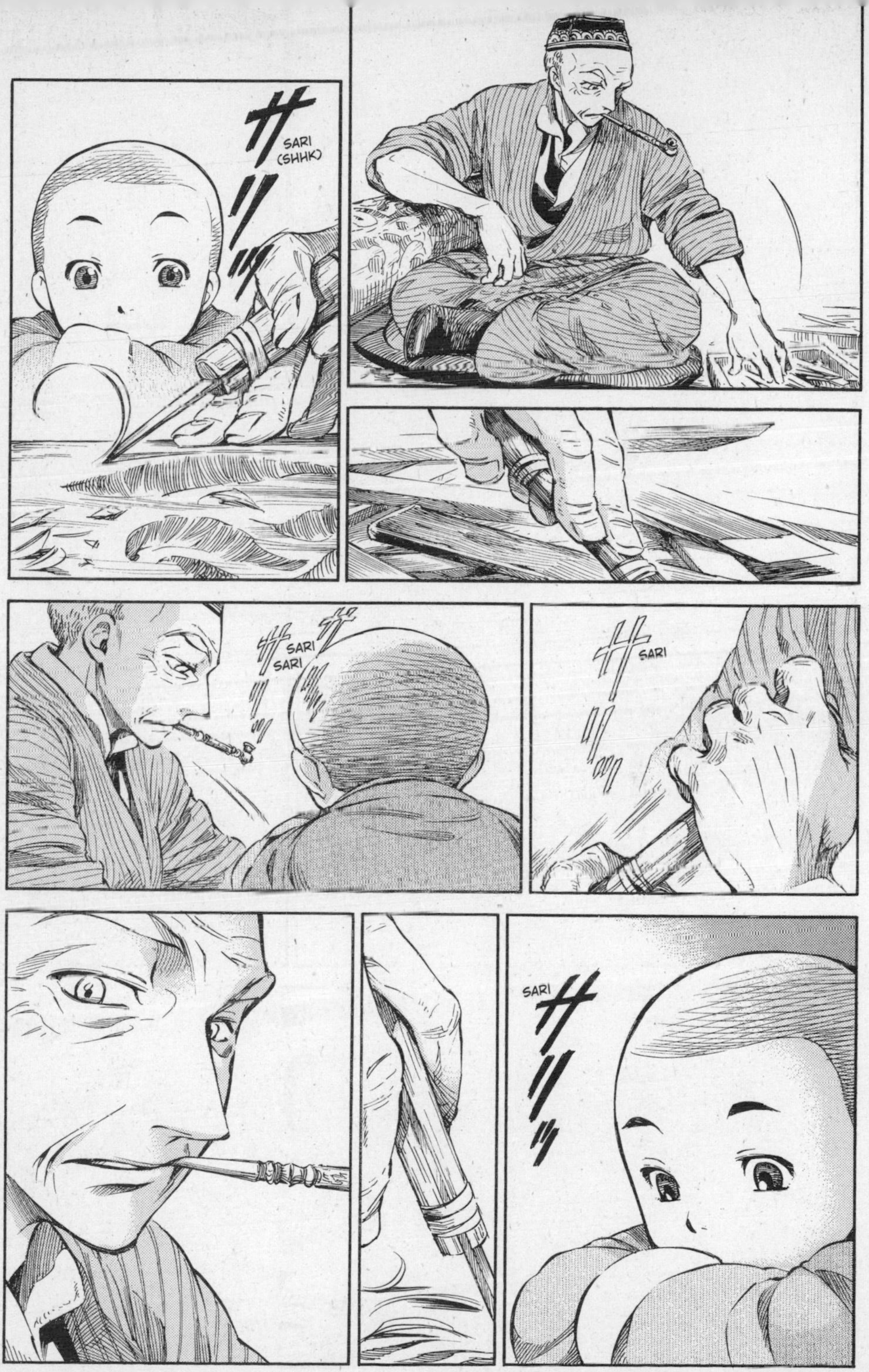
SARI
(SHHK)
SARI
SARI
SARI
SARI

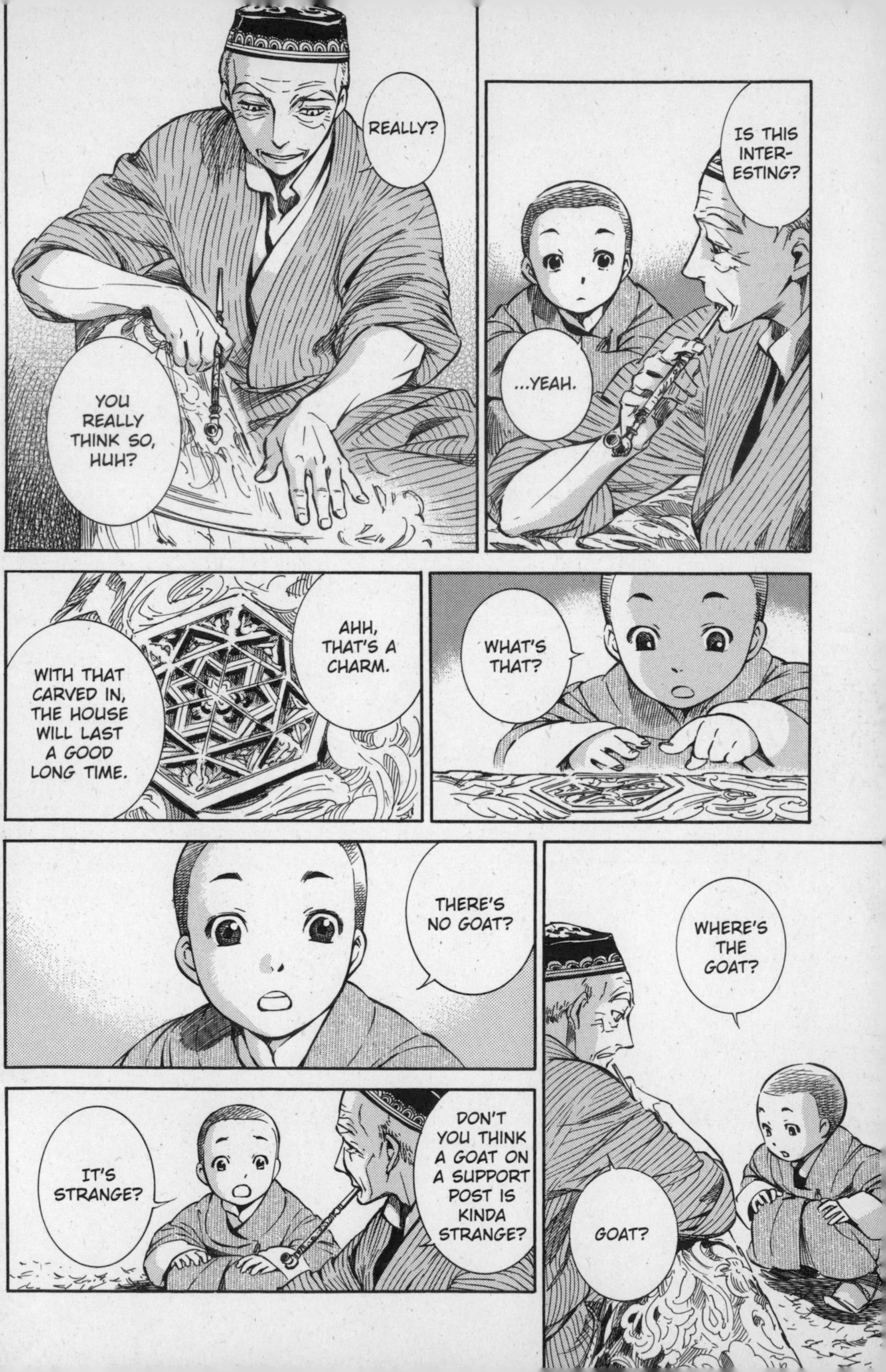
IS THIS INTER-ESTING?
...YEAH.
REALLY?
YOU REALLY THINK SO, HUH?
WHAT'S THAT?
AHH, THAT'S A CHARM.
WITH THAT CARVED IN, THE HOUSE WILL LAST A GOOD LONG TIME.
WHERE'S THE GOAT?
GOAT?
THERE'S NO GOAT?
DON'T YOU THINK A GOAT ON A SUPPORT POST IS KINDA STRANGE?
IT'S STRANGE?

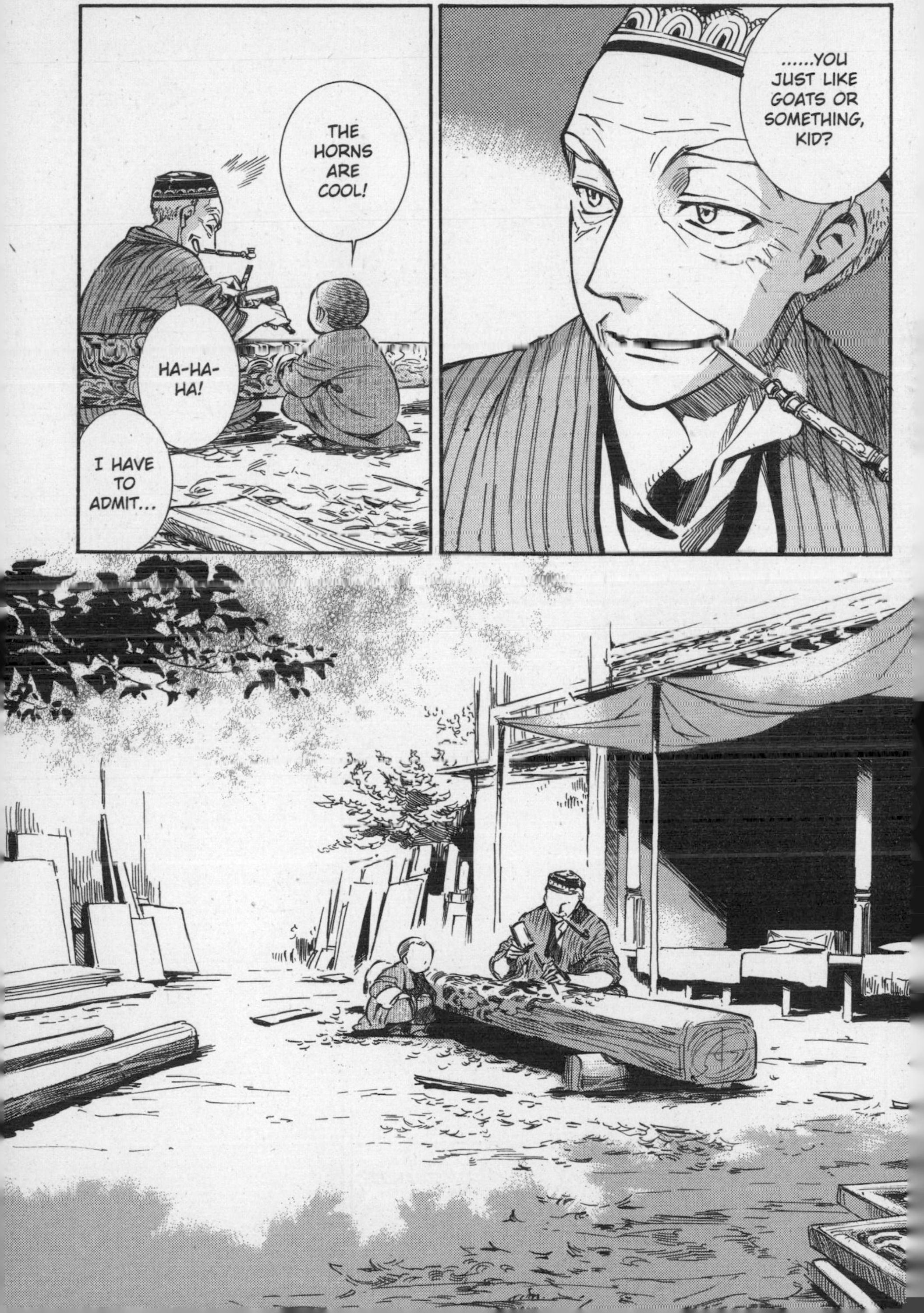

......YOU JUST LIKE GOATS OR SOMETHING, KID?
THE HORNS ARE COOL!
HA-HA-HA!
I HAVE TO ADMIT...

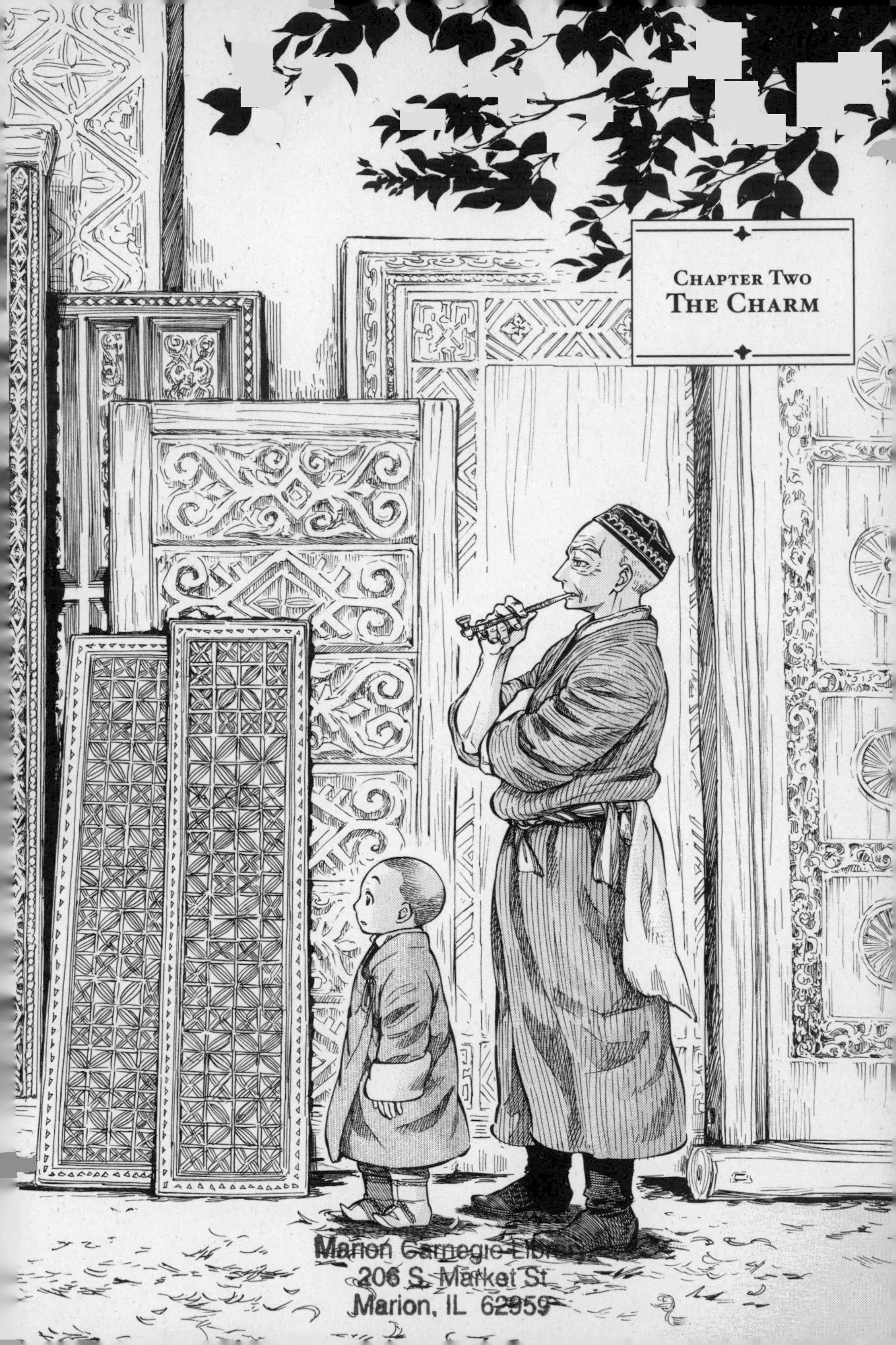
CHAPTER TWO
THE CHARM

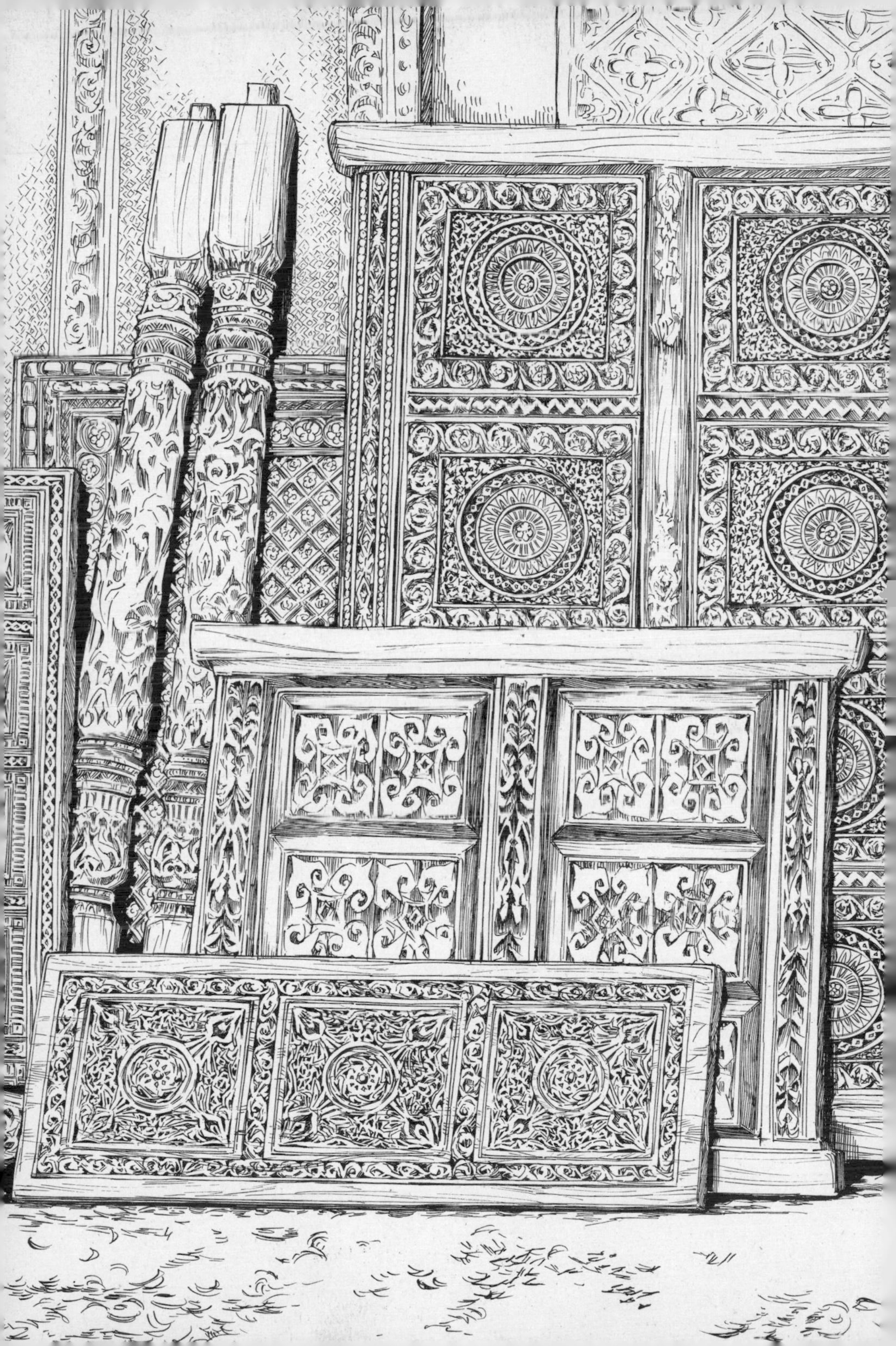

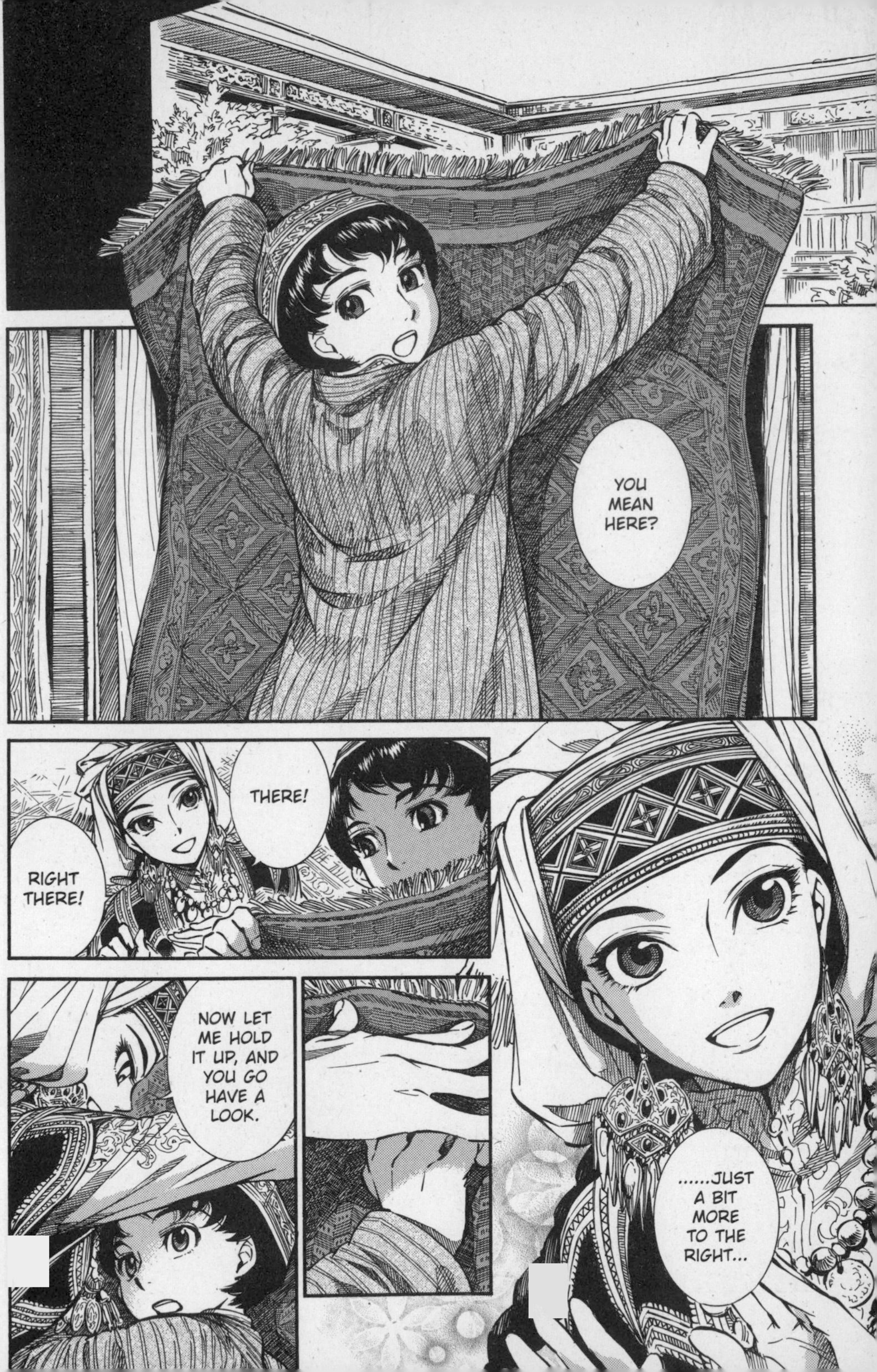
YOU MEAN HERE?
......JUST A BIT MORE TO THE RIGHT...
THERE!
RIGHT THERE!
NOW LET ME HOLD IT UP, AND YOU GO HAVE A LOOK.

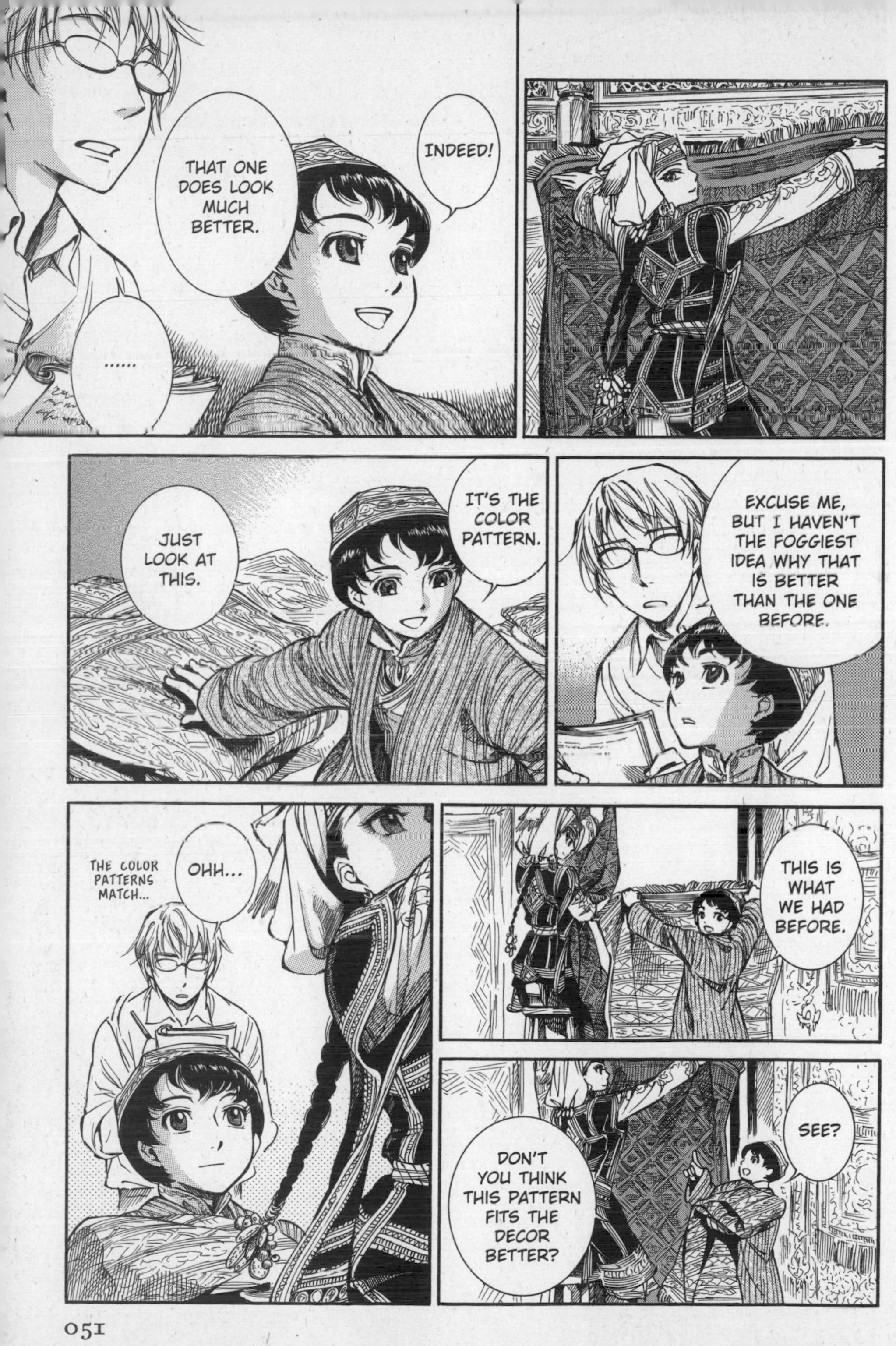
INDEED!
THAT ONE DOES LOOK MUCH BETTER.
......
EXCUSE ME, BUT I HAVEN'T THE FOGGIEST IDEA WHY THAT IS BETTER THAN THE ONE BEFORE.
IT'S THE COLOR PATTERN.
JUST LOOK AT THIS.
THIS IS WHAT WE HAD BEFORE.
SEE?
DON'T YOU THINK THIS PATTERN FITS THE DECOR BETTER?
OHH...
THE COLOR PATTERNS MATCH...

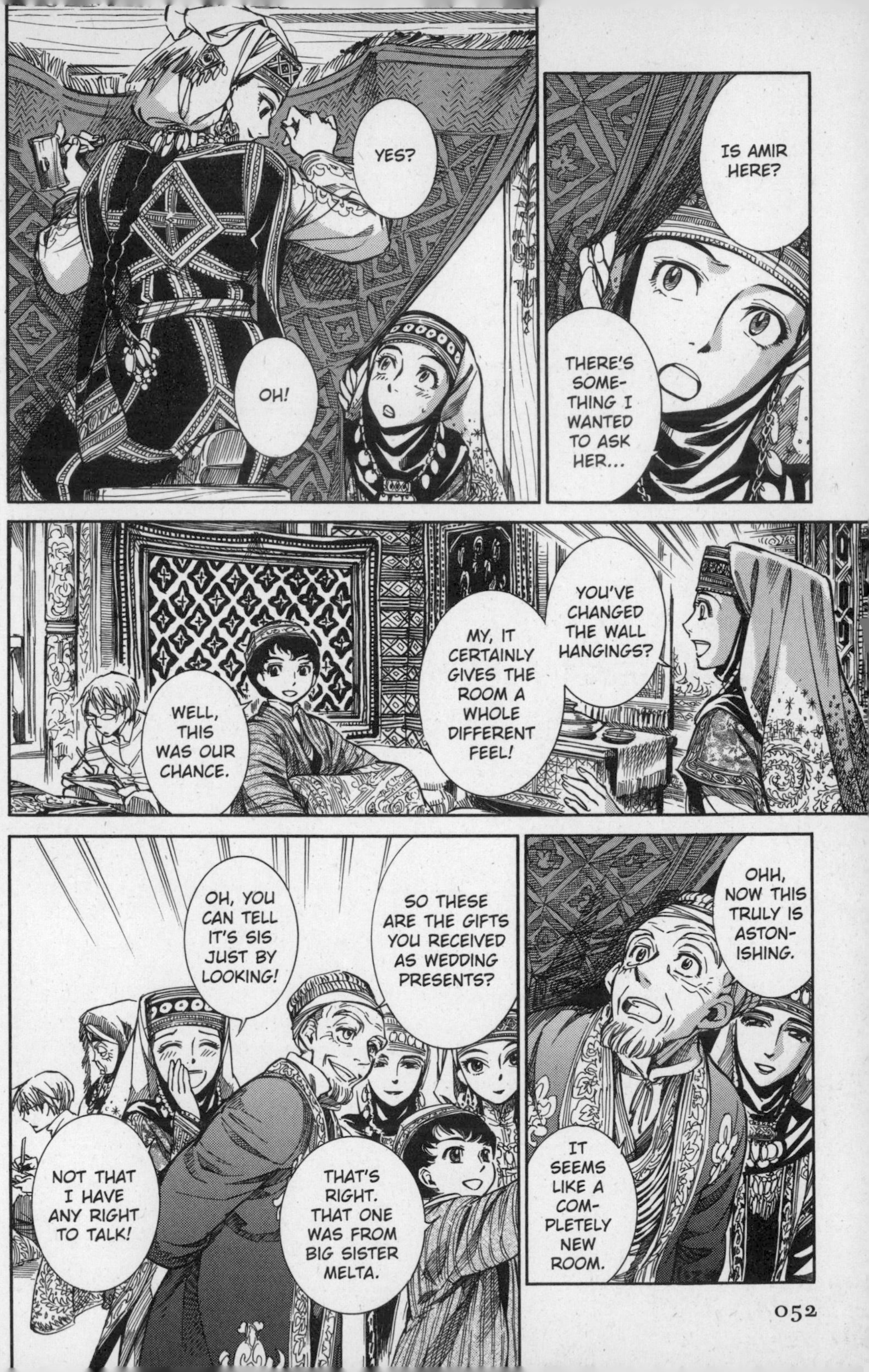
IS AMIR HERE?
THERE'S SOME-THING I WANTED TO ASK HER...
YES?
OH!
YOU'VE CHANGED THE WALL HANGINGS?
MY, IT CERTAINLY GIVES THE ROOM A WHOLE DIFFERENT FEEL!
WELL, THIS WAS OUR CHANCE.
OHH, NOW THIS TRULY IS ASTON-ISHING.
IT SEEMS LIKE A COM-PLETELY NEW ROOM.
SO THESE ARE THE GIFTS YOU RECEIVED AS WEDDING PRESENTS?
OH, YOU CAN TELL IT'S SIS JUST BY LOOKING!
THAT'S RIGHT. THAT ONE WAS FROM BIG SISTER MELTA.
NOT THAT I HAVE ANY RIGHT TO TALK!

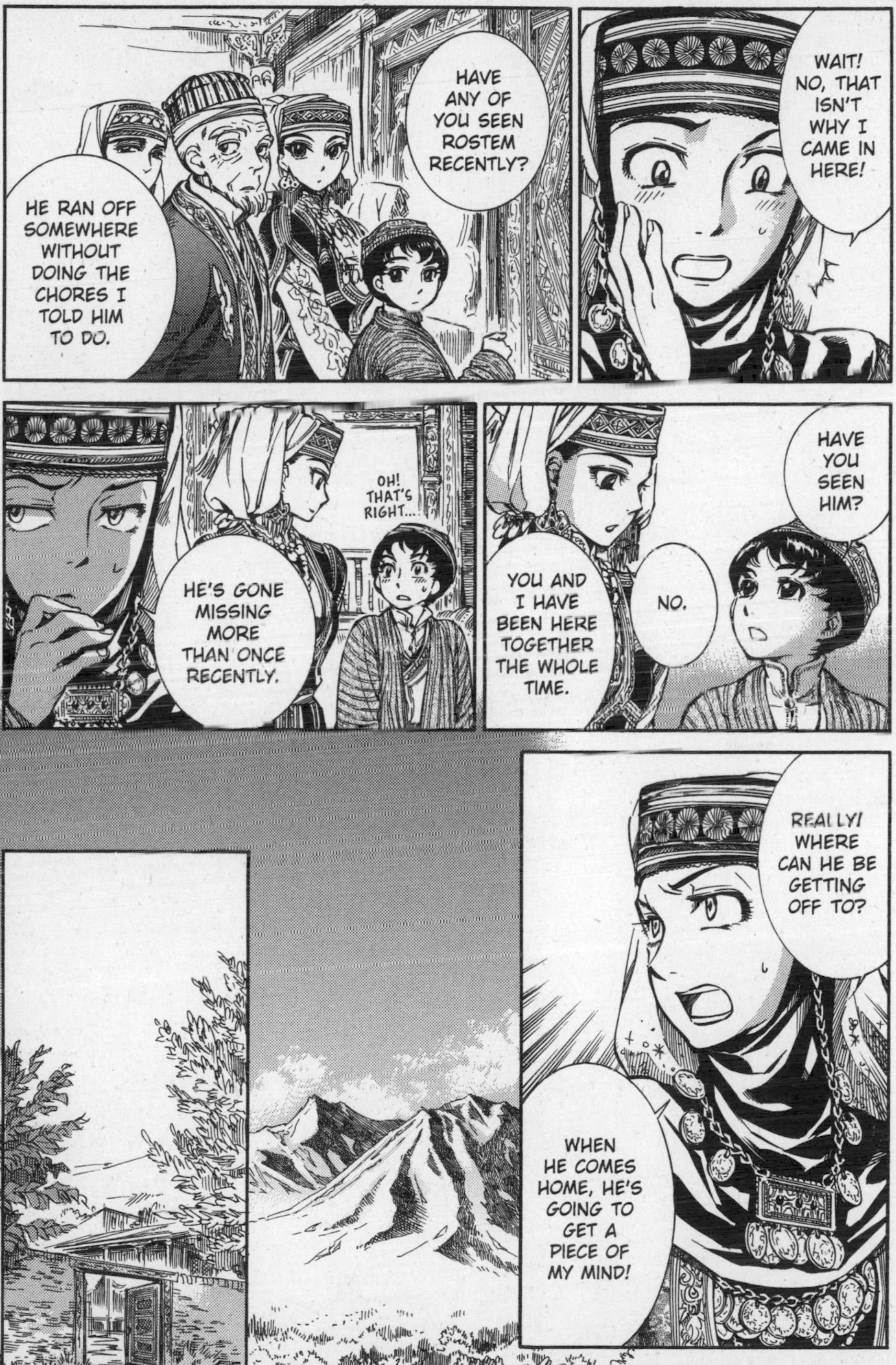
WAIT! NO, THAT ISN'T WHY I CAME IN HERE!
HAVE ANY OF YOU SEEN ROSTEM RECENTLY?
HE RAN OFF SOMEWHERE WITHOUT DOING THE CHORES I TOLD HIM TO DO.
HAVE YOU SEEN HIM?
NO.
YOU AND I HAVE BEEN HERE TOGETHER THE WHOLE TIME.
OH! THAT'S RIGHT...
HE'S GONE MISSING MORE THAN ONCE RECENTLY.
REALLY! WHERE CAN HE BE GETTING OFF TO?
WHEN HE COMES HOME, HE'S GOING TO GET A PIECE OF MY MIND!

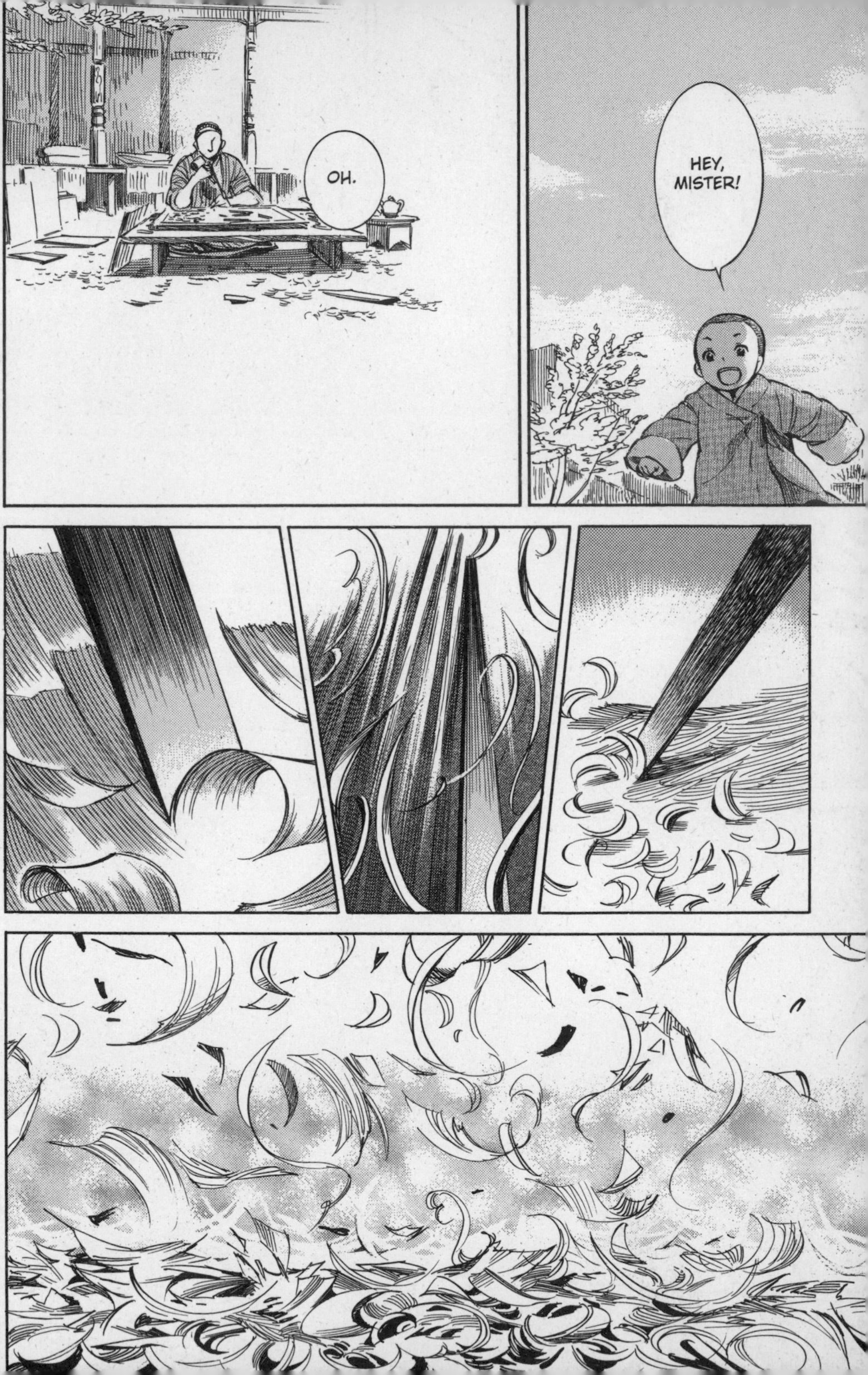
HEY, MISTER!
OH.

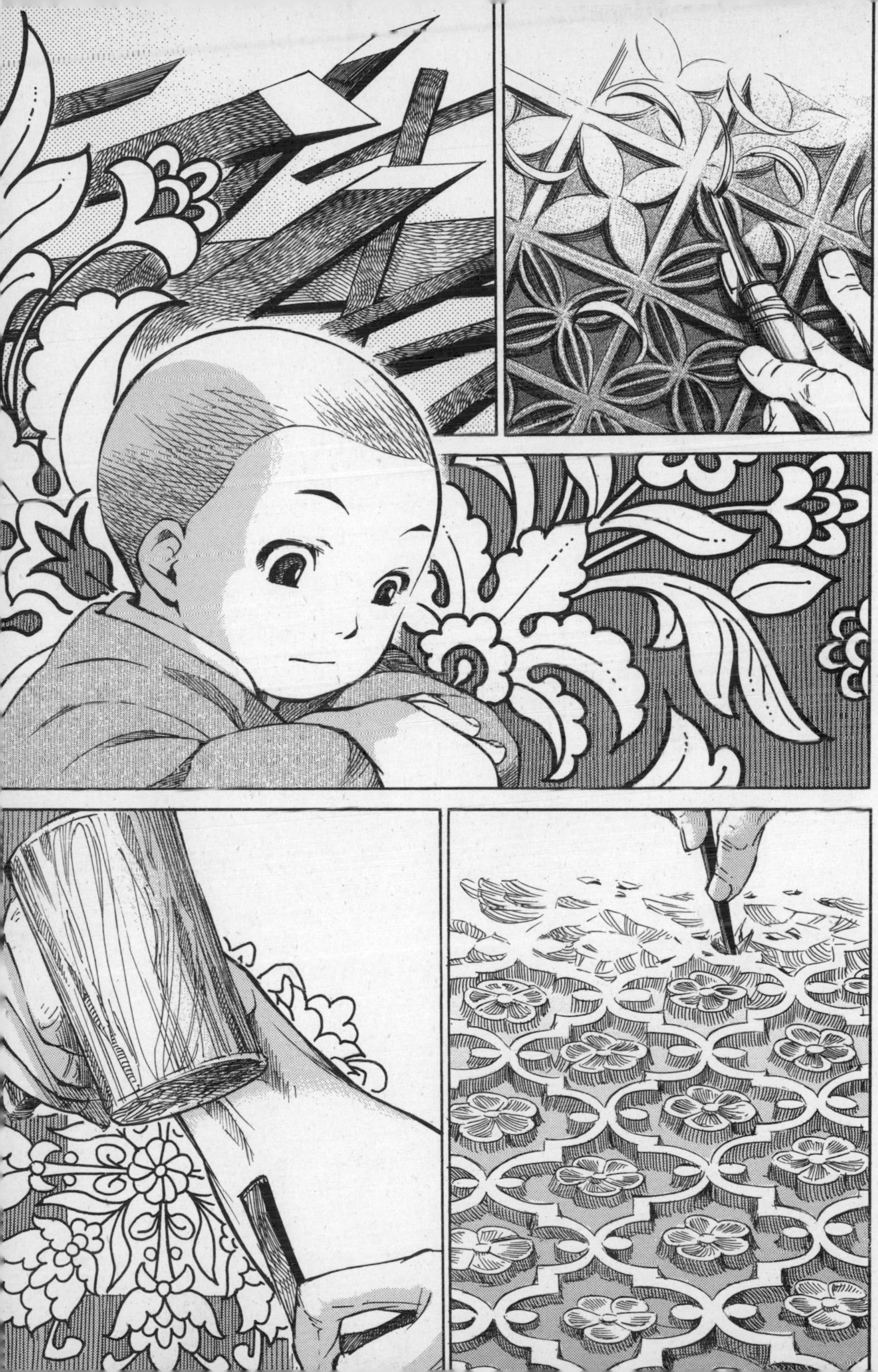

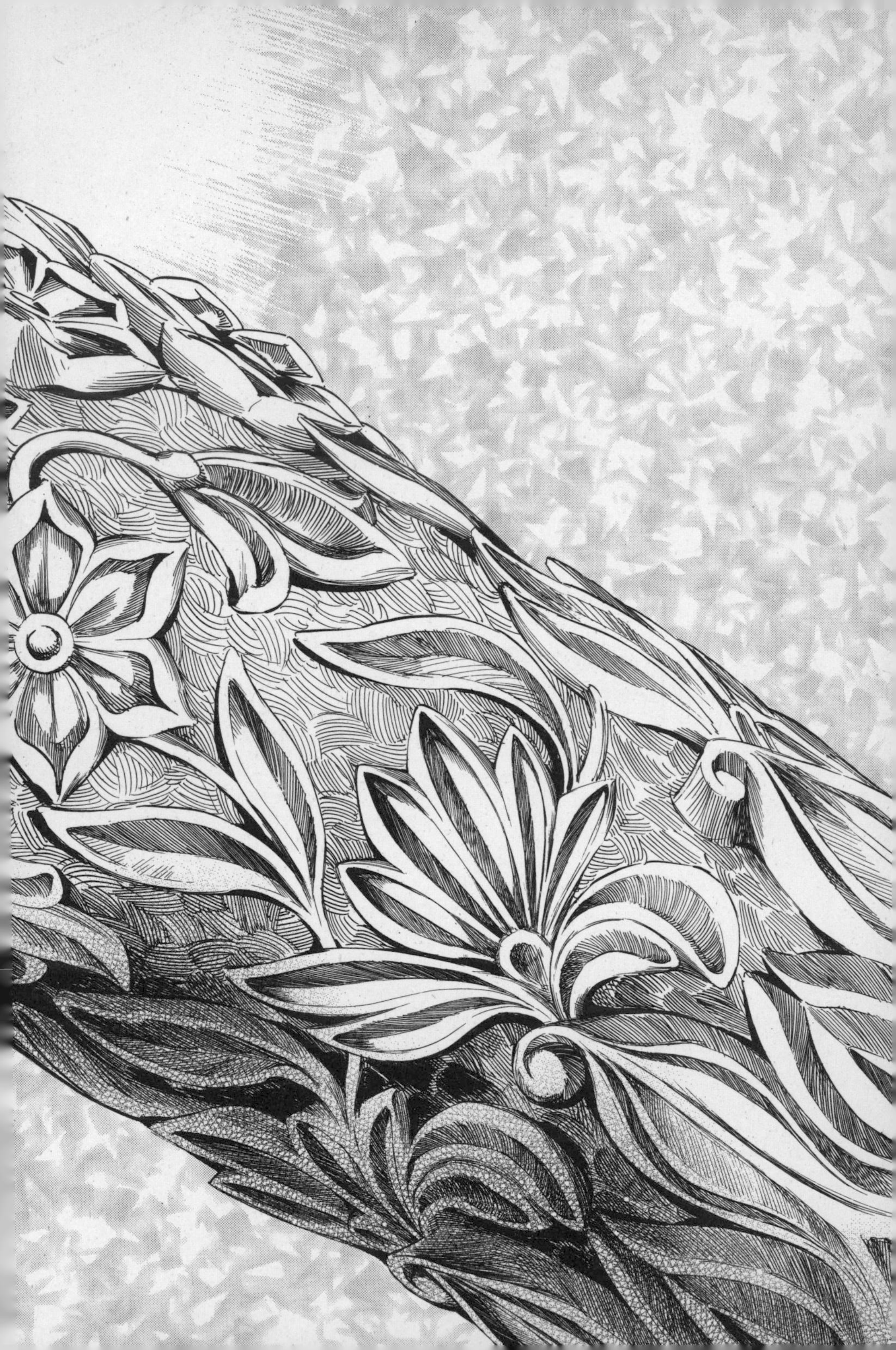

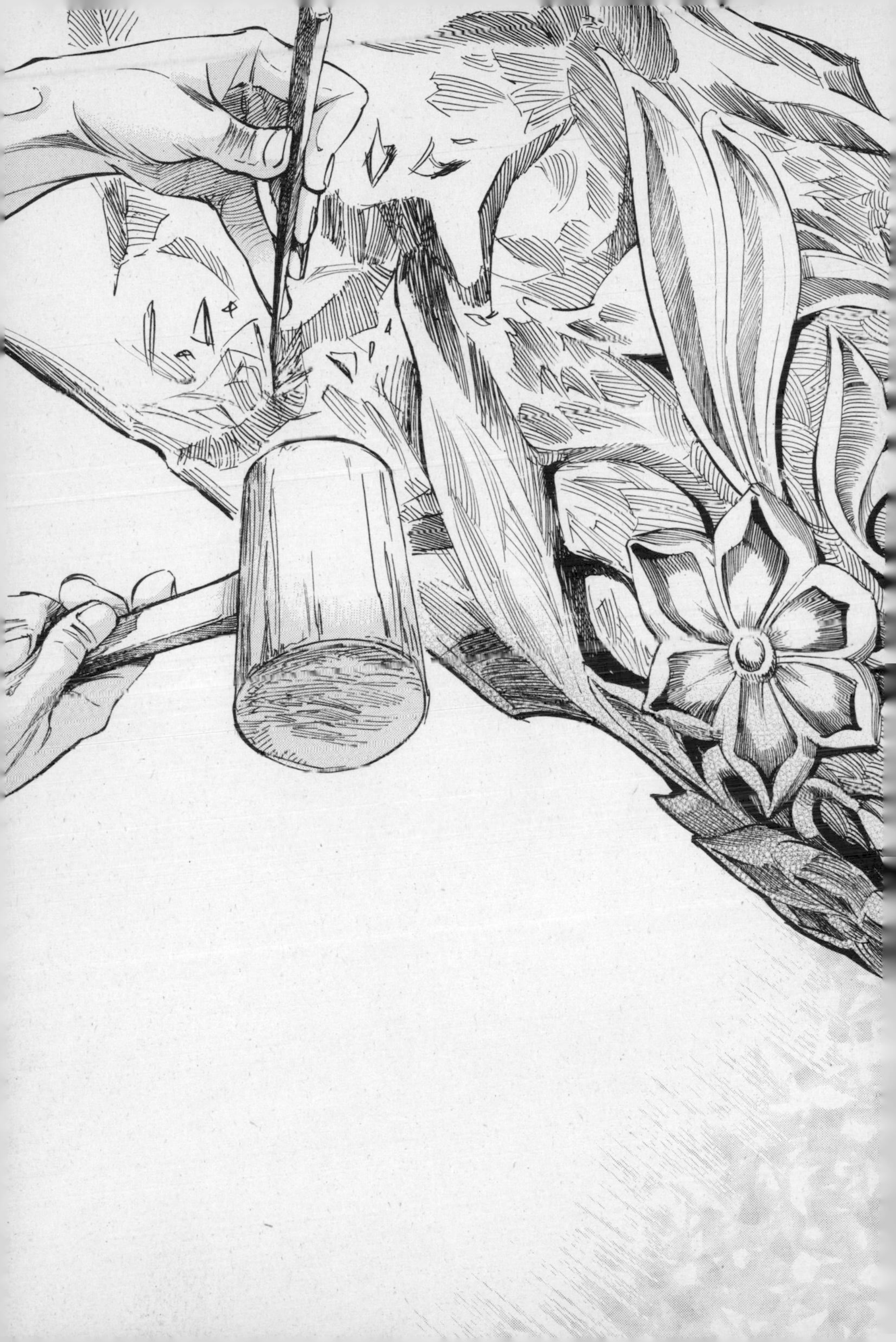

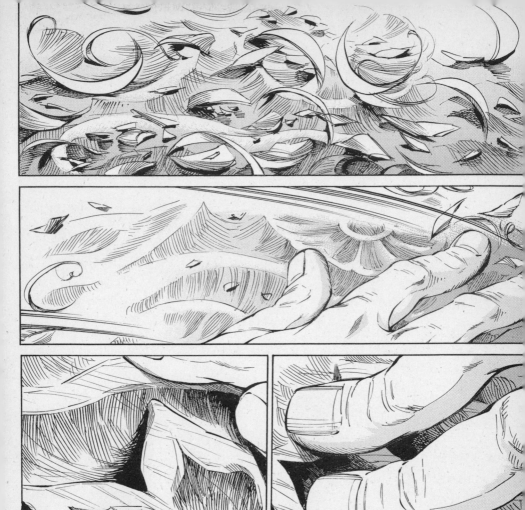

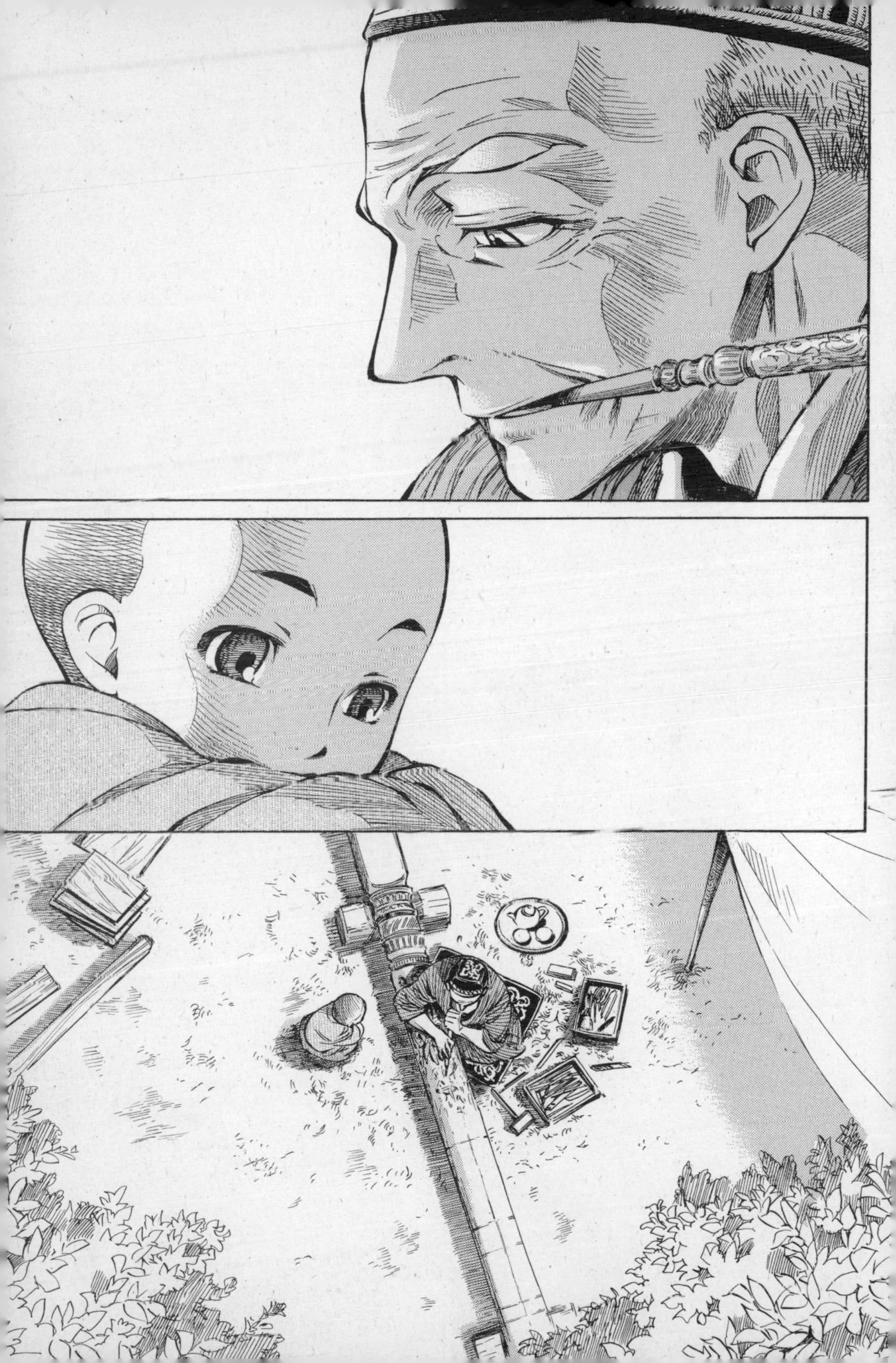

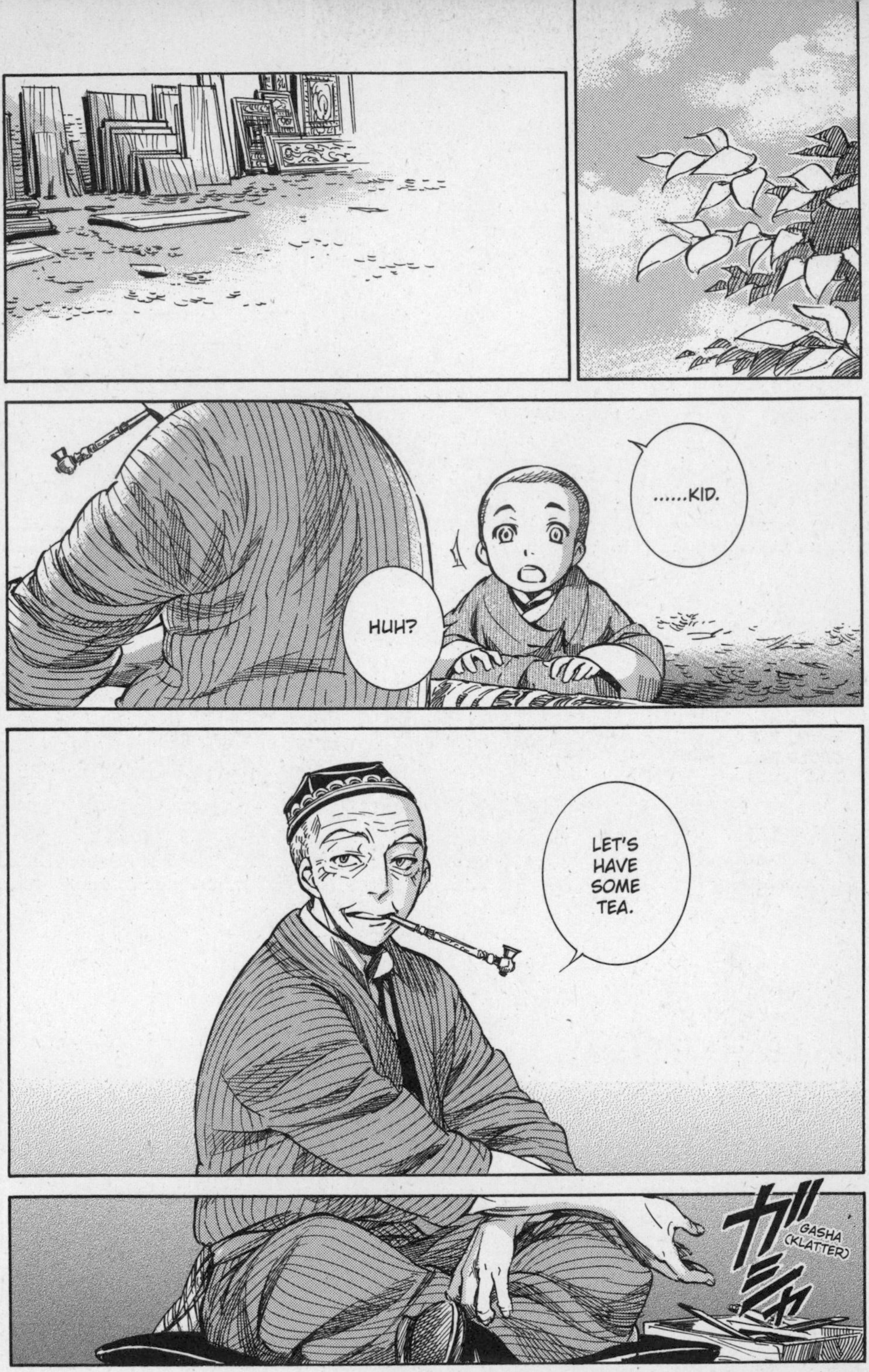
......KID.
HUH?
LET'S HAVE SOME TEA.
ガシャ
GASHA (KLATTER)

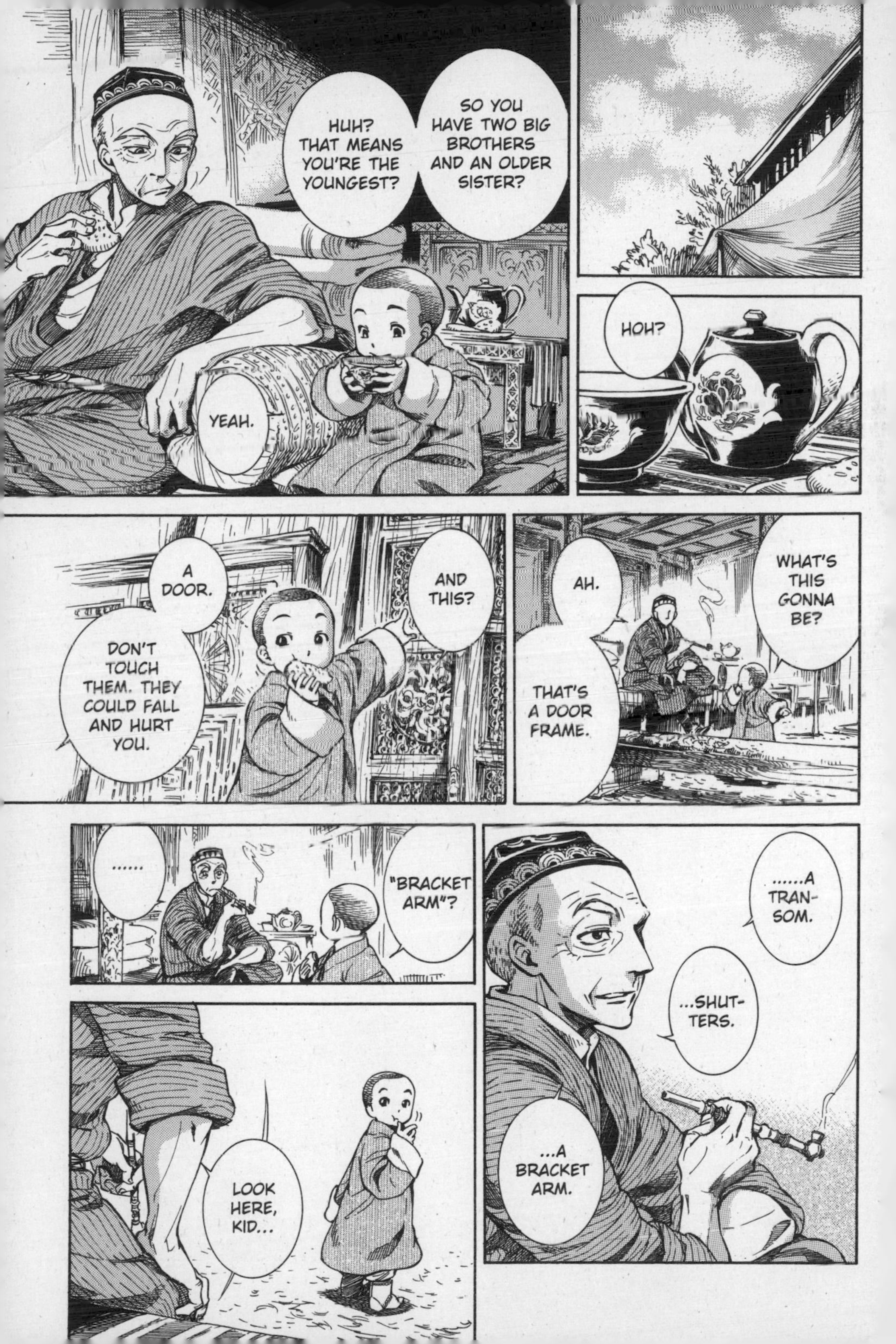
HOH?
SO YOU HAVE TWO BIG BROTHERS AND AN OLDER SISTER?
HUH? THAT MEANS YOU'RE THE YOUNGEST?
YEAH.
WHAT'S THIS GONNA BE?
AH.
THAT'S A DOOR FRAME.
AND THIS?
A DOOR.
DON'T TOUCH THEM. THEY COULD FALL AND HURT YOU.
......A TRAN-SOM.
...SHUT-TERS.
...A BRACKET ARM.
"BRACKET ARM"?
......
LOOK HERE, KID...

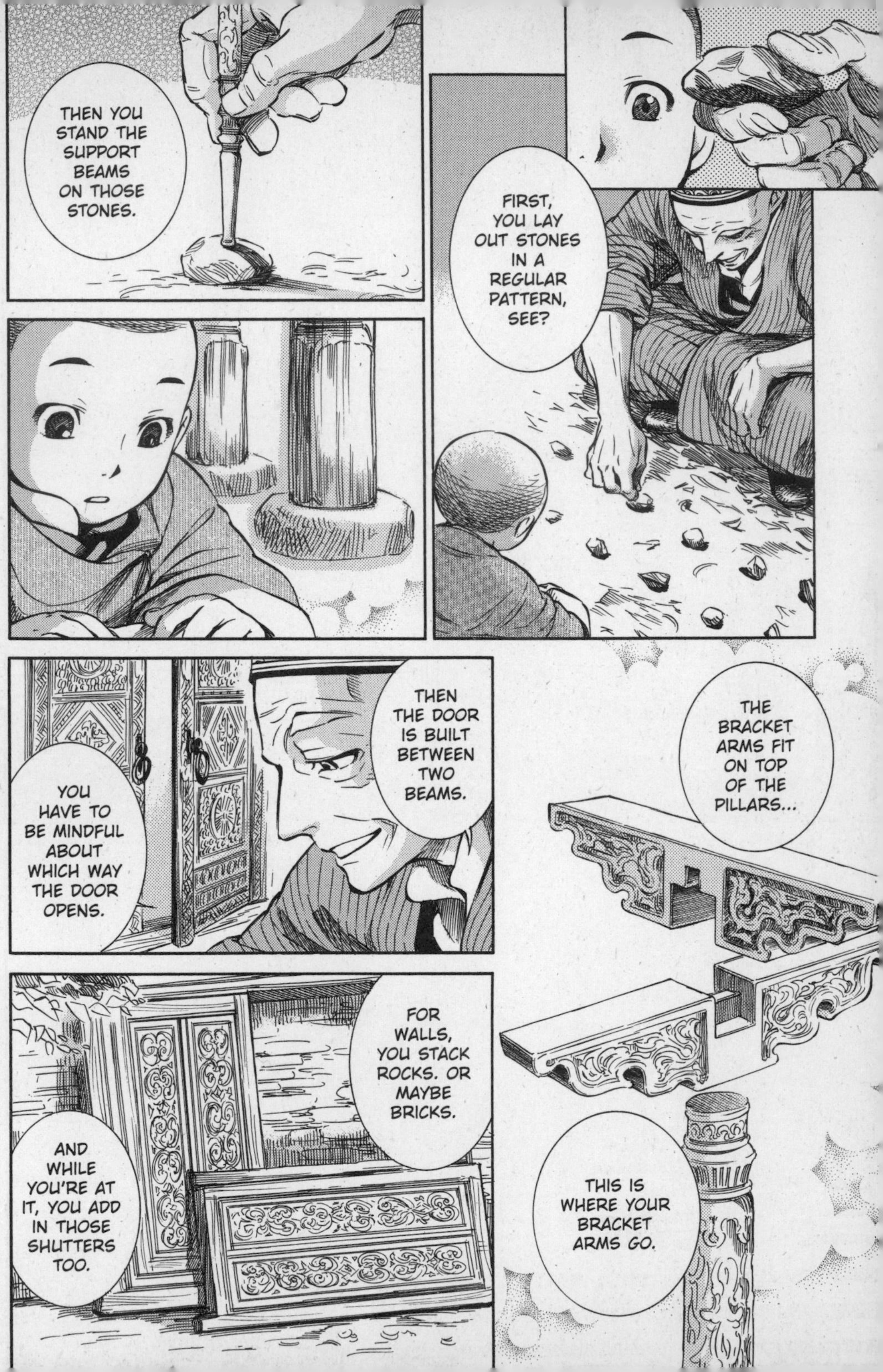
FIRST, YOU LAY OUT STONES IN A REGULAR PATTERN, SEE?
THEN YOU STAND THE SUPPORT BEAMS ON THOSE STONES.
THE BRACKET ARMS FIT ON TOP OF THE PILLARS...
THIS IS WHERE YOUR BRACKET ARMS GO.
THEN THE DOOR IS BUILT BETWEEN TWO BEAMS.
YOU HAVE TO BE MINDFUL ABOUT WHICH WAY THE DOOR OPENS.
FOR WALLS, YOU STACK ROCKS. OR MAYBE BRICKS.
AND WHILE YOU'RE AT IT, YOU ADD IN THOSE SHUTTERS TOO.

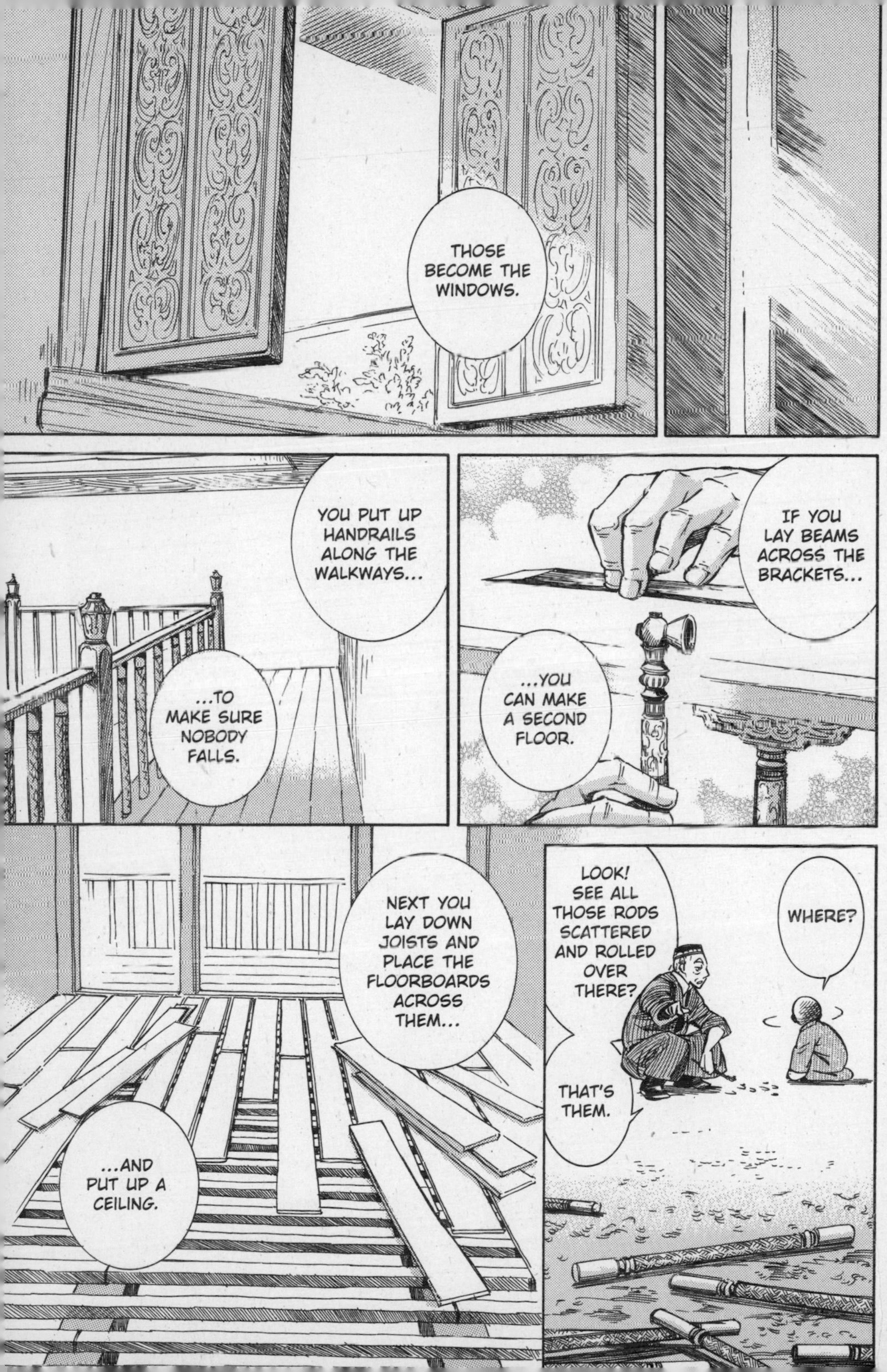
THOSE BECOME THE WINDOWS.
IF YOU LAY BEAMS ACROSS THE BRACKETS...
...YOU CAN MAKE A SECOND FLOOR.
YOU PUT UP HANDRAILS ALONG THE WALKWAYS...
...TO MAKE SURE NOBODY FALLS.
LOOK! SEE ALL THOSE RODS SCATTERED AND ROLLED OVER THERE?
WHERE?
THAT'S THEM.
NEXT YOU LAY DOWN JOISTS AND PLACE THE FLOORBOARDS ACROSS THEM...
...AND PUT UP A CEILING.

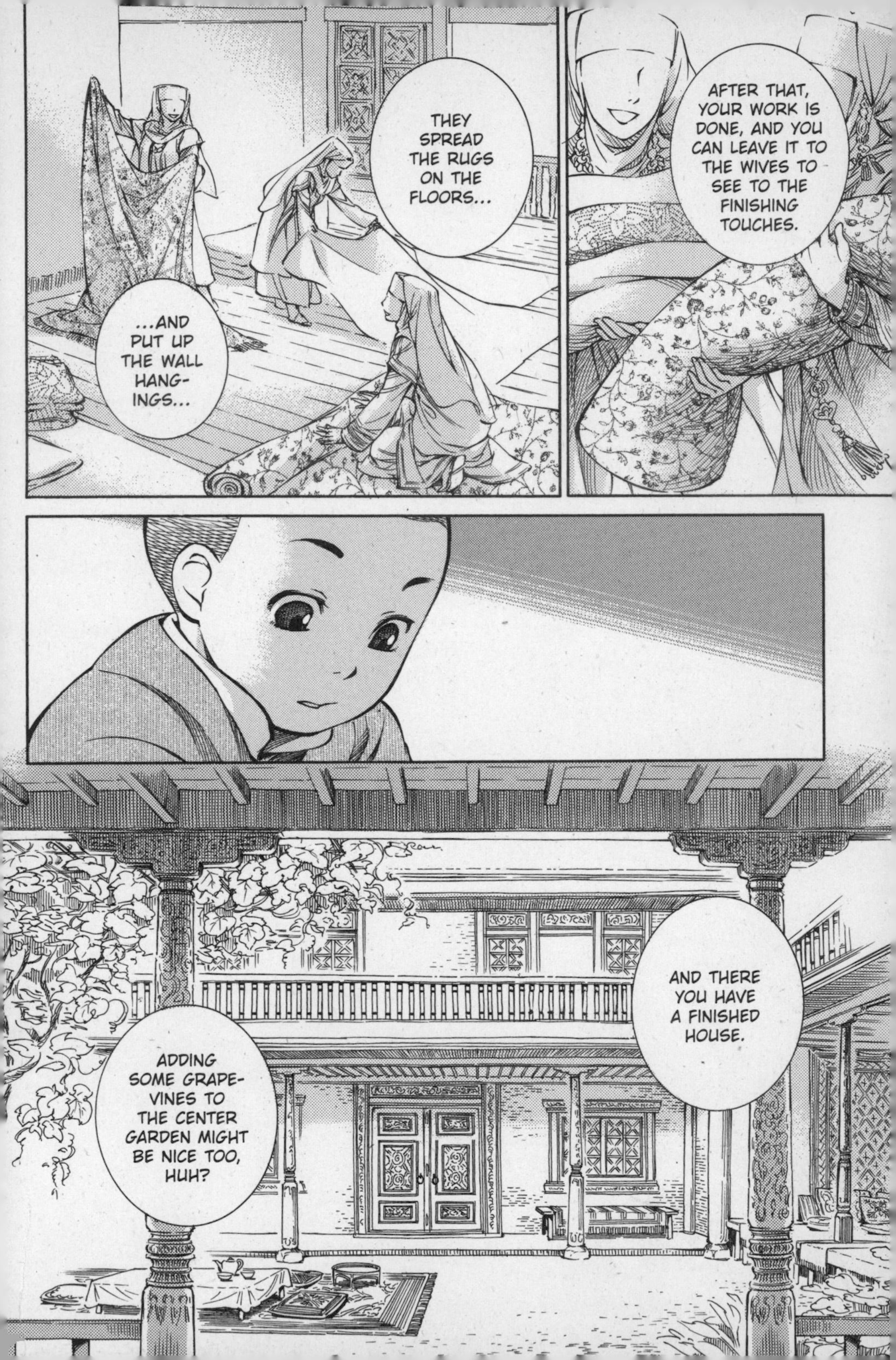
AFTER THAT, YOUR WORK IS DONE, AND YOU CAN LEAVE IT TO THE WIVES TO SEE TO THE FINISHING TOUCHES.
THEY SPREAD THE RUGS ON THE FLOORS...
...AND PUT UP THE WALL HANG-INGS...
AND THERE YOU HAVE A FINISHED HOUSE.
ADDING SOME GRAPE-VINES TO THE CENTER GARDEN MIGHT BE NICE TOO, HUH?

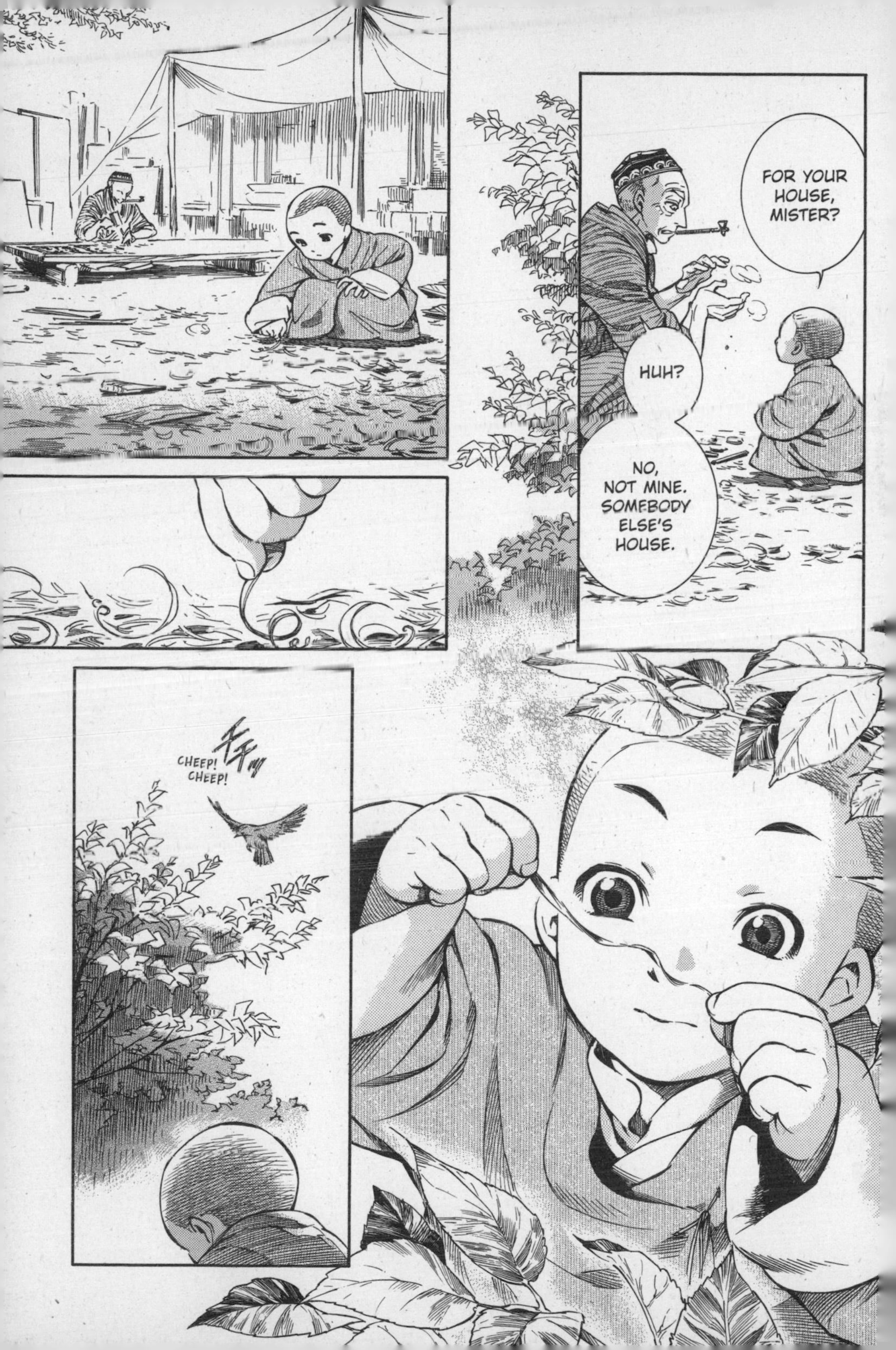
FOR YOUR HOUSE, MISTER?
HUH?
NO, NOT MINE. SOMEBODY ELSE'S HOUSE.
CHEEP! CHEEP!

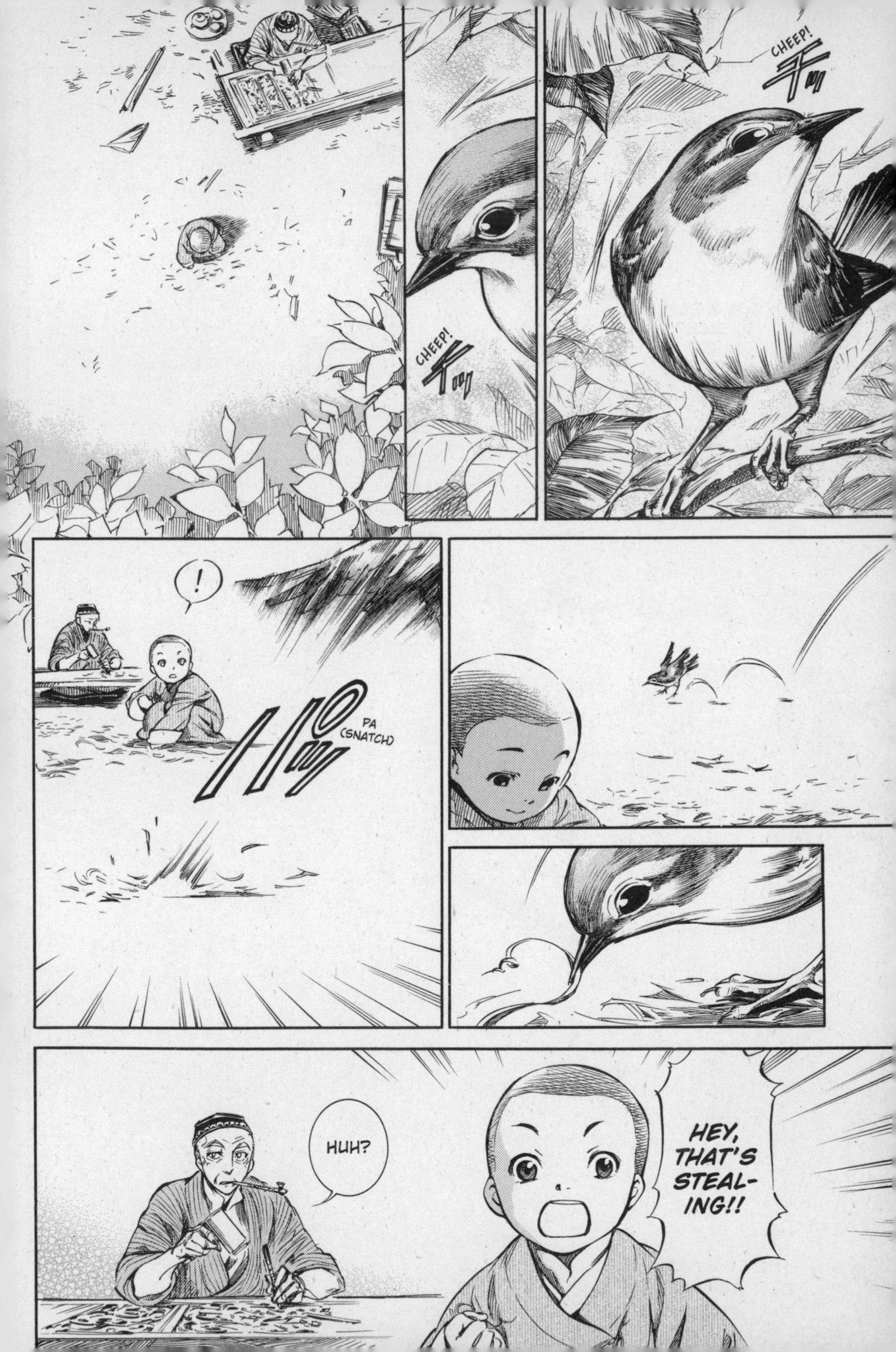

CHEEP!
CHEEP!
!
PA (SNATCH)
HEY, THAT'S STEAL-ING!!
HUH?

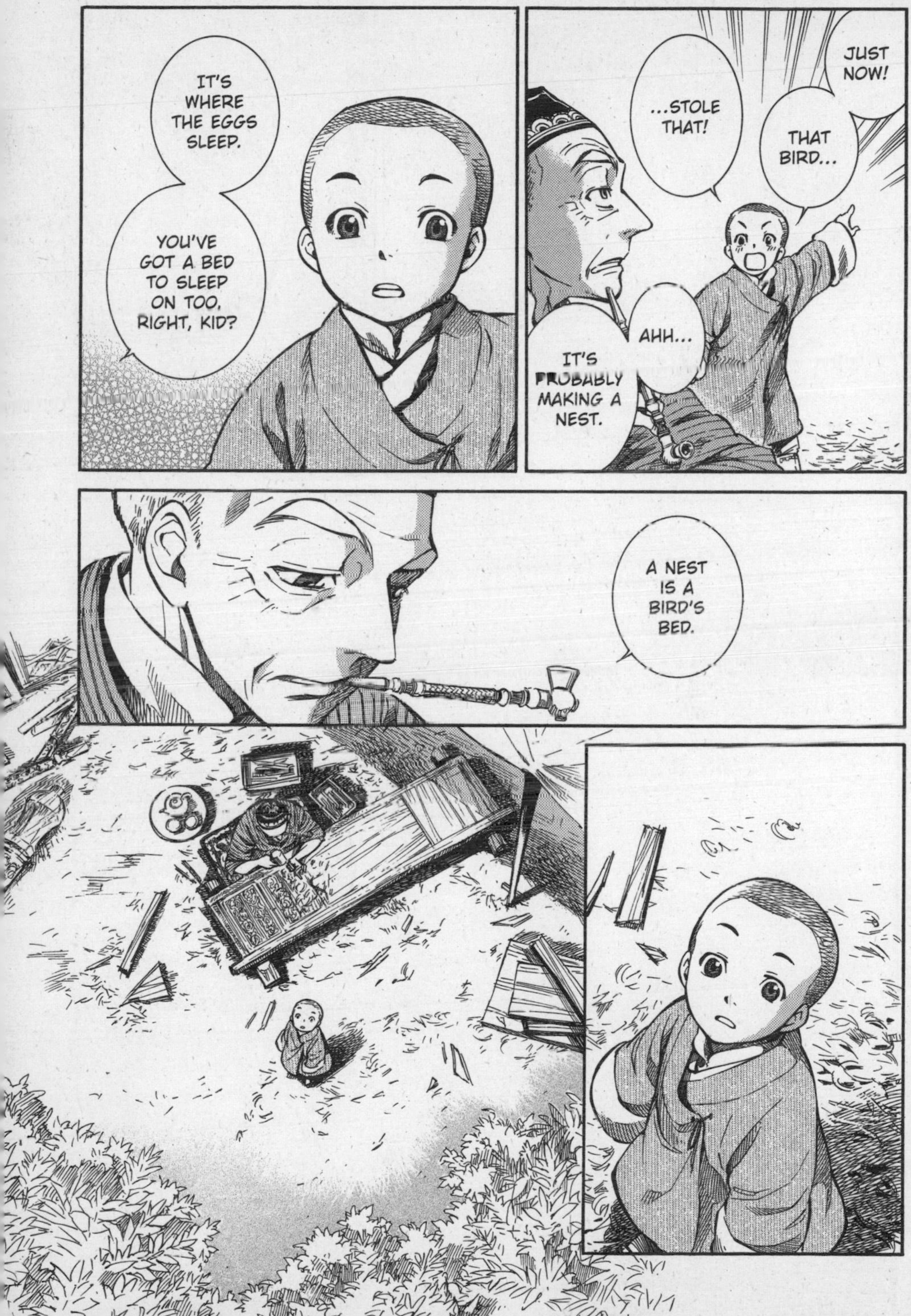
JUST NOW!
THAT BIRD...
...STOLE THAT!
AHH...
IT'S PROBABLY MAKING A NEST.
IT'S WHERE THE EGGS SLEEP.
YOU'VE GOT A BED TO SLEEP ON TOO, RIGHT, KID?
A NEST IS A BIRD'S BED.

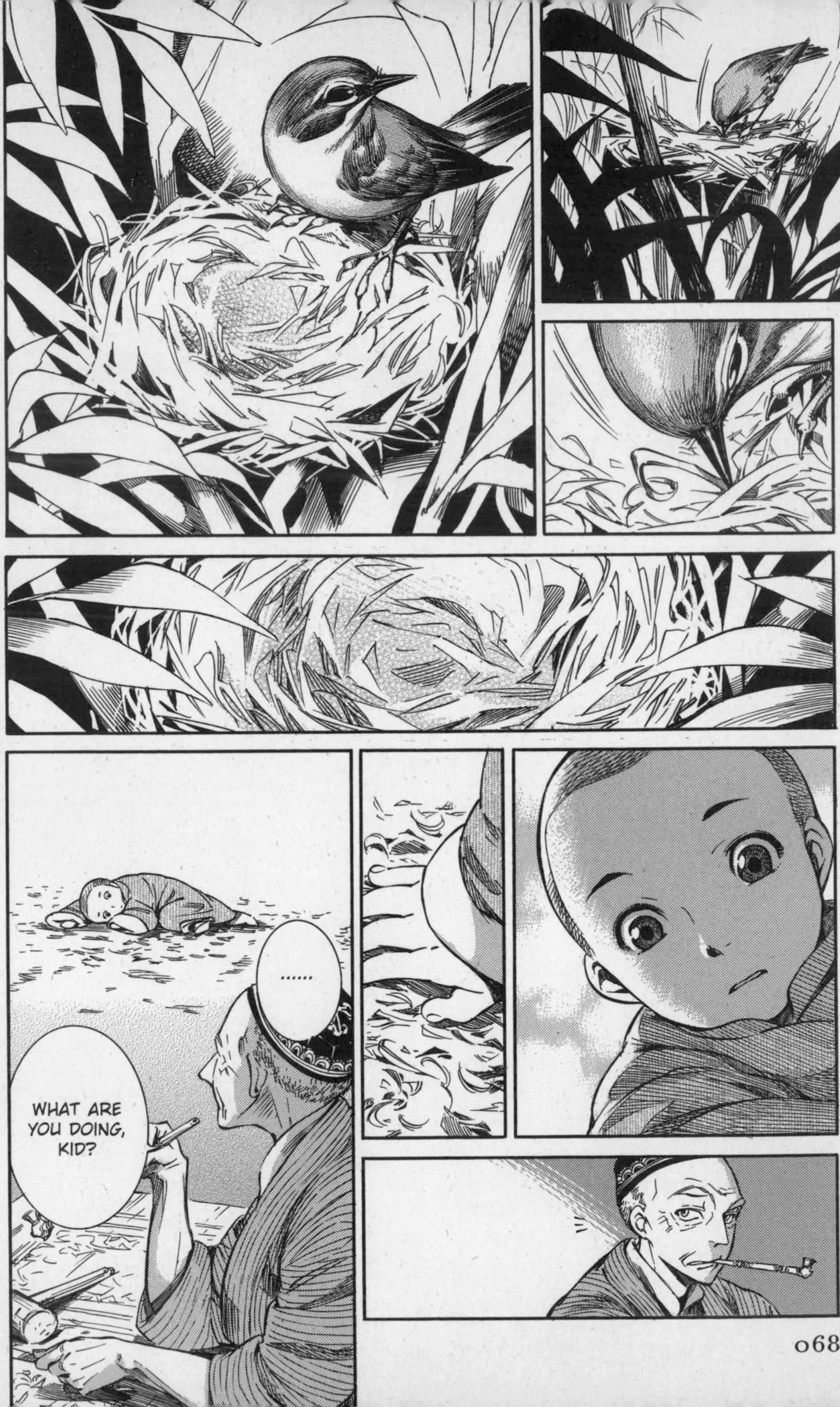
......
WHAT ARE YOU DOING, KID?

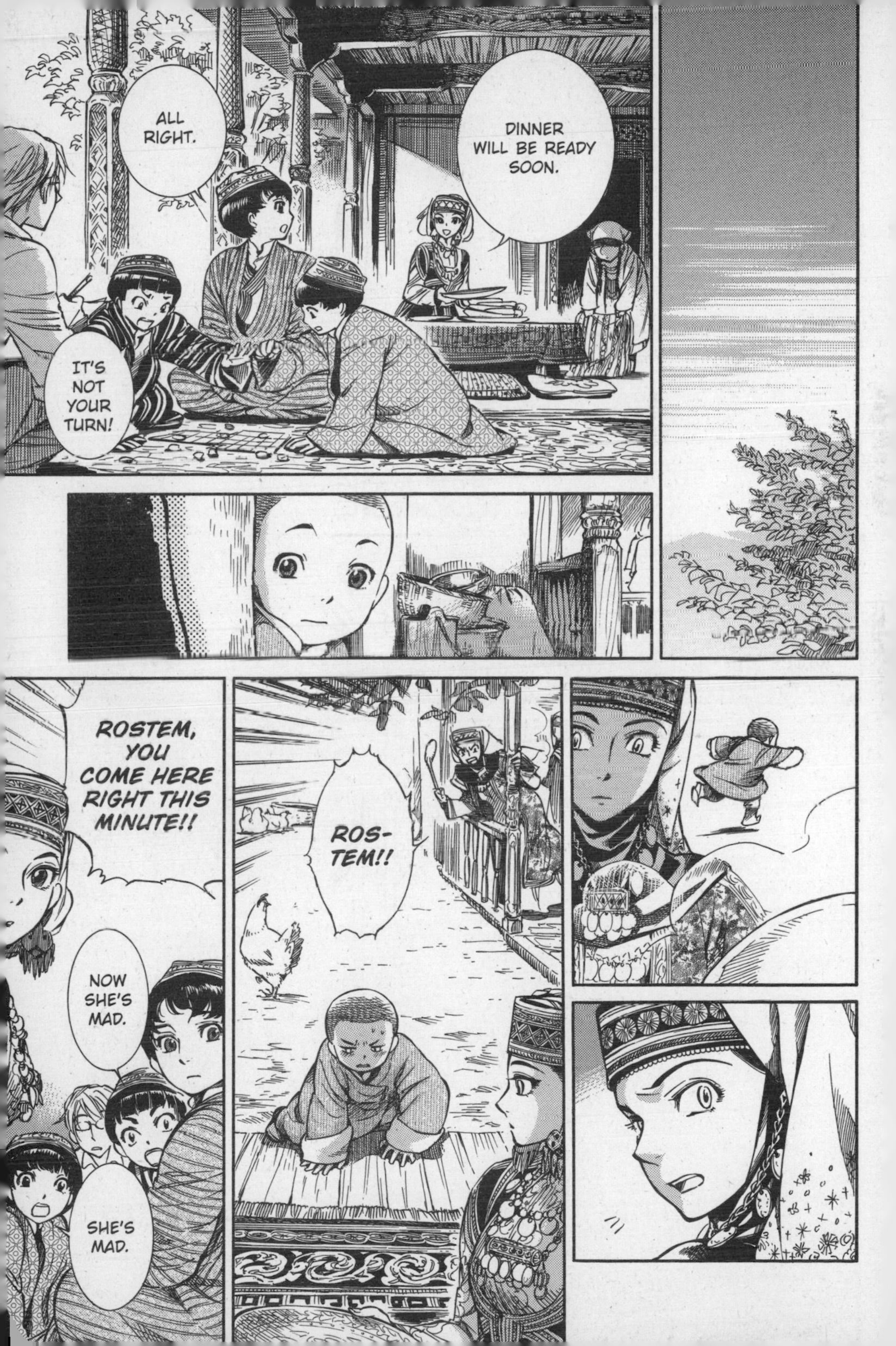
DINNER WILL BE READY SOON.
ALL RIGHT.
IT'S NOT YOUR TURN!
ROS-TEM!!
ROSTEM, YOU COME HERE RIGHT THIS MINUTE!!
NOW SHE'S MAD.
SHE'S MAD.

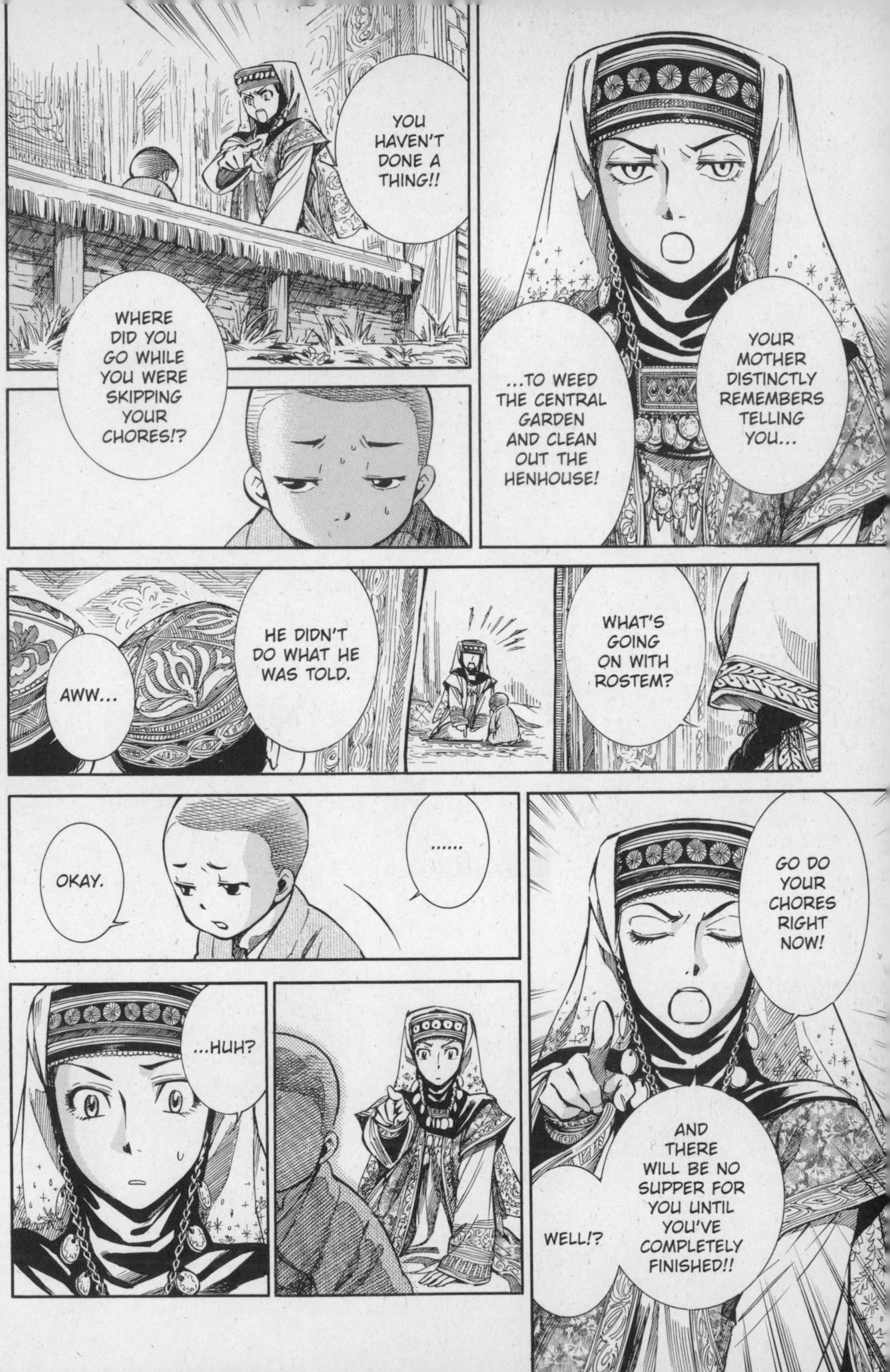
YOUR MOTHER DISTINCTLY REMEMBERS TELLING YOU...
...TO WEED THE CENTRAL GARDEN AND CLEAN OUT THE HENHOUSE!
YOU HAVEN'T DONE A THING!!
WHERE DID YOU GO WHILE YOU WERE SKIPPING YOUR CHORES!?
WHAT'S GOING ON WITH ROSTEM?
HE DIDN'T DO WHAT HE WAS TOLD.
AWW...
GO DO YOUR CHORES RIGHT NOW!
AND THERE WILL BE NO SUPPER FOR YOU UNTIL YOU'VE COMPLETELY FINISHED!!
WELL!?
......
OKAY.
...HUH?

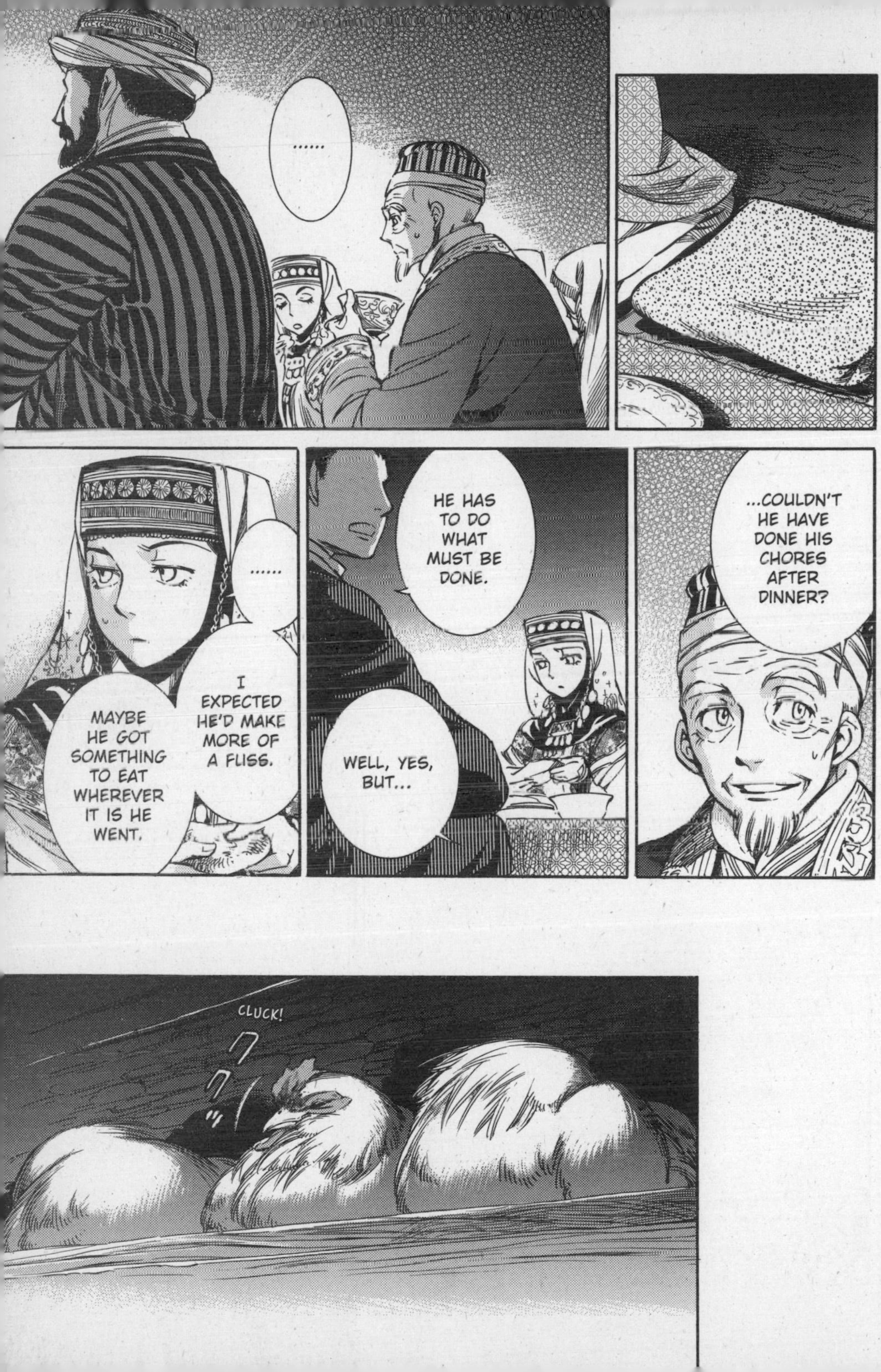
......
...COULDN'T HE HAVE DONE HIS CHORES AFTER DINNER?
HE HAS TO DO WHAT MUST BE DONE.
WELL, YES, BUT...
......
I EXPECTED HE'D MAKE MORE OF A FUSS.
MAYBE HE GOT SOMETHING TO EAT WHEREVER IT IS HE WENT.
CLUCK!

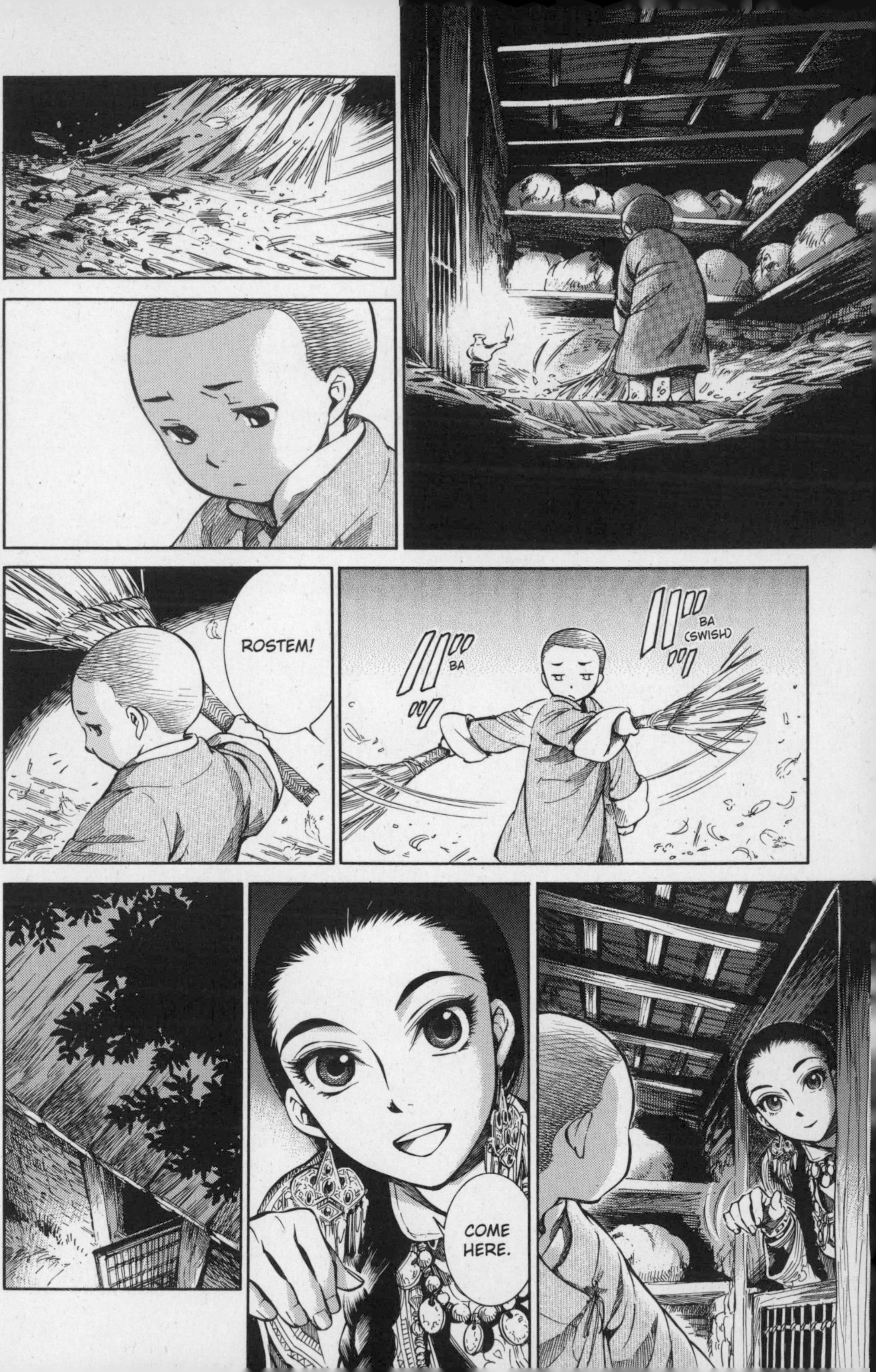
BA (SWISH)
BA
ROSTEM!
COME HERE.

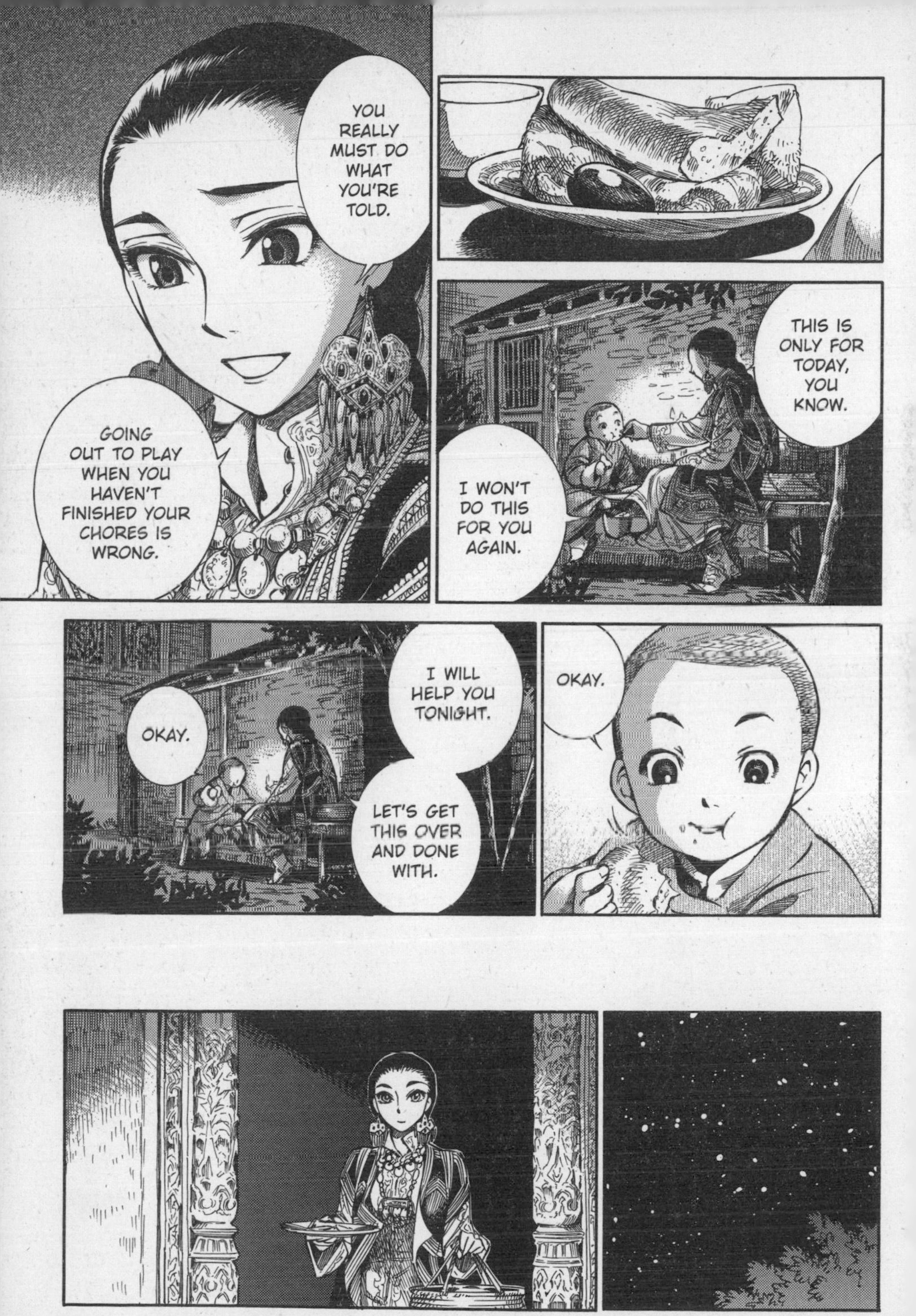
THIS IS ONLY FOR TODAY, YOU KNOW.
I WON'T DO THIS FOR YOU AGAIN.
YOU REALLY MUST DO WHAT YOU'RE TOLD.
GOING OUT TO PLAY WHEN YOU HAVEN'T FINISHED YOUR CHORES IS WRONG.
OKAY.
I WILL HELP YOU TONIGHT.
OKAY.
LET'S GET THIS OVER AND DONE WITH.

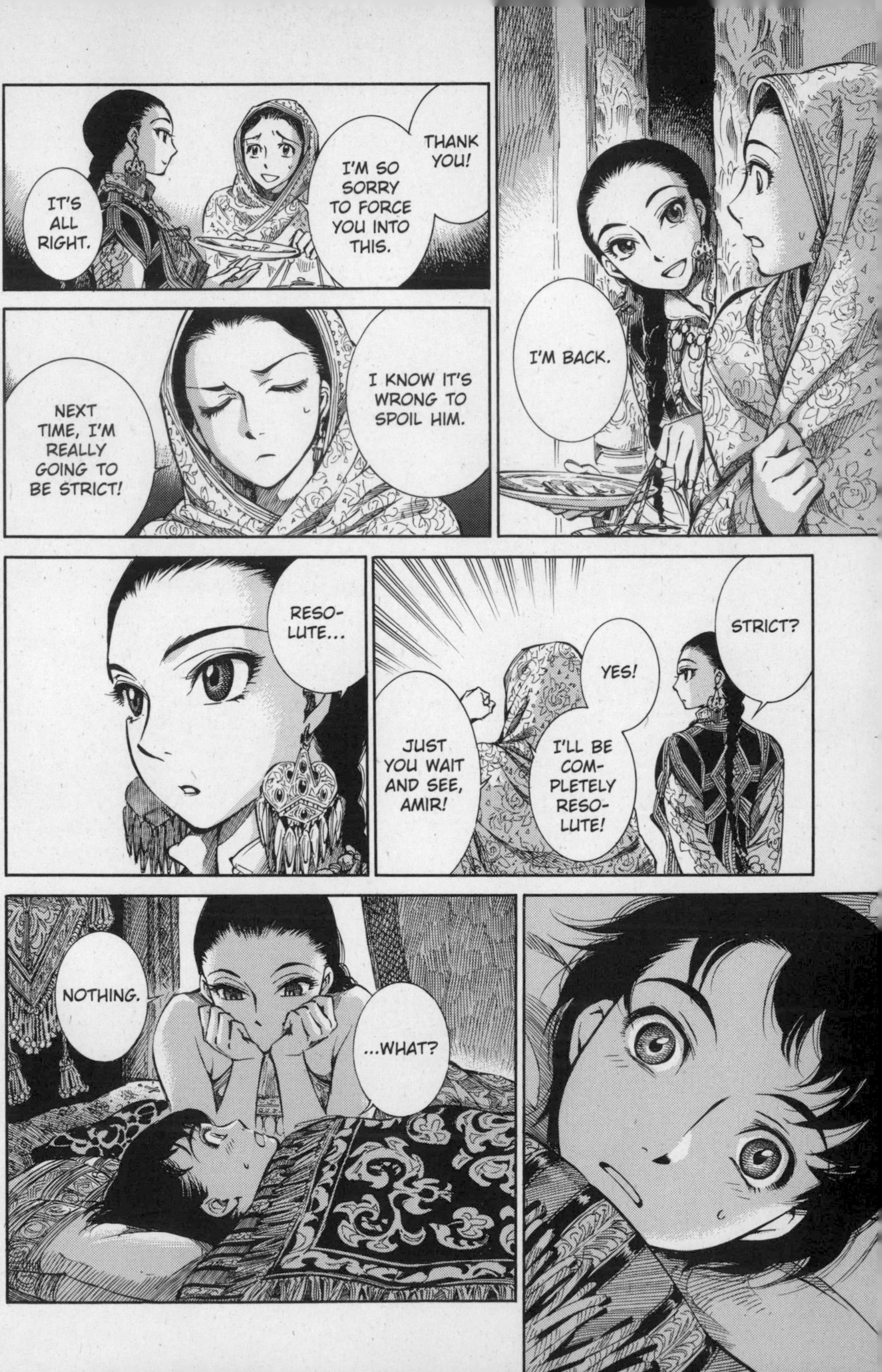
I'M BACK.
THANK YOU!
I'M SO SORRY TO FORCE YOU INTO THIS.
IT'S ALL RIGHT.
I KNOW IT'S WRONG TO SPOIL HIM.
NEXT TIME, I'M REALLY GOING TO BE STRICT!
STRICT?
YES!
I'LL BE COM-PLETELY RESO-LUTE!
JUST YOU WAIT AND SEE, AMIR!
RESO-LUTE...
...WHAT?
NOTHING.

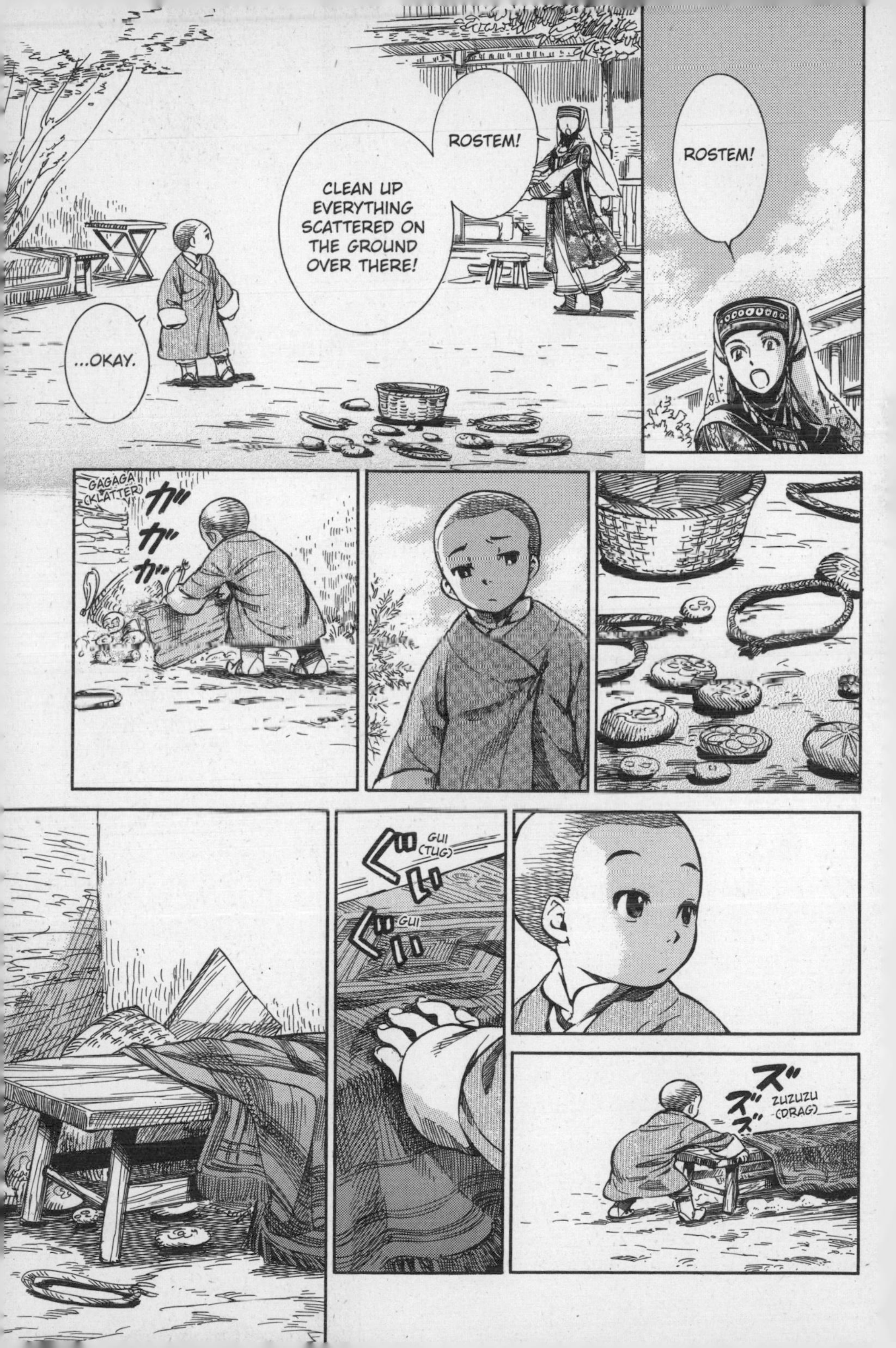
ROSTEM!
ROSTEM!
CLEAN UP EVERYTHING SCATTERED ON THE GROUND OVER THERE!
...OKAY.
ガガガ
GAGAGA (KLATTER)
ズズズ
ZUZUZU (DRAG)
ぐい
GUI (TUG)
ぐい
GUI

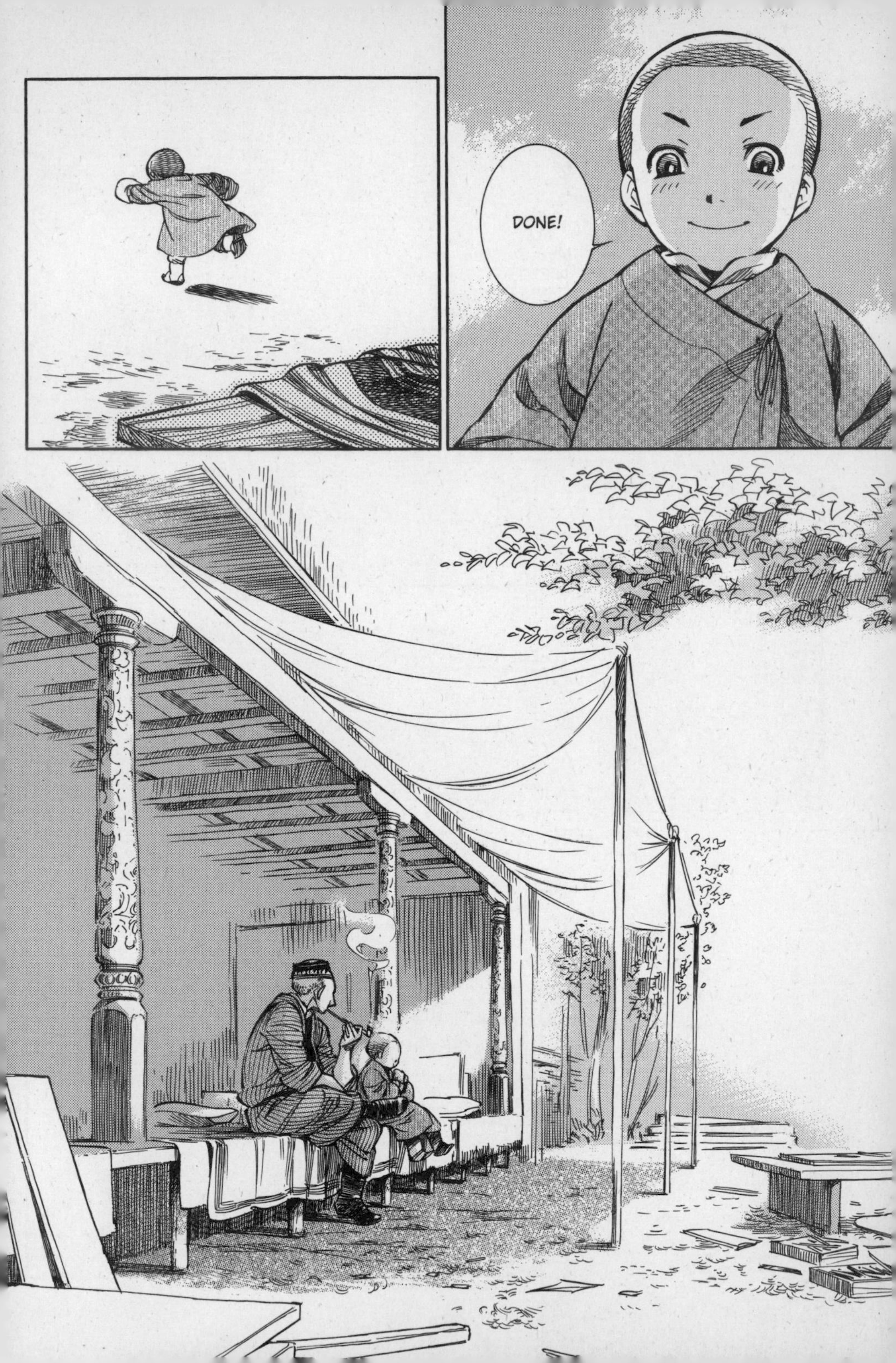
DONE!

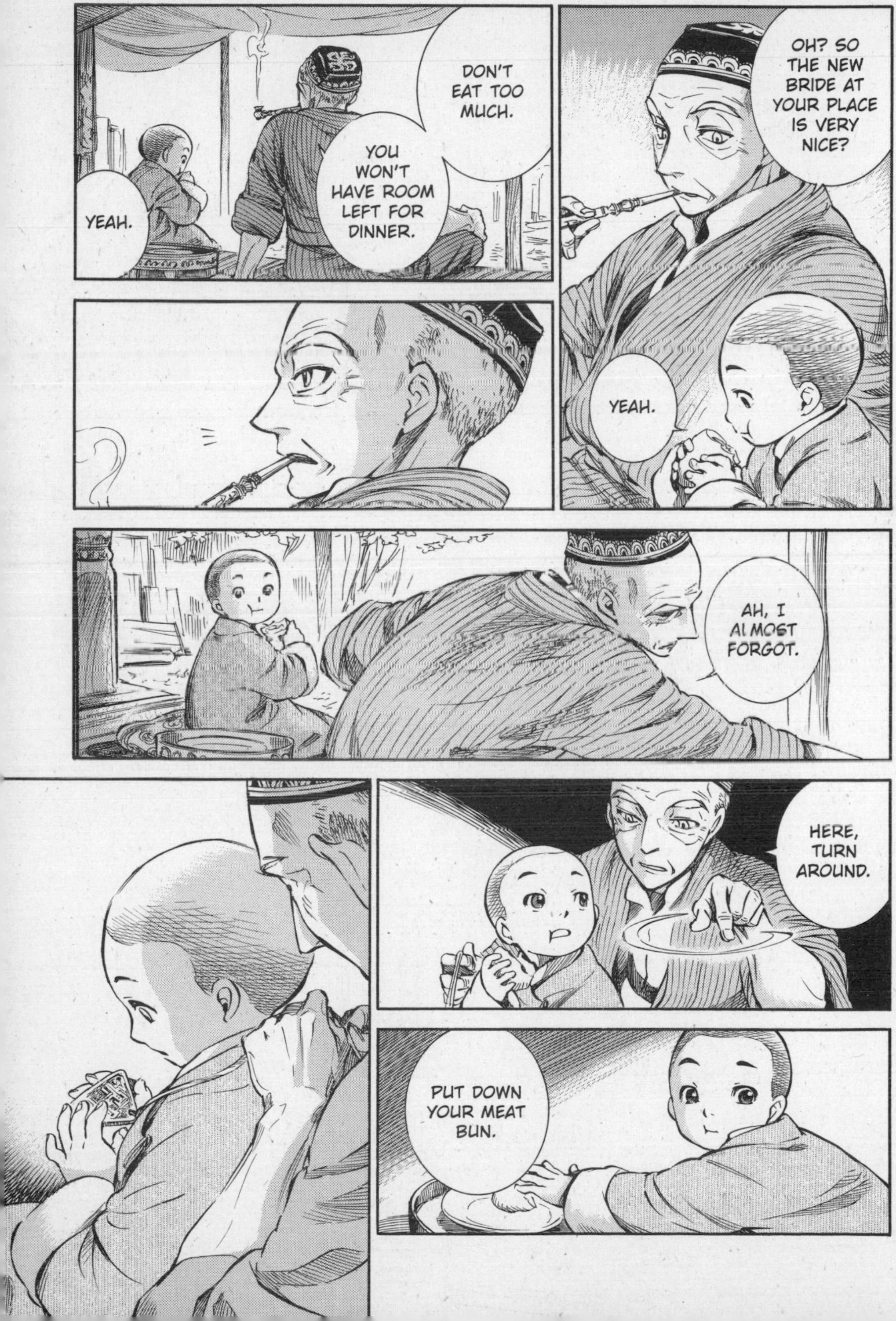
OH? SO THE NEW BRIDE AT YOUR PLACE IS VERY NICE?
YEAH.
DON'T EAT TOO MUCH.
YOU WON'T HAVE ROOM LEFT FOR DINNER.
YEAH.
AH, I ALMOST FORGOT.
HERE, TURN AROUND.
PUT DOWN YOUR MEAT BUN.

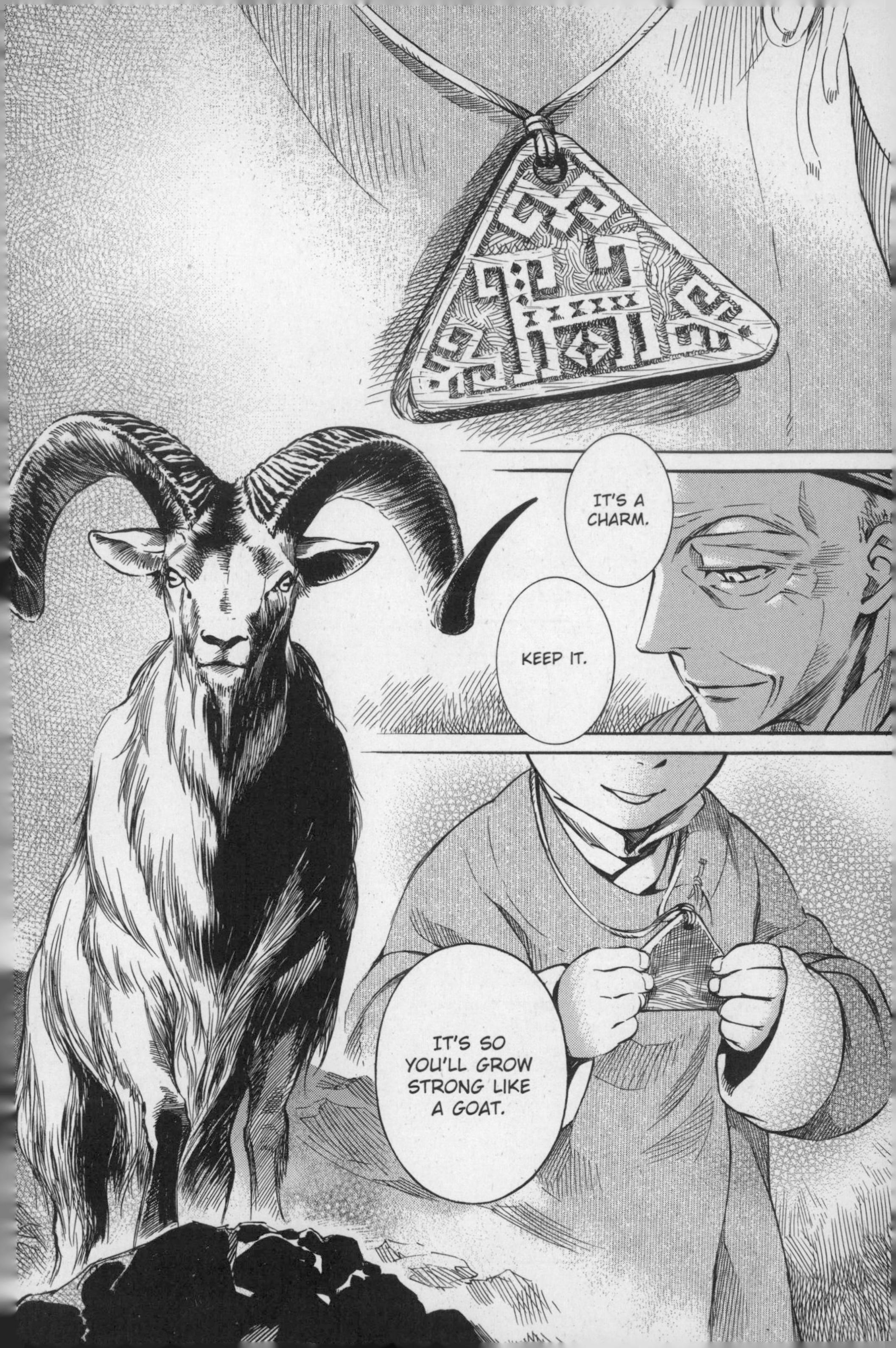
IT'S A CHARM.
KEEP IT.
IT'S SO YOU'LL GROW STRONG LIKE A GOAT.

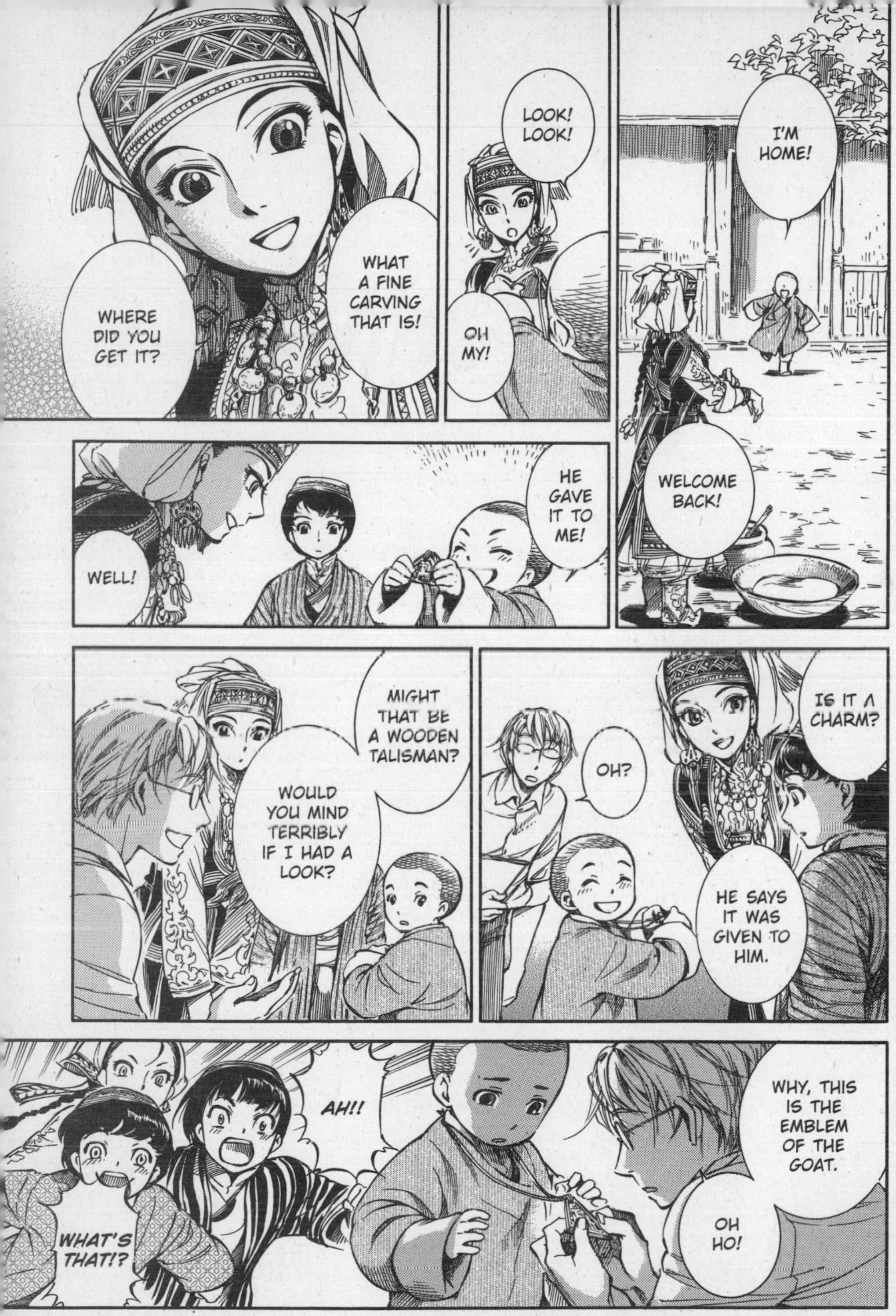
I'M HOME!
WELCOME BACK!
LOOK! LOOK!
OH MY!
WHAT A FINE CARVING THAT IS!
WHERE DID YOU GET IT?
HE GAVE IT TO ME!
WELL!
IS IT A CHARM?
OH?
HE SAYS IT WAS GIVEN TO HIM.
MIGHT THAT BE A WOODEN TALISMAN?
WOULD YOU MIND TERRIBLY IF I HAD A LOOK?
WHY, THIS IS THE EMBLEM OF THE GOAT.
OH HO!
AH!!
WHAT'S THAT!?

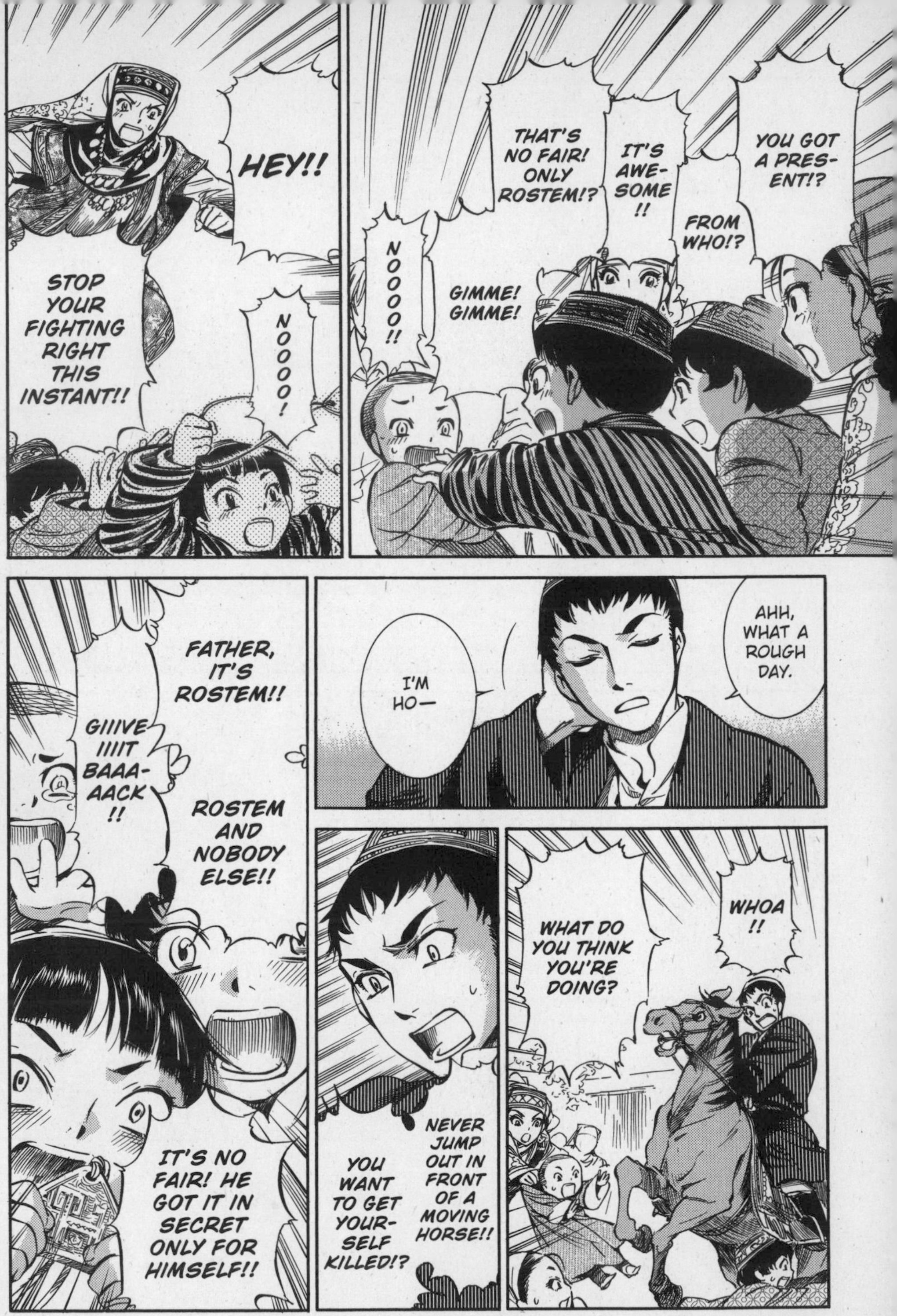
YOU GOT A PRESENT!?
FROM WHO!?
IT'S AWESOME!!
THAT'S NO FAIR! ONLY ROSTEM!?
GIMME! GIMME!
NOOOOO!!
HEY!!
NOOOOO!
STOP YOUR FIGHTING RIGHT THIS INSTANT!!
AHH, WHAT A ROUGH DAY.
I'M HO—
WHOA!!
WHAT DO YOU THINK YOU'RE DOING?
NEVER JUMP OUT IN FRONT OF A MOVING HORSE!!
YOU WANT TO GET YOURSELF KILLED!?
FATHER, IT'S ROSTEM!!
GIIIVE IIIIT BAAAAACK!!
ROSTEM AND NOBODY ELSE!!
IT'S NO FAIR! HE GOT IT IN SECRET ONLY FOR HIMSELF!!

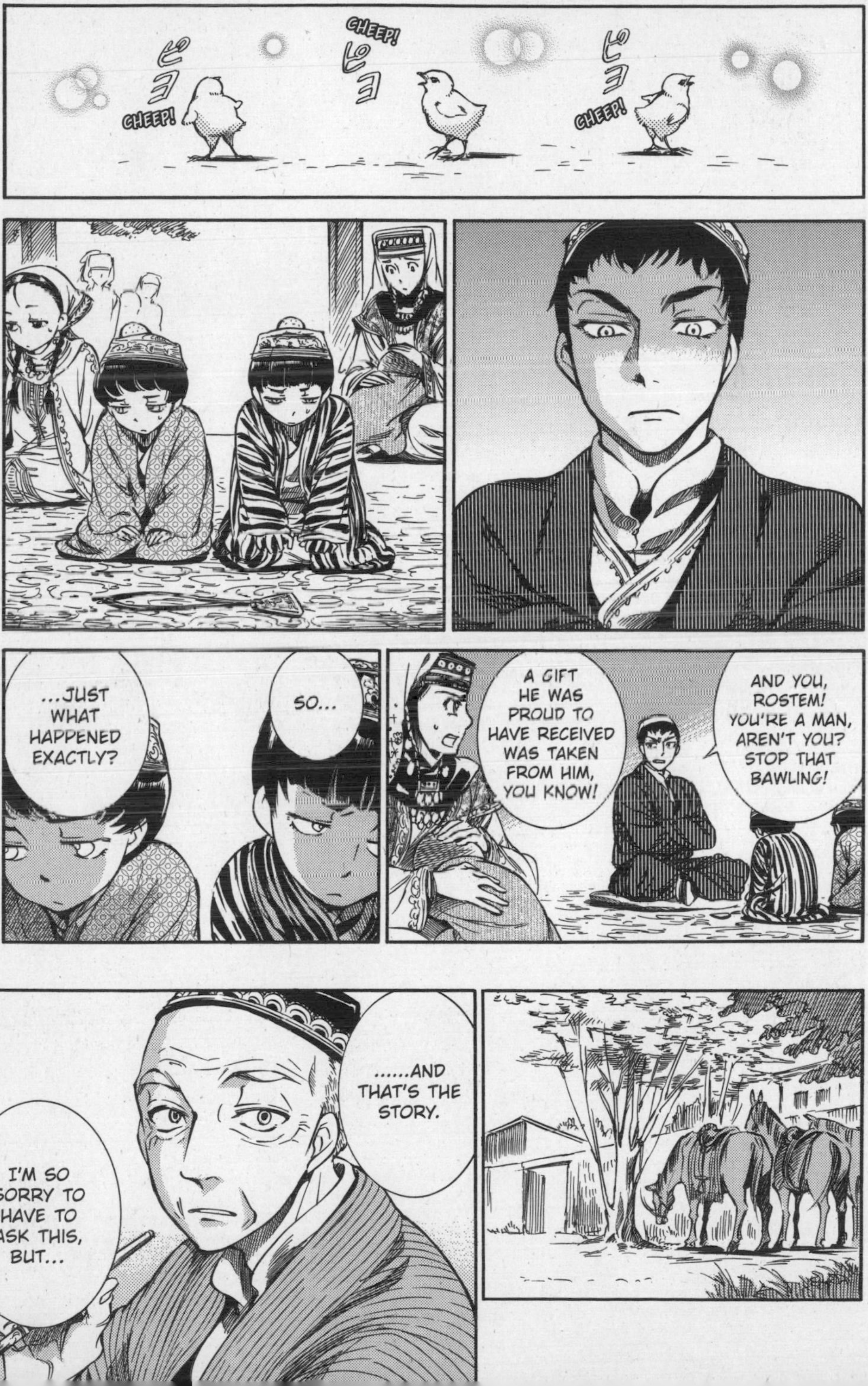
ピヨ
CHEEP!
CHEEP!
ピヨ
ピヨ
CHEEP!
AND YOU, ROSTEM! YOU'RE A MAN, AREN'T YOU? STOP THAT BAWLING!
A GIFT HE WAS PROUD TO HAVE RECEIVED WAS TAKEN FROM HIM, YOU KNOW!
SO...
...JUST WHAT HAPPENED EXACTLY?
......AND THAT'S THE STORY.
I'M SO SORRY TO HAVE TO ASK THIS, BUT...

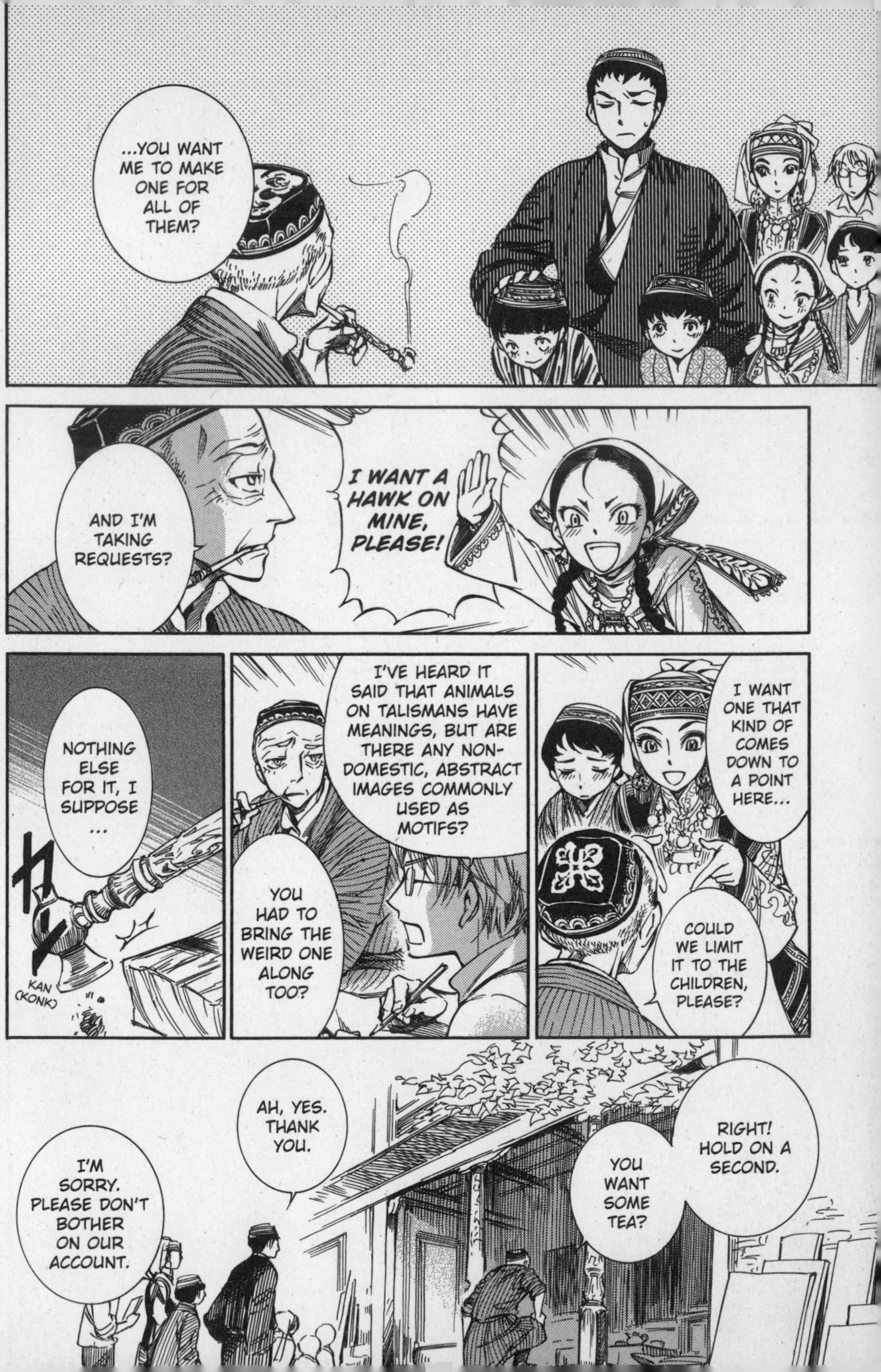
...YOU WANT ME TO MAKE ONE FOR ALL OF THEM?
I WANT A HAWK ON MINE, PLEASE!
AND I'M TAKING REQUESTS?
I WANT ONE THAT KIND OF COMES DOWN TO A POINT HERE...
COULD WE LIMIT IT TO THE CHILDREN, PLEASE?
I'VE HEARD IT SAID THAT ANIMALS ON TALISMANS HAVE MEANINGS, BUT ARE THERE ANY NON-DOMESTIC, ABSTRACT IMAGES COMMONLY USED AS MOTIFS?
YOU HAD TO BRING THE WEIRD ONE ALONG TOO?
NOTHING ELSE FOR IT, I SUPPOSE...
KAN (KONK)
RIGHT! HOLD ON A SECOND.
YOU WANT SOME TEA?
AH, YES. THANK YOU.
I'M SORRY. PLEASE DON'T BOTHER ON OUR ACCOUNT.

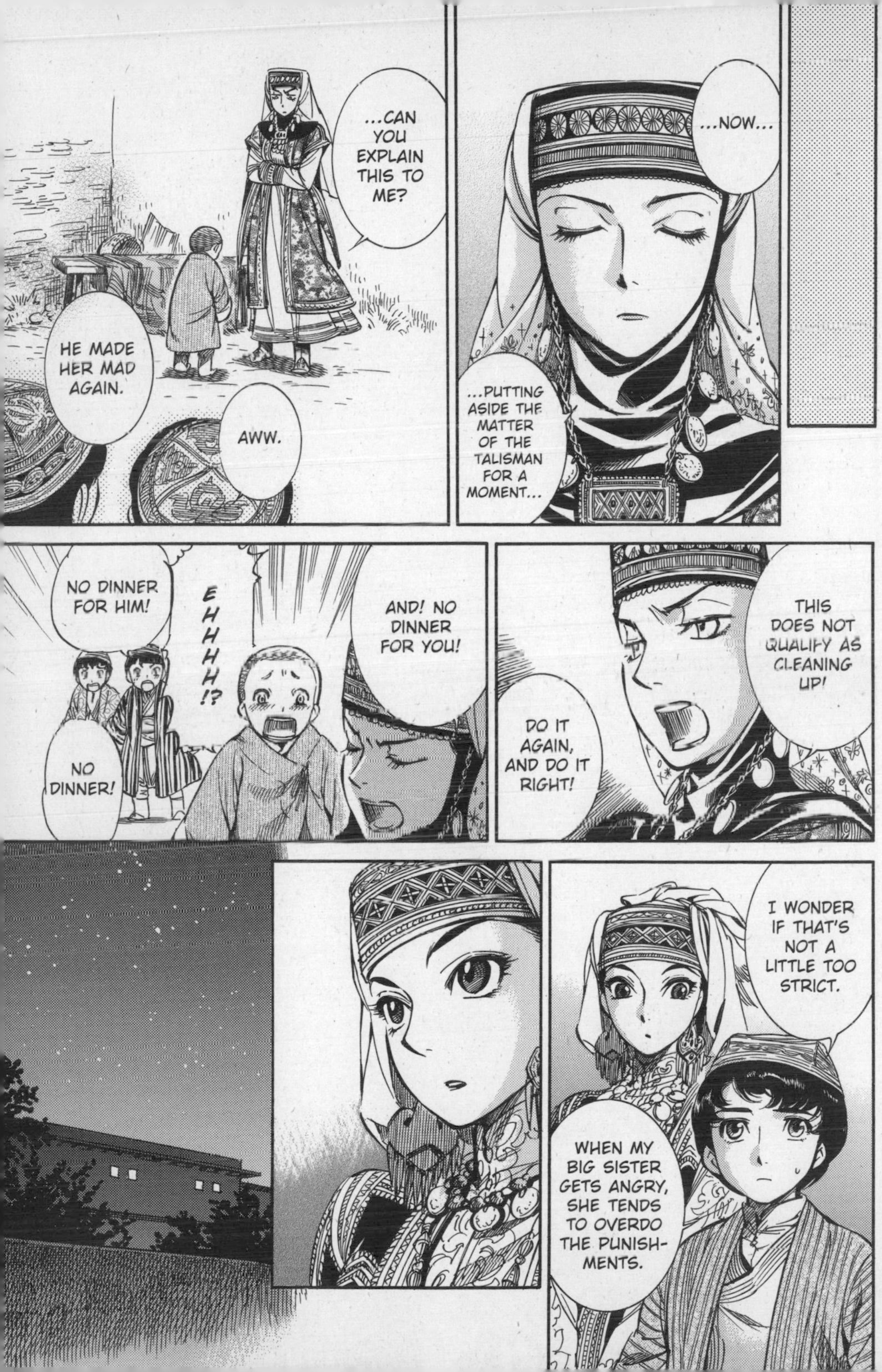
...NOW...
...PUTTING ASIDE THE MATTER OF THE TALISMAN FOR A MOMENT...
...CAN YOU EXPLAIN THIS TO ME?
HE MADE HER MAD AGAIN.
AWW.
THIS DOES NOT QUALIFY AS CLEANING UP!
DO IT AGAIN, AND DO IT RIGHT!
AND! NO DINNER FOR YOU!
EHHHHH!?
NO DINNER FOR HIM!
NO DINNER!
I WONDER IF THAT'S NOT A LITTLE TOO STRICT.
WHEN MY BIG SISTER GETS ANGRY, SHE TENDS TO OVERDO THE PUNISHMENTS.

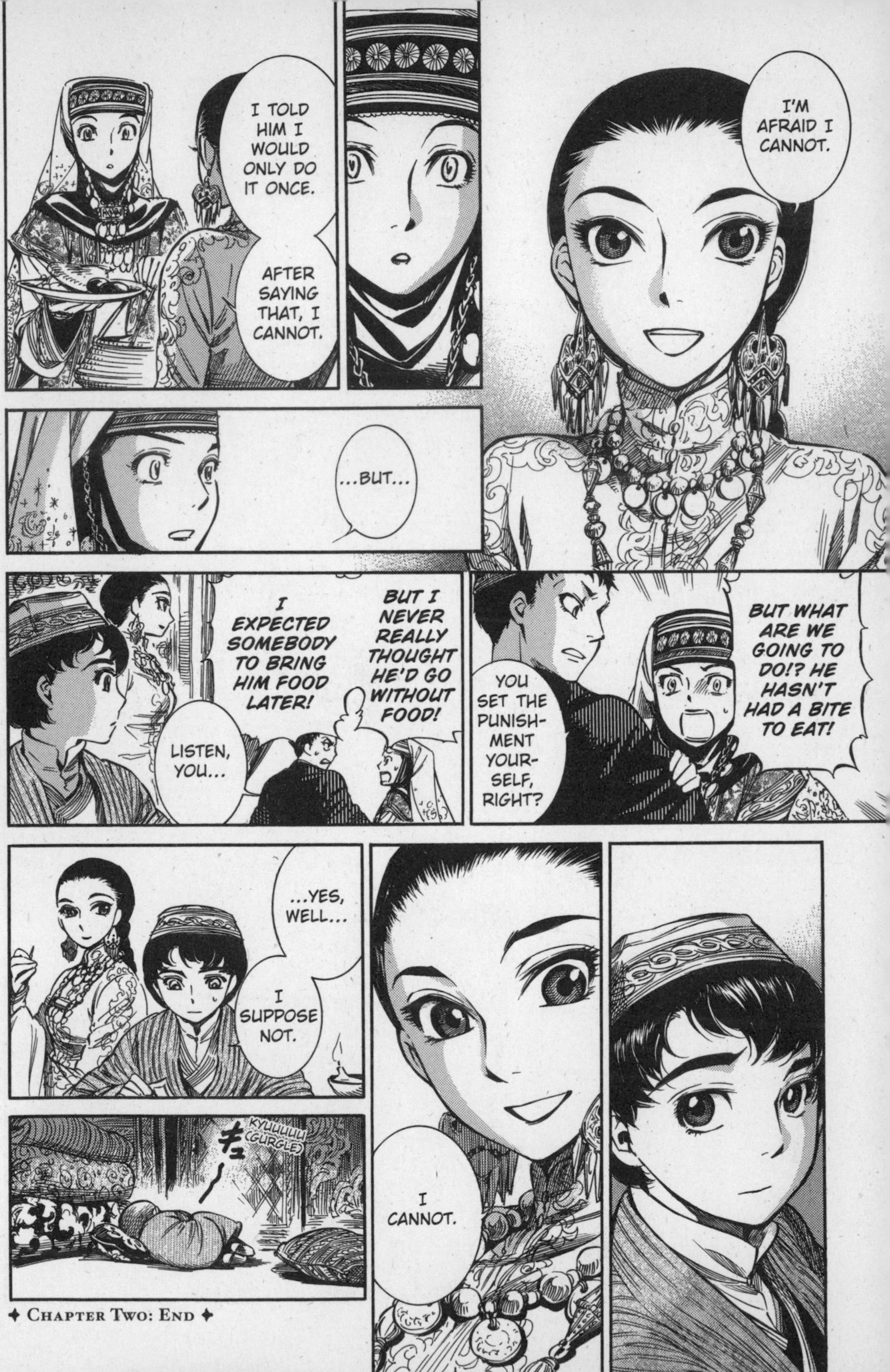
I'M AFRAID I CANNOT.
I TOLD HIM I WOULD ONLY DO IT ONCE.
AFTER SAYING THAT, I CANNOT.
...BUT...
BUT WHAT ARE WE GOING TO DO!? HE HASN'T HAD A BITE TO EAT!
YOU SET THE PUNISHMENT YOURSELF, RIGHT?
BUT I NEVER REALLY THOUGHT HE'D GO WITHOUT FOOD!
I EXPECTED SOMEBODY TO BRING HIM FOOD LATER!
LISTEN, YOU...
I CANNOT.
...YES, WELL...
I SUPPOSE NOT.
KYUUUUU (GURGLE)

✦ Chapter Two: End ✦

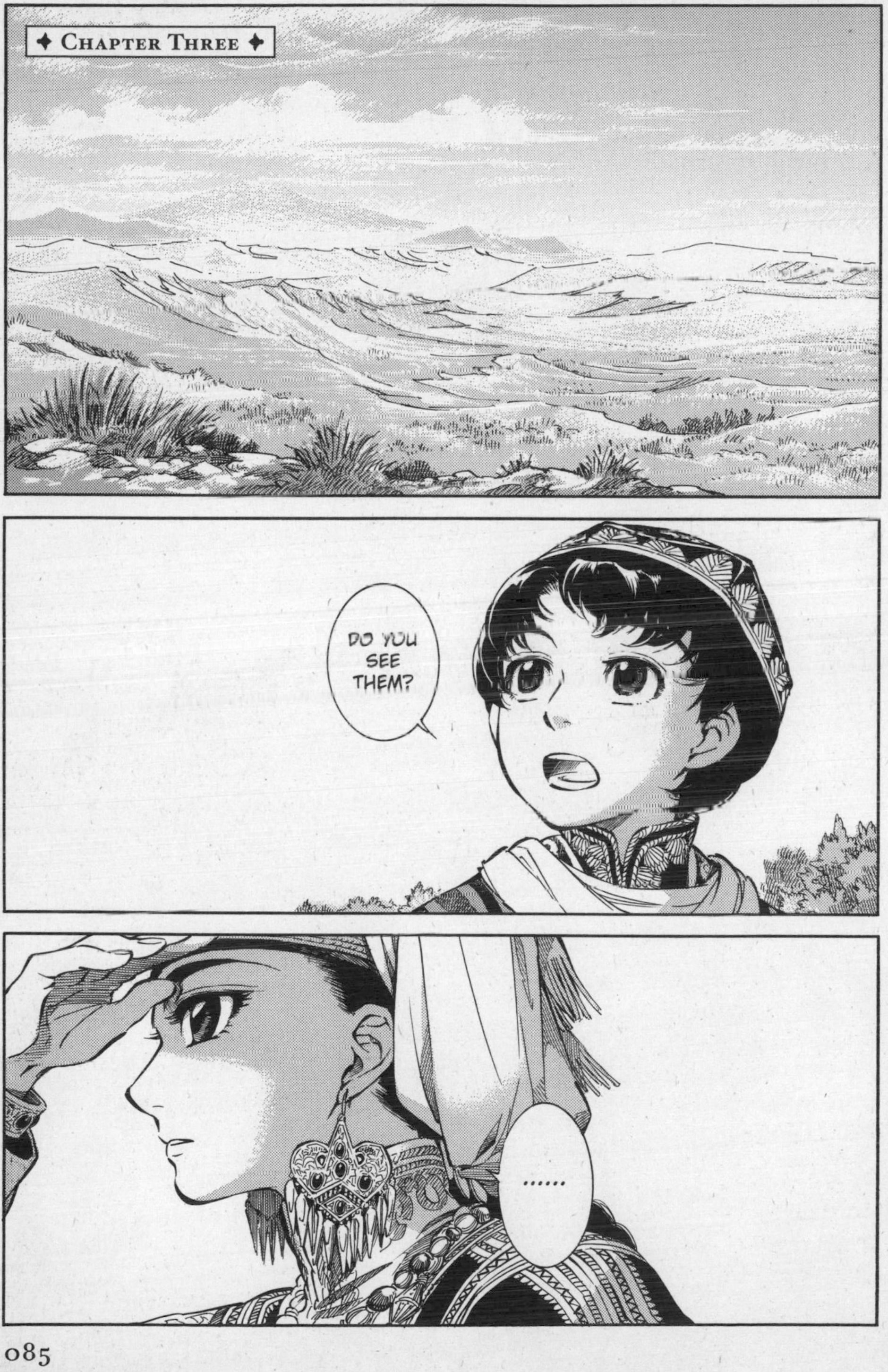
Chapter Three
DO YOU SEE THEM?
......

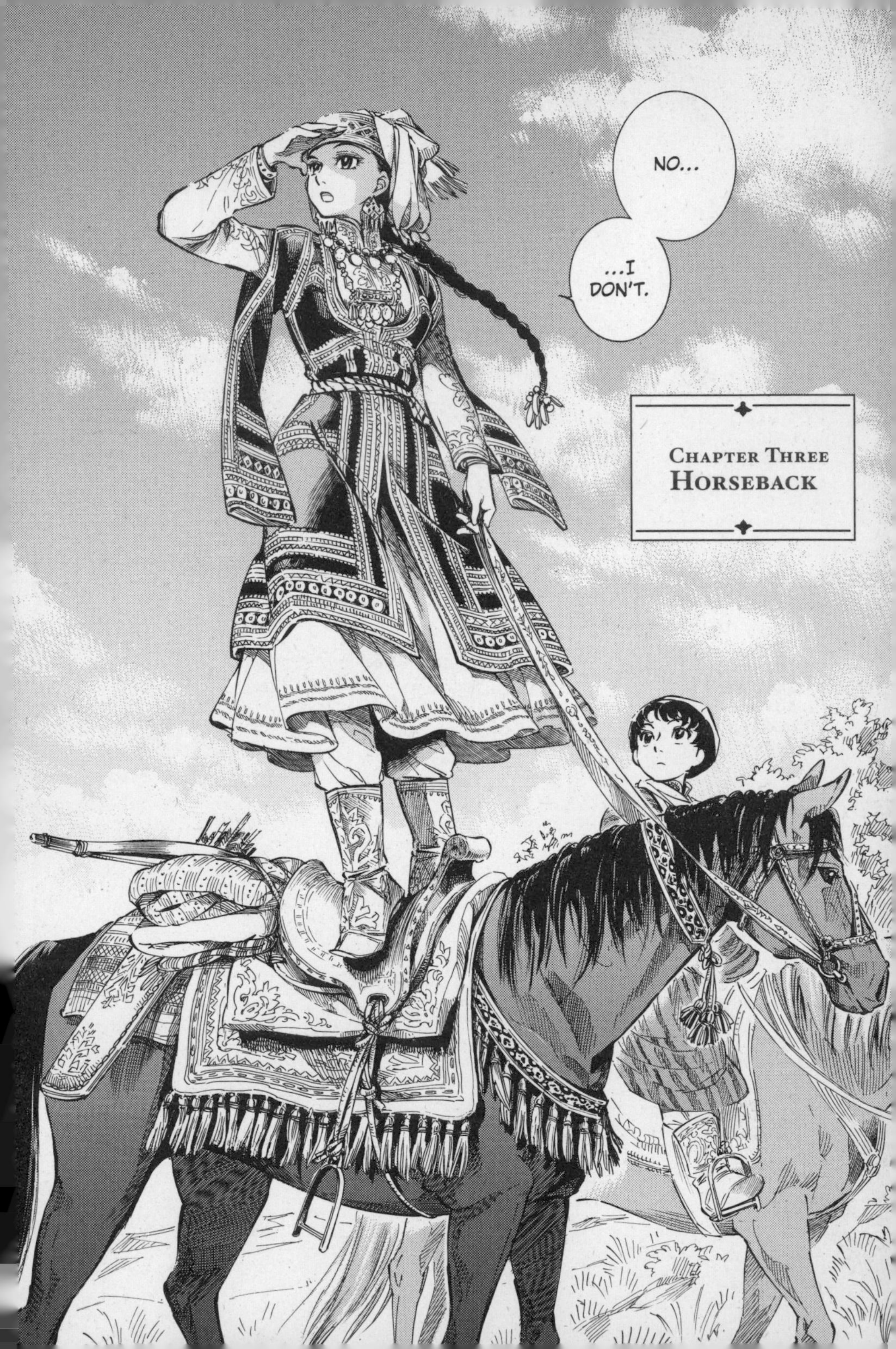
NO...
...I DON'T.
CHAPTER THREE
HORSEBACK

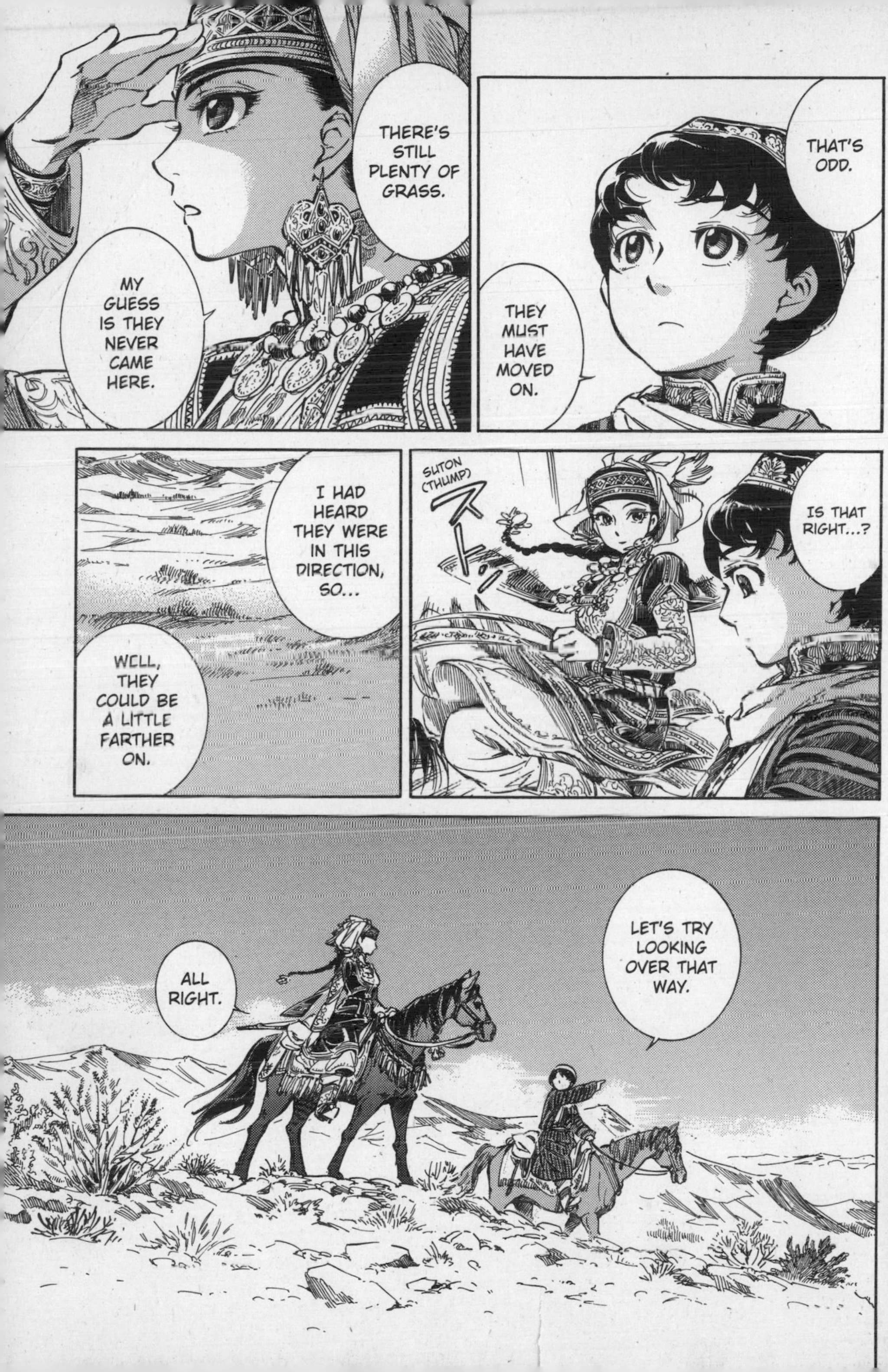
THAT'S ODD.
THEY MUST HAVE MOVED ON.
THERE'S STILL PLENTY OF GRASS.
MY GUESS IS THEY NEVER CAME HERE.
IS THAT RIGHT...?
SUTON (THUMP)
I HAD HEARD THEY WERE IN THIS DIRECTION, SO...
WELL, THEY COULD BE A LITTLE FARTHER ON.
LET'S TRY LOOKING OVER THAT WAY.
ALL RIGHT.

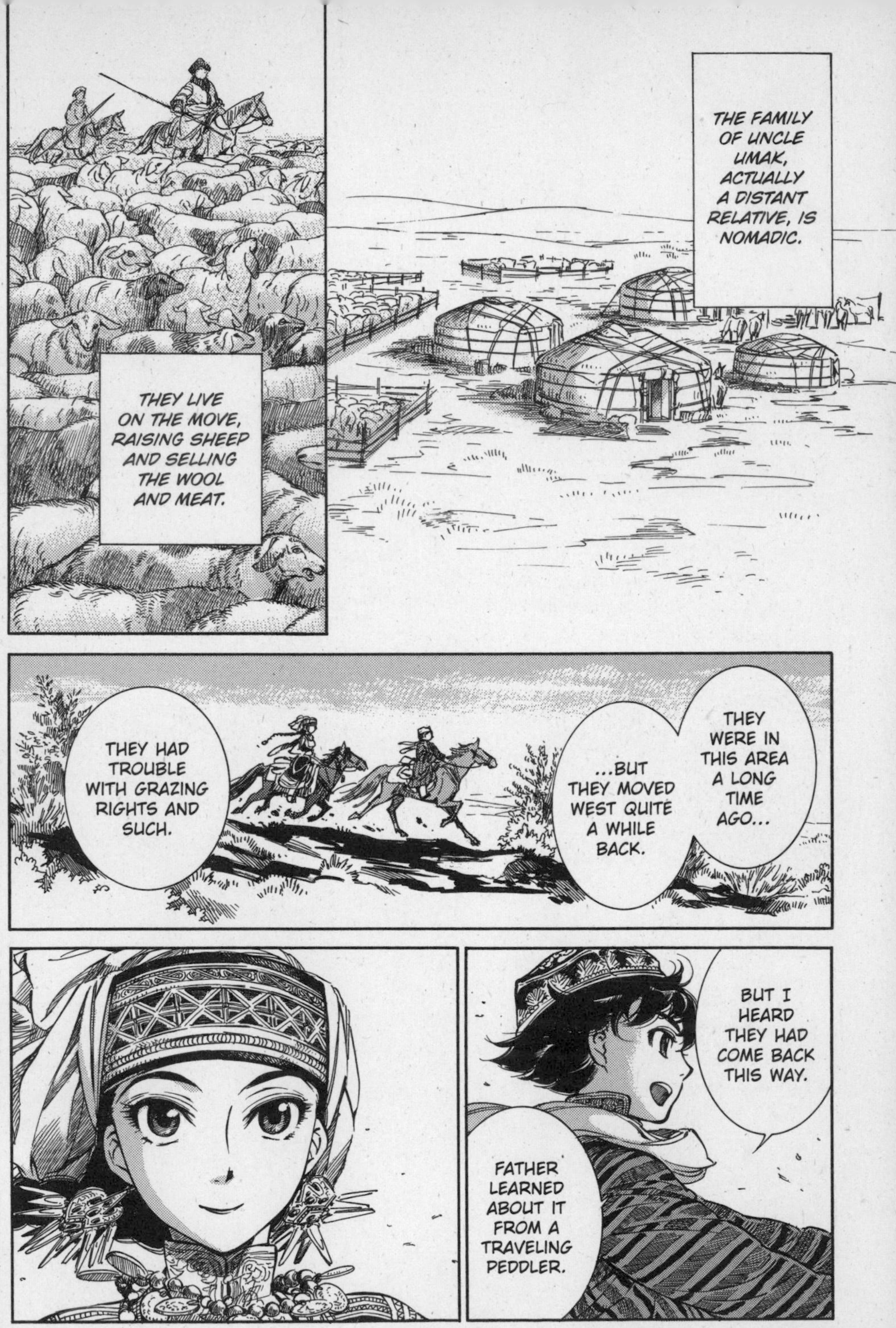
THE FAMILY OF UNCLE UMAK, ACTUALLY A DISTANT RELATIVE, IS NOMADIC.
THEY LIVE ON THE MOVE, RAISING SHEEP AND SELLING THE WOOL AND MEAT.
THEY WERE IN THIS AREA A LONG TIME AGO...
...BUT THEY MOVED WEST QUITE A WHILE BACK.
THEY HAD TROUBLE WITH GRAZING RIGHTS AND SUCH.
BUT I HEARD THEY HAD COME BACK THIS WAY.
FATHER LEARNED ABOUT IT FROM A TRAVELING PEDDLER.

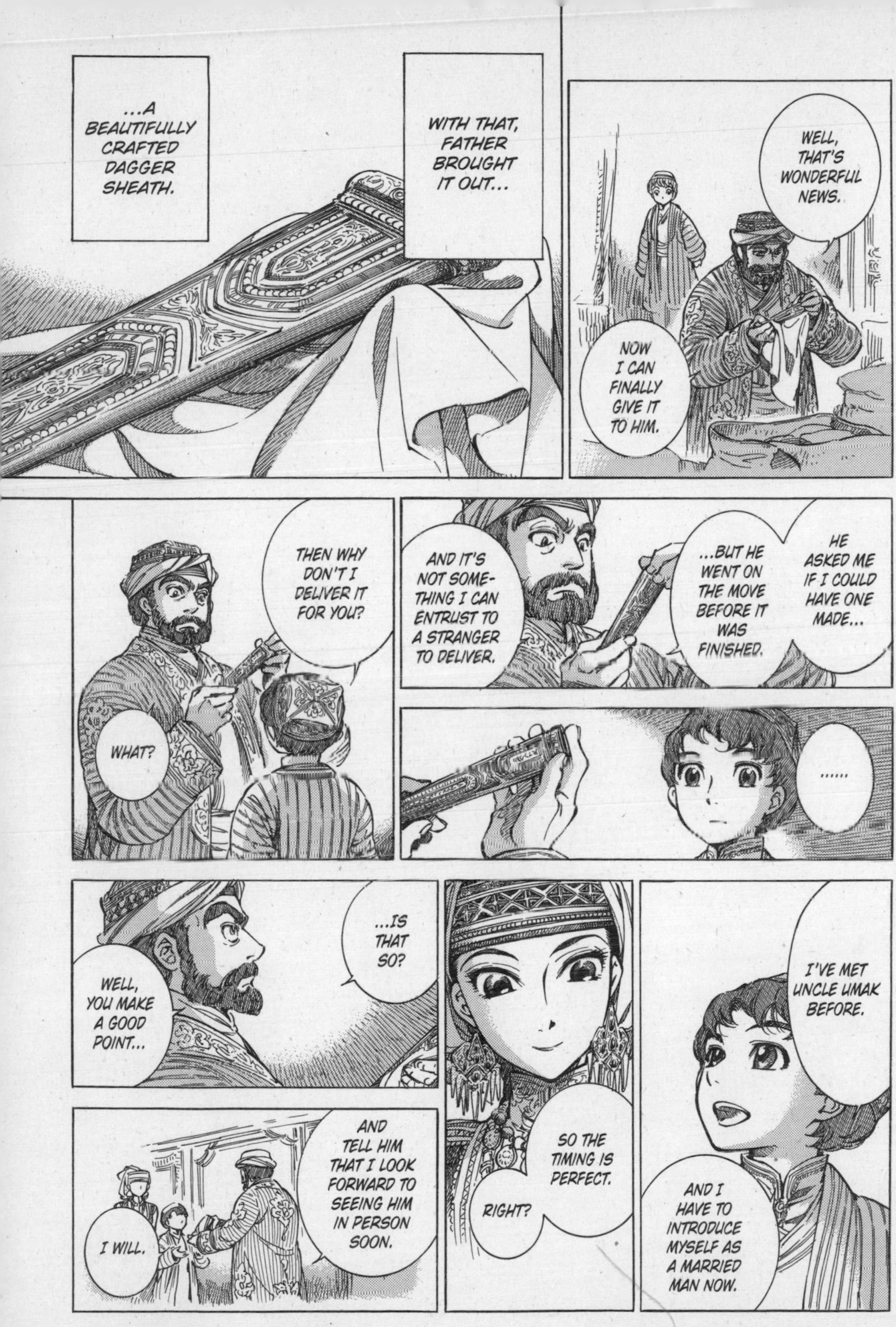
WELL, THAT'S WONDERFUL NEWS.
NOW I CAN FINALLY GIVE IT TO HIM.
WITH THAT, FATHER BROUGHT IT OUT...
...A BEAUTIFULLY CRAFTED DAGGER SHEATH.
HE ASKED ME IF I COULD HAVE ONE MADE...
...BUT HE WENT ON THE MOVE BEFORE IT WAS FINISHED.
AND IT'S NOT SOME-THING I CAN ENTRUST TO A STRANGER TO DELIVER.
......
THEN WHY DON'T I DELIVER IT FOR YOU?
WHAT?
I'VE MET UNCLE UMAK BEFORE.
AND I HAVE TO INTRODUCE MYSELF AS A MARRIED MAN NOW.
SO THE TIMING IS PERFECT.
RIGHT?
...IS THAT SO?
WELL, YOU MAKE A GOOD POINT...
AND TELL HIM THAT I LOOK FORWARD TO SEEING HIM IN PERSON SOON.
I WILL.

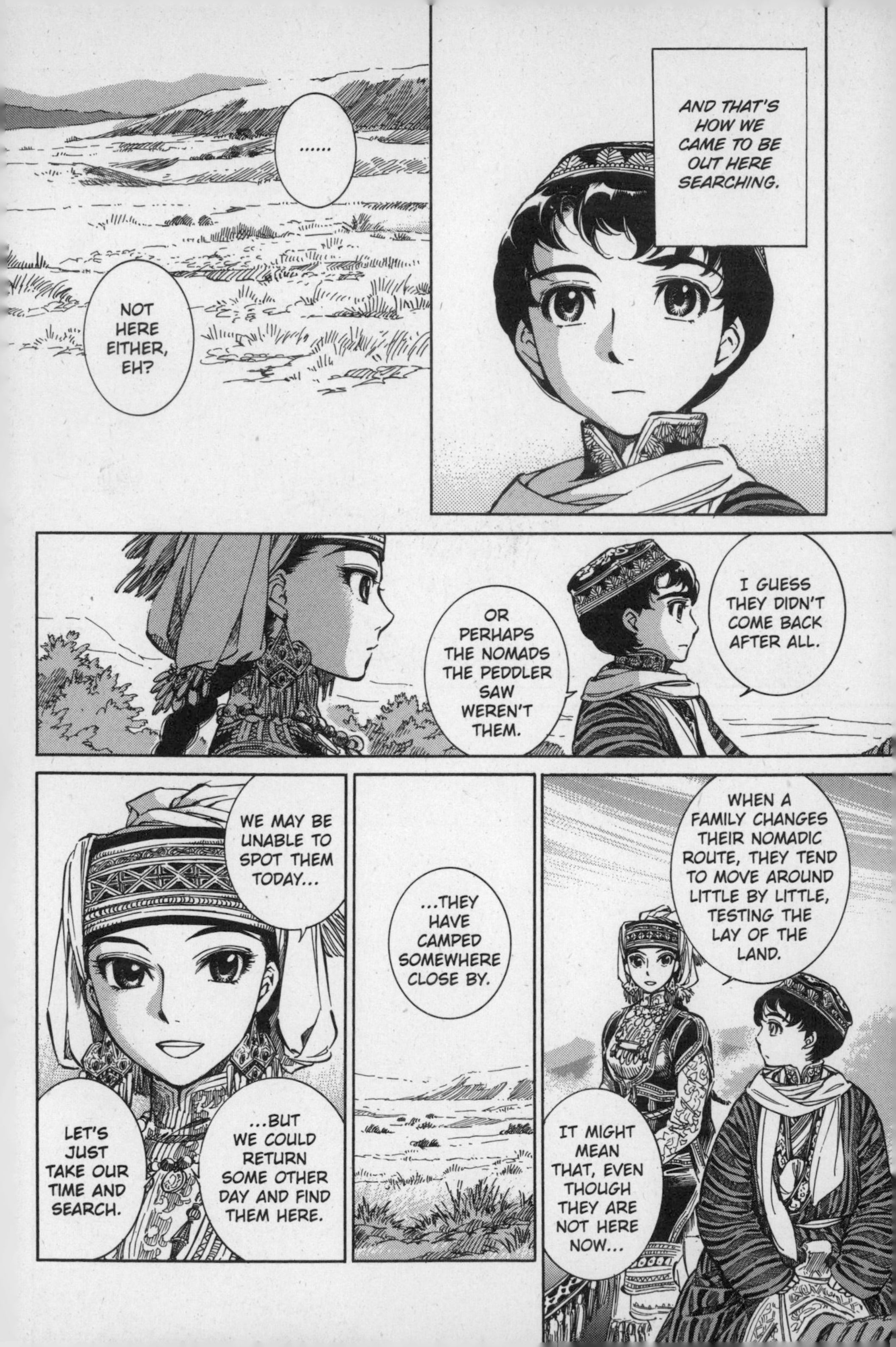
AND THAT'S HOW WE CAME TO BE OUT HERE SEARCHING.
......
NOT HERE EITHER, EH?
I GUESS THEY DIDN'T COME BACK AFTER ALL.
OR PERHAPS THE NOMADS THE PEDDLER SAW WEREN'T THEM.
WHEN A FAMILY CHANGES THEIR NOMADIC ROUTE, THEY TEND TO MOVE AROUND LITTLE BY LITTLE, TESTING THE LAY OF THE LAND.
IT MIGHT MEAN THAT, EVEN THOUGH THEY ARE NOT HERE NOW...
...THEY HAVE CAMPED SOMEWHERE CLOSE BY.
WE MAY BE UNABLE TO SPOT THEM TODAY...
...BUT WE COULD RETURN SOME OTHER DAY AND FIND THEM HERE.
LET'S JUST TAKE OUR TIME AND SEARCH.

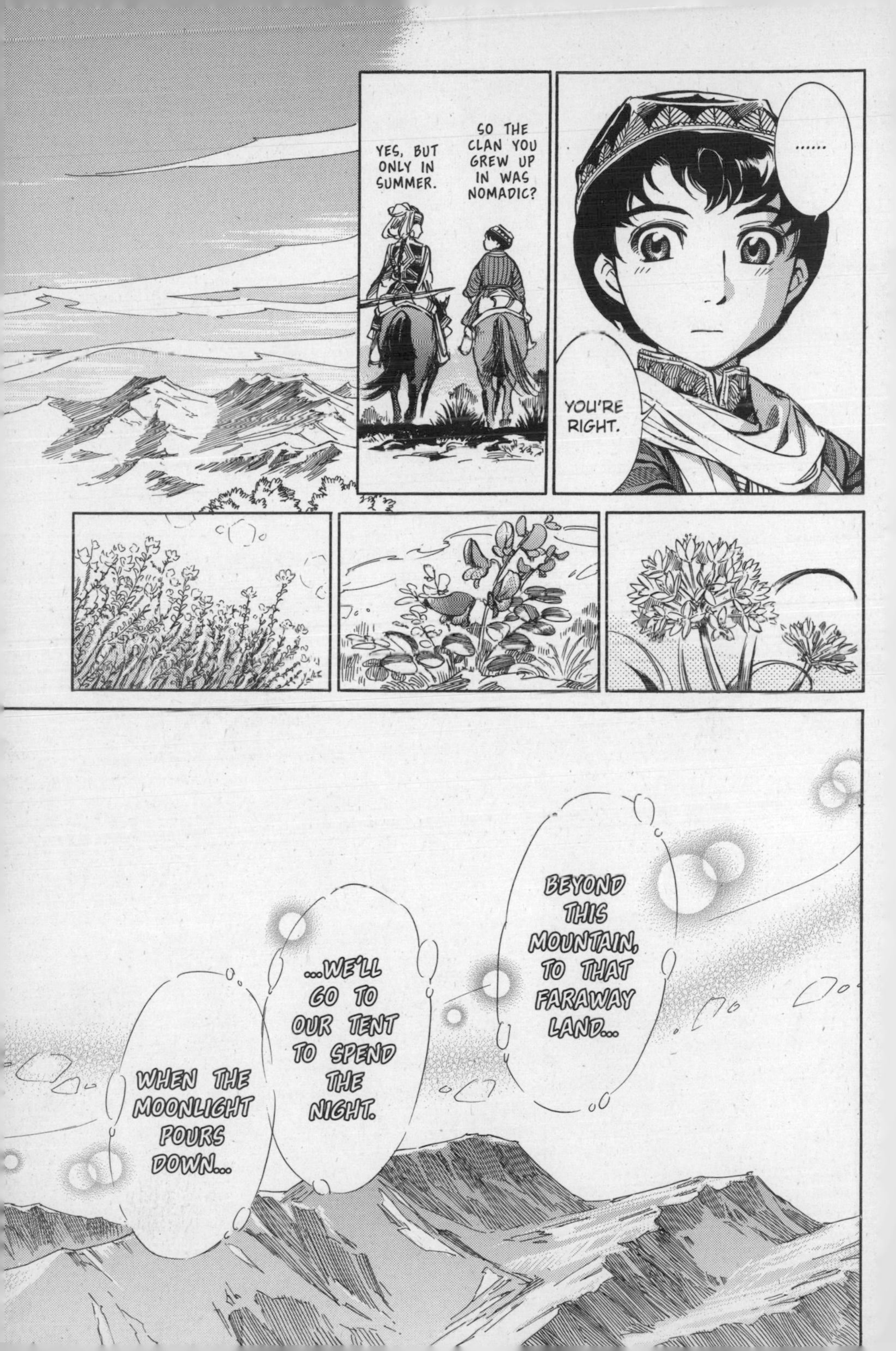
......
YOU'RE RIGHT.
SO THE CLAN YOU GREW UP IN WAS NOMADIC?
YES, BUT ONLY IN SUMMER.
BEYOND THIS MOUNTAIN, TO THAT FARAWAY LAND...
...WE'LL GO TO OUR TENT TO SPEND THE NIGHT.
WHEN THE MOONLIGHT POURS DOWN...

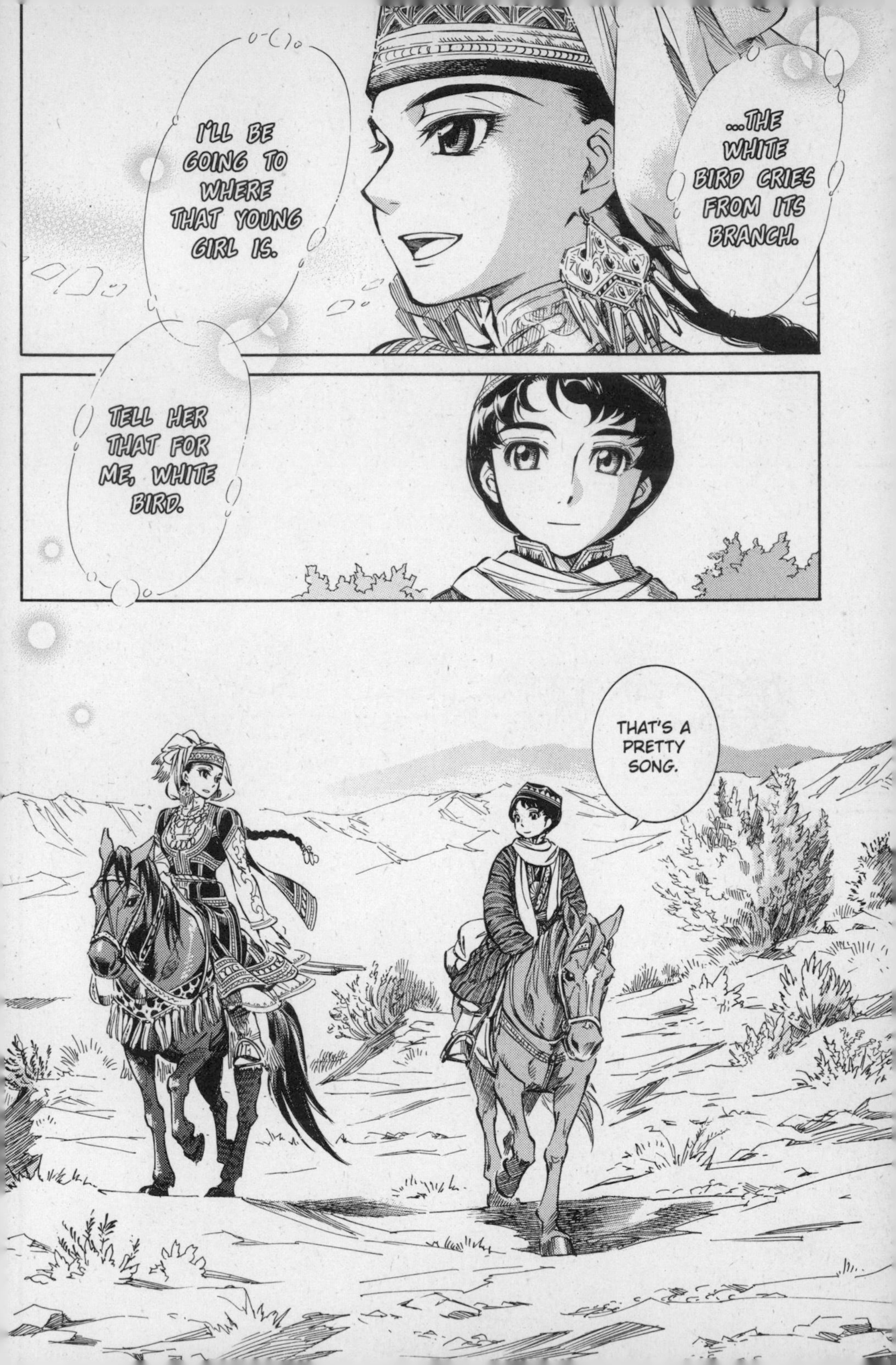
...THE WHITE BIRD CRIES FROM ITS BRANCH.
I'LL BE GOING TO WHERE THAT YOUNG GIRL IS.
TELL HER THAT FOR ME, WHITE BIRD.
THAT'S A PRETTY SONG.

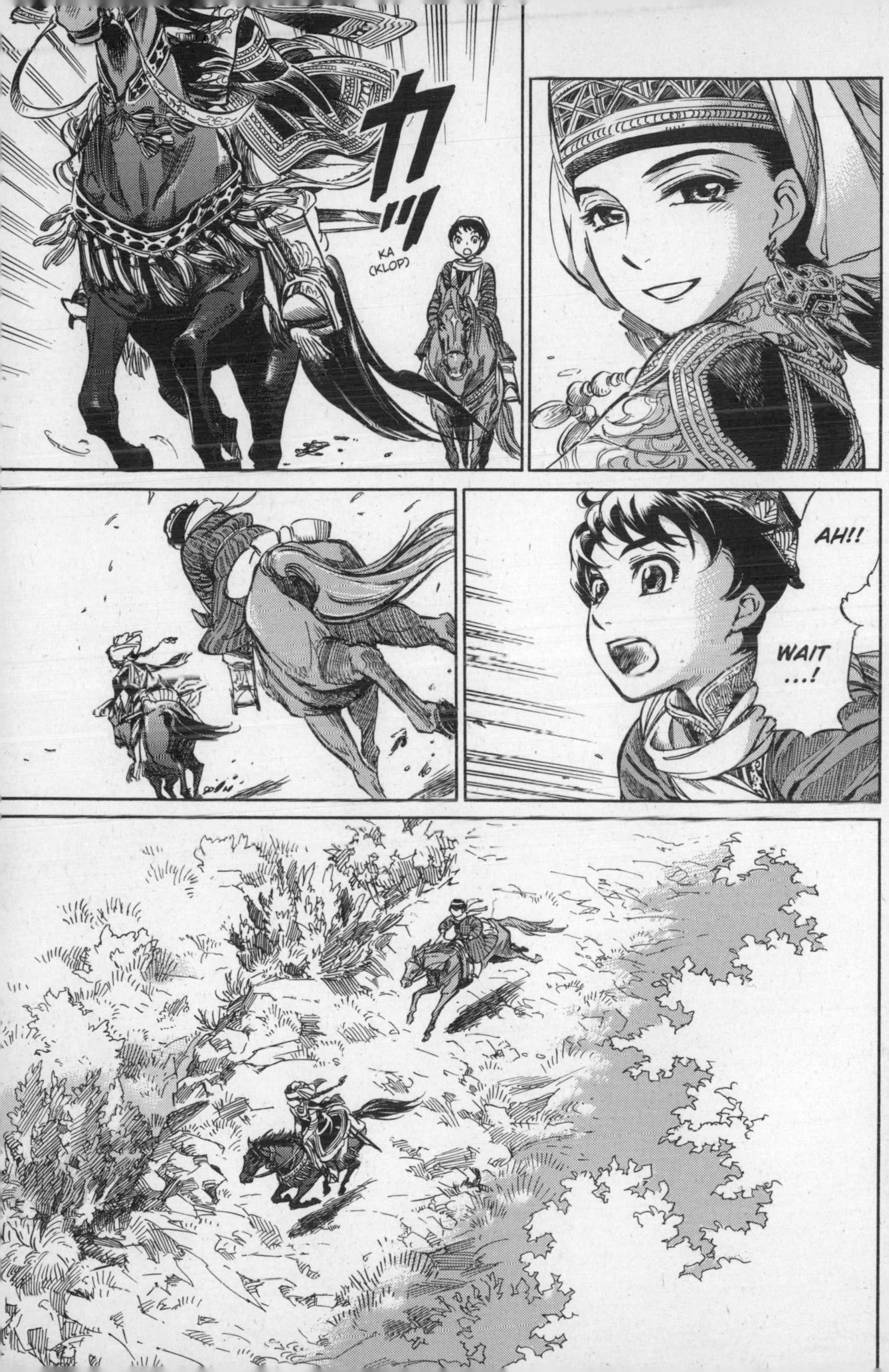
カッ
KA (KLOP)
AH!!
WAIT ...!

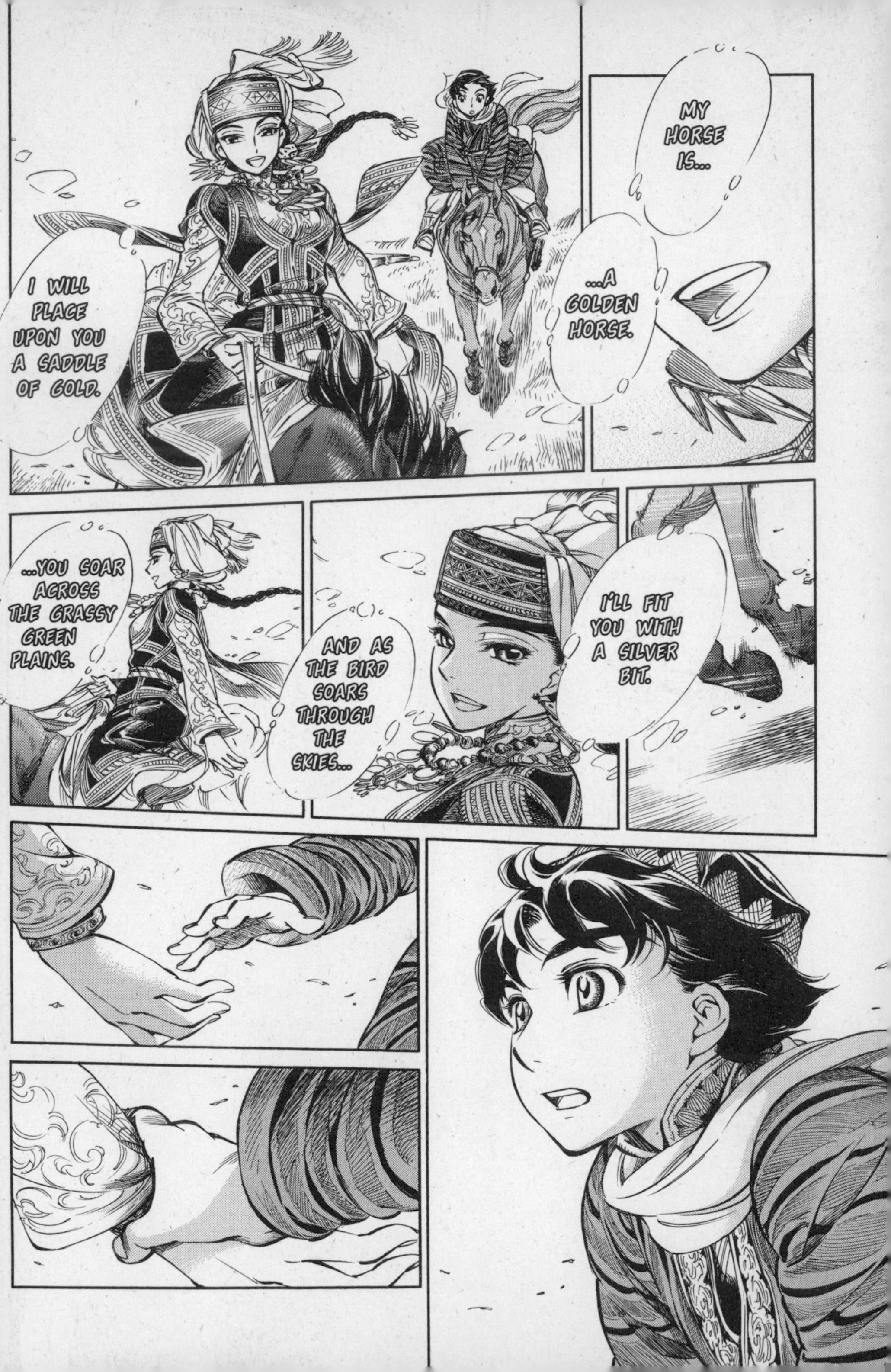
MY HORSE IS...
...A GOLDEN HORSE.
I WILL PLACE UPON YOU A SADDLE OF GOLD.
I'LL FIT YOU WITH A SILVER BIT.
AND AS THE BIRD SOARS THROUGH THE SKIES...
...YOU SOAR ACROSS THE GRASSY GREEN PLAINS.

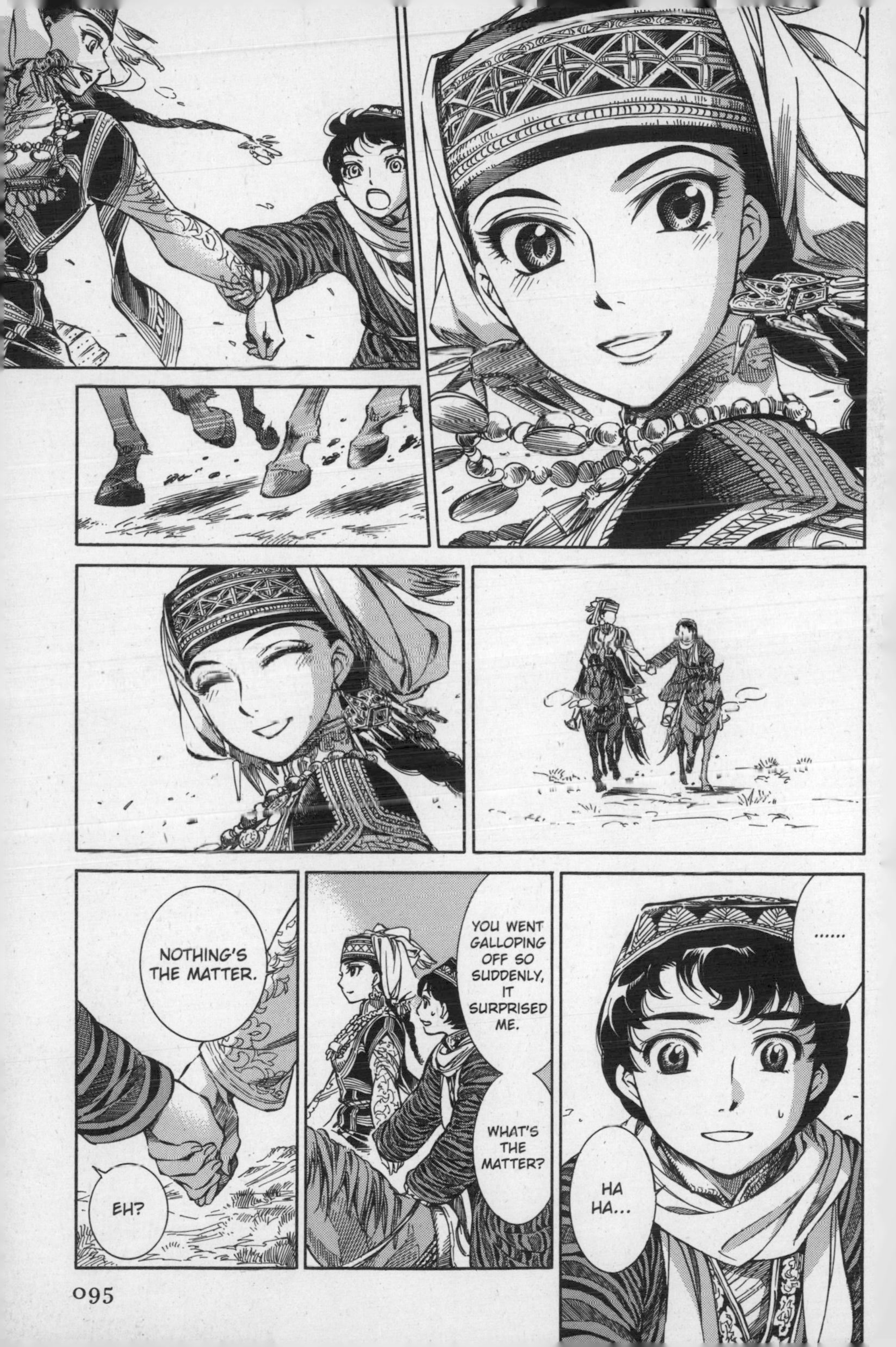
......
HA HA...
YOU WENT GALLOPING OFF SO SUDDENLY, IT SURPRISED ME.
WHAT'S THE MATTER?
NOTHING'S THE MATTER.
EH?

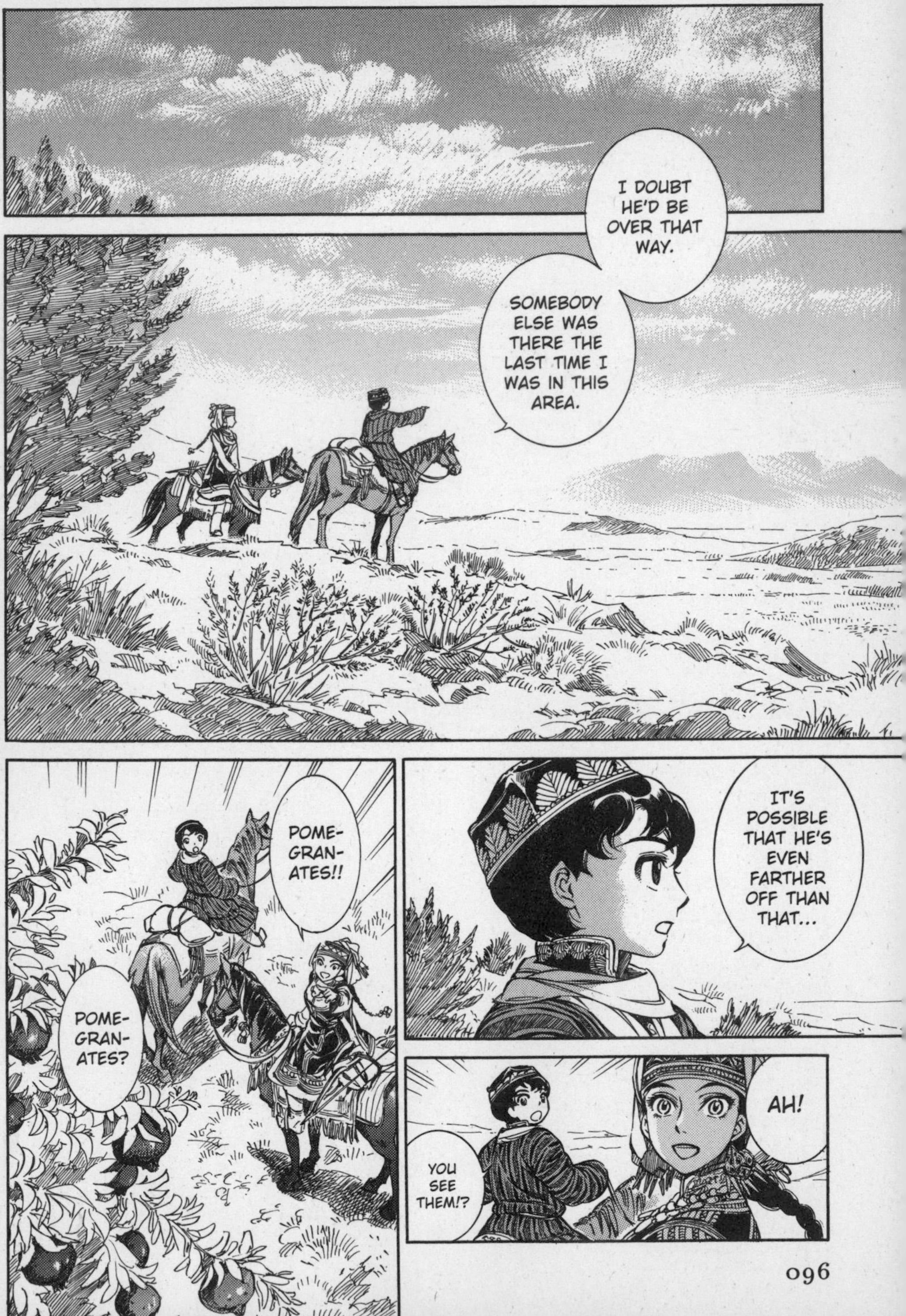
I DOUBT HE'D BE OVER THAT WAY.
SOMEBODY ELSE WAS THERE THE LAST TIME I WAS IN THIS AREA.
IT'S POSSIBLE THAT HE'S EVEN FARTHER OFF THAN THAT...
AH!
YOU SEE THEM!?
POME-GRAN-ATES!!
POME-GRAN-ATES?

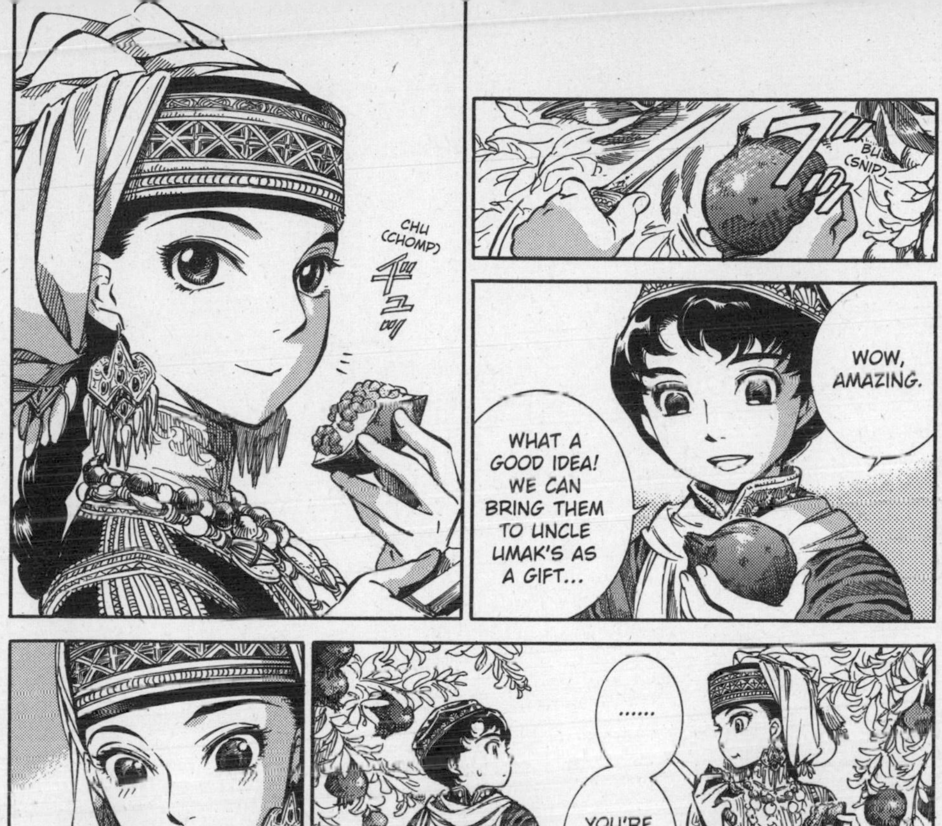
BLI (SNIP)
WOW, AMAZING.
WHAT A GOOD IDEA! WE CAN BRING THEM TO UNCLE UMAK'S AS A GIFT...
CHU (CHOMP)
......
YOU'RE EATING IT NOW?

SFX: PIIIYORORORO (NEEEIGH)

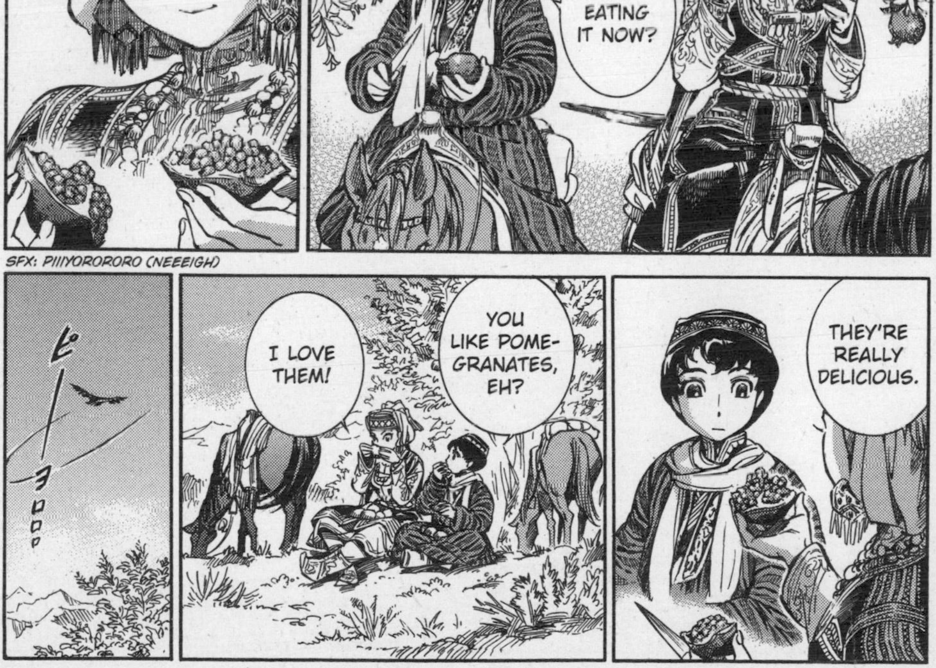
THEY'RE REALLY DELICIOUS.
YOU LIKE POME-GRANATES, EH?
I LOVE THEM!

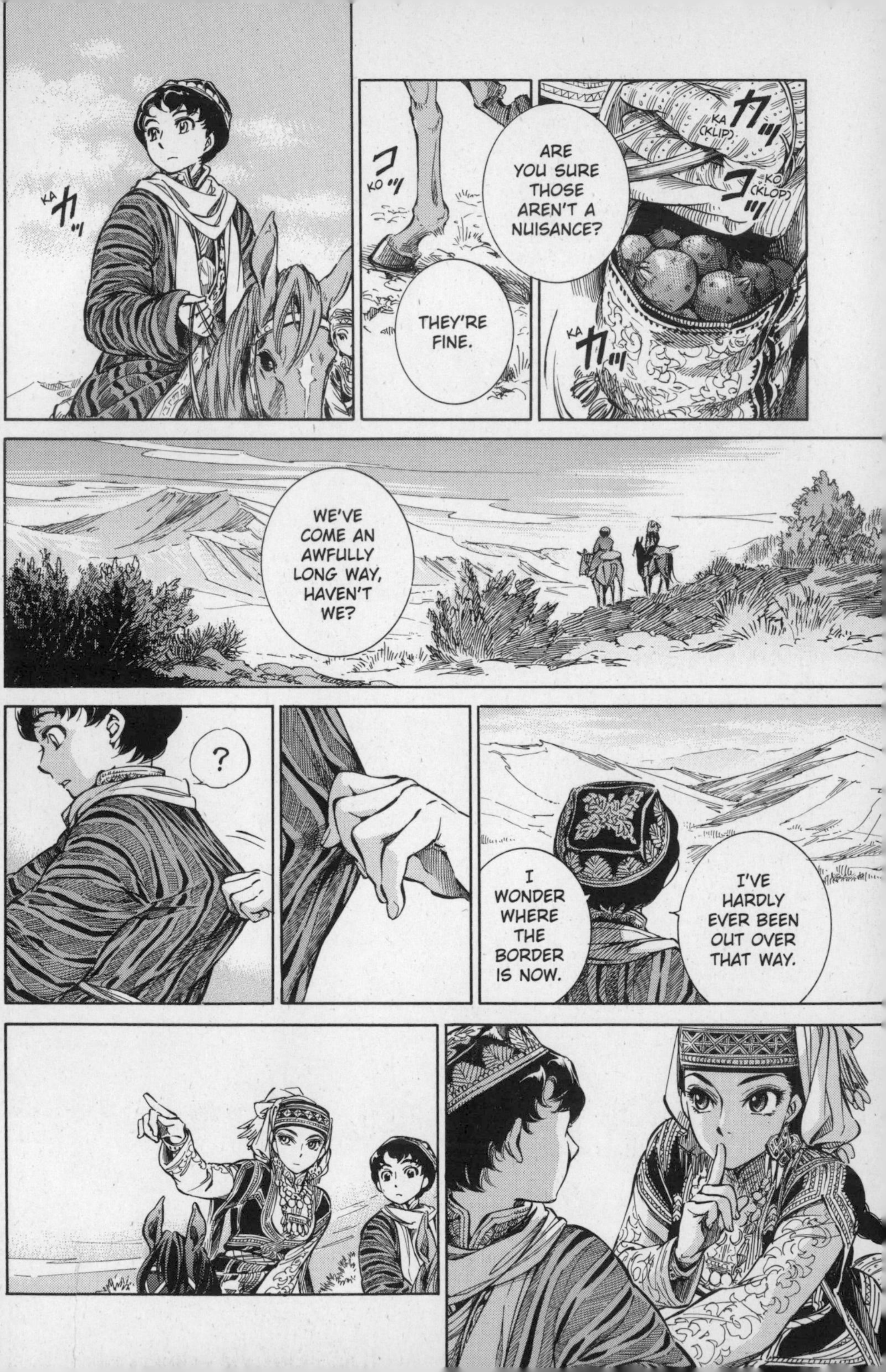
KA (KLIP)
KO (KLOP)
ARE YOU SURE THOSE AREN'T A NUISANCE?
KA
KO
THEY'RE FINE.
KA
WE'VE COME AN AWFULLY LONG WAY, HAVEN'T WE?
I'VE HARDLY EVER BEEN OUT OVER THAT WAY.
I WONDER WHERE THE BORDER IS NOW.
?

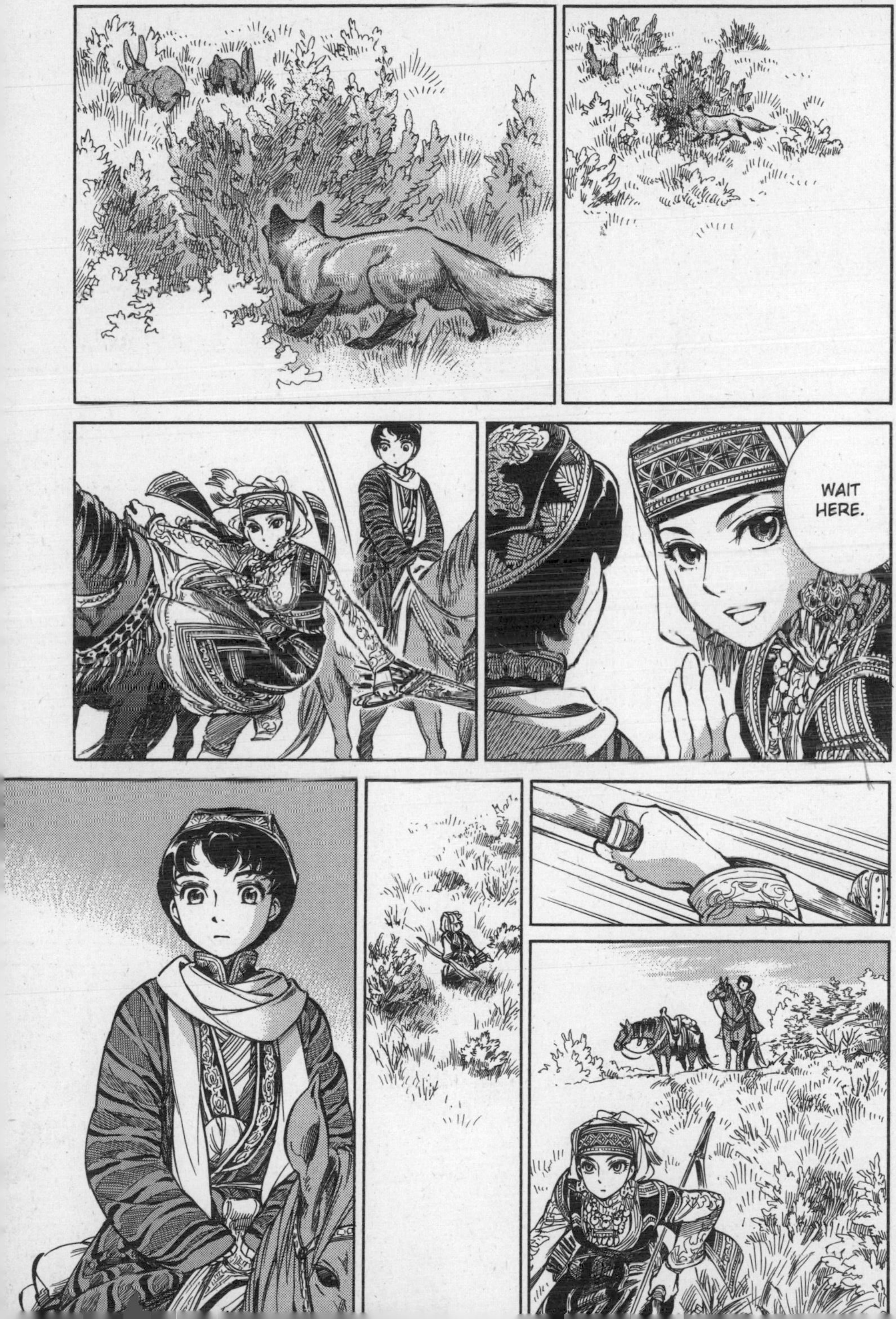
WAIT HERE.

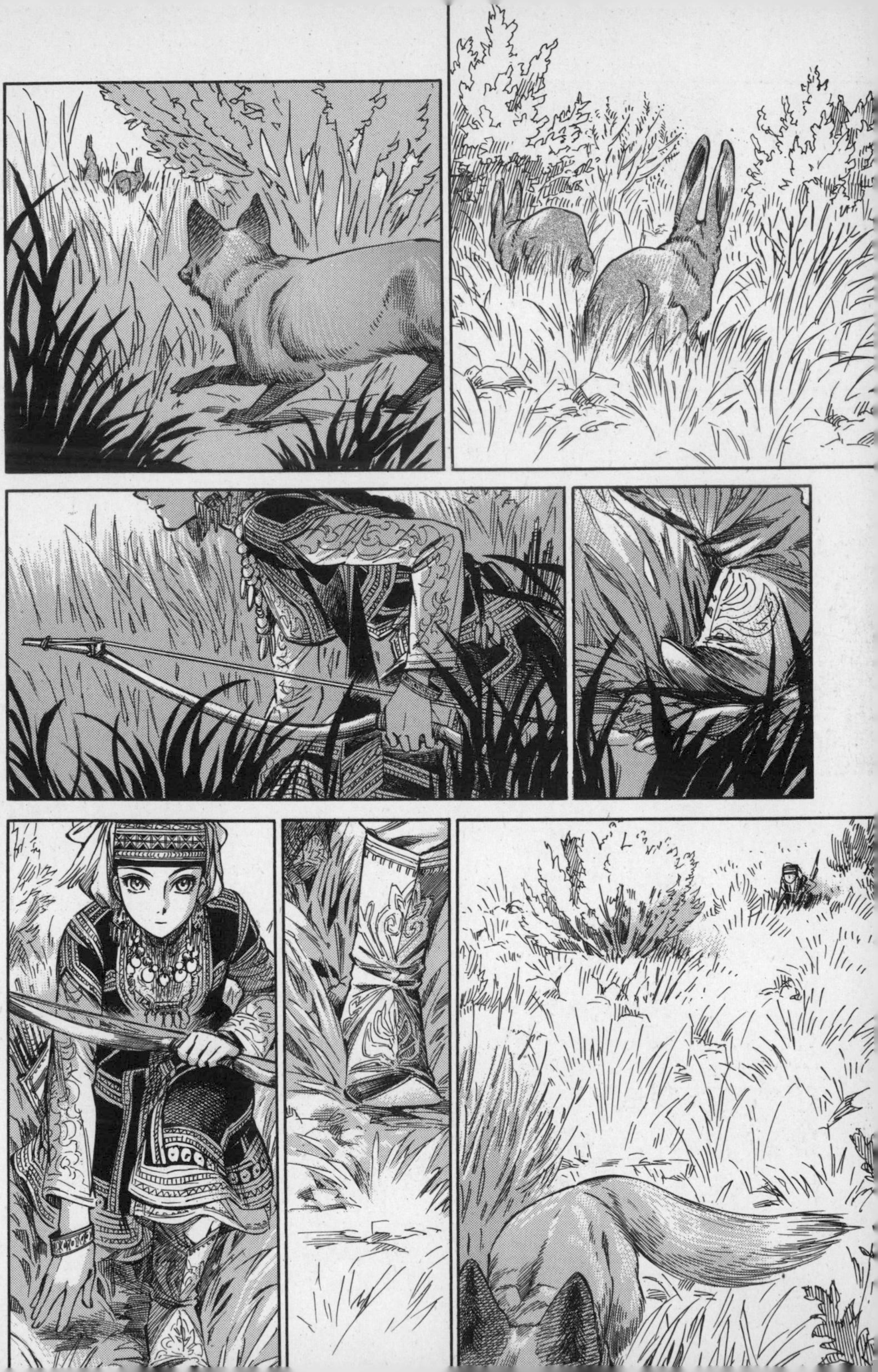

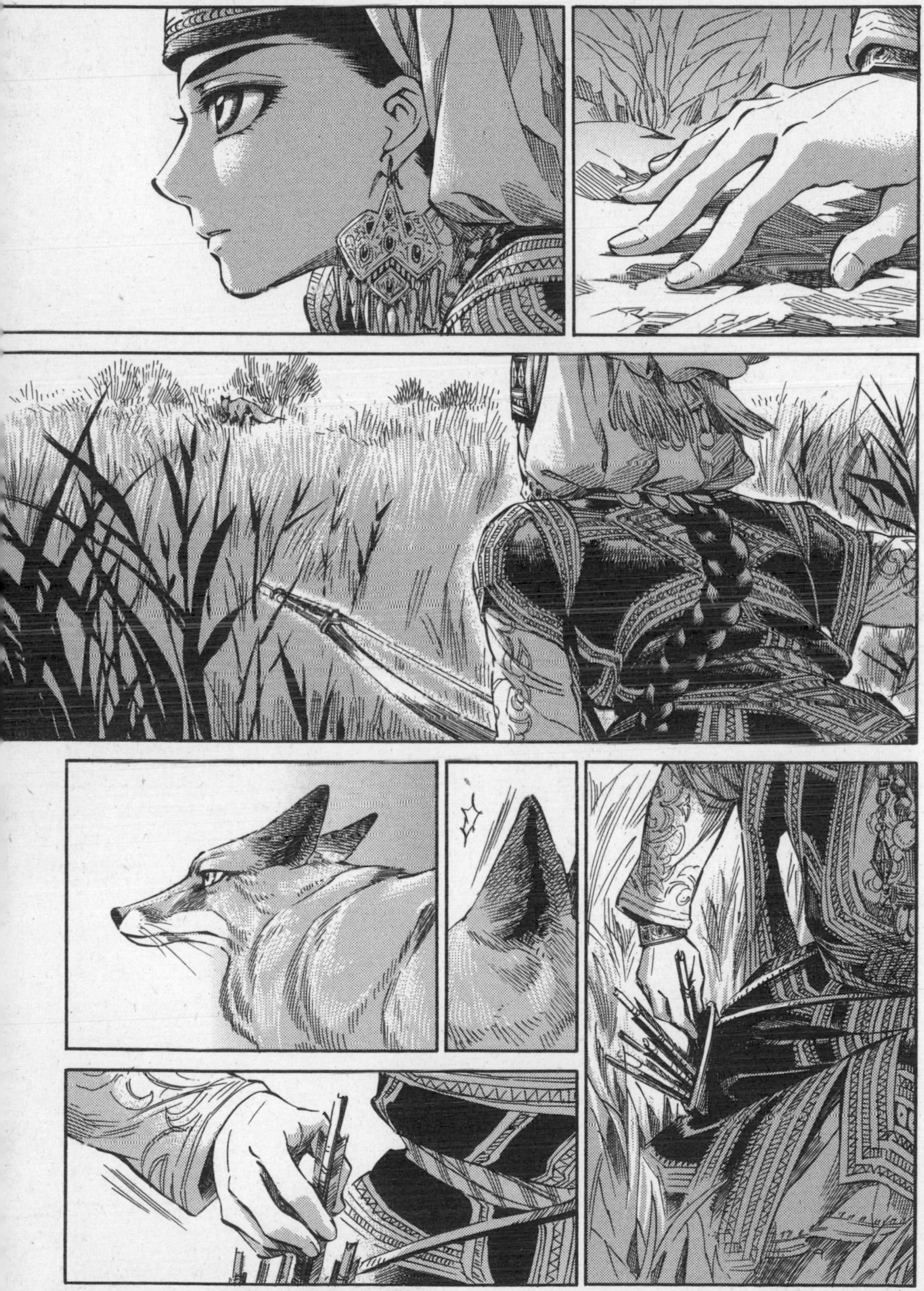

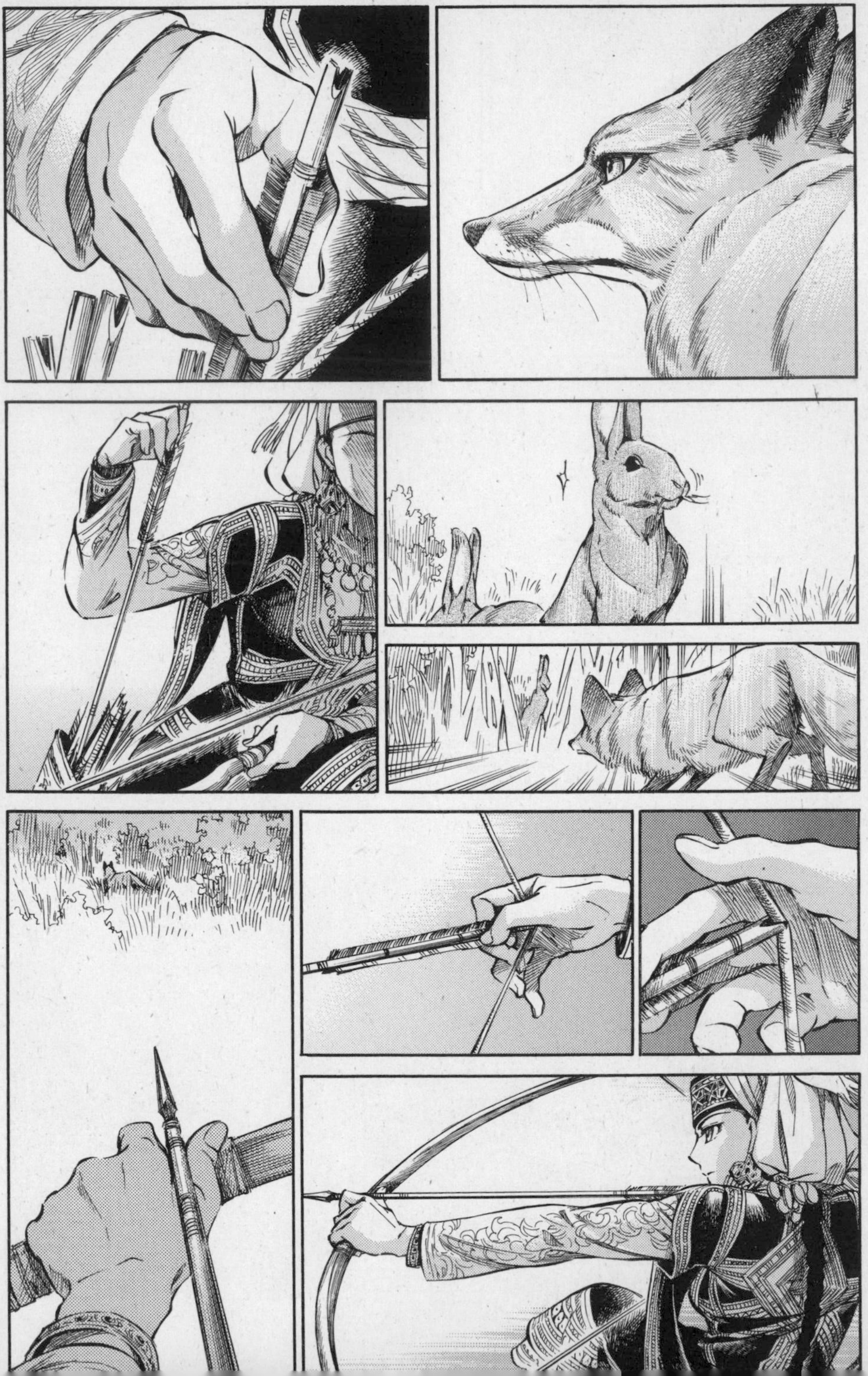

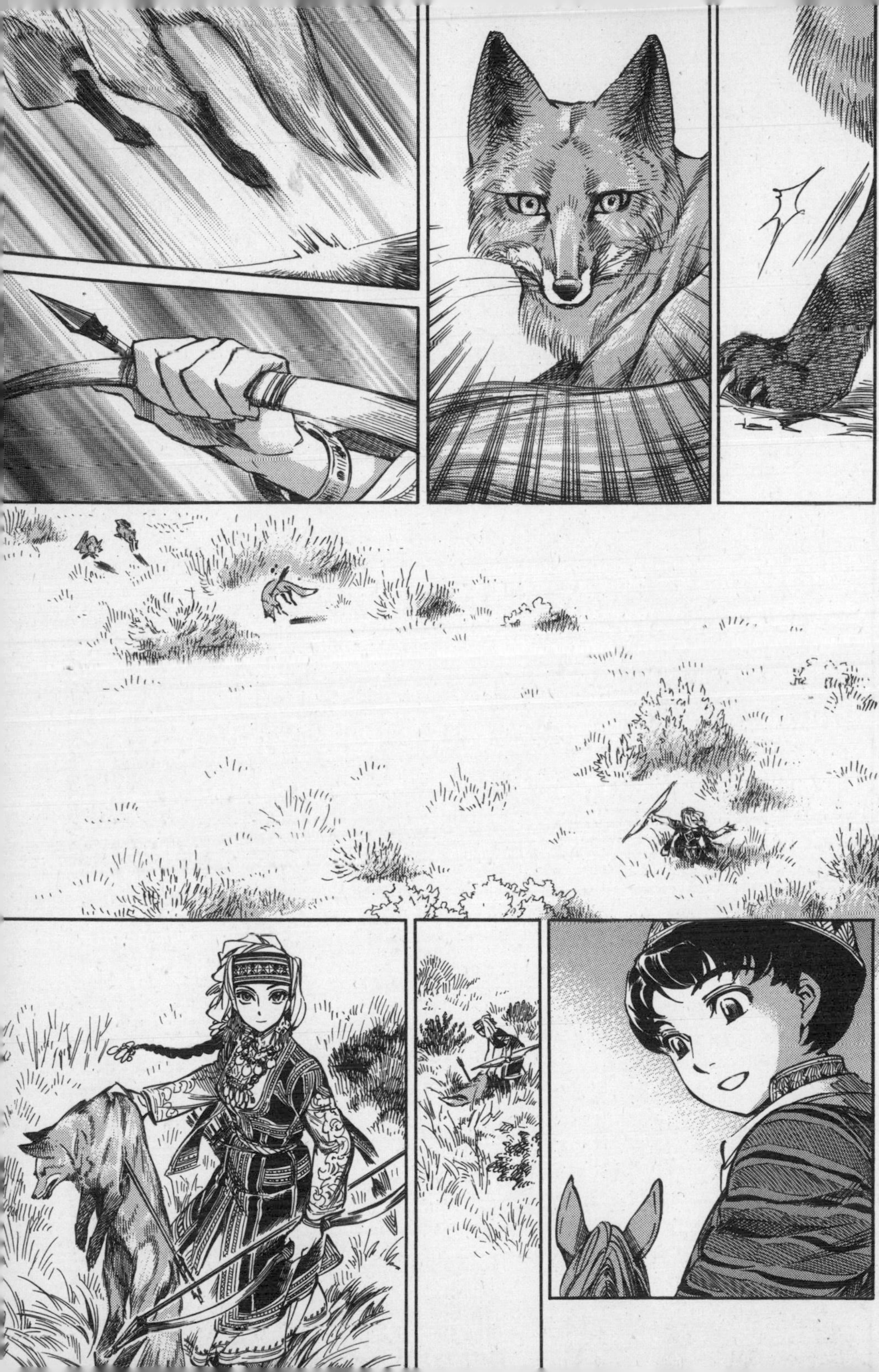

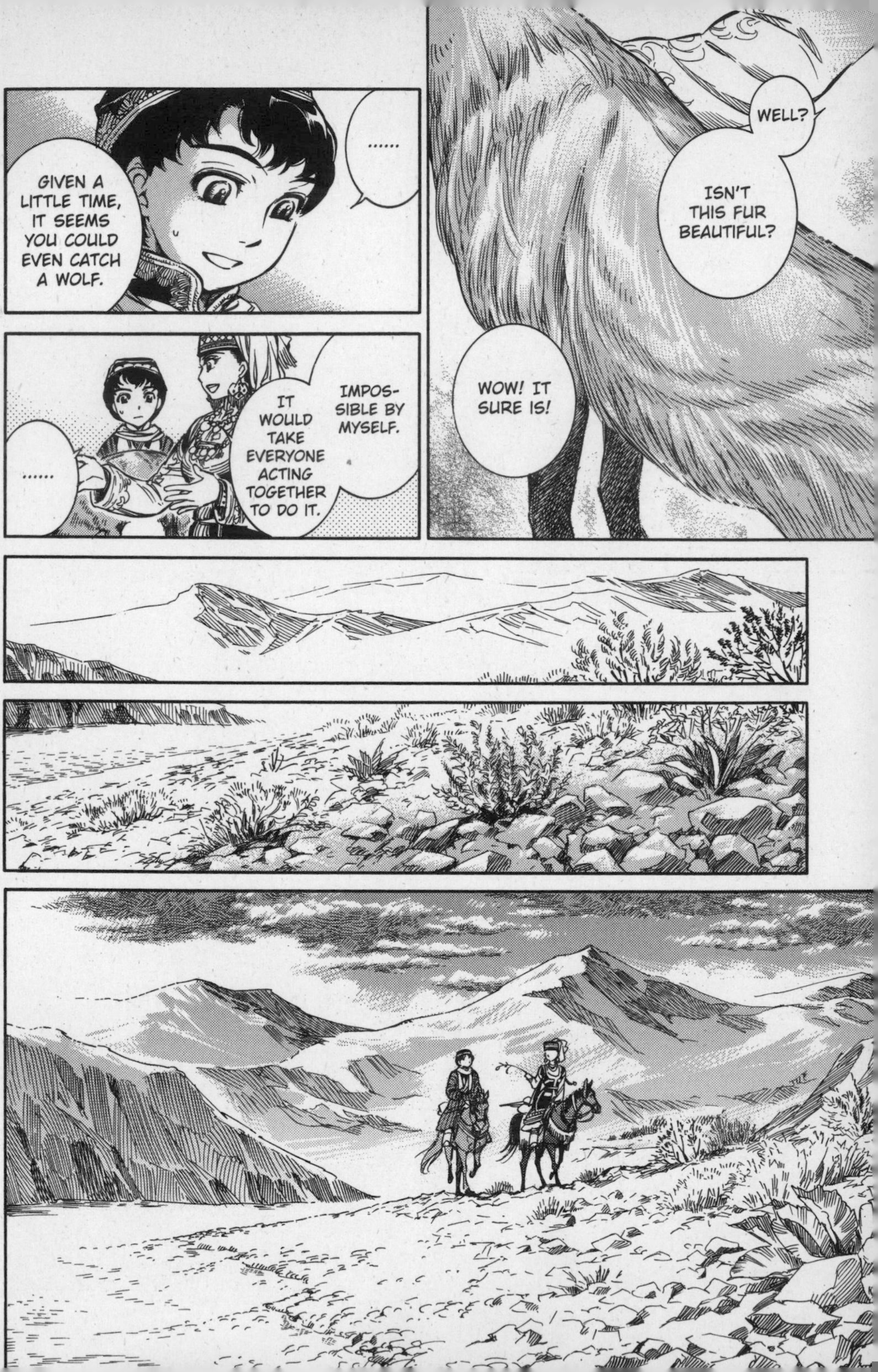
WELL?
ISN'T THIS FUR BEAUTIFUL?
WOW! IT SURE IS!
......
GIVEN A LITTLE TIME, IT SEEMS YOU COULD EVEN CATCH A WOLF.
IMPOS-SIBLE BY MYSELF.
IT WOULD TAKE EVERYONE ACTING TOGETHER TO DO IT.
......

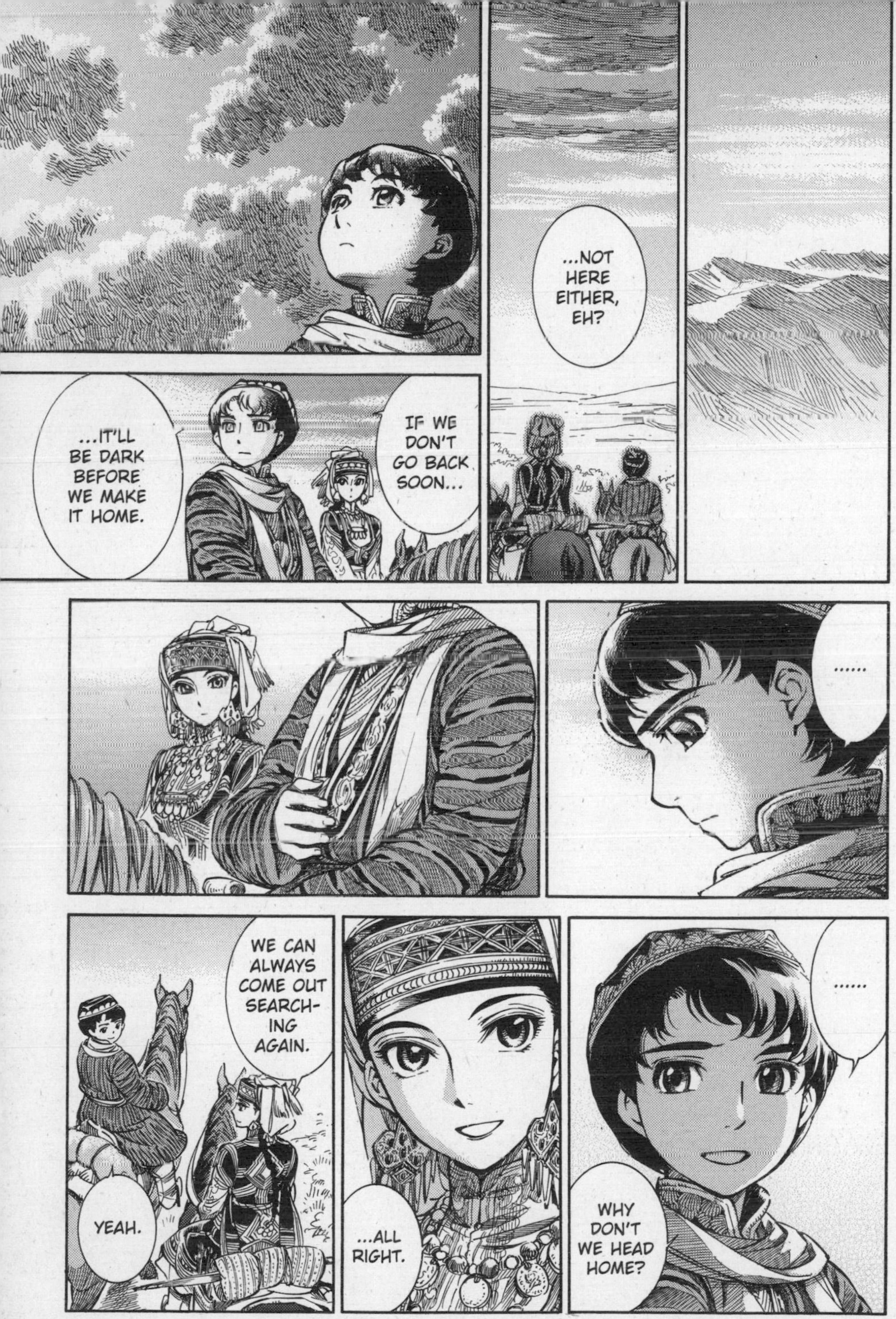
...NOT HERE EITHER, EH?
IF WE DON'T GO BACK SOON...
...IT'LL BE DARK BEFORE WE MAKE IT HOME.
......
......
WHY DON'T WE HEAD HOME?
...ALL RIGHT.
WE CAN ALWAYS COME OUT SEARCHING AGAIN.
YEAH.

LET'S HAVE SOME MORE POMEGRANATES WHEN WE GET HOME.

OKAY.

WE'LL GIVE THE FUR TO FATHER...

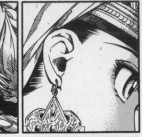

カコ カコ
KAKO
KAKO
(KAKLOP)

カッ
KA
(KLIP)

WHAT IS IT?

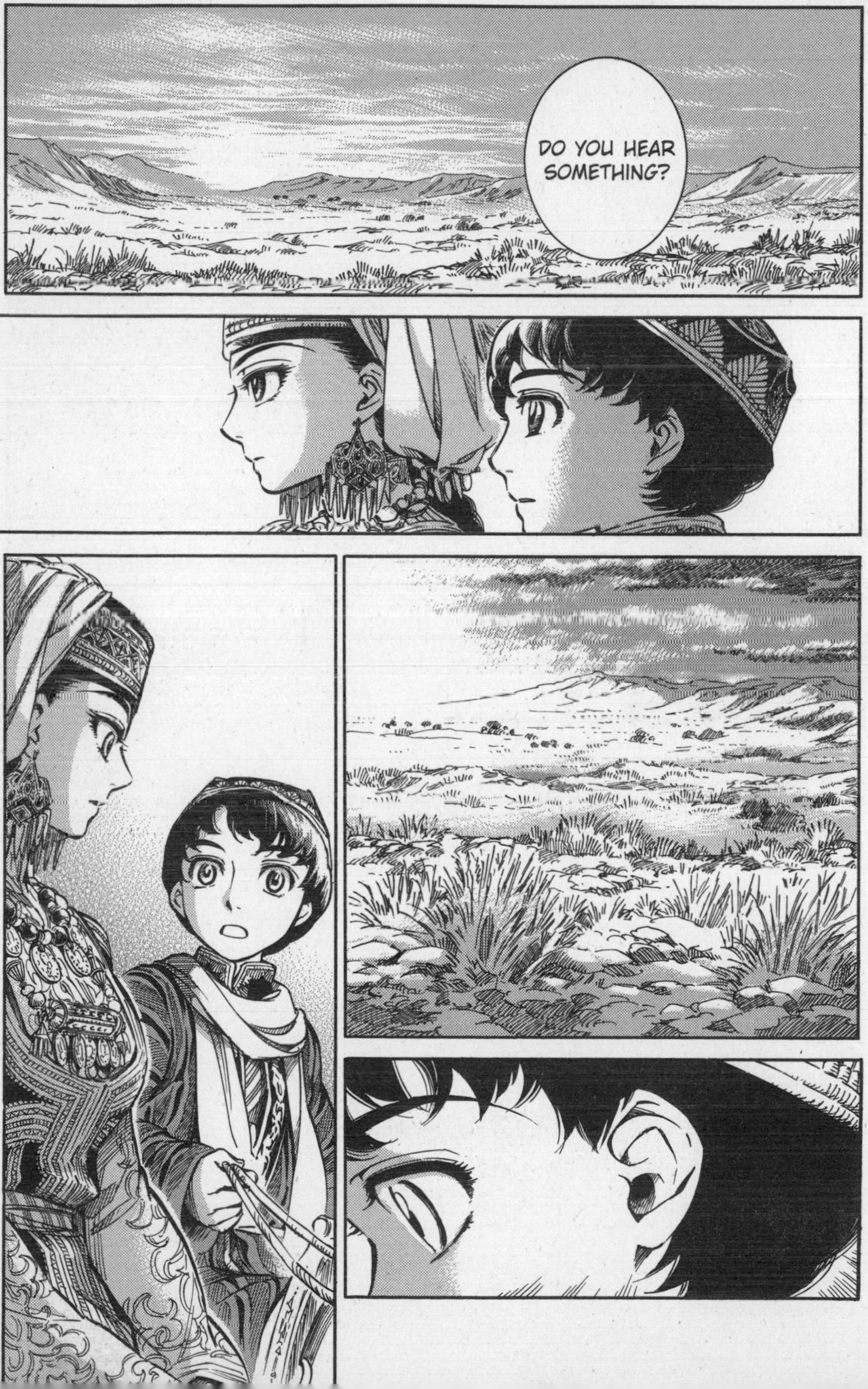
DO YOU HEAR SOMETHING?

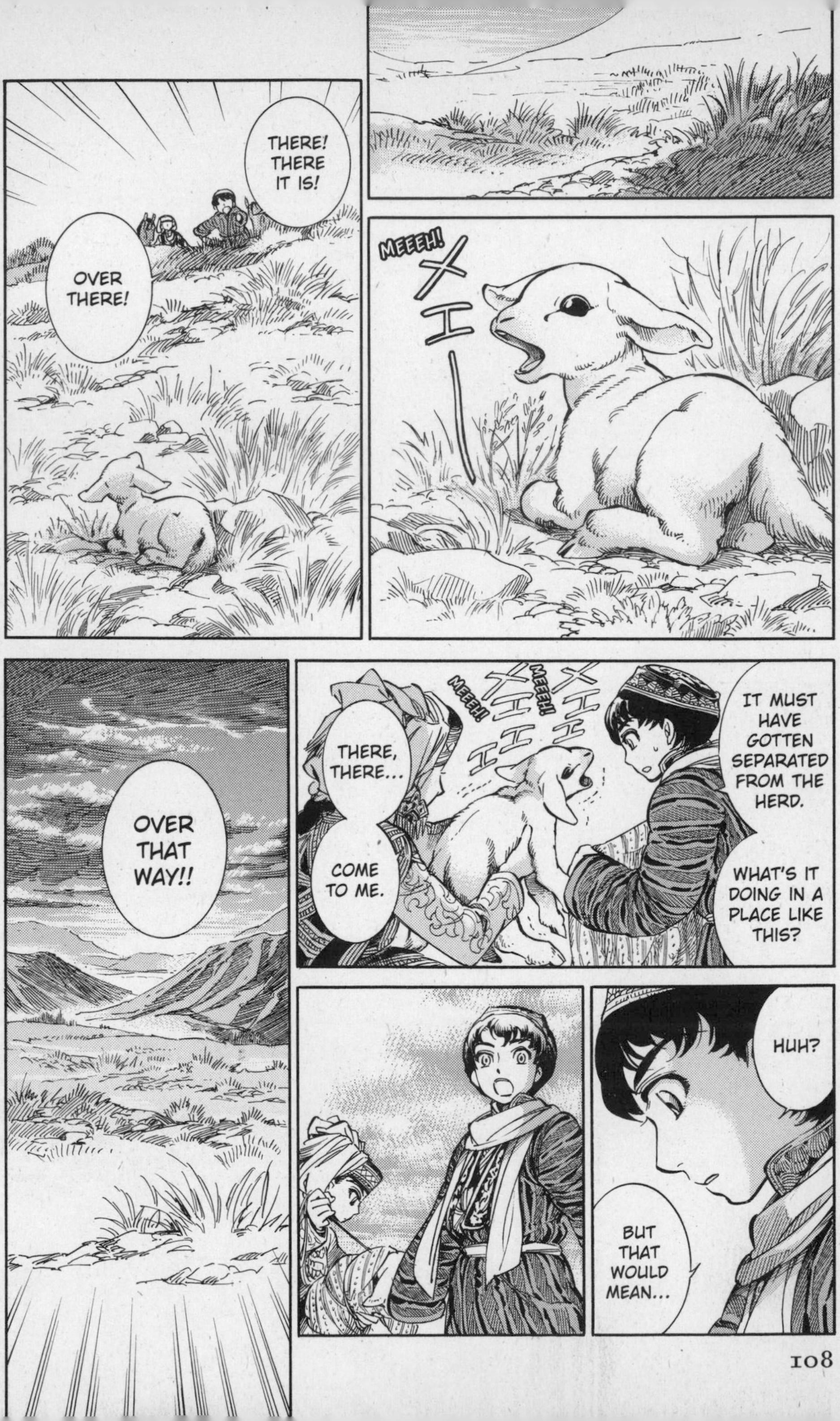
MEEEH!
THERE! THERE IT IS!
OVER THERE!
IT MUST HAVE GOTTEN SEPARATED FROM THE HERD.
WHAT'S IT DOING IN A PLACE LIKE THIS?
MEEEH!
MEEEH!
THERE, THERE...
COME TO ME.
HUH?
BUT THAT WOULD MEAN...
OVER THAT WAY!!

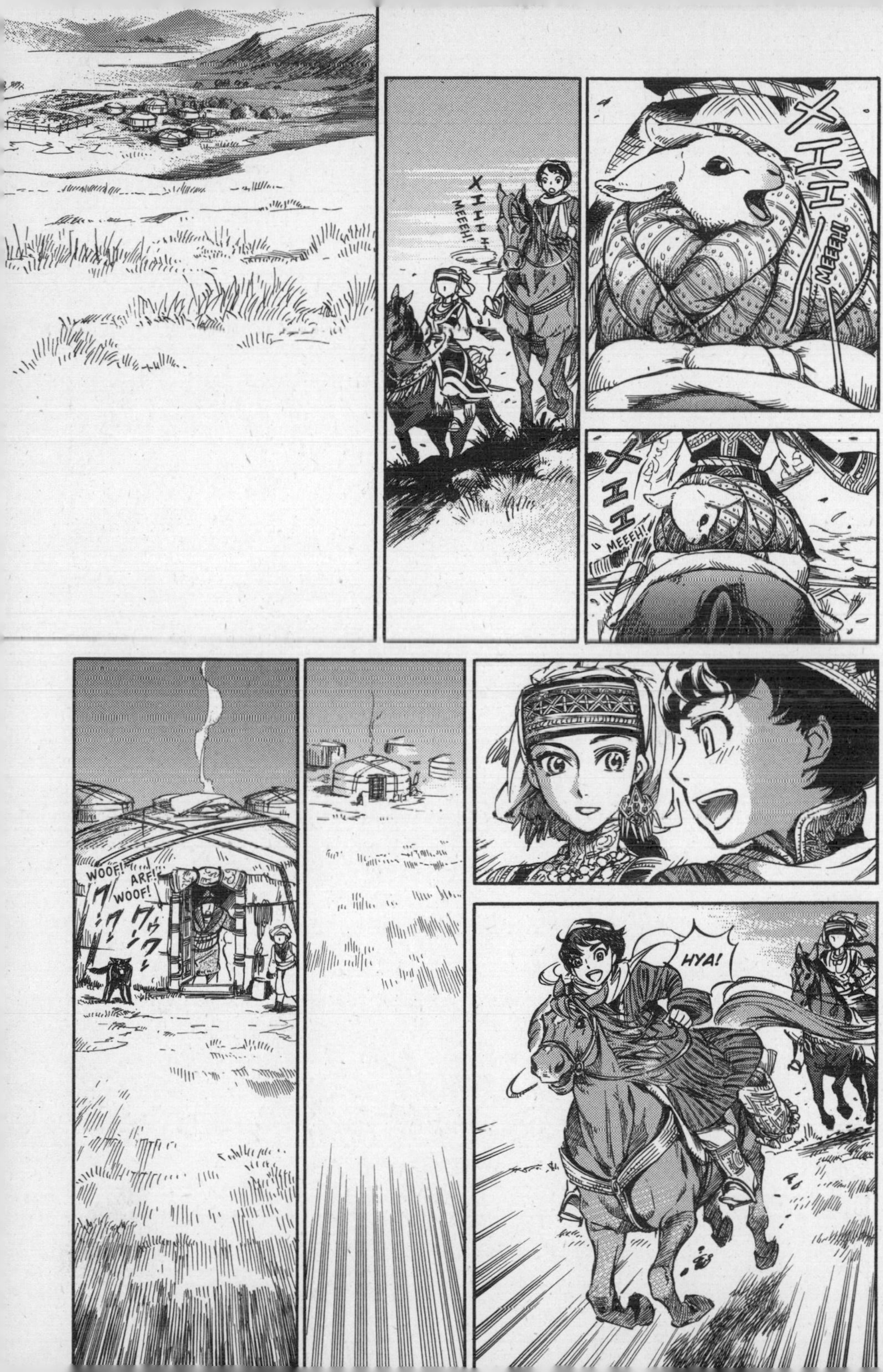
MEEEH!
MEEEH!
MEEEH!
HYA!
WOOF!
ARF!
WOOF!

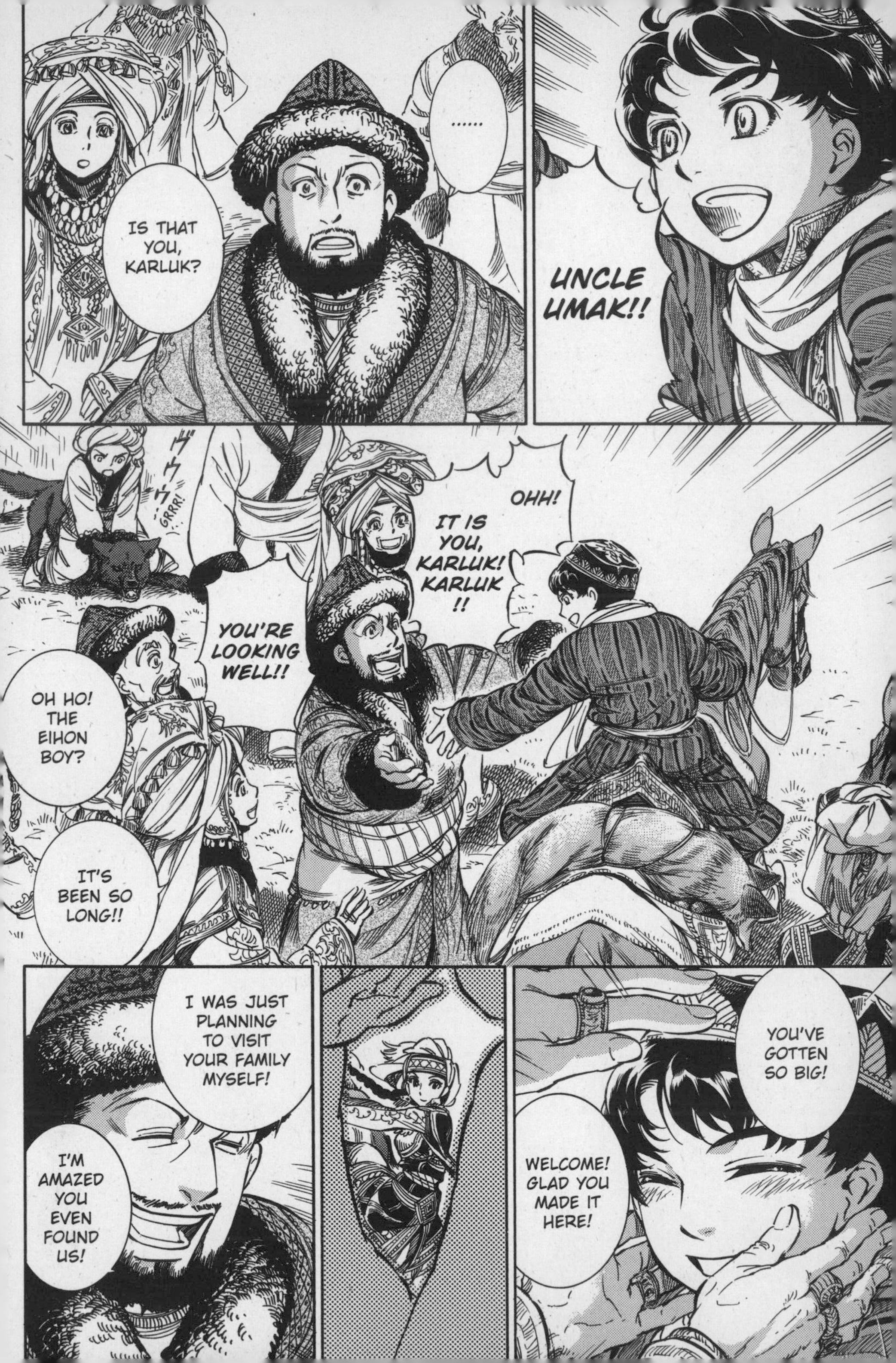
UNCLE UMAK!!
......
IS THAT YOU, KARLUK?
OHH!
IT IS YOU, KARLUK! KARLUK !!
ヴゥゥ GRRR!
YOU'RE LOOKING WELL!!
OH HO! THE EIHON BOY?
IT'S BEEN SO LONG!!
YOU'VE GOTTEN SO BIG!
WELCOME! GLAD YOU MADE IT HERE!
I WAS JUST PLANNING TO VISIT YOUR FAMILY MYSELF!
I'M AMAZED YOU EVEN FOUND US!

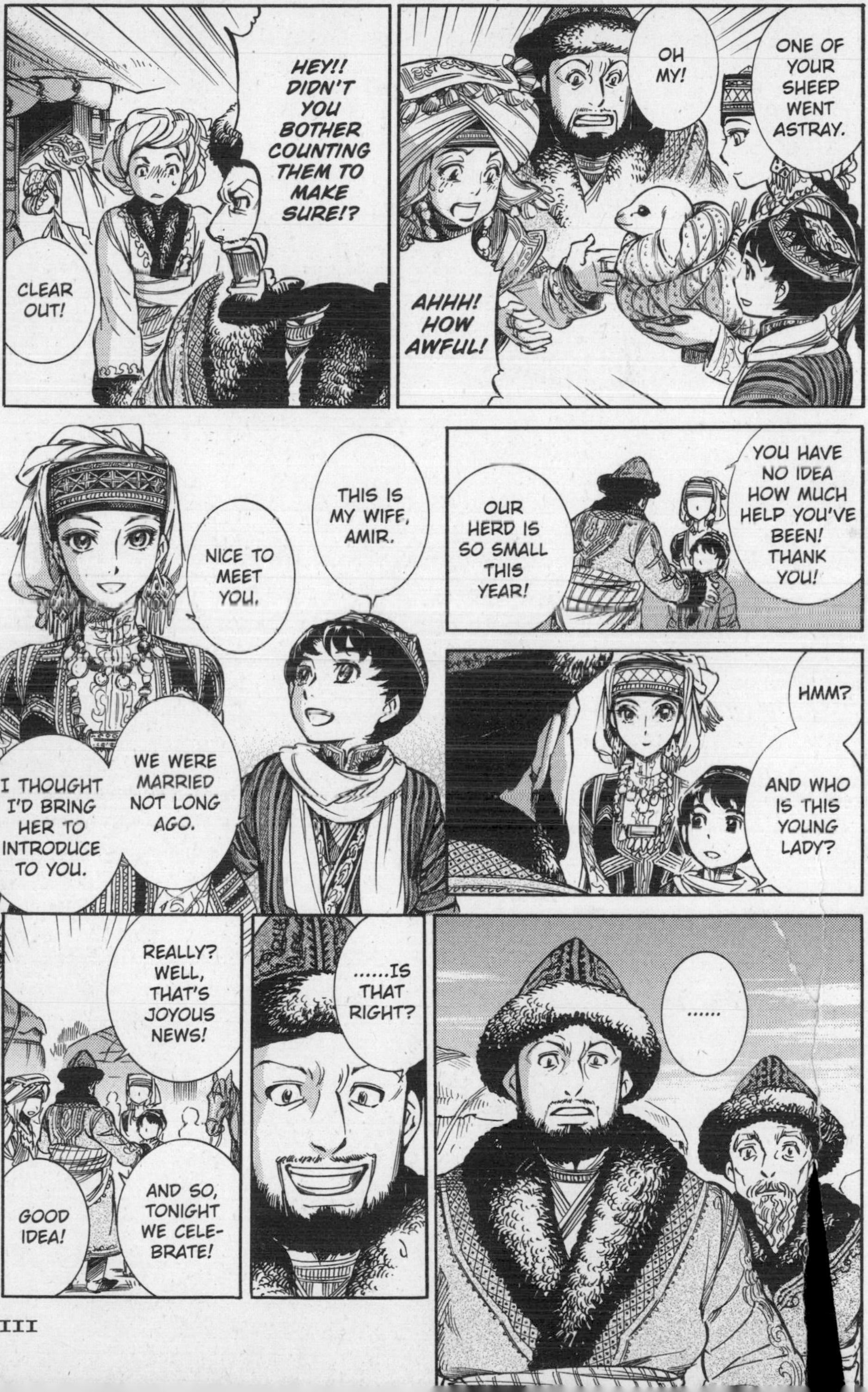
ONE OF YOUR SHEEP WENT ASTRAY.
OH MY!
AHHH! HOW AWFUL!
HEY!! DIDN'T YOU BOTHER COUNTING THEM TO MAKE SURE!?
CLEAR OUT!
YOU HAVE NO IDEA HOW MUCH HELP YOU'VE BEEN! THANK YOU!
OUR HERD IS SO SMALL THIS YEAR!
HMM?
AND WHO IS THIS YOUNG LADY?
THIS IS MY WIFE, AMIR.
NICE TO MEET YOU.
WE WERE MARRIED NOT LONG AGO.
I THOUGHT I'D BRING HER TO INTRODUCE TO YOU.
......
......IS THAT RIGHT?
REALLY? WELL, THAT'S JOYOUS NEWS!
AND SO, TONIGHT WE CELEBRATE!
GOOD IDEA!

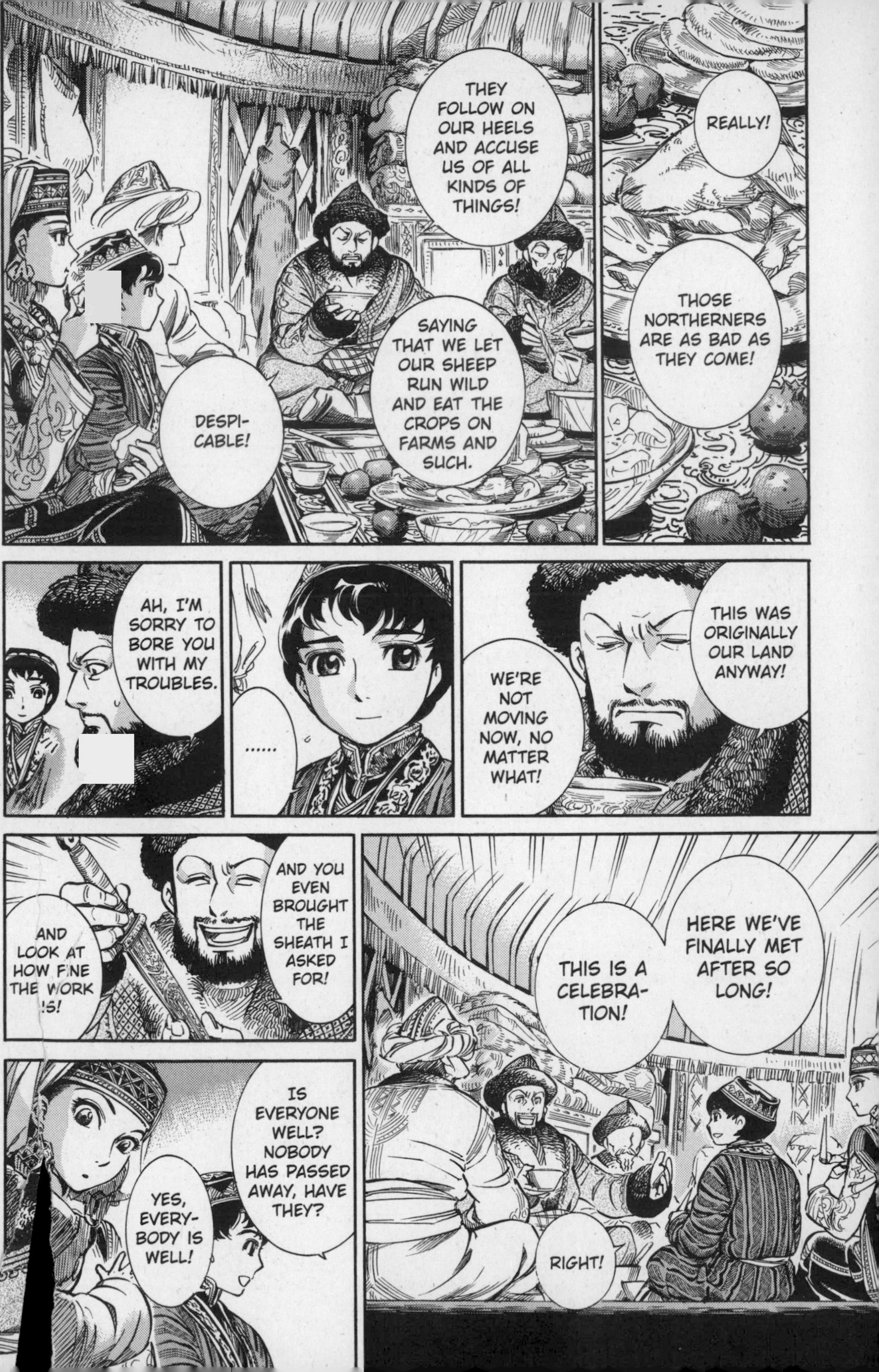
REALLY!
THOSE NORTHERNERS ARE AS BAD AS THEY COME!
THEY FOLLOW ON OUR HEELS AND ACCUSE US OF ALL KINDS OF THINGS!
SAYING THAT WE LET OUR SHEEP RUN WILD AND EAT THE CROPS ON FARMS AND SUCH.
DESPI-CABLE!
THIS WAS ORIGINALLY OUR LAND ANYWAY!
WE'RE NOT MOVING NOW, NO MATTER WHAT!
......
AH, I'M SORRY TO BORE YOU WITH MY TROUBLES.
HERE WE'VE FINALLY MET AFTER SO LONG!
THIS IS A CELEBRA-TION!
RIGHT!
AND YOU EVEN BROUGHT THE SHEATH I ASKED FOR!
AND LOOK AT HOW FINE THE WORK IS!
IS EVERYONE WELL? NOBODY HAS PASSED AWAY, HAVE THEY?
YES, EVERY-BODY IS WELL!

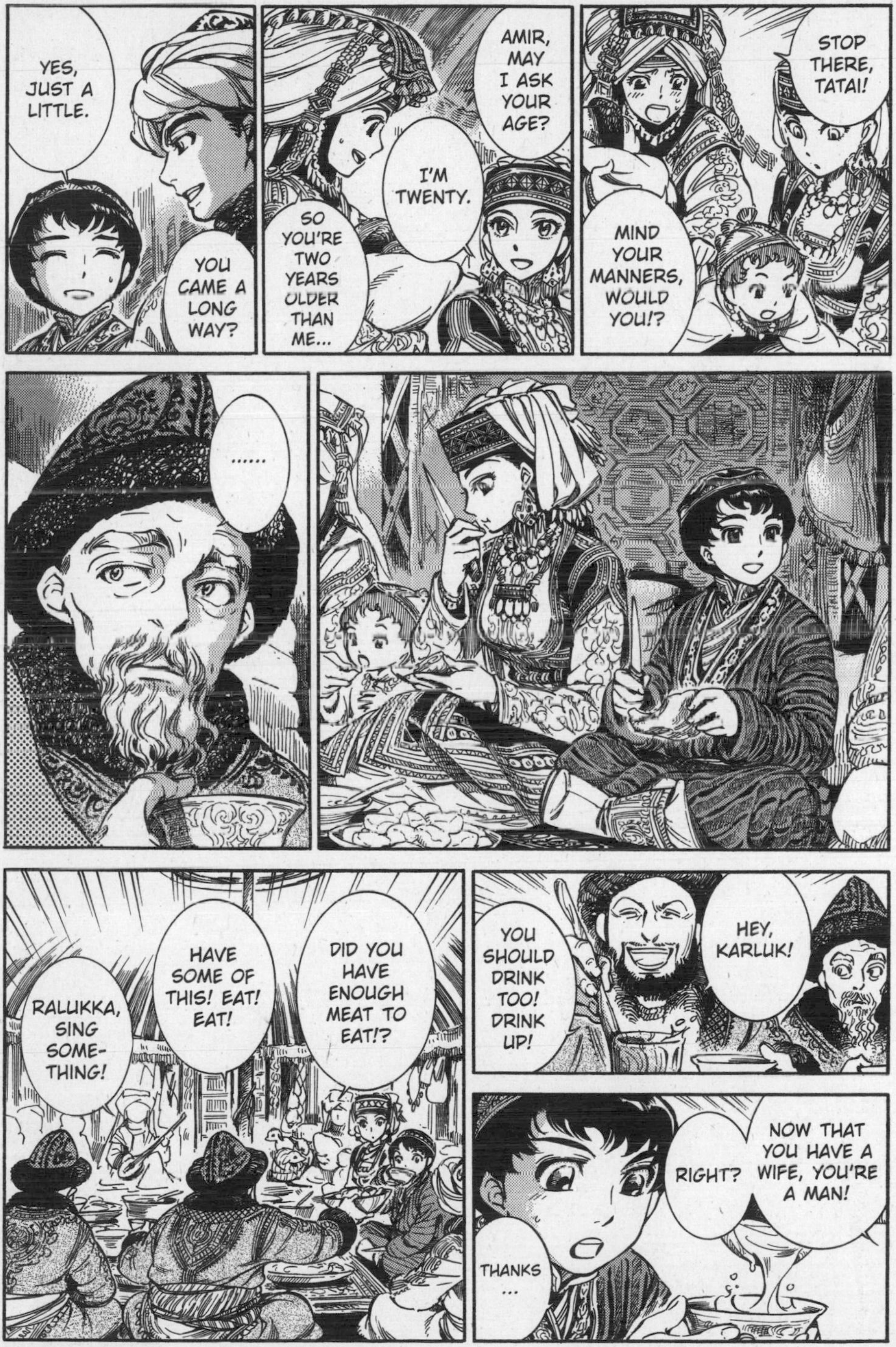
STOP THERE, TATAI!
MIND YOUR MANNERS, WOULD YOU!?
AMIR, MAY I ASK YOUR AGE?
I'M TWENTY.
SO YOU'RE TWO YEARS OLDER THAN ME...
YOU CAME A LONG WAY?
YES, JUST A LITTLE.
......
HEY, KARLUK!
YOU SHOULD DRINK TOO! DRINK UP!
NOW THAT YOU HAVE A WIFE, YOU'RE A MAN!
RIGHT?
THANKS...
DID YOU HAVE ENOUGH MEAT TO EAT!?
HAVE SOME OF THIS! EAT! EAT!
RALUKKA, SING SOMETHING!

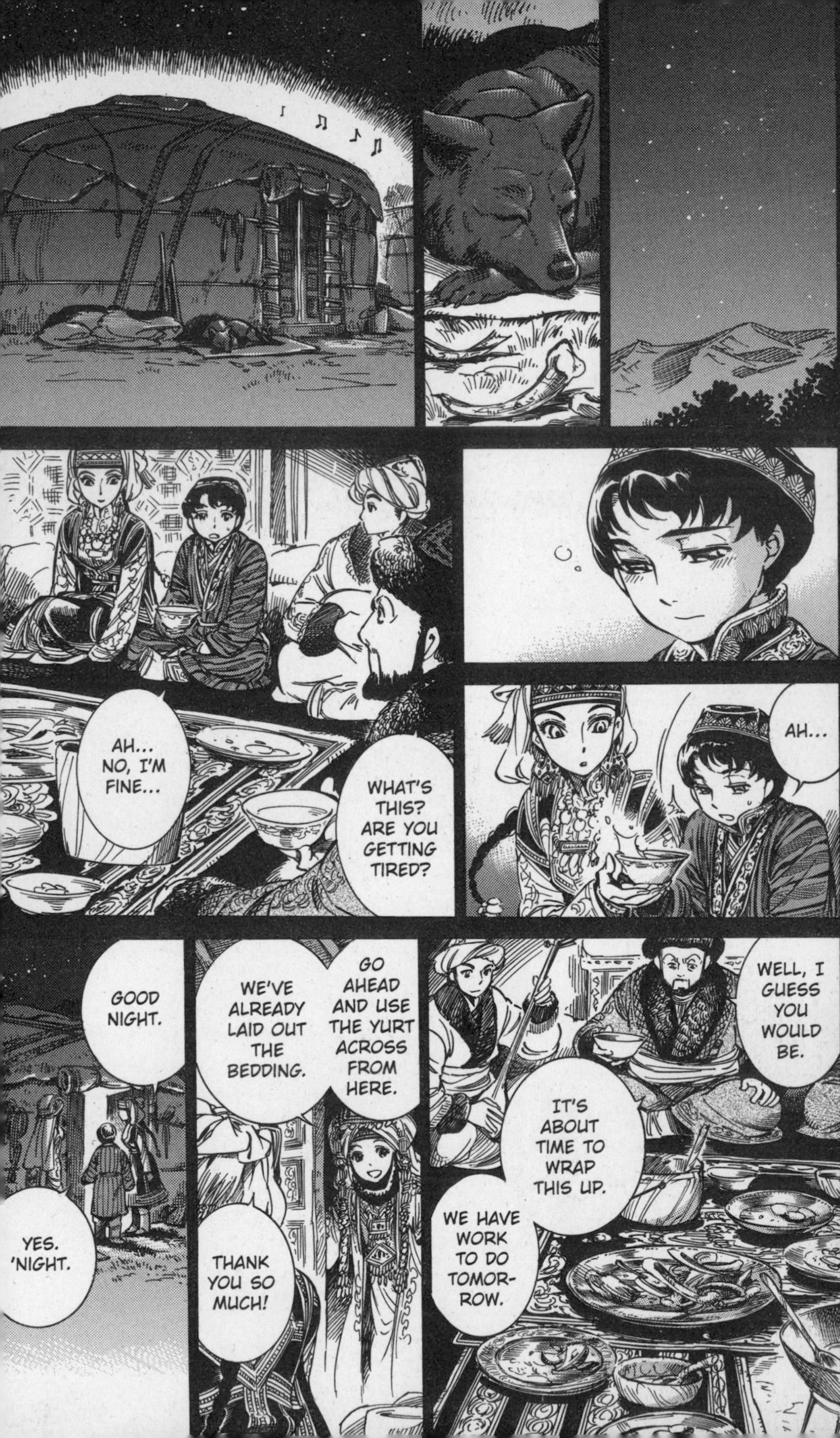
AH...
WHAT'S THIS? ARE YOU GETTING TIRED?
AH... NO, I'M FINE...
WELL, I GUESS YOU WOULD BE.
IT'S ABOUT TIME TO WRAP THIS UP.
WE HAVE WORK TO DO TOMOR-ROW.
GO AHEAD AND USE THE YURT ACROSS FROM HERE.
WE'VE ALREADY LAID OUT THE BEDDING.
THANK YOU SO MUCH!
GOOD NIGHT.
YES. 'NIGHT.

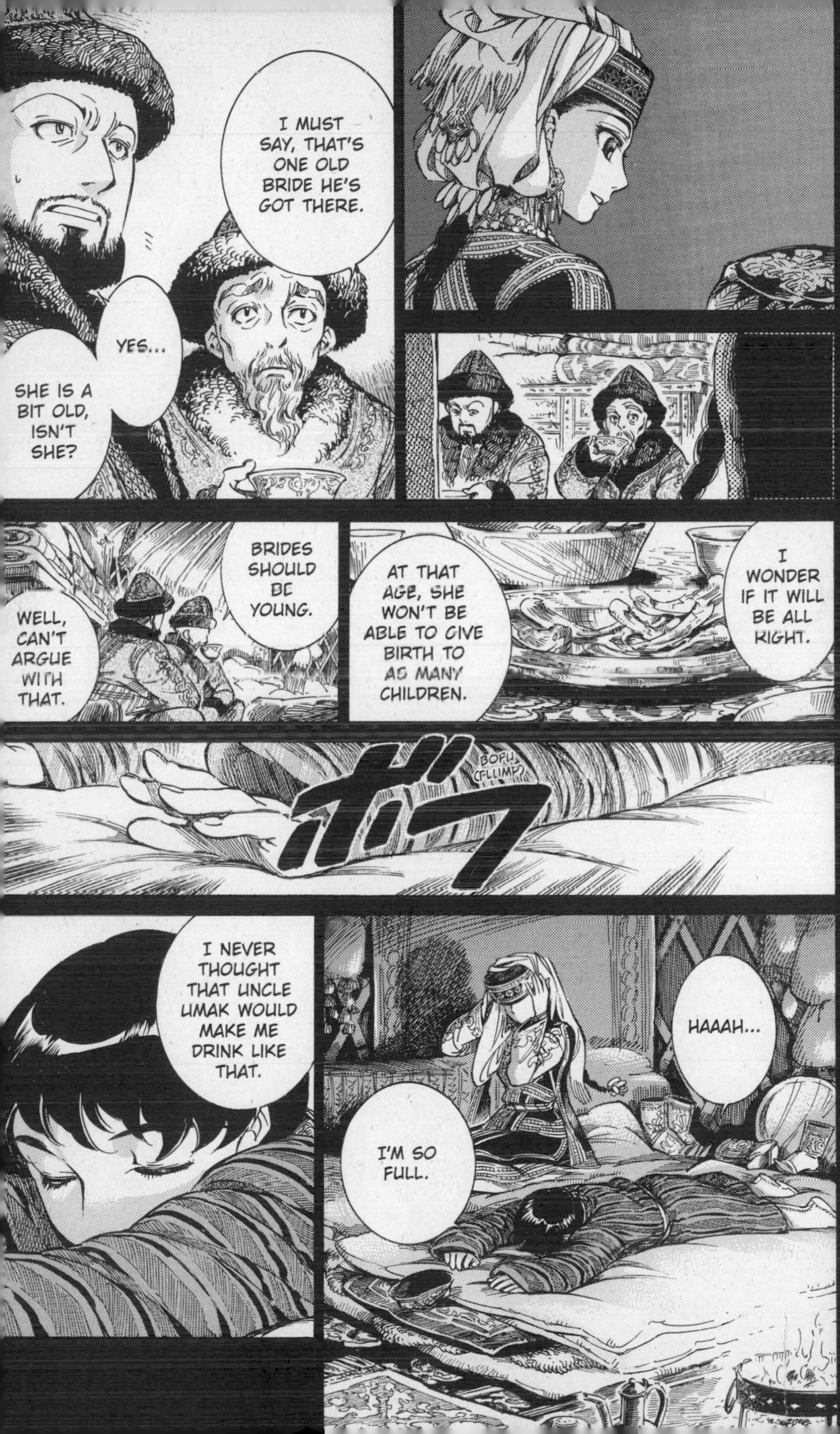
I MUST SAY, THAT'S ONE OLD BRIDE HE'S GOT THERE.
YES...
SHE IS A BIT OLD, ISN'T SHE?
I WONDER IF IT WILL BE ALL RIGHT.
AT THAT AGE, SHE WON'T BE ABLE TO GIVE BIRTH TO AS MANY CHILDREN.
BRIDES SHOULD BE YOUNG.
WELL, CAN'T ARGUE WITH THAT.
ボフ
BOFU (FLUMP)
HAAAH...
I'M SO FULL.
I NEVER THOUGHT THAT UNCLE UMAK WOULD MAKE ME DRINK LIKE THAT.

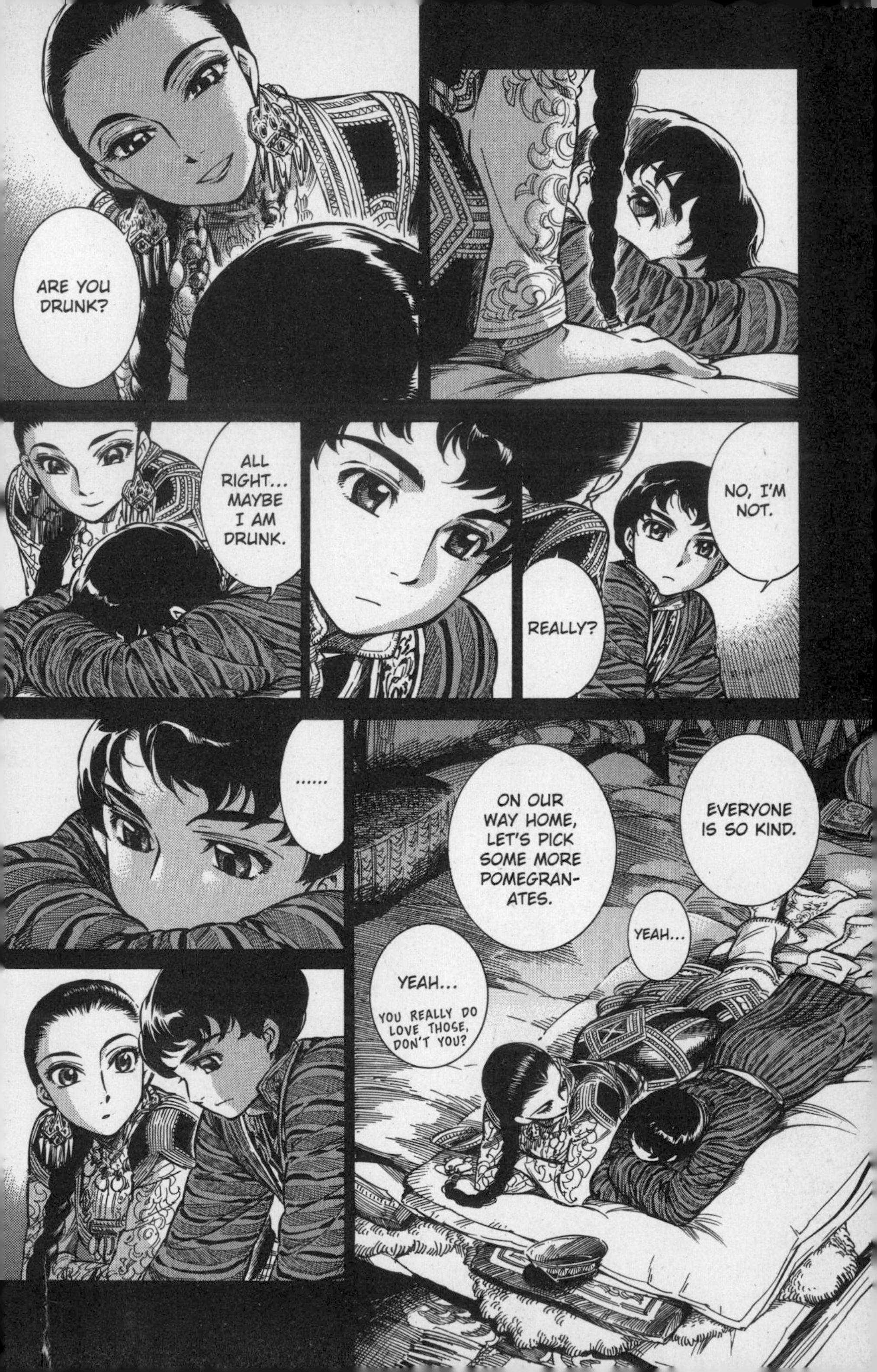
ARE YOU DRUNK?
NO, I'M NOT.
REALLY?
ALL RIGHT... MAYBE I AM DRUNK.
EVERYONE IS SO KIND.
ON OUR WAY HOME, LET'S PICK SOME MORE POMEGRAN-ATES.
YEAH...
YEAH...
YOU REALLY DO LOVE THOSE, DON'T YOU?
......

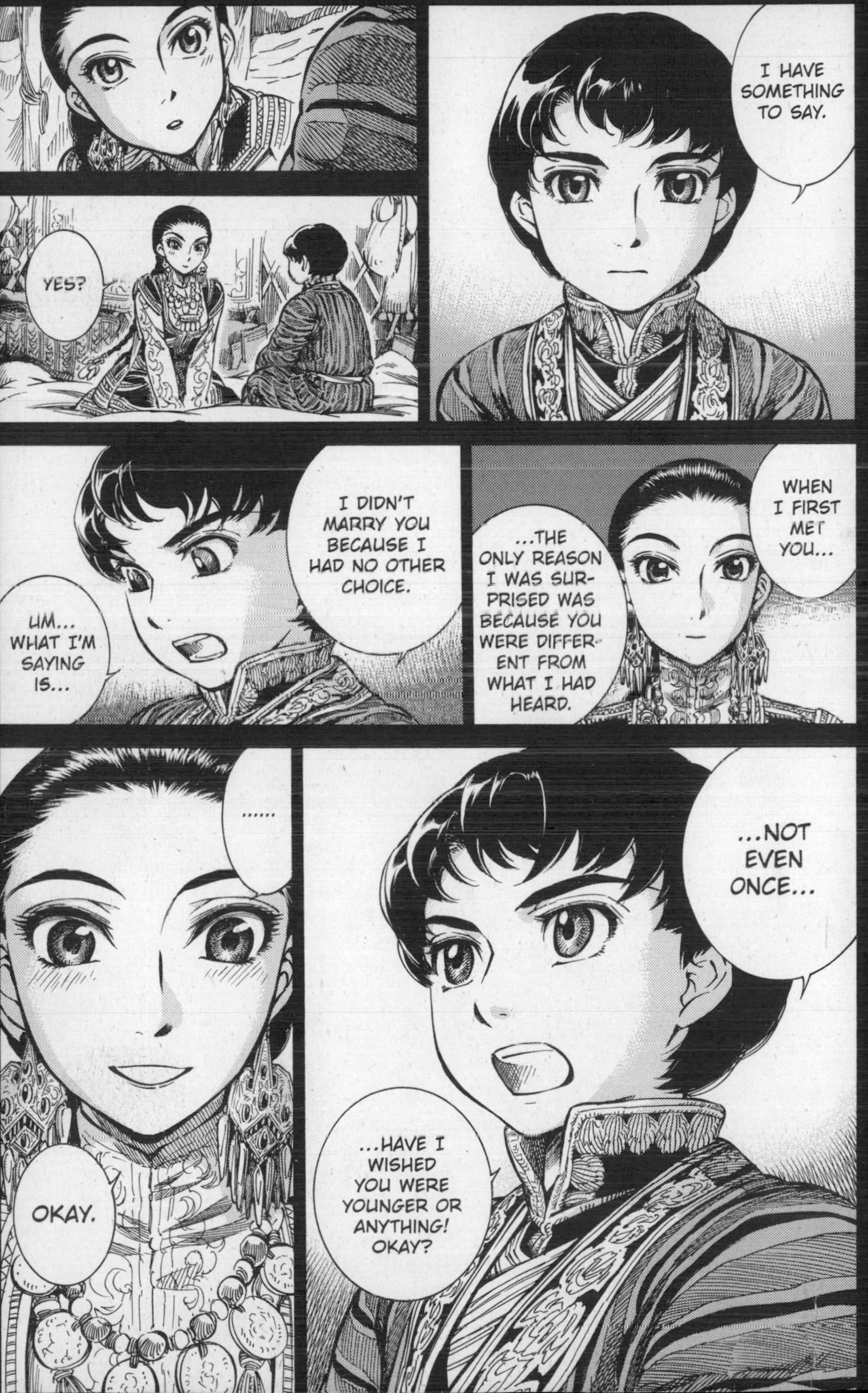
I HAVE SOMETHING TO SAY.
YES?
WHEN I FIRST MET YOU...
...THE ONLY REASON I WAS SUR- PRISED WAS BECAUSE YOU WERE DIFFER- ENT FROM WHAT I HAD HEARD.
I DIDN'T MARRY YOU BECAUSE I HAD NO OTHER CHOICE.
UM... WHAT I'M SAYING IS...
...NOT EVEN ONCE...
...HAVE I WISHED YOU WERE YOUNGER OR ANYTHING! OKAY?
......
OKAY.

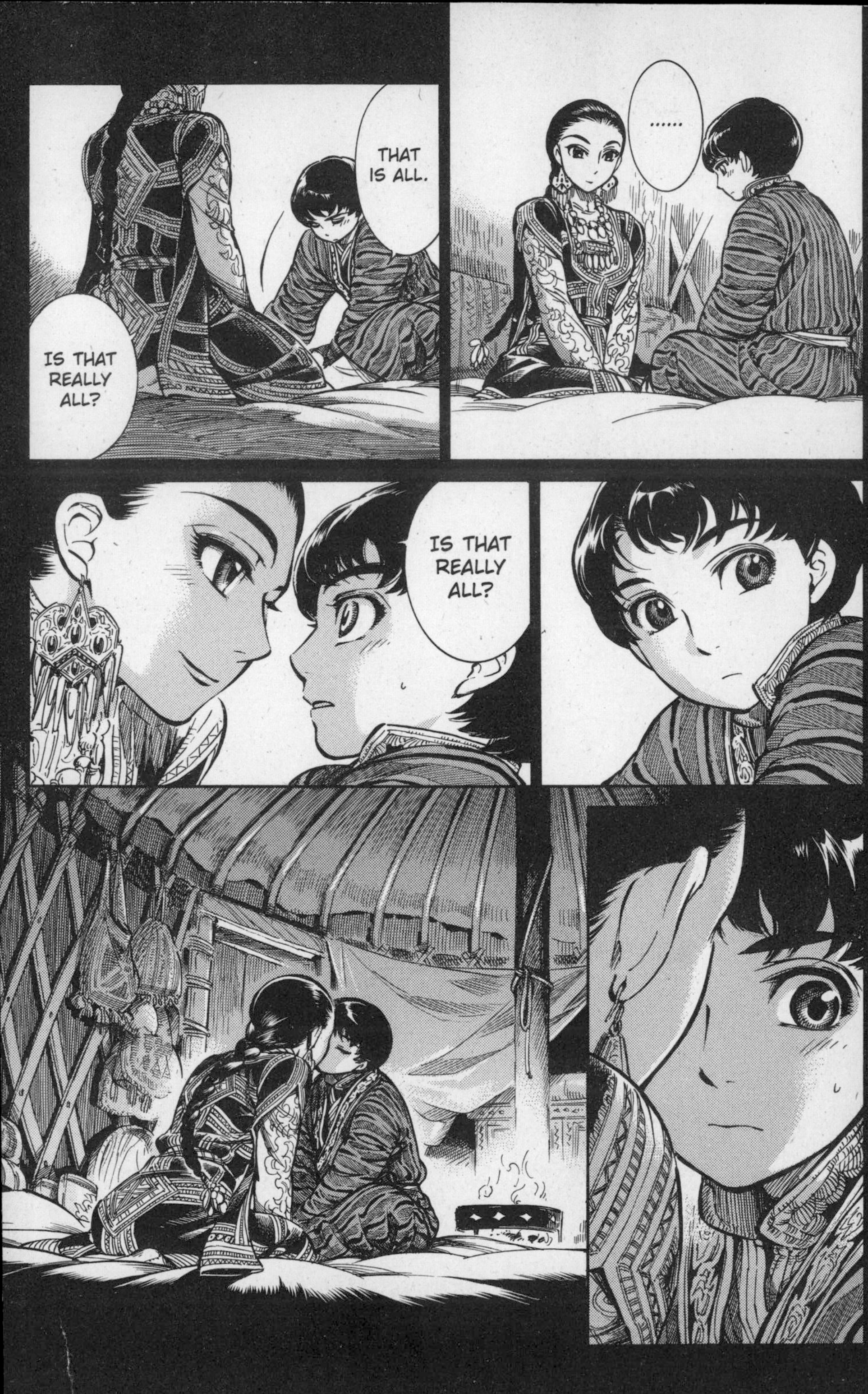
......
THAT IS ALL.
IS THAT REALLY ALL?
IS THAT REALLY ALL?

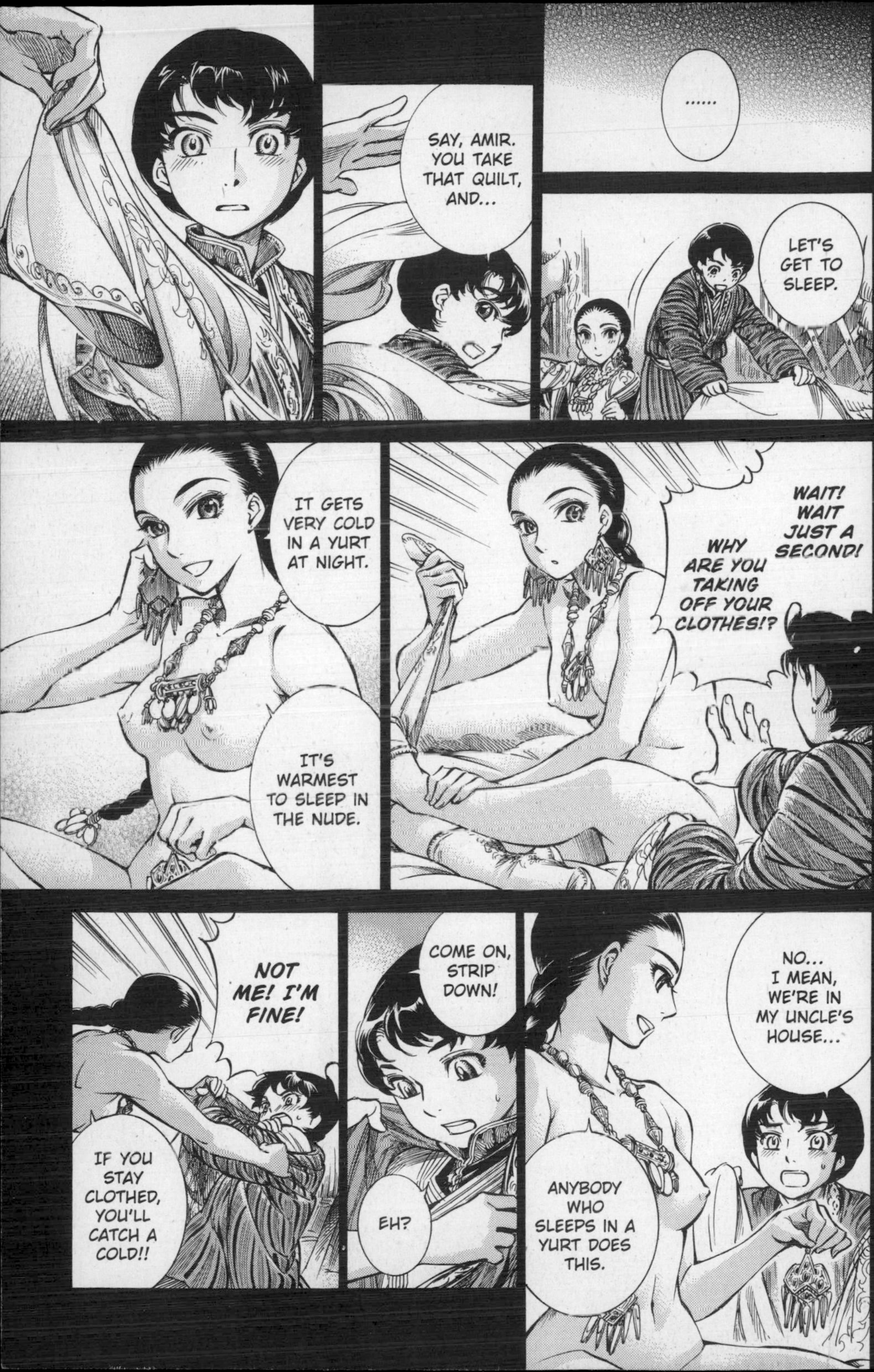
......
LET'S GET TO SLEEP.
SAY, AMIR. YOU TAKE THAT QUILT, AND...
WAIT! WAIT JUST A SECOND!
WHY ARE YOU TAKING OFF YOUR CLOTHES!?
IT GETS VERY COLD IN A YURT AT NIGHT.
IT'S WARMEST TO SLEEP IN THE NUDE.
NO... I MEAN, WE'RE IN MY UNCLE'S HOUSE...
ANYBODY WHO SLEEPS IN A YURT DOES THIS.
COME ON, STRIP DOWN!
EH?
NOT ME! I'M FINE!
IF YOU STAY CLOTHED, YOU'LL CATCH A COLD!!

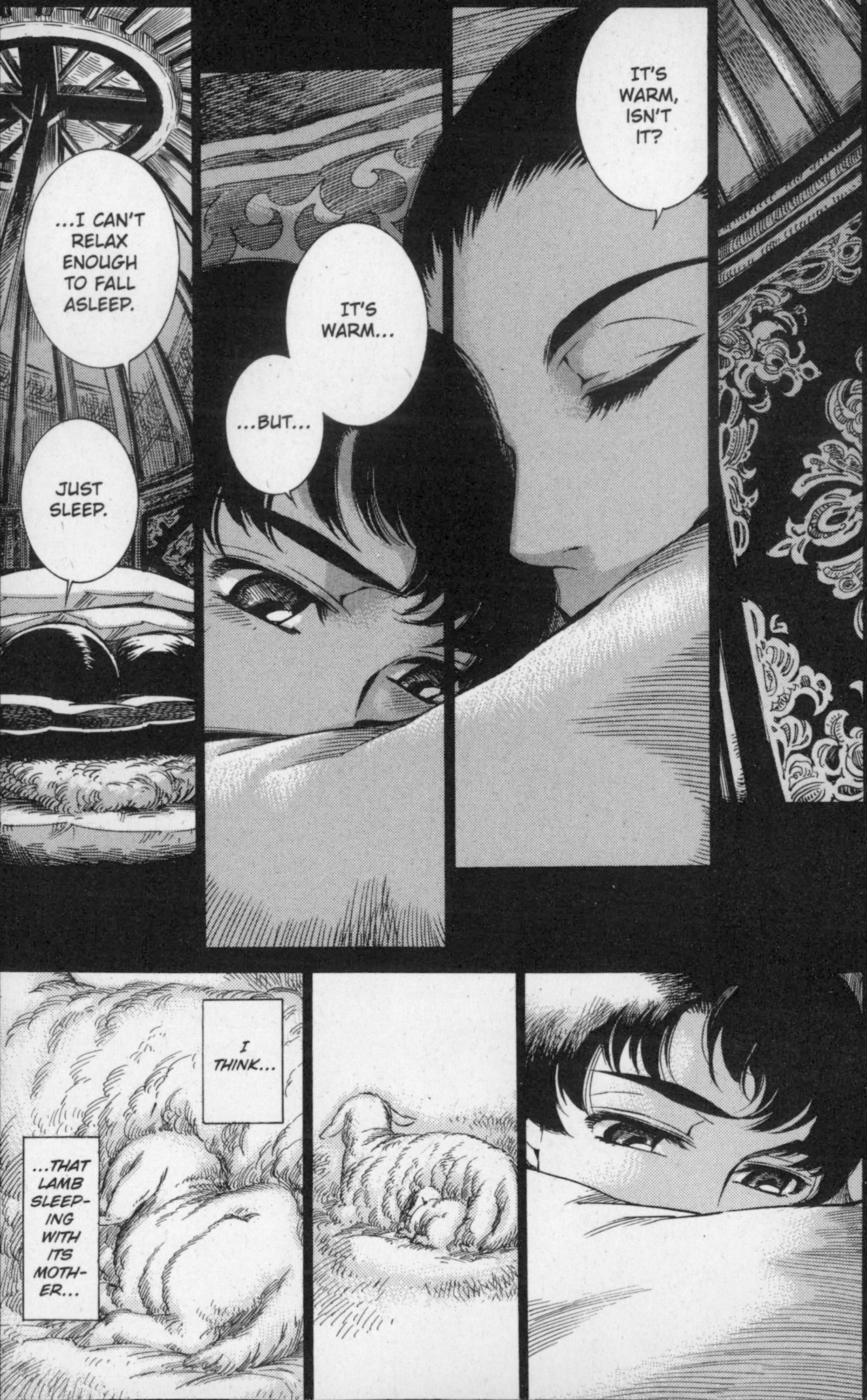
IT'S WARM, ISN'T IT?
IT'S WARM...
...BUT...
...I CAN'T RELAX ENOUGH TO FALL ASLEEP.
JUST SLEEP.
I THINK...
...THAT LAMB SLEEPING WITH ITS MOTHER...

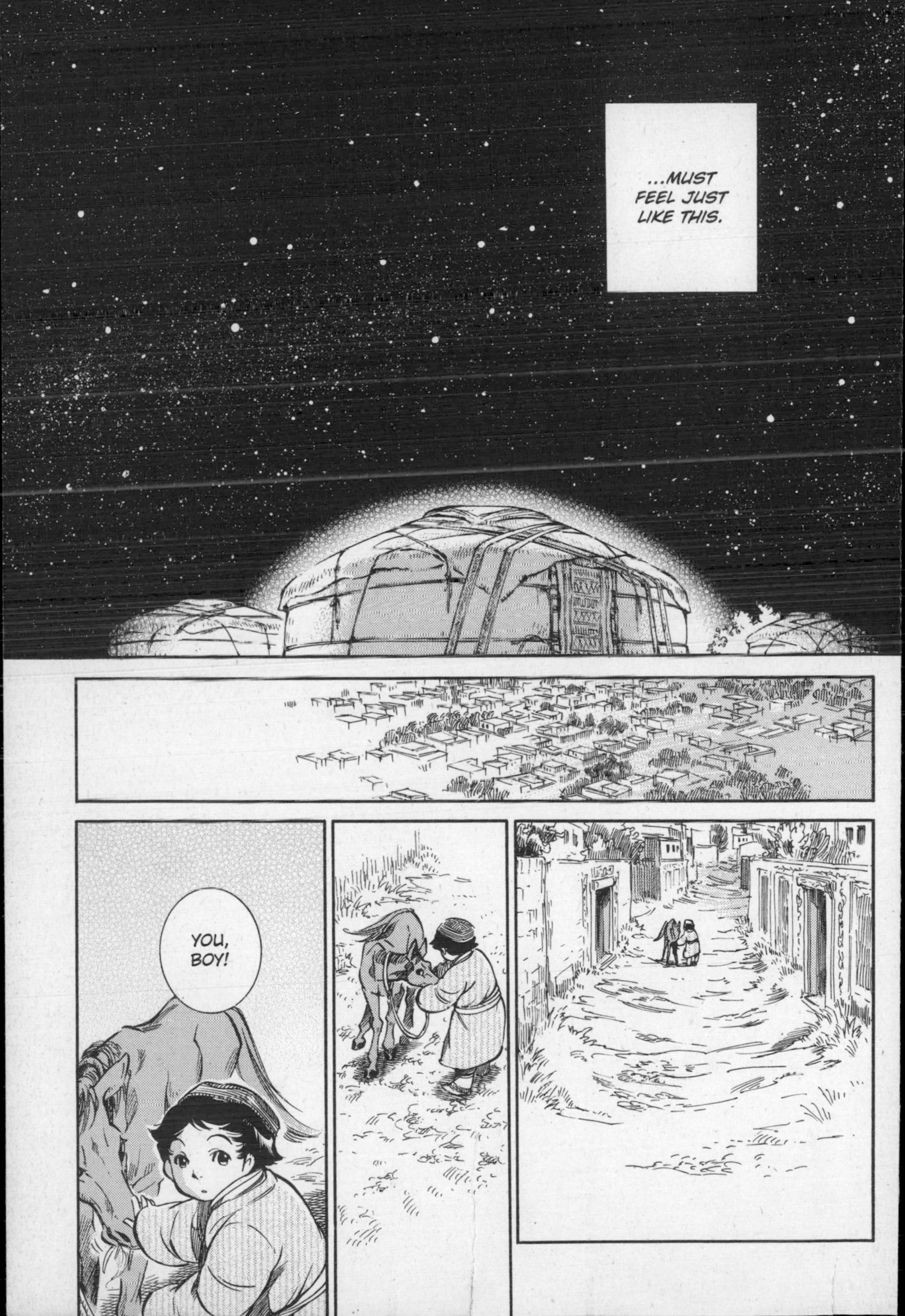
...MUST FEEL JUST LIKE THIS.
YOU, BOY!

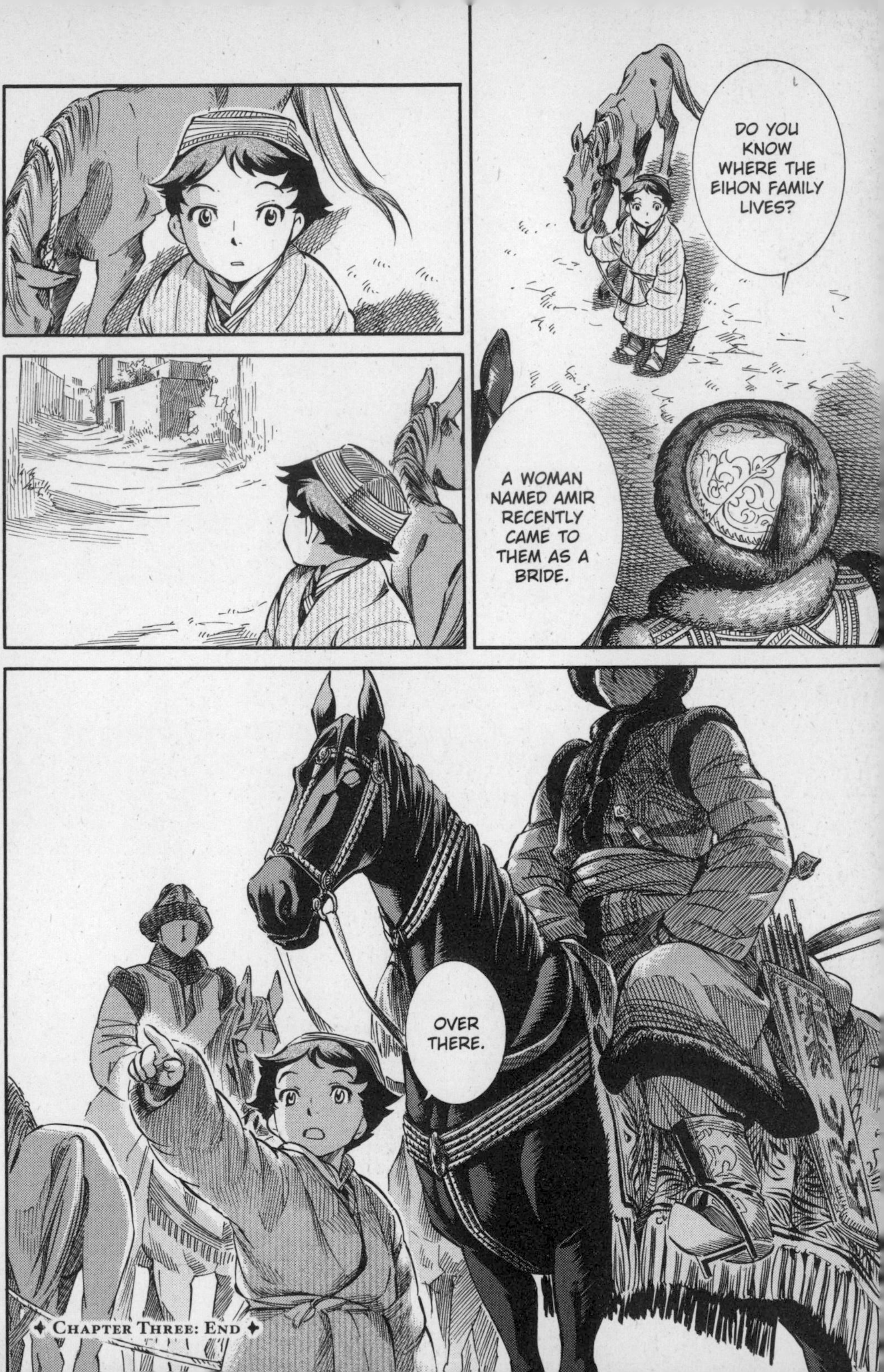
DO YOU KNOW WHERE THE EIHON FAMILY LIVES?
A WOMAN NAMED AMIR RECENTLY CAME TO THEM AS A BRIDE.
OVER THERE.
Chapter Three: End

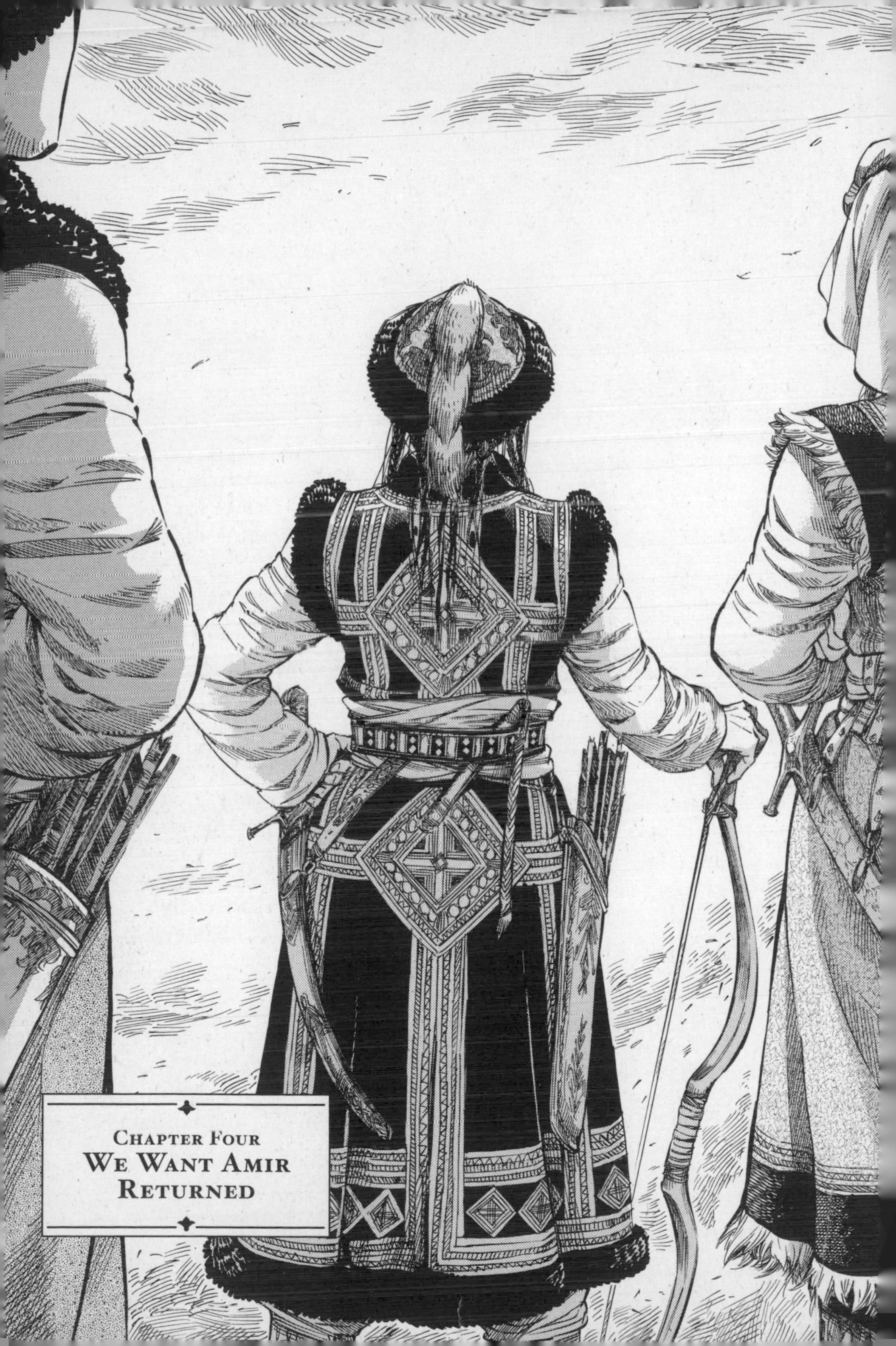
Chapter Four
We Want Amir
Returned

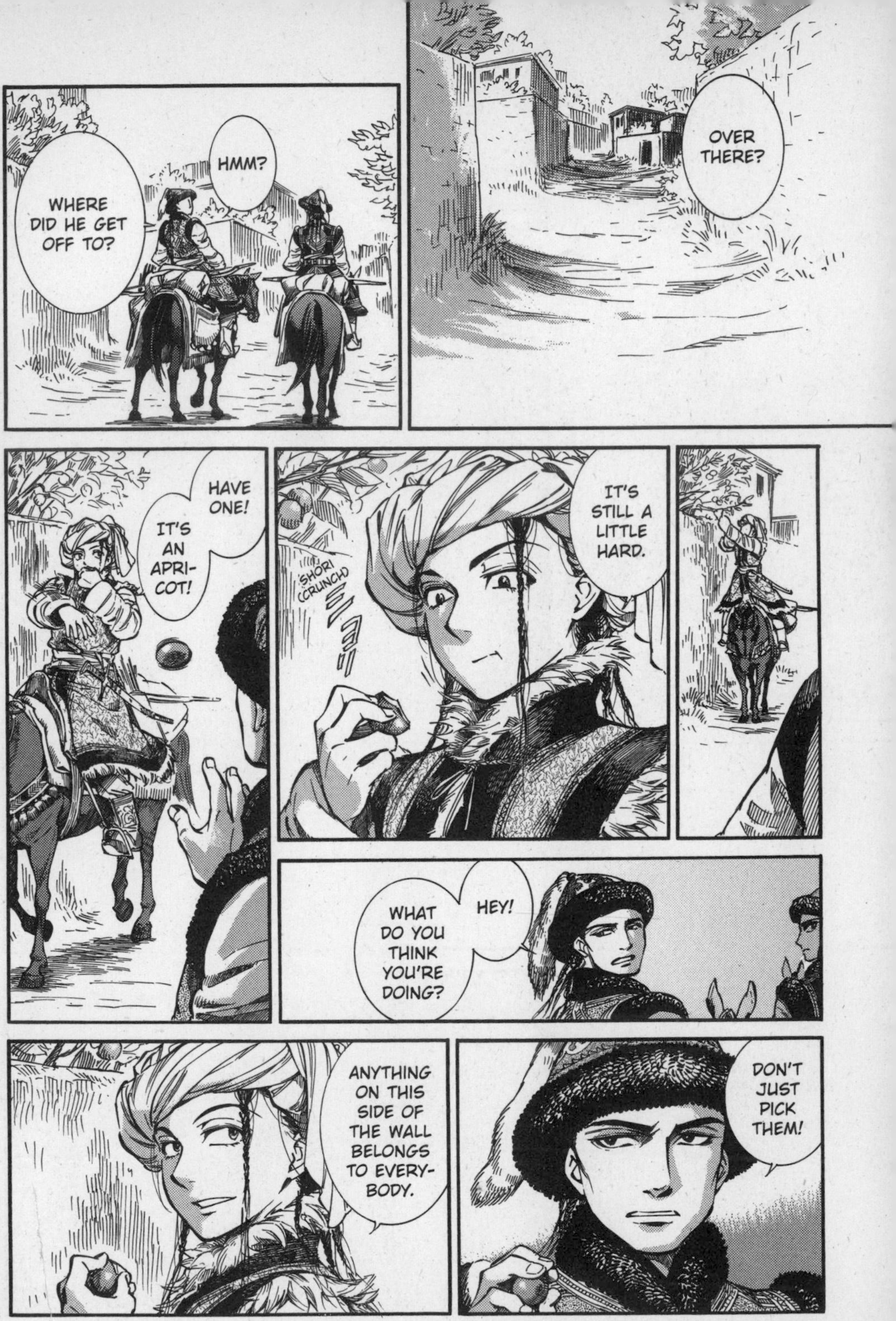
OVER THERE?
HMM?
WHERE DID HE GET OFF TO?
IT'S STILL A LITTLE HARD.
SHORI (CRUNCH)
HEY!
WHAT DO YOU THINK YOU'RE DOING?
HAVE ONE!
IT'S AN APRICOT!
DON'T JUST PICK THEM!
ANYTHING ON THIS SIDE OF THE WALL BELONGS TO EVERYBODY.

HERE!

YOU HAVE ONE TOO!

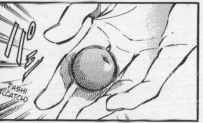

PASHI
(CATCH)

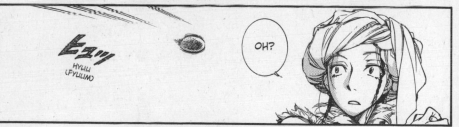

HYUU
(FYUUN)

OH?

WAIT!

I'M GOING.

······

KA
(KLOP)

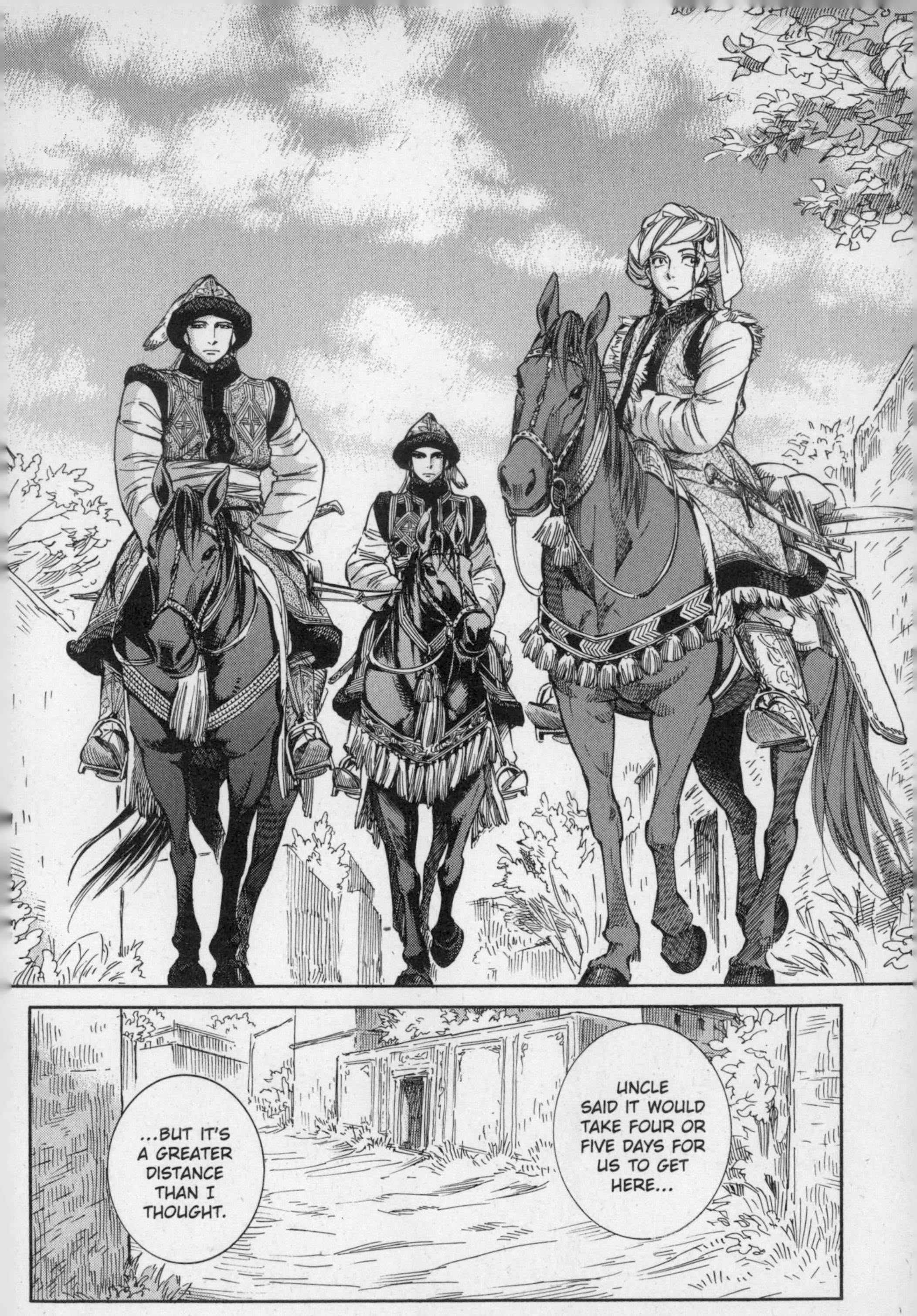
UNCLE SAID IT WOULD TAKE FOUR OR FIVE DAYS FOR US TO GET HERE...
...BUT IT'S A GREATER DISTANCE THAN I THOUGHT.

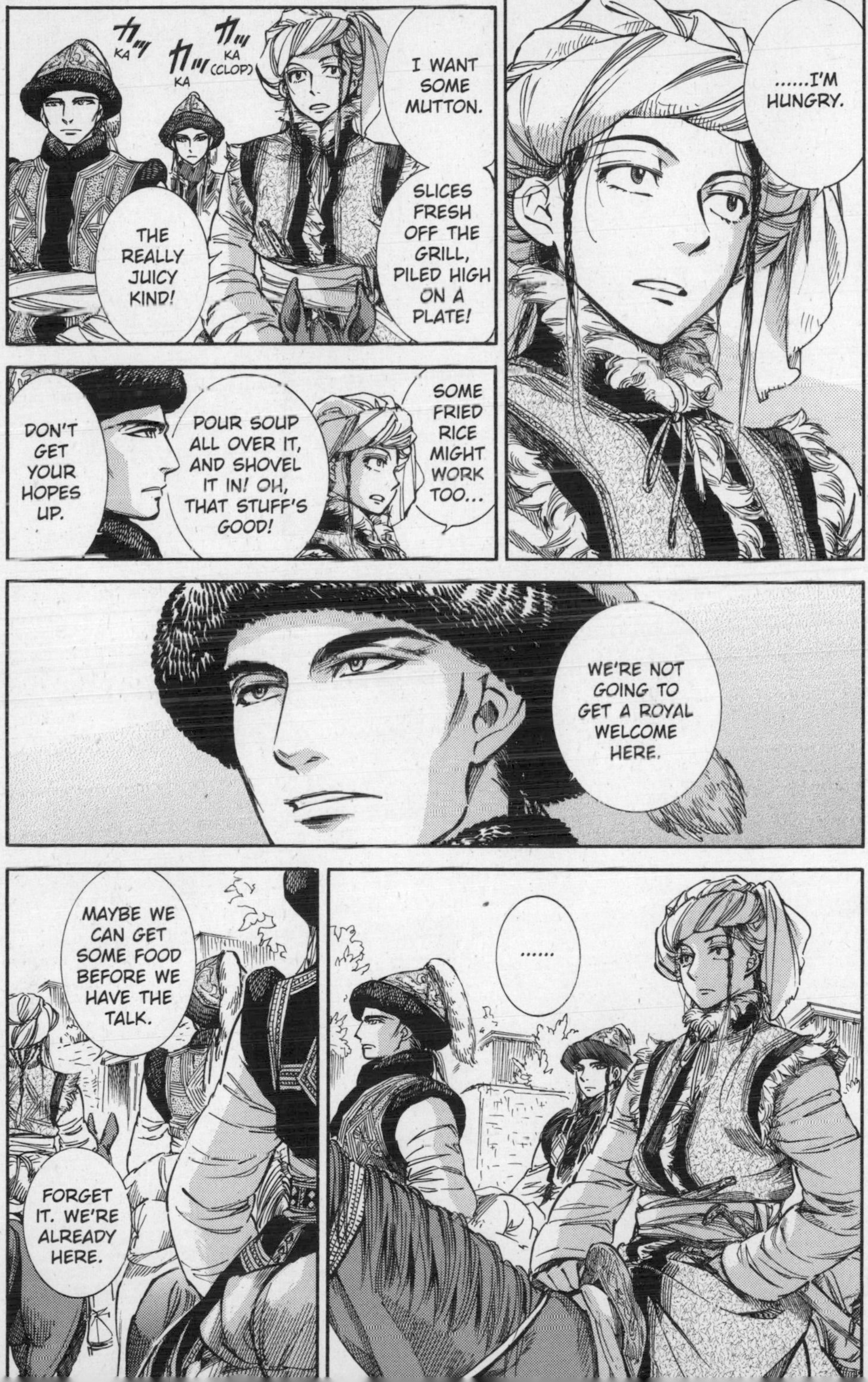
......I'M HUNGRY.
I WANT SOME MUTTON.
カッ KA
カッ KA
カッ KA (CLOP)
SLICES FRESH OFF THE GRILL, PILED HIGH ON A PLATE!
THE REALLY JUICY KIND!
SOME FRIED RICE MIGHT WORK TOO...
POUR SOUP ALL OVER IT, AND SHOVEL IT IN! OH, THAT STUFF'S GOOD!
DON'T GET YOUR HOPES UP.
WE'RE NOT GOING TO GET A ROYAL WELCOME HERE.
......
MAYBE WE CAN GET SOME FOOD BEFORE WE HAVE THE TALK.
FORGET IT. WE'RE ALREADY HERE.

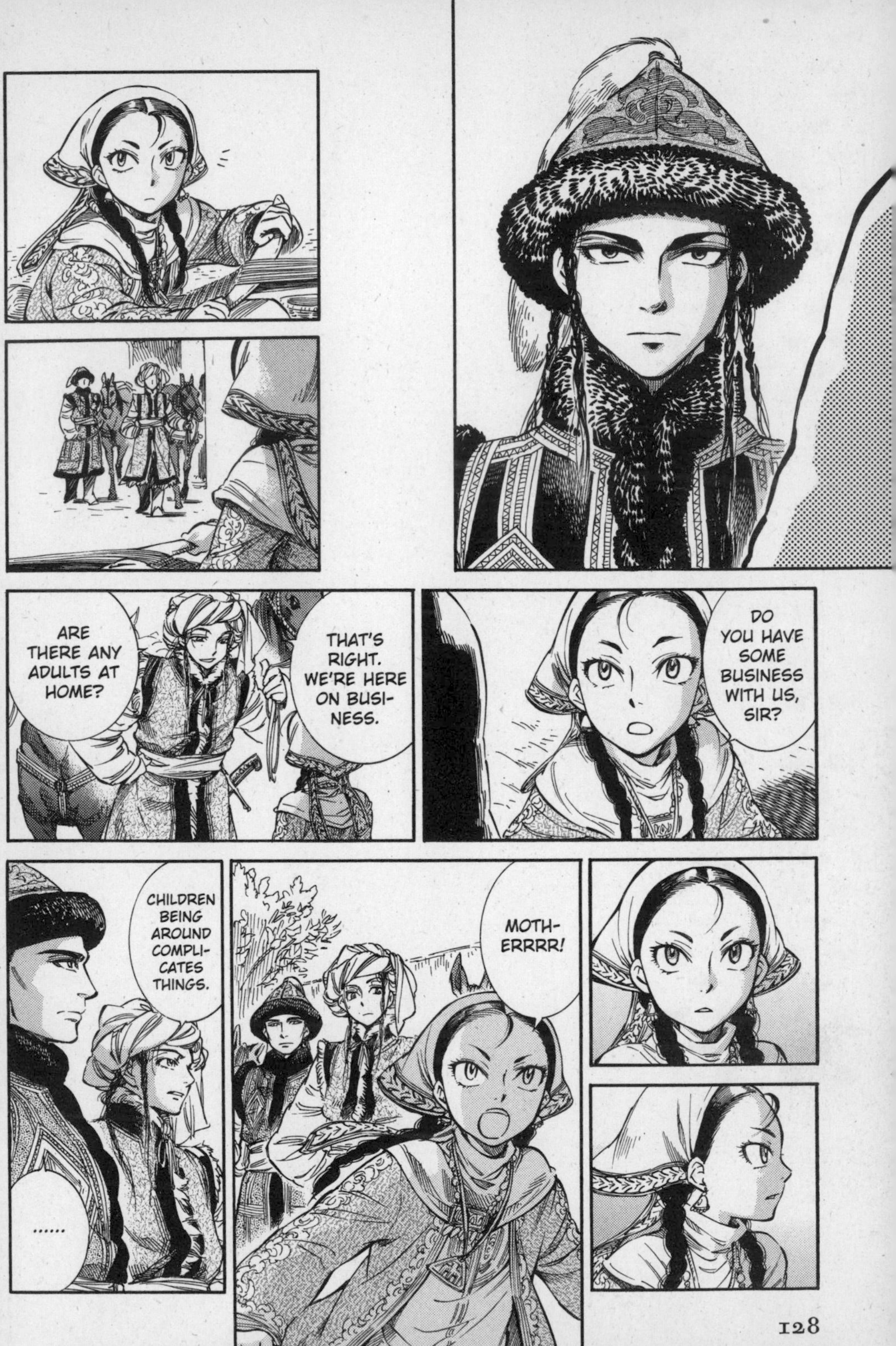
DO YOU HAVE SOME BUSINESS WITH US, SIR?
THAT'S RIGHT. WE'RE HERE ON BUSI-NESS.
ARE THERE ANY ADULTS AT HOME?
MOTH-ERRRR!
CHILDREN BEING AROUND COMPLI-CATES THINGS.
......

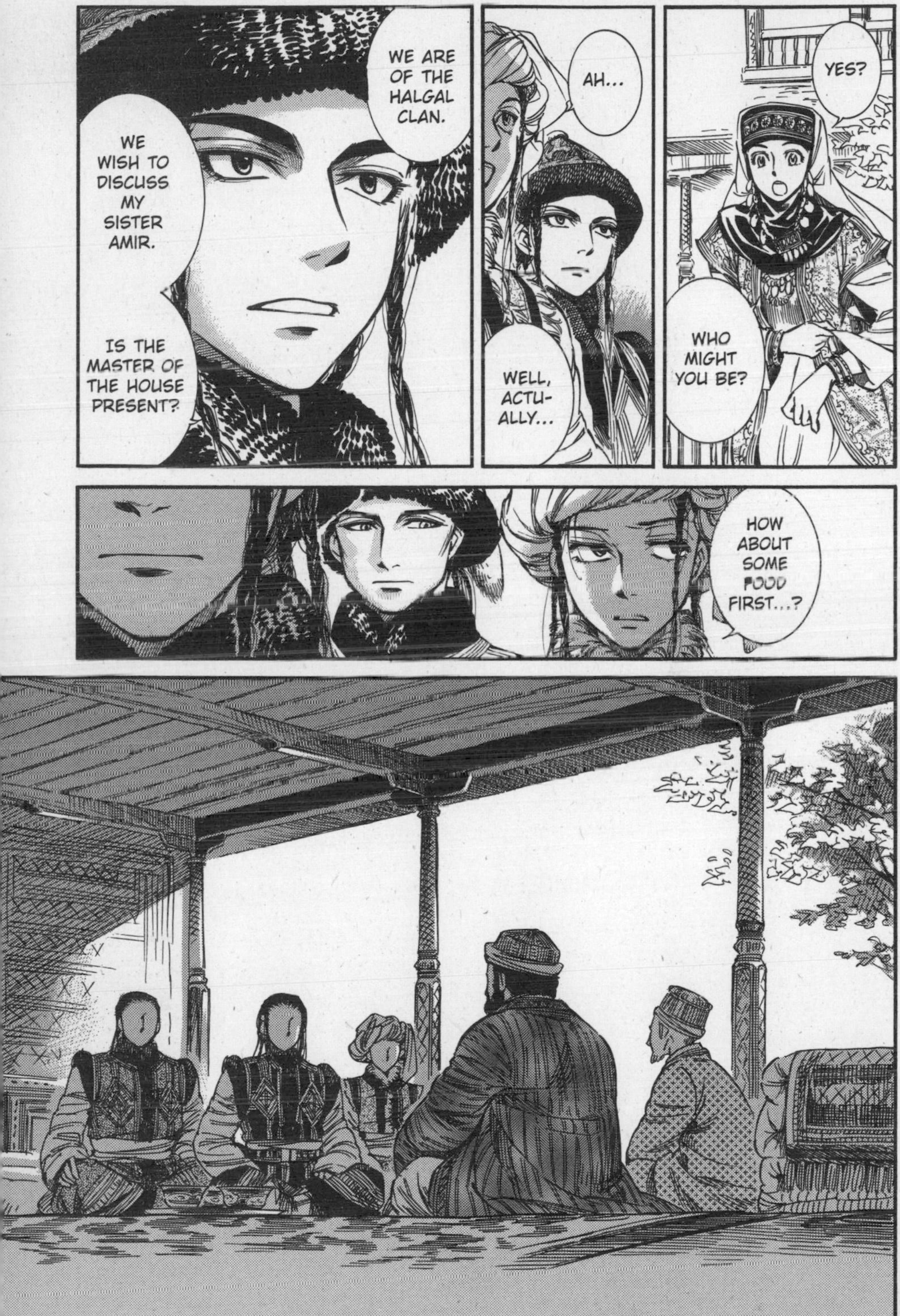
YES?
WHO MIGHT YOU BE?
AH...
WELL, ACTUALLY...
WE ARE OF THE HALGAL CLAN.
WE WISH TO DISCUSS MY SISTER AMIR.
IS THE MASTER OF THE HOUSE PRESENT?
HOW ABOUT SOME FOOD FIRST...?

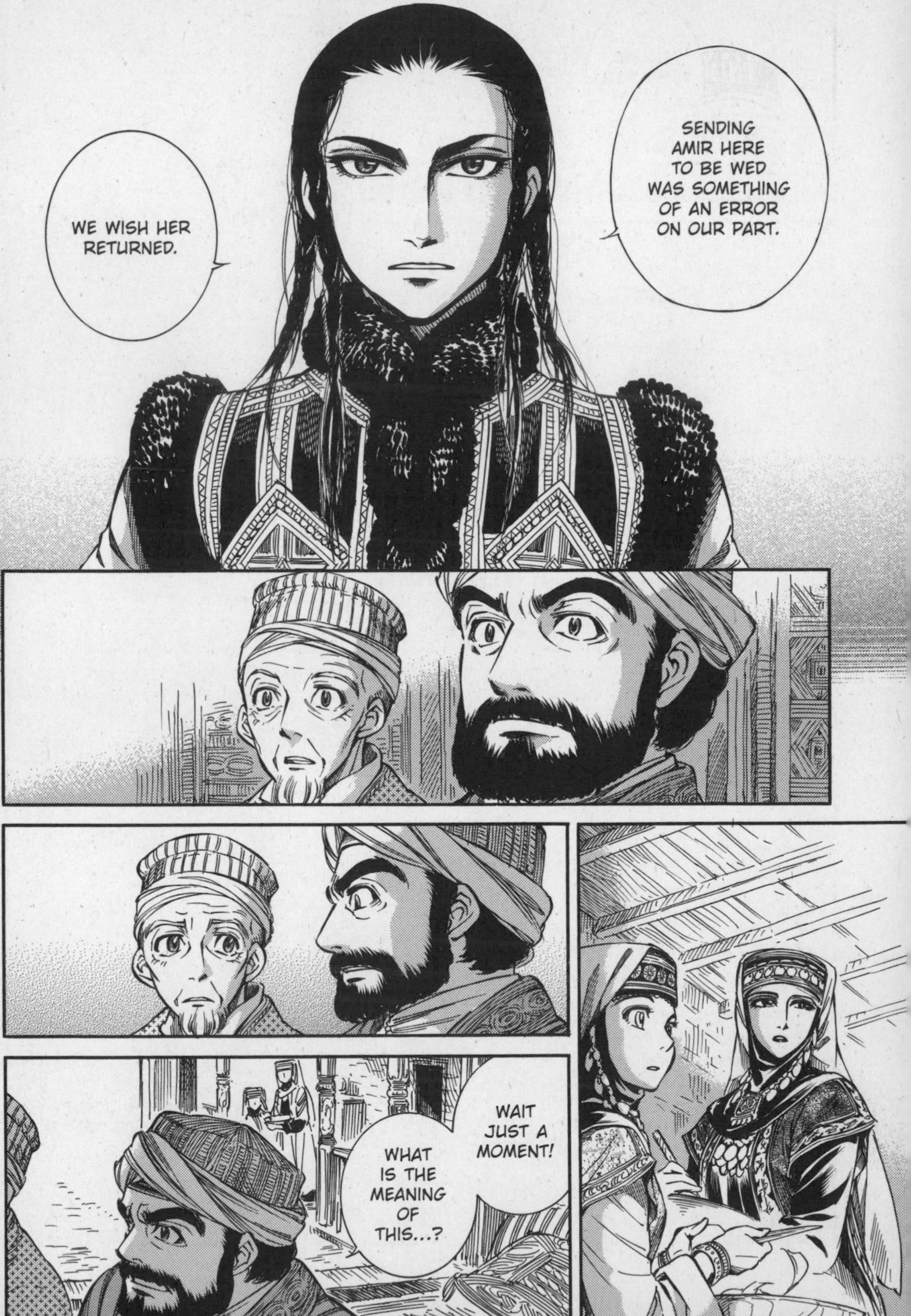
SENDING AMIR HERE TO BE WED WAS SOMETHING OF AN ERROR ON OUR PART.
WE WISH HER RETURNED.
WAIT JUST A MOMENT!
WHAT IS THE MEANING OF THIS...?

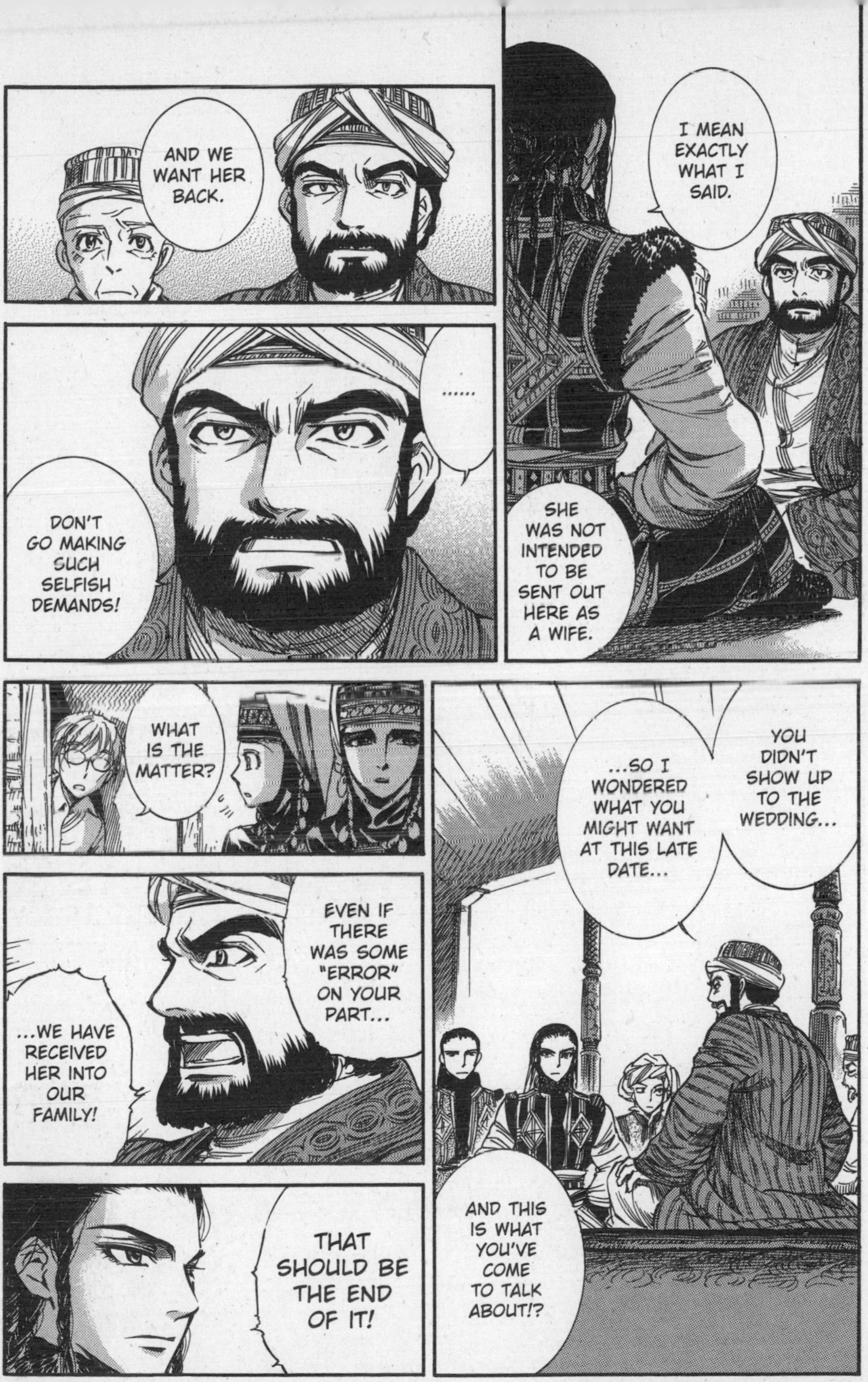
I MEAN EXACTLY WHAT I SAID.
SHE WAS NOT INTENDED TO BE SENT OUT HERE AS A WIFE.
AND WE WANT HER BACK.
......
DON'T GO MAKING SUCH SELFISH DEMANDS!
YOU DIDN'T SHOW UP TO THE WEDDING...
...SO I WONDERED WHAT YOU MIGHT WANT AT THIS LATE DATE...
AND THIS IS WHAT YOU'VE COME TO TALK ABOUT!?
WHAT IS THE MATTER?
EVEN IF THERE WAS SOME "ERROR" ON YOUR PART...
...WE HAVE RECEIVED HER INTO OUR FAMILY!
THAT SHOULD BE THE END OF IT!

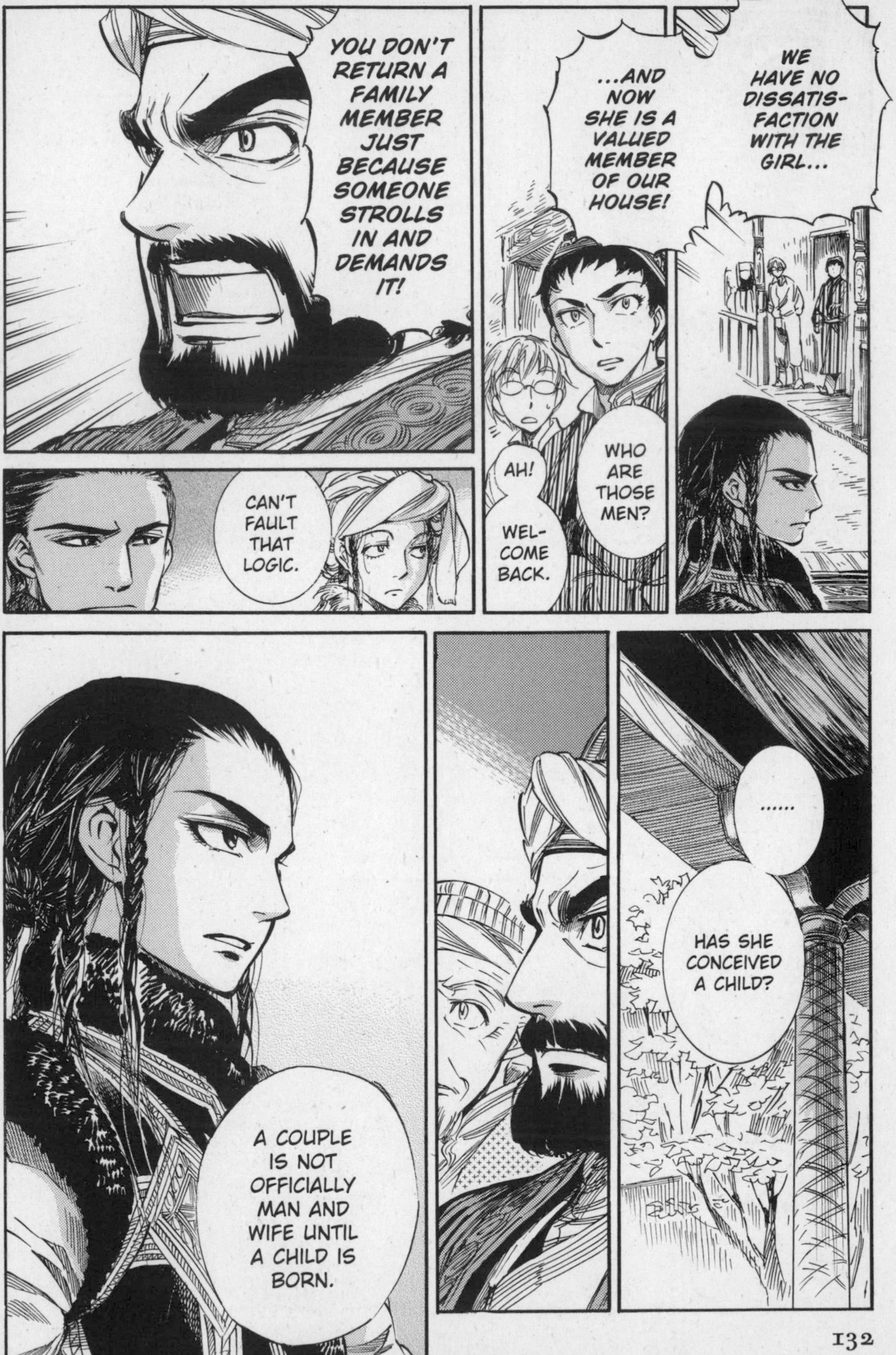
WE HAVE NO DISSATIS-FACTION WITH THE GIRL...
...AND NOW SHE IS A VALUED MEMBER OF OUR HOUSE!
WHO ARE THOSE MEN?
AH!
WEL-COME BACK.
YOU DON'T RETURN A FAMILY MEMBER JUST BECAUSE SOMEONE STROLLS IN AND DEMANDS IT!
CAN'T FAULT THAT LOGIC.
......
HAS SHE CONCEIVED A CHILD?
A COUPLE IS NOT OFFICIALLY MAN AND WIFE UNTIL A CHILD IS BORN.

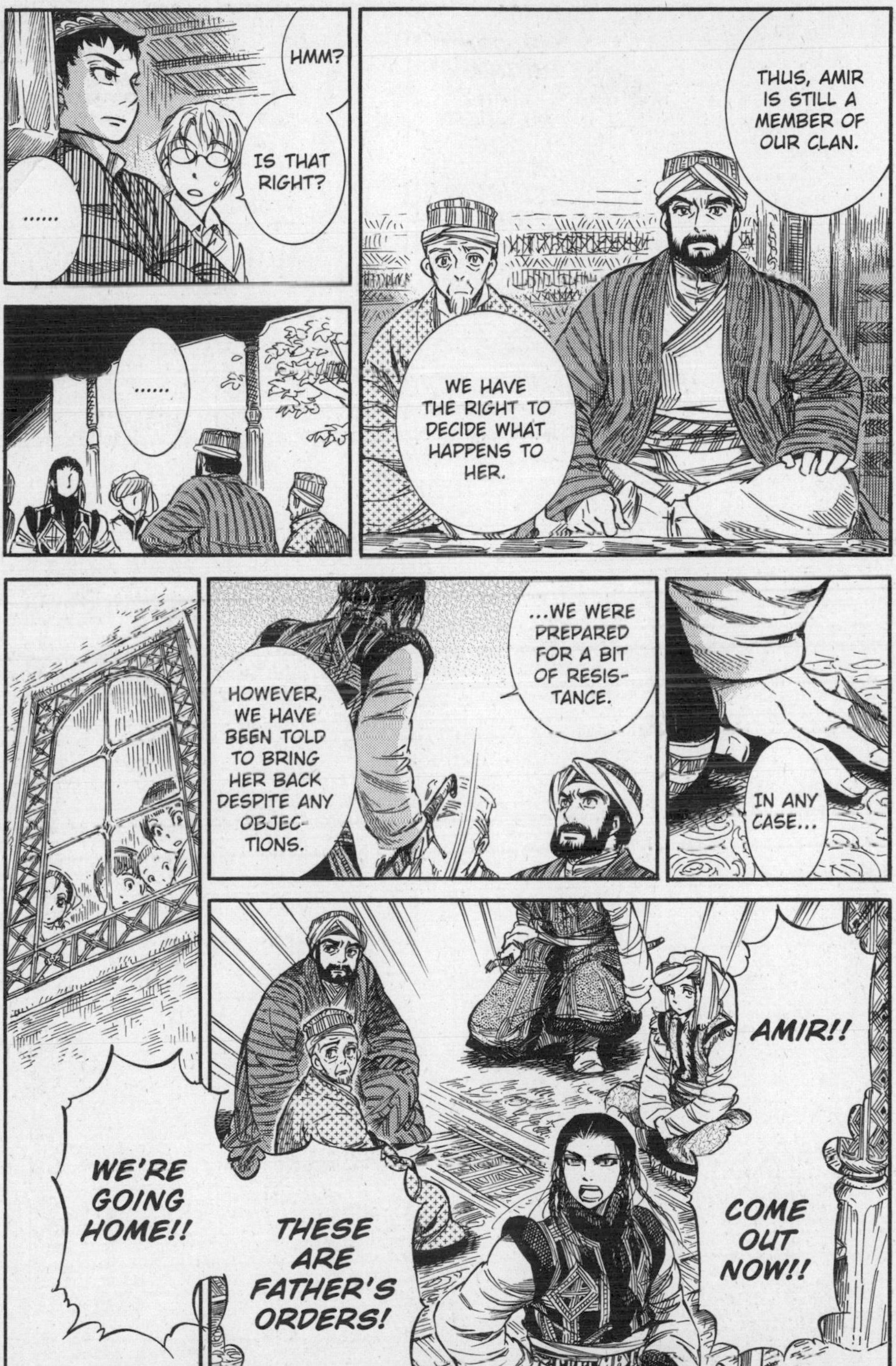
THUS, AMIR IS STILL A MEMBER OF OUR CLAN.
WE HAVE THE RIGHT TO DECIDE WHAT HAPPENS TO HER.
HMM?
IS THAT RIGHT?
......
......
IN ANY CASE...
...WE WERE PREPARED FOR A BIT OF RESIS-TANCE.
HOWEVER, WE HAVE BEEN TOLD TO BRING HER BACK DESPITE ANY OBJEC-TIONS.
AMIR!!
COME OUT NOW!!
THESE ARE FATHER'S ORDERS!
WE'RE GOING HOME!!

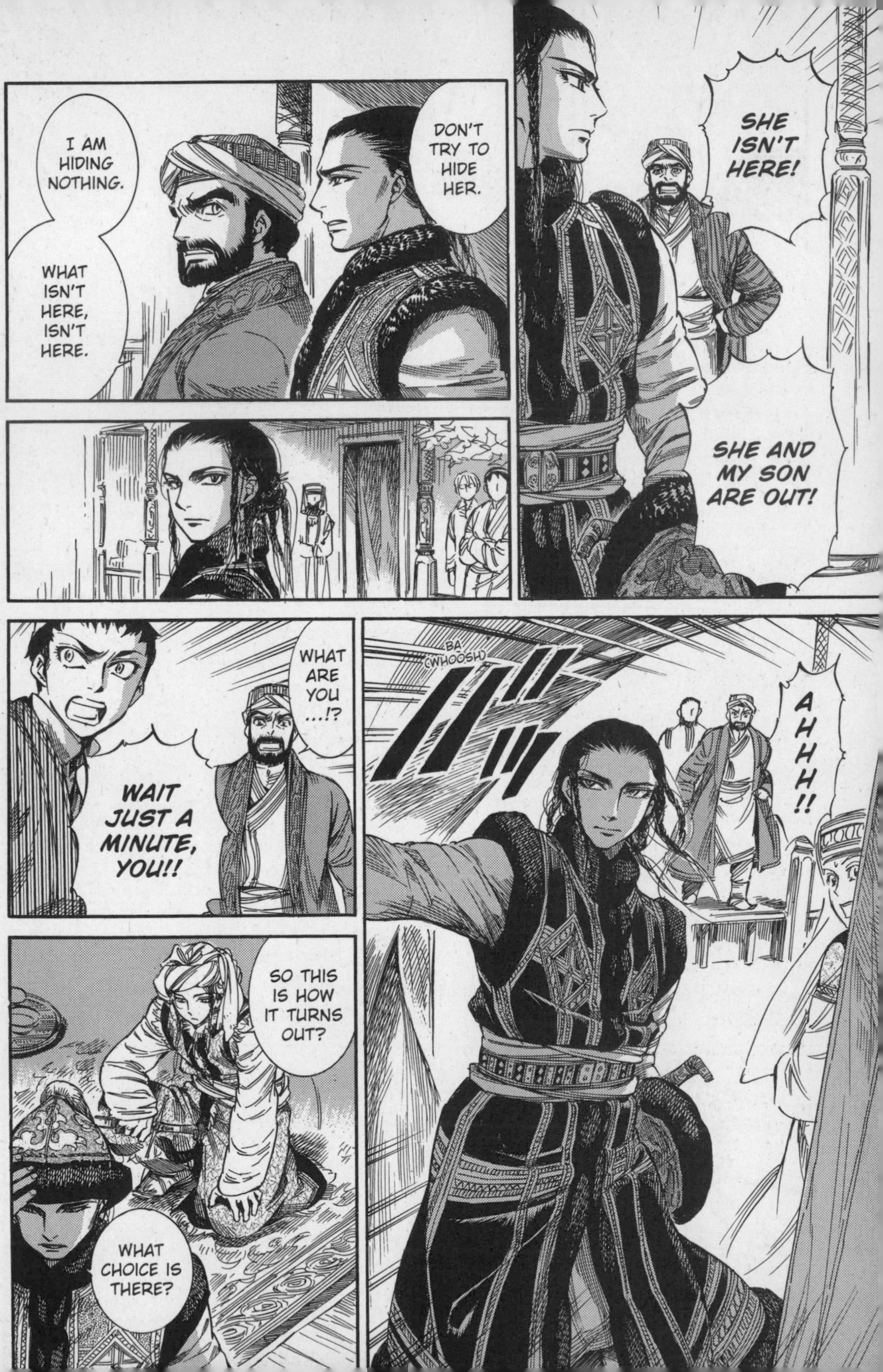
SHE ISN'T HERE!
SHE AND MY SON ARE OUT!
DON'T TRY TO HIDE HER.
I AM HIDING NOTHING.
WHAT ISN'T HERE, ISN'T HERE.
BA (WHOOSH)
AHHH!!
WHAT ARE YOU ...!?
WAIT JUST A MINUTE, YOU!!
SO THIS IS HOW IT TURNS OUT?
WHAT CHOICE IS THERE?

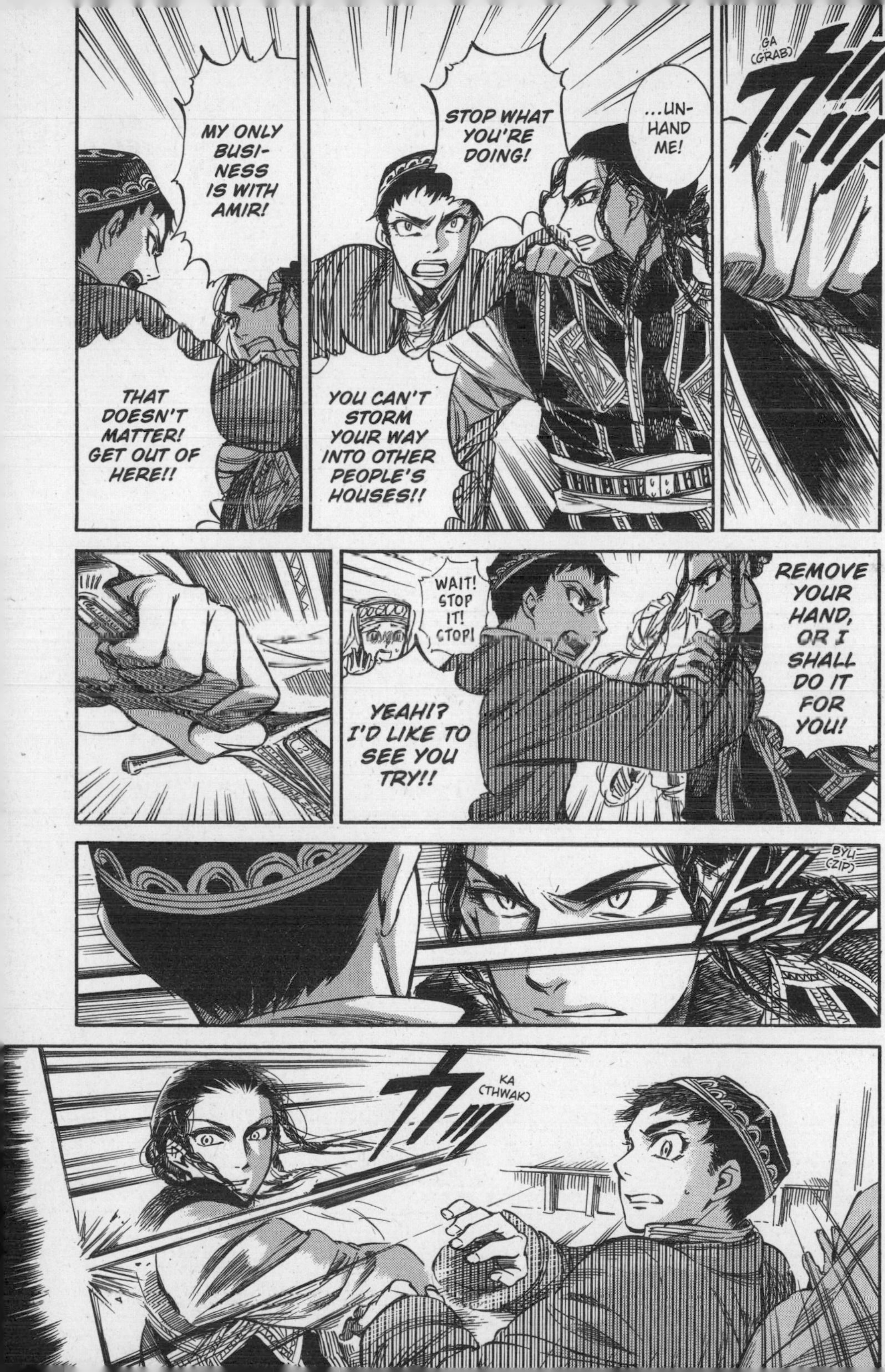
GA (GRAB)
...UN-HAND ME!
STOP WHAT YOU'RE DOING!
YOU CAN'T STORM YOUR WAY INTO OTHER PEOPLE'S HOUSES!!
MY ONLY BUSI-NESS IS WITH AMIR!
THAT DOESN'T MATTER! GET OUT OF HERE!!
REMOVE YOUR HAND, OR I SHALL DO IT FOR YOU!
WAIT! STOP IT! STOP!
YEAH!? I'D LIKE TO SEE YOU TRY!!
BYU (ZIP)
KA (THWAK)

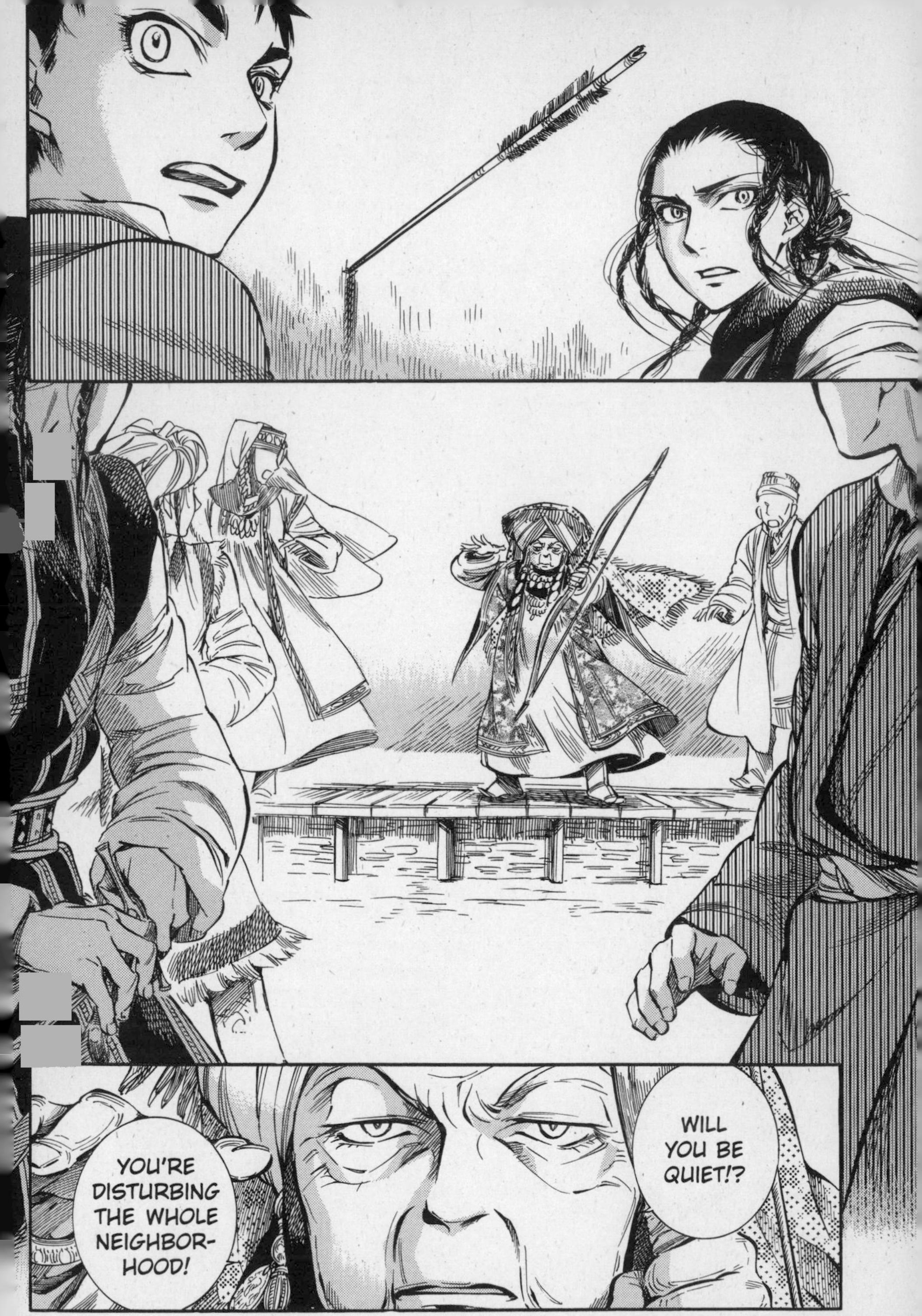
WILL YOU BE QUIET!?
YOU'RE DISTURBING THE WHOLE NEIGHBOR-HOOD!

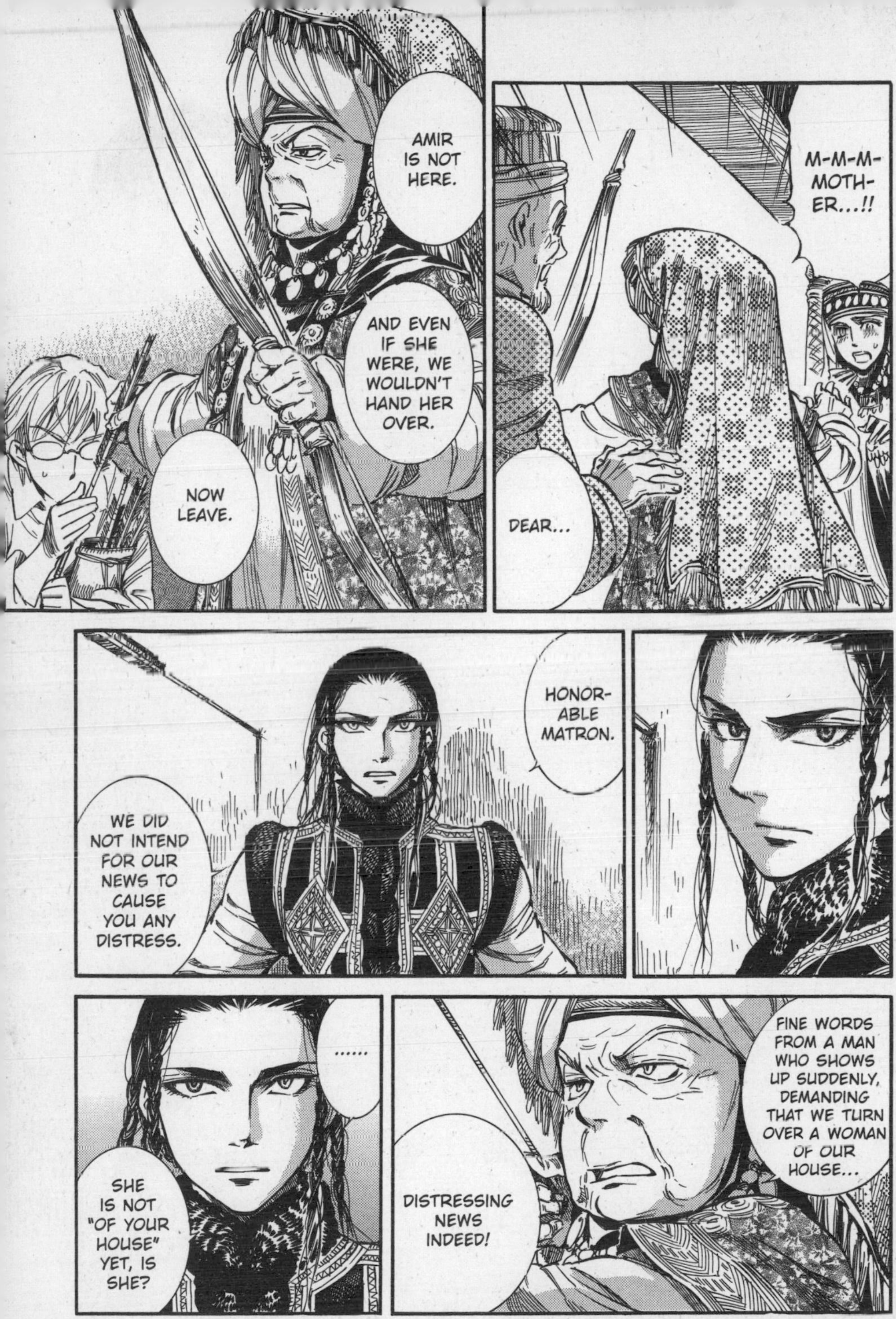
M-M-M-MOTHER...!!
DEAR...
AMIR IS NOT HERE.
AND EVEN IF SHE WERE, WE WOULDN'T HAND HER OVER.
NOW LEAVE.
HONORABLE MATRON.
WE DID NOT INTEND FOR OUR NEWS TO CAUSE YOU ANY DISTRESS.
FINE WORDS FROM A MAN WHO SHOWS UP SUDDENLY, DEMANDING THAT WE TURN OVER A WOMAN OF OUR HOUSE...
DISTRESSING NEWS INDEED!
......
SHE IS NOT "OF YOUR HOUSE" YET, IS SHE?

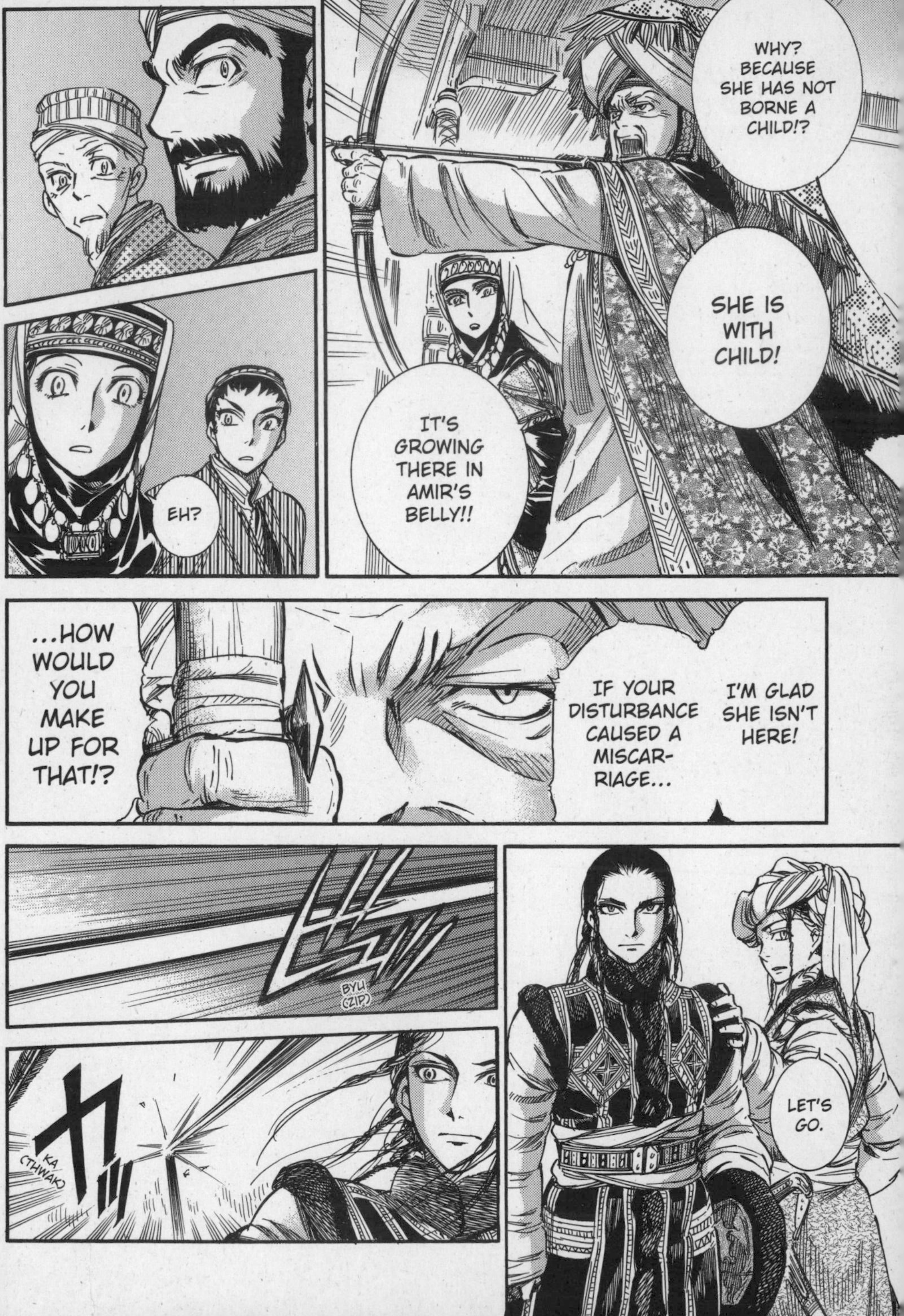
WHY? BECAUSE SHE HAS NOT BORNE A CHILD!?
SHE IS WITH CHILD!
IT'S GROWING THERE IN AMIR'S BELLY!!
EH?
I'M GLAD SHE ISN'T HERE!
IF YOUR DISTURBANCE CAUSED A MISCAR-RIAGE...
...HOW WOULD YOU MAKE UP FOR THAT!?
LET'S GO.
BYU (ZIP)
KA (THWAK)

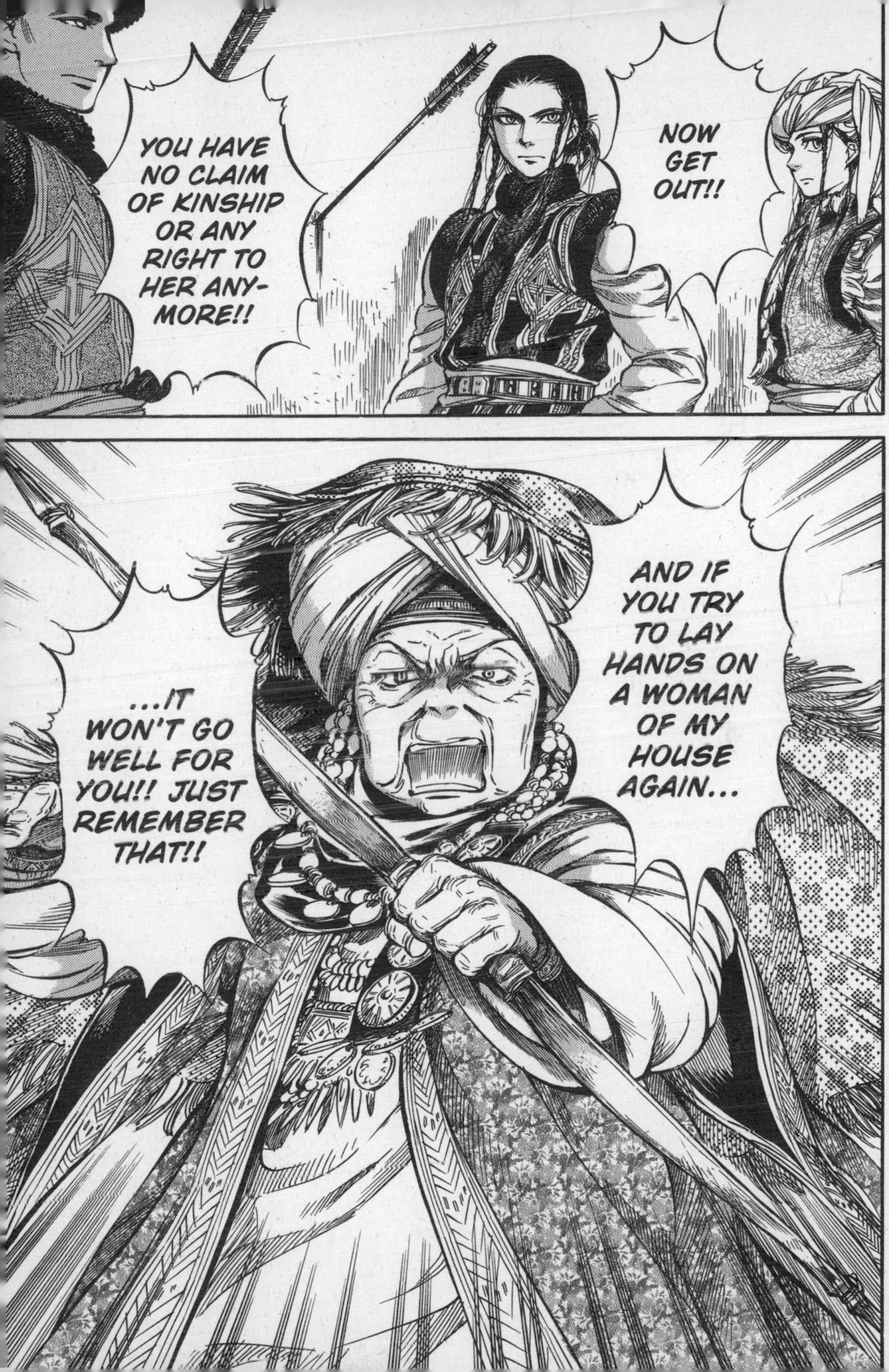
NOW GET OUT!!
YOU HAVE NO CLAIM OF KINSHIP OR ANY RIGHT TO HER ANY-MORE!!
AND IF YOU TRY TO LAY HANDS ON A WOMAN OF MY HOUSE AGAIN...
...IT WON'T GO WELL FOR YOU!! JUST REMEMBER THAT!!

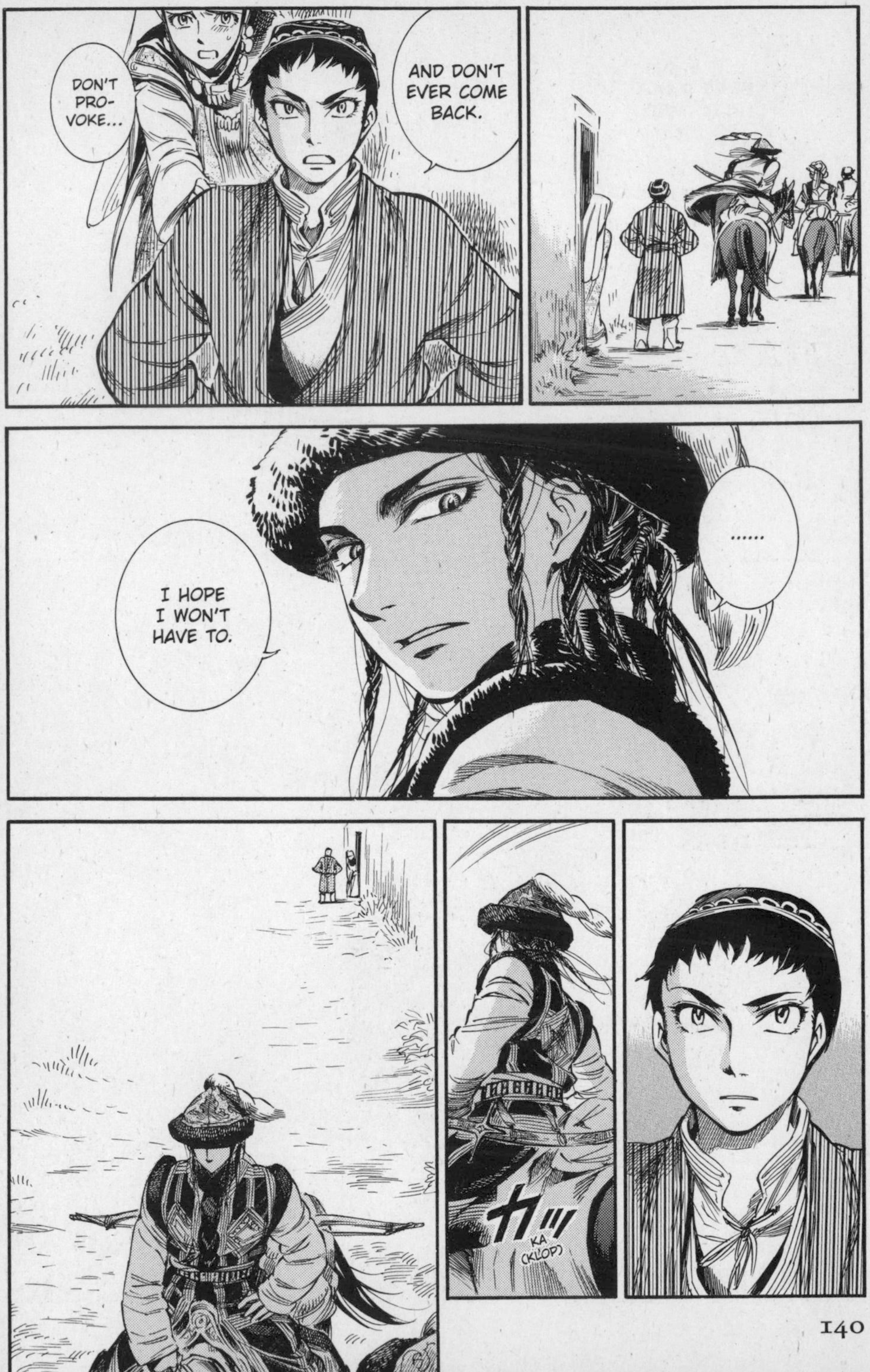
AND DON'T EVER COME BACK.
DON'T PROVOKE...
......
I HOPE I WON'T HAVE TO.
カッ
KA (KLOP)

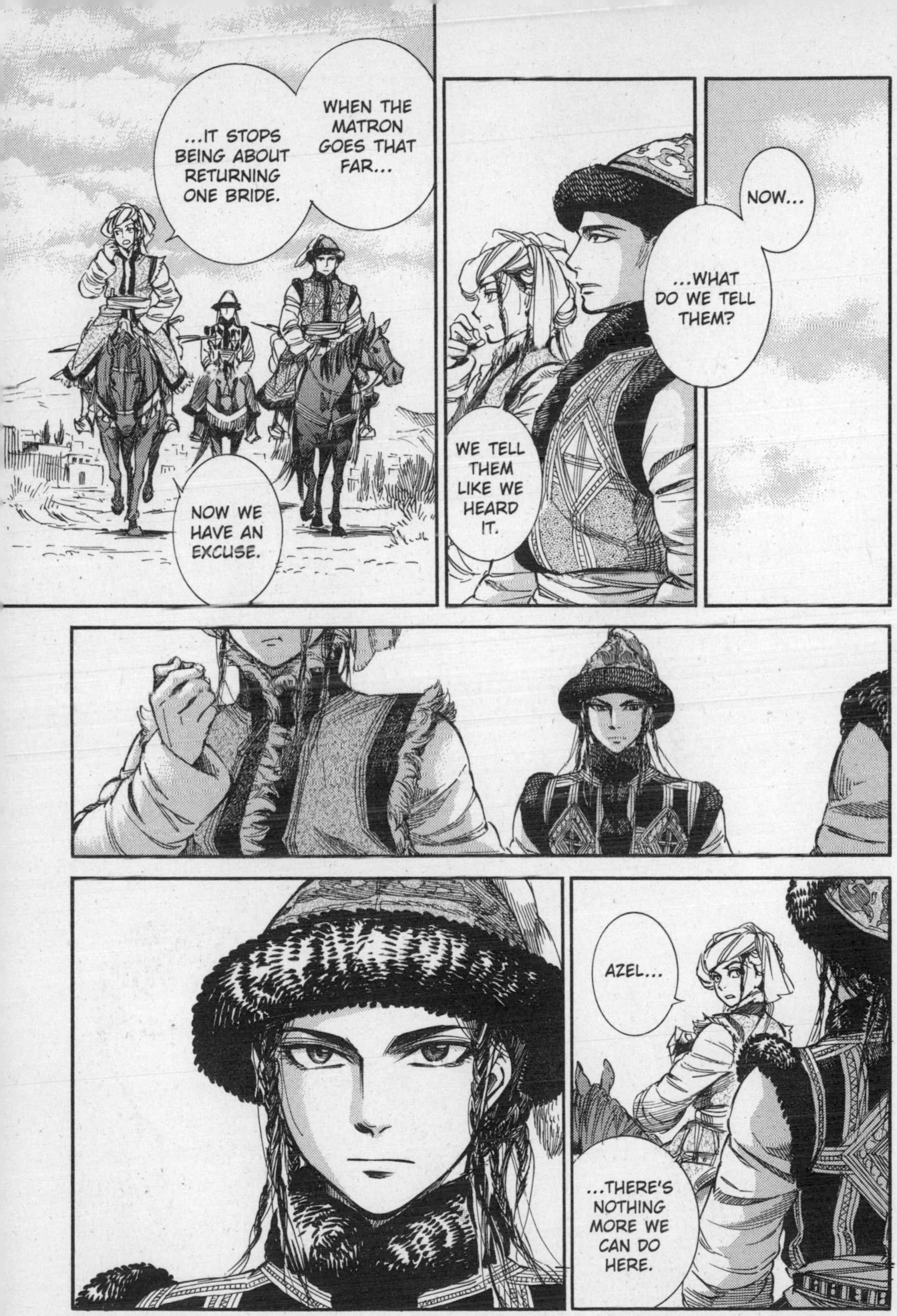
NOW...
...WHAT DO WE TELL THEM?
WE TELL THEM LIKE WE HEARD IT.
WHEN THE MATRON GOES THAT FAR...
...IT STOPS BEING ABOUT RETURNING ONE BRIDE.
NOW WE HAVE AN EXCUSE.
AZEL...
...THERE'S NOTHING MORE WE CAN DO HERE.

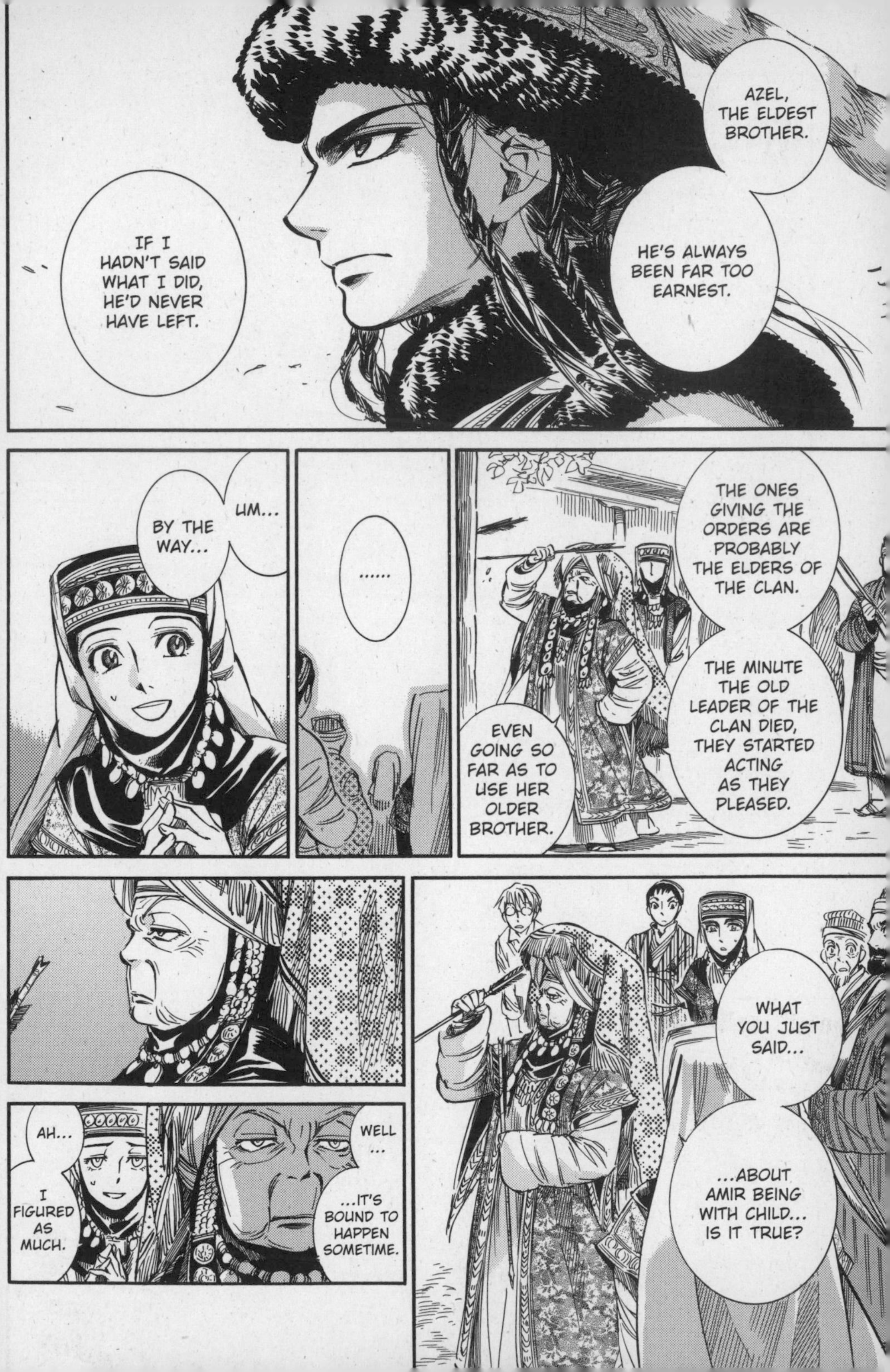
AZEL, THE ELDEST BROTHER.
HE'S ALWAYS BEEN FAR TOO EARNEST.
IF I HADN'T SAID WHAT I DID, HE'D NEVER HAVE LEFT.
THE ONES GIVING THE ORDERS ARE PROBABLY THE ELDERS OF THE CLAN.
THE MINUTE THE OLD LEADER OF THE CLAN DIED, THEY STARTED ACTING AS THEY PLEASED.
EVEN GOING SO FAR AS TO USE HER OLDER BROTHER.
......
UM...
BY THE WAY...
WHAT YOU JUST SAID...
...ABOUT AMIR BEING WITH CHILD... IS IT TRUE?
WELL...
...IT'S BOUND TO HAPPEN SOMETIME.
AH...
I FIGURED AS MUCH.

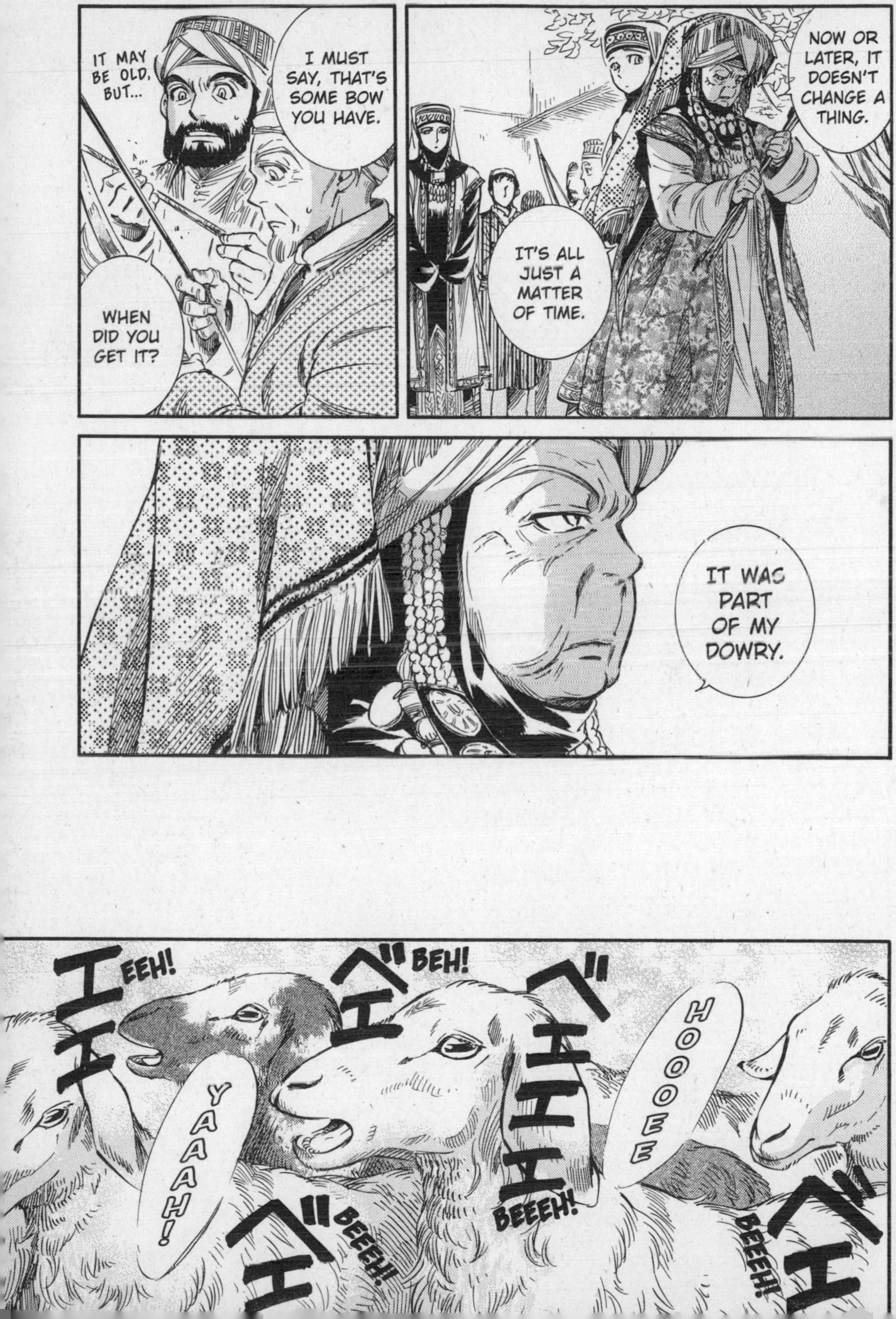
NOW OR LATER, IT DOESN'T CHANGE A THING.
IT'S ALL JUST A MATTER OF TIME.
I MUST SAY, THAT'S SOME BOW YOU HAVE.
IT MAY BE OLD, BUT...
WHEN DID YOU GET IT?
IT WAS PART OF MY DOWRY.
HOOOOEE
BEEEH!
BEEEH!
BEH!
EEEH!
YAAAAH!
BEEEH!

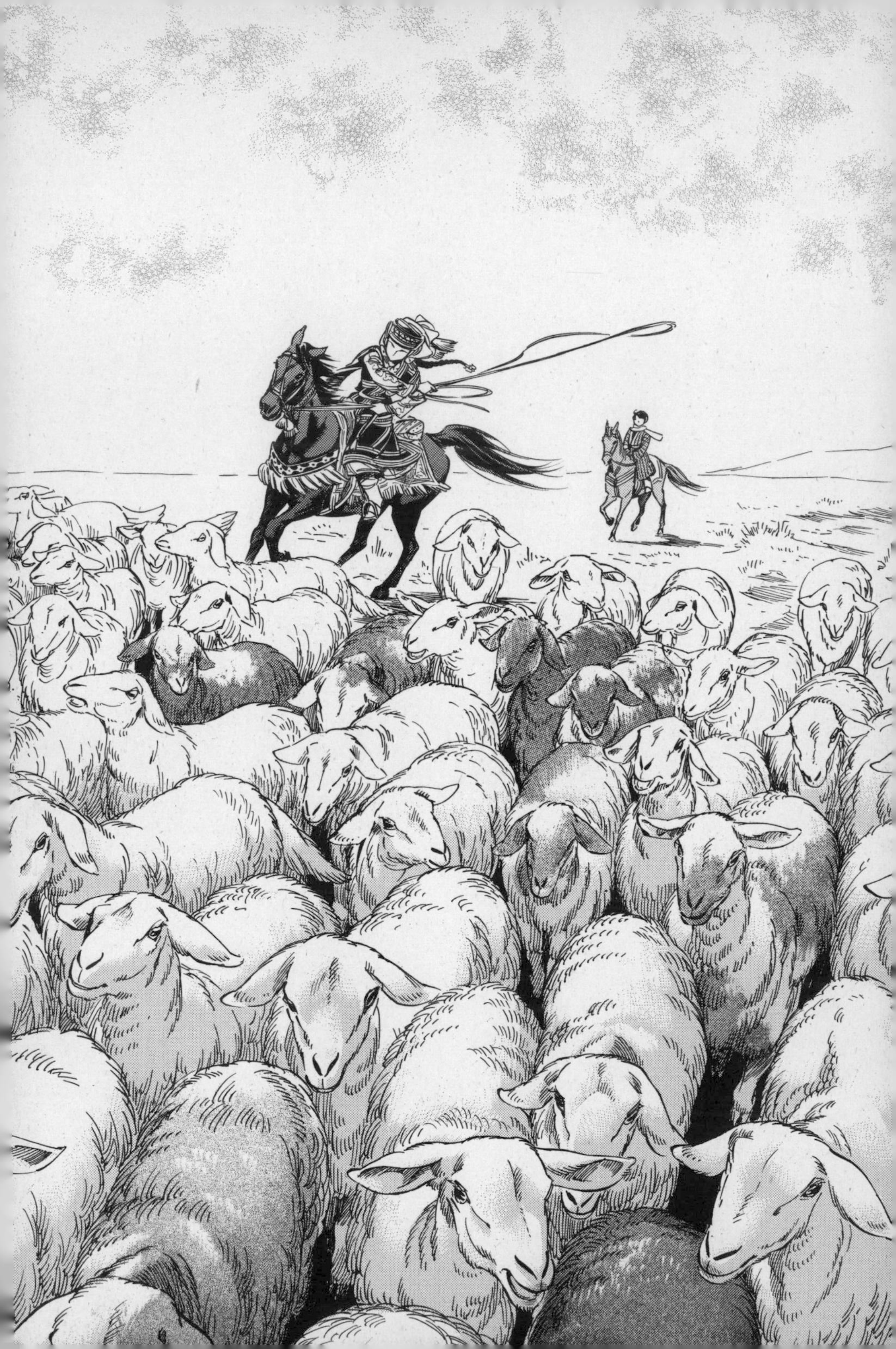

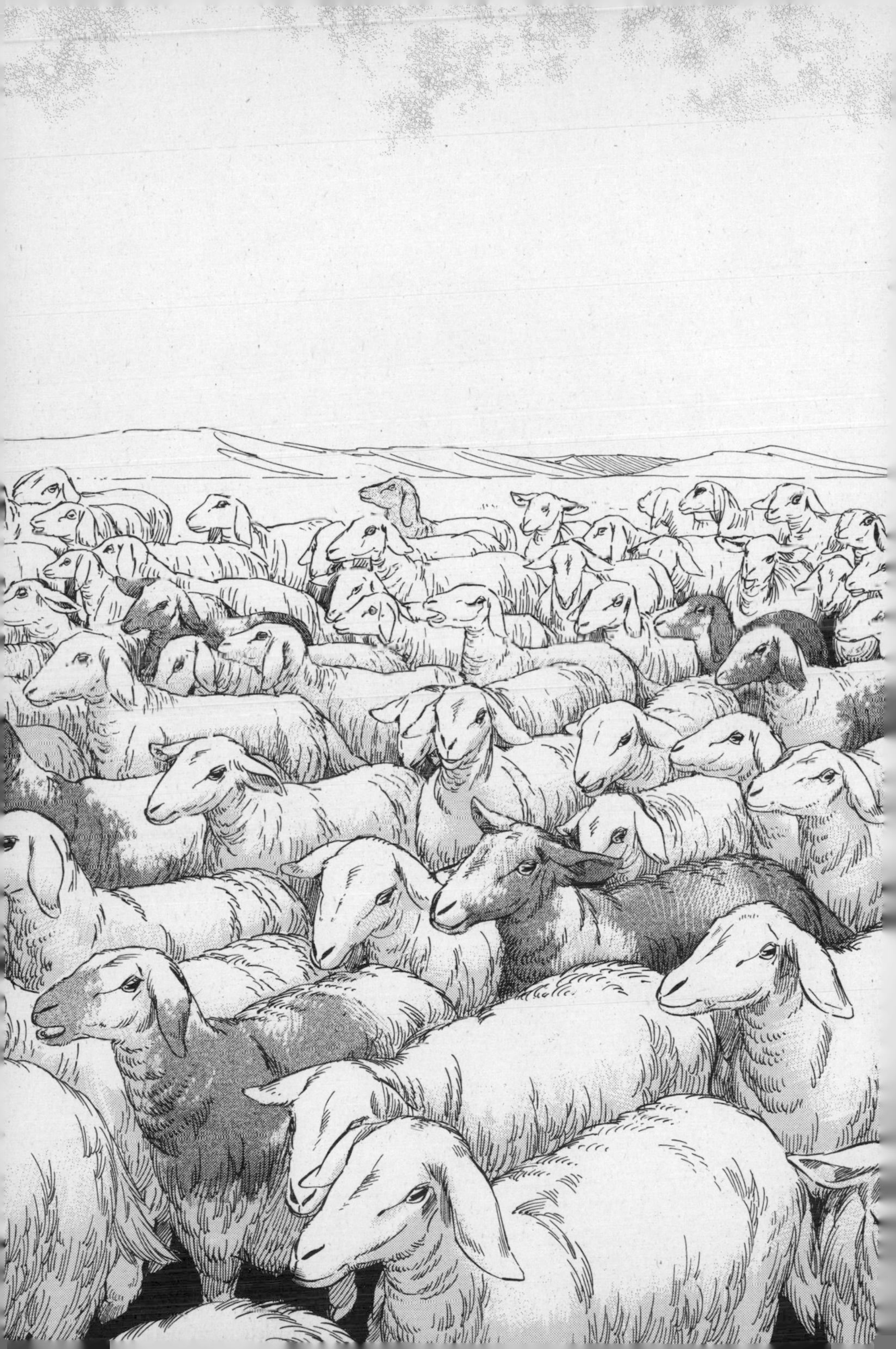

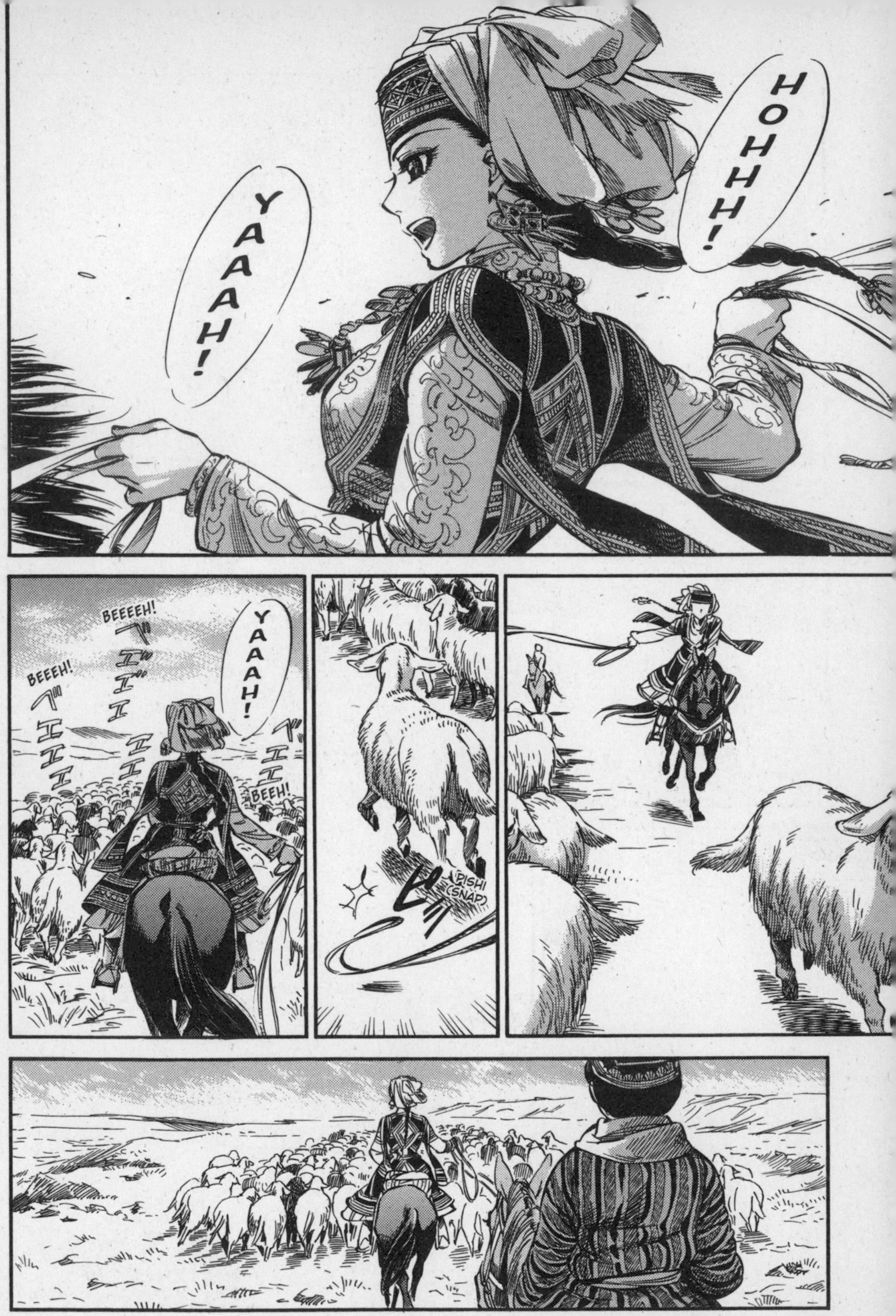
HOHHH!
YAAAAH!
PISHI (SNAP)
YAAAAH!
BEEEEH!
BEEEH!
BEEH!

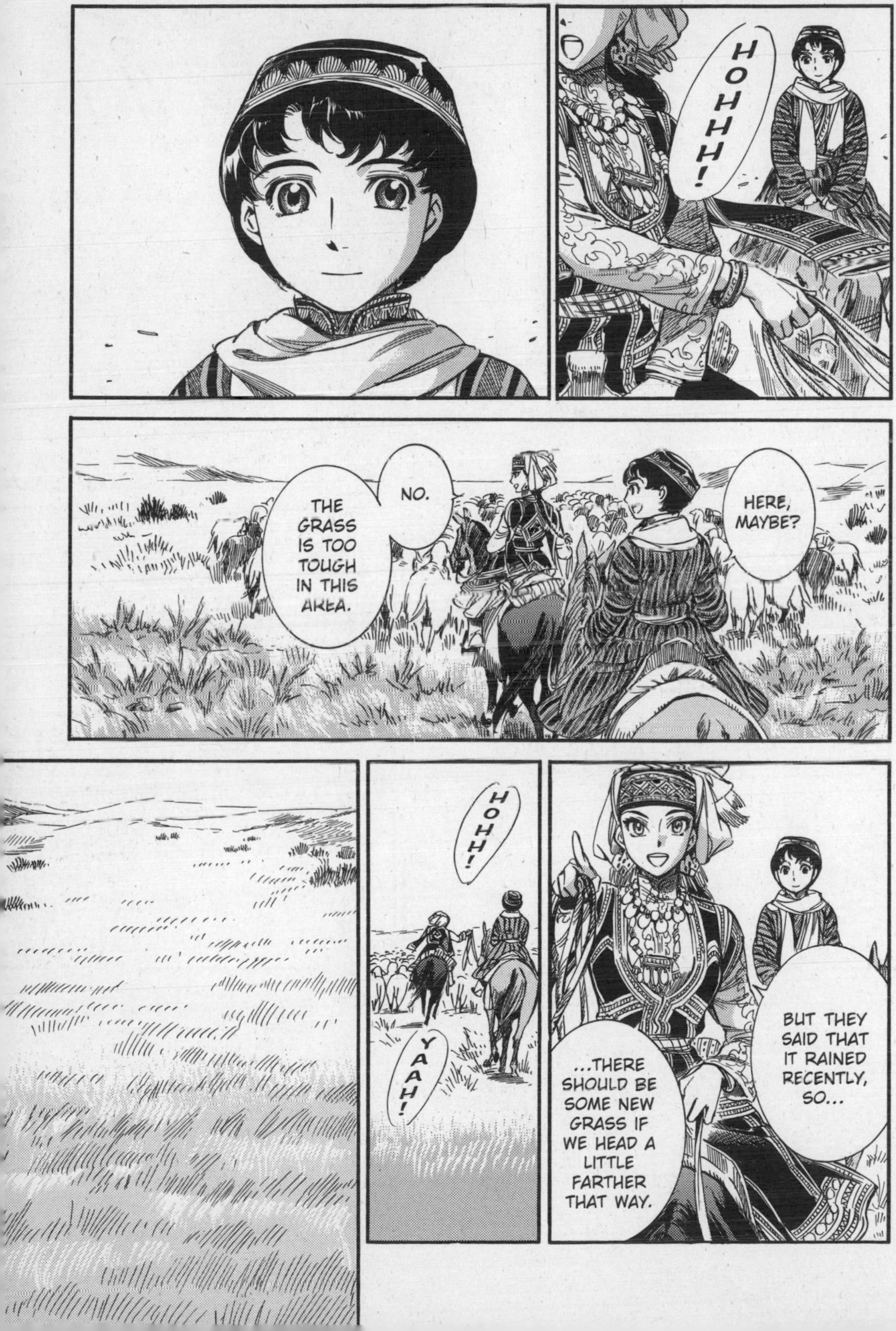
HOHHHH!
HERE, MAYBE?
NO.
THE GRASS IS TOO TOUGH IN THIS AREA.
BUT THEY SAID THAT IT RAINED RECENTLY, SO...
...THERE SHOULD BE SOME NEW GRASS IF WE HEAD A LITTLE FARTHER THAT WAY.
HOHHH!
YAAAH!

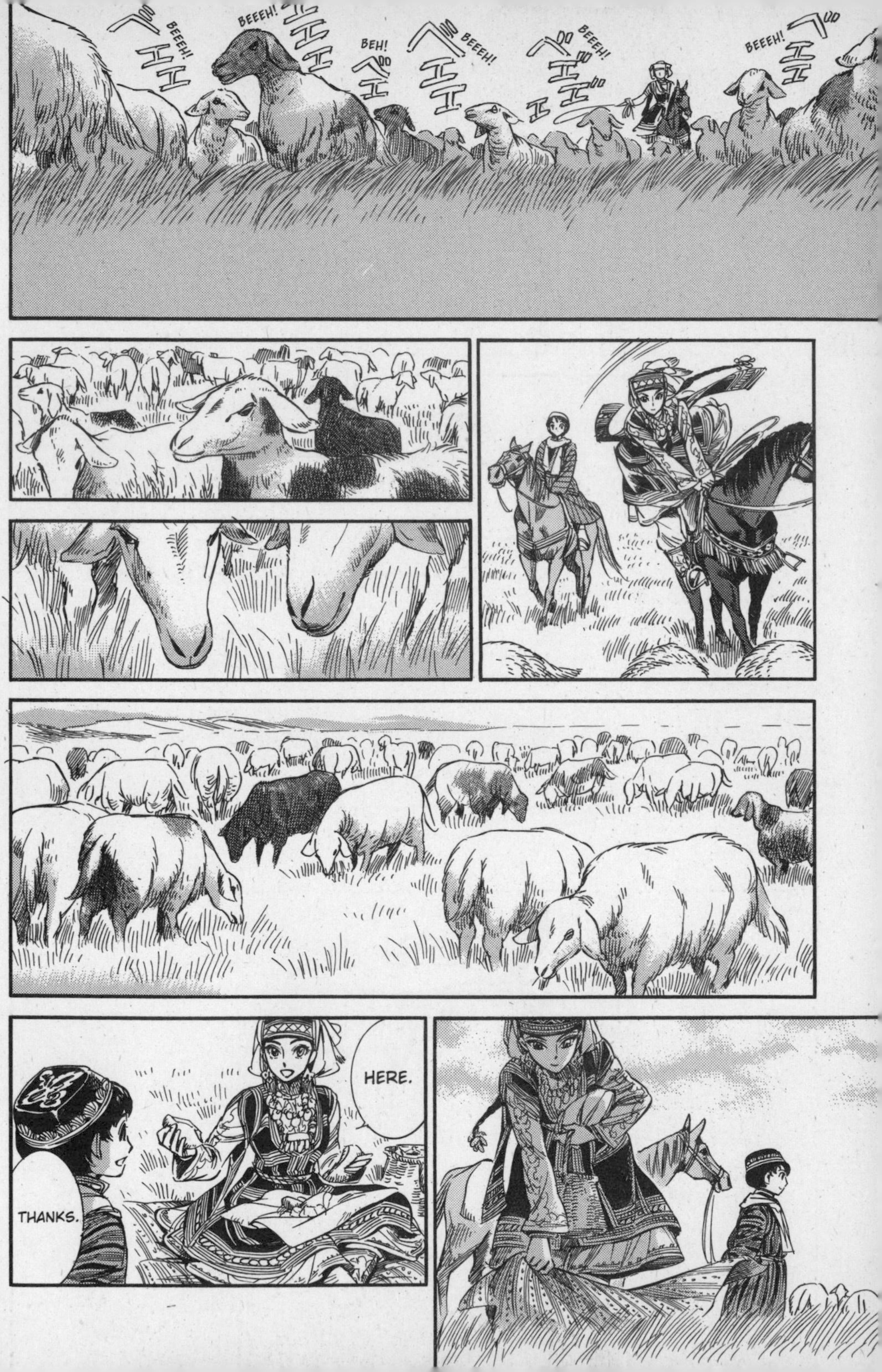
BEEEH!
BEEEH!
BEEEH!
BEH!
BEEEH!
BEEEH!
HERE.
THANKS.

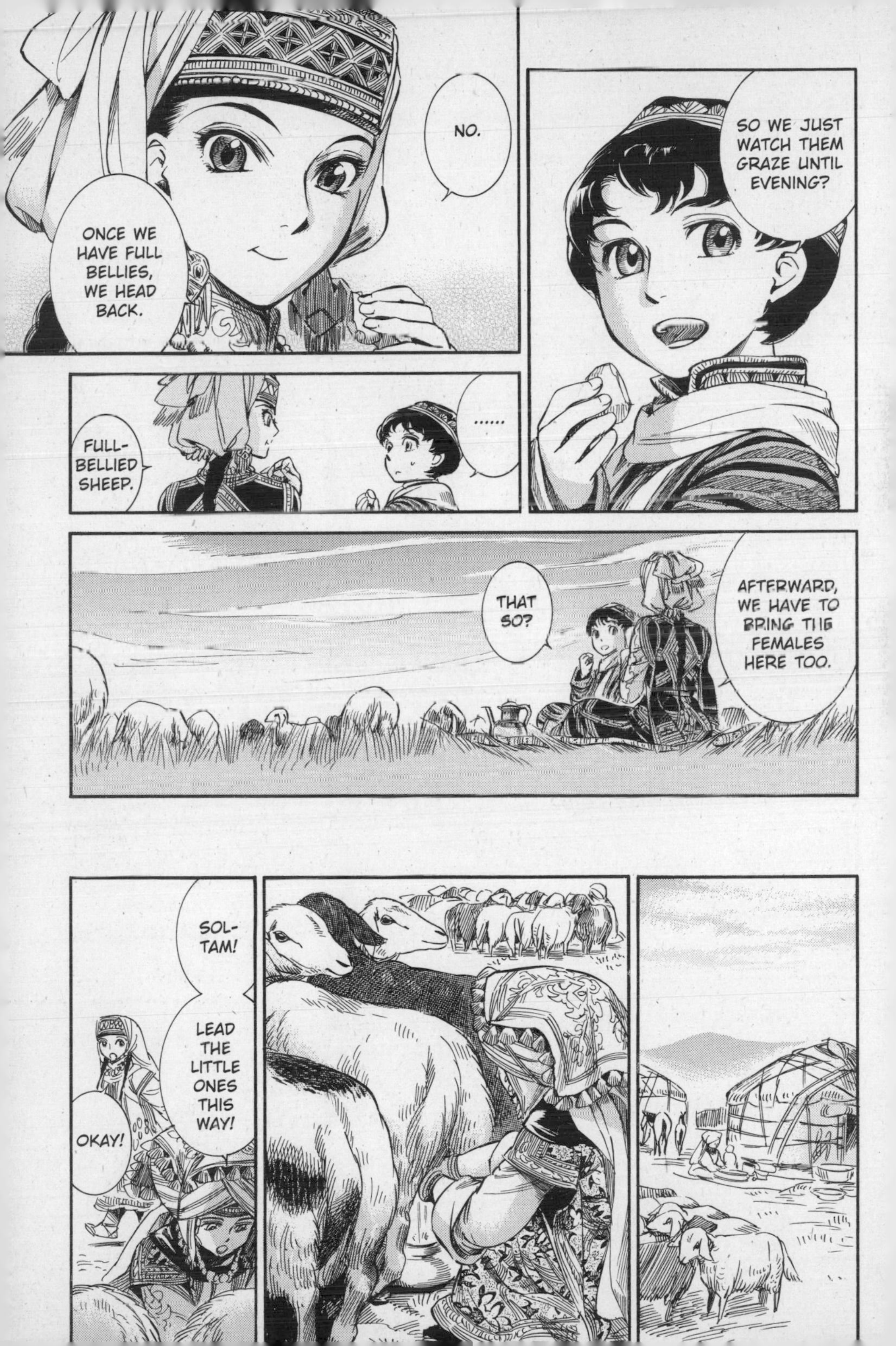
SO WE JUST WATCH THEM GRAZE UNTIL EVENING?
NO.
ONCE WE HAVE FULL BELLIES, WE HEAD BACK.
......
FULL-BELLIED SHEEP.
AFTERWARD, WE HAVE TO BRING THE FEMALES HERE TOO.
THAT SO?
SOL-TAM!
LEAD THE LITTLE ONES THIS WAY!
OKAY!

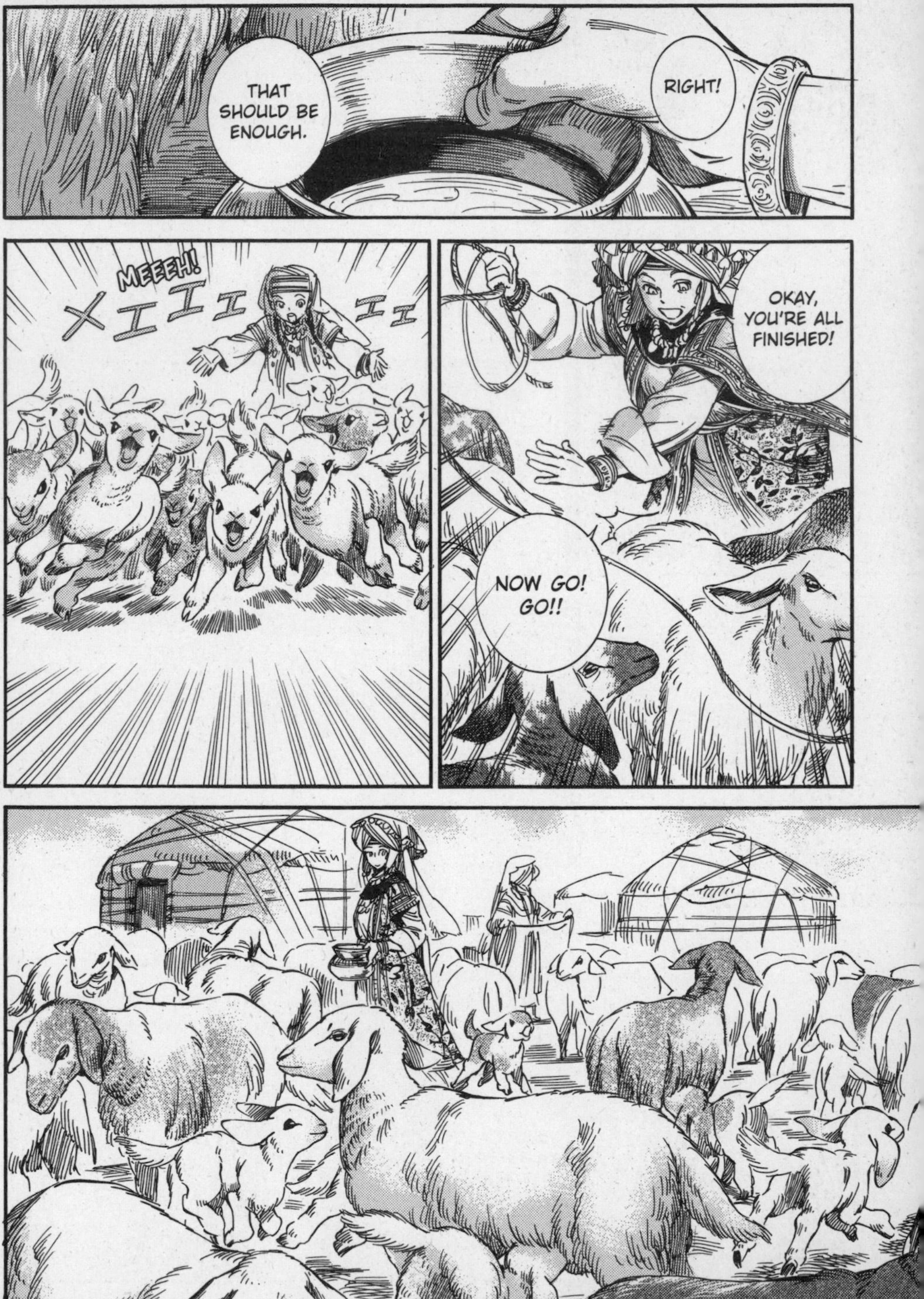

RIGHT!
THAT SHOULD BE ENOUGH.
OKAY, YOU'RE ALL FINISHED!
NOW GO! GO!!
MEEEH!

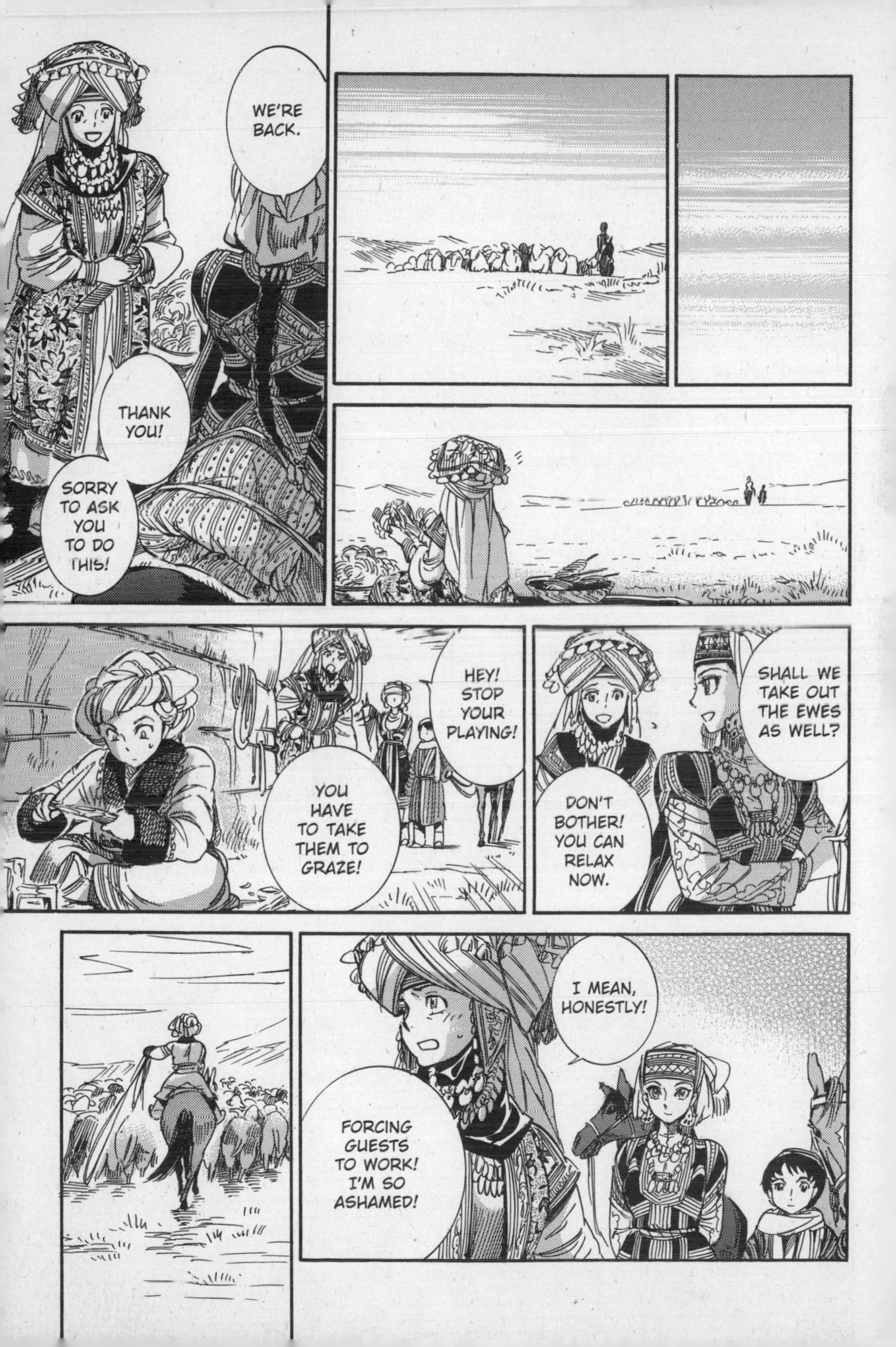
WE'RE BACK.
THANK YOU!
SORRY TO ASK YOU TO DO THIS!
SHALL WE TAKE OUT THE EWES AS WELL?
DON'T BOTHER! YOU CAN RELAX NOW.
HEY! STOP YOUR PLAYING!
YOU HAVE TO TAKE THEM TO GRAZE!
I MEAN, HONESTLY!
FORCING GUESTS TO WORK! I'M SO ASHAMED!

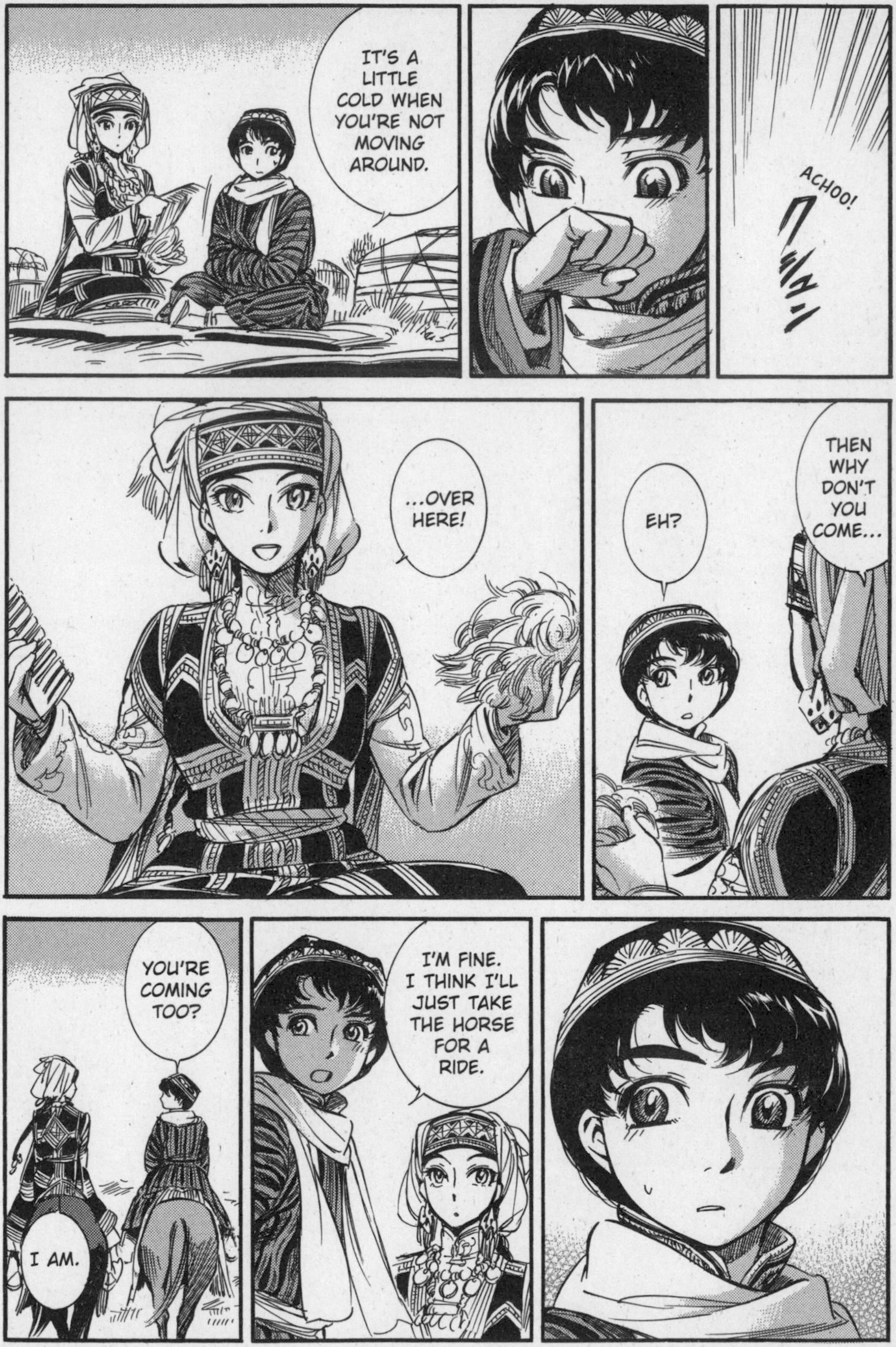
ACHOO!
IT'S A LITTLE COLD WHEN YOU'RE NOT MOVING AROUND.
THEN WHY DON'T YOU COME...
EH?
...OVER HERE!
I'M FINE. I THINK I'LL JUST TAKE THE HORSE FOR A RIDE.
YOU'RE COMING TOO?
I AM.

✦ Chapter Four: End ✦

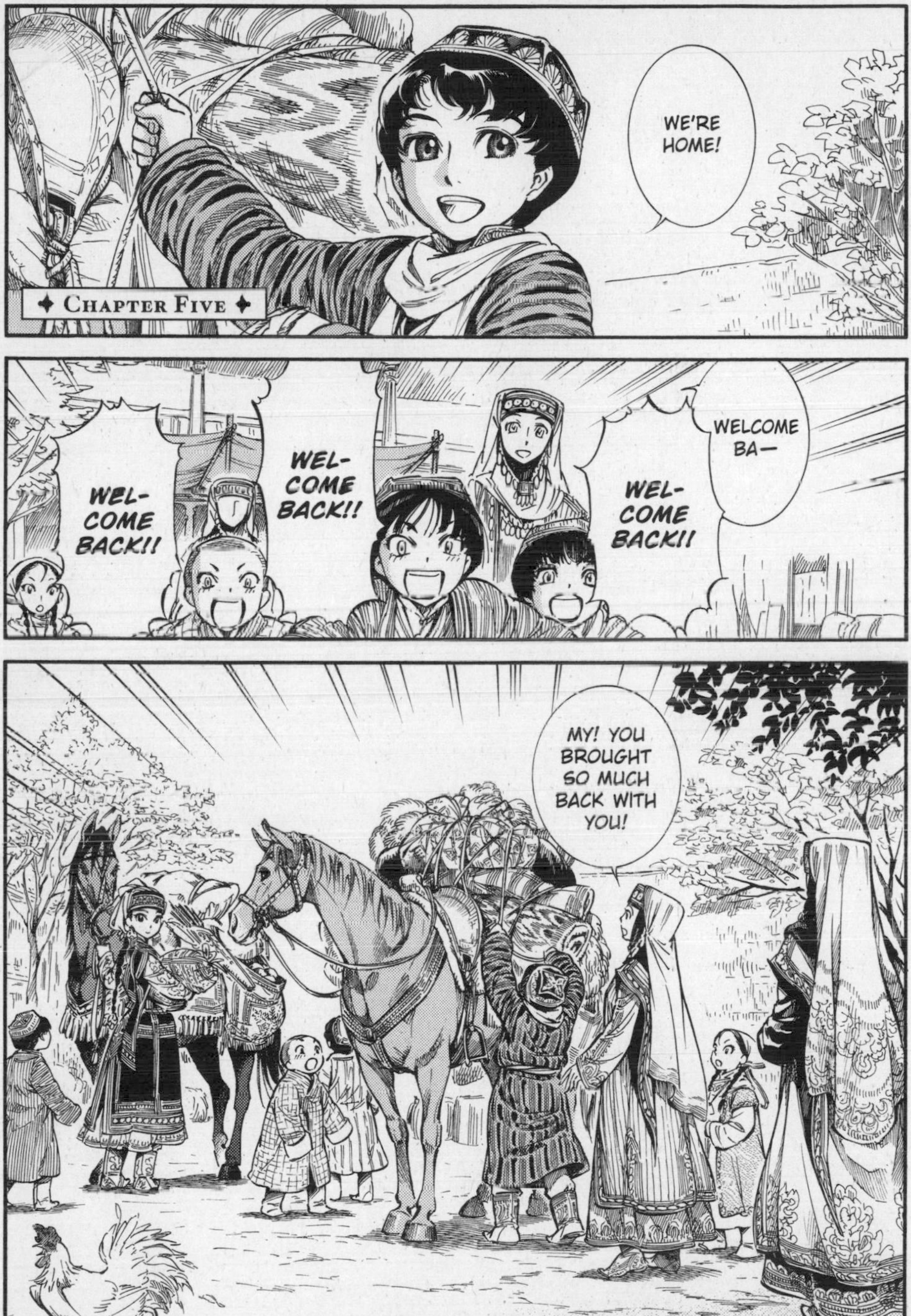
WE'RE HOME!
✦ CHAPTER FIVE ✦
WELCOME BA—
WEL-COME BACK!!
WEL-COME BACK!!
WEL-COME BACK!!
MY! YOU BROUGHT SO MUCH BACK WITH YOU!

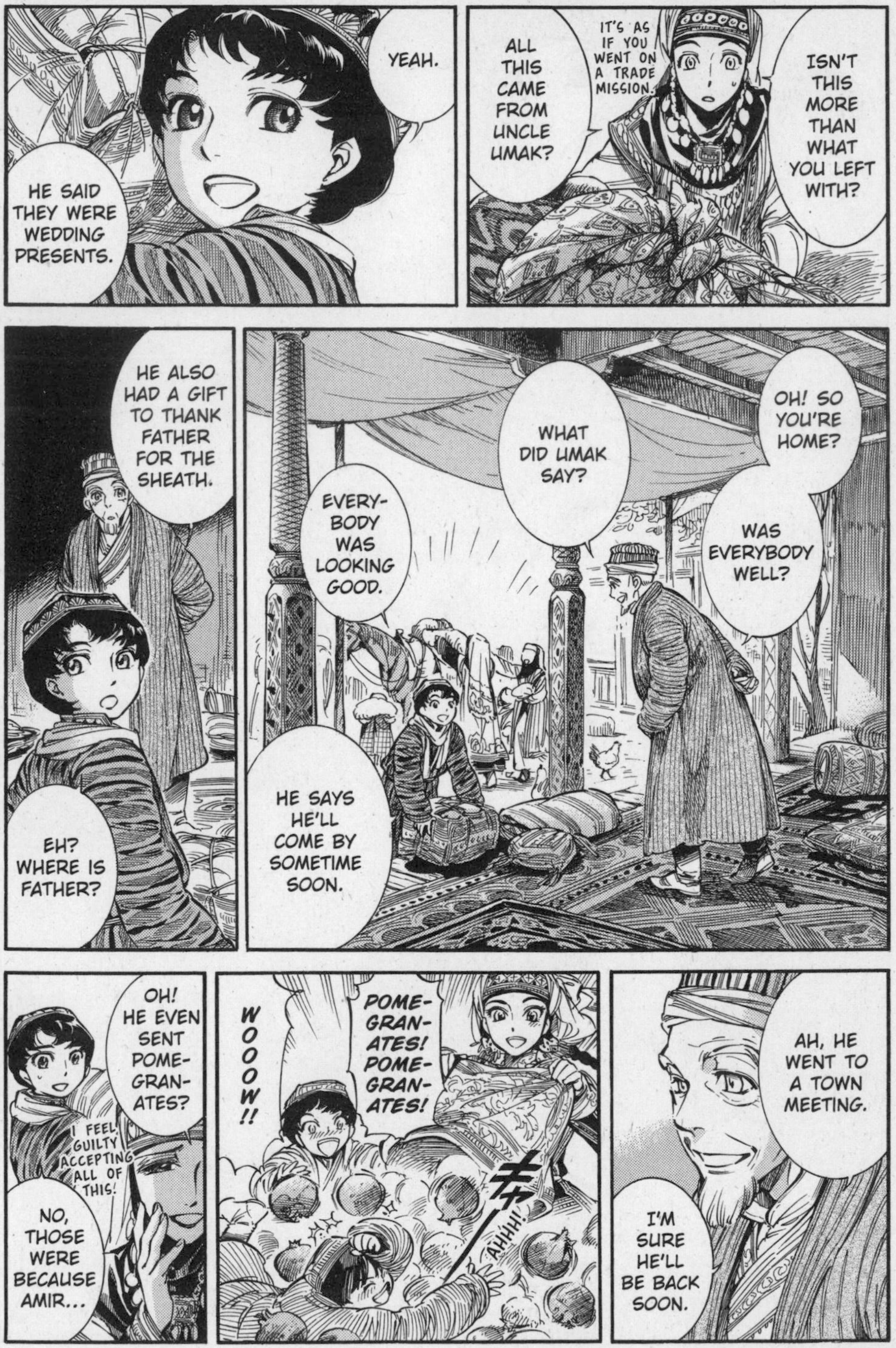
ISN'T THIS MORE THAN WHAT YOU LEFT WITH?
IT'S AS IF YOU WENT ON A TRADE MISSION.
ALL THIS CAME FROM UNCLE UMAK?
YEAH.
HE SAID THEY WERE WEDDING PRESENTS.
OH! SO YOU'RE HOME?
WHAT DID UMAK SAY?
WAS EVERYBODY WELL?
EVERY-BODY WAS LOOKING GOOD.
HE SAYS HE'LL COME BY SOMETIME SOON.
HE ALSO HAD A GIFT TO THANK FATHER FOR THE SHEATH.
EH? WHERE IS FATHER?
AH, HE WENT TO A TOWN MEETING.
I'M SURE HE'LL BE BACK SOON.
POME-GRAN-ATES! POME-GRAN-ATES!
WOOOOW!!
キャ
AHHH!
OH! HE EVEN SENT POME-GRAN-ATES?
I FEEL GUILTY ACCEPTING ALL OF THIS!
NO, THOSE WERE BECAUSE AMIR...

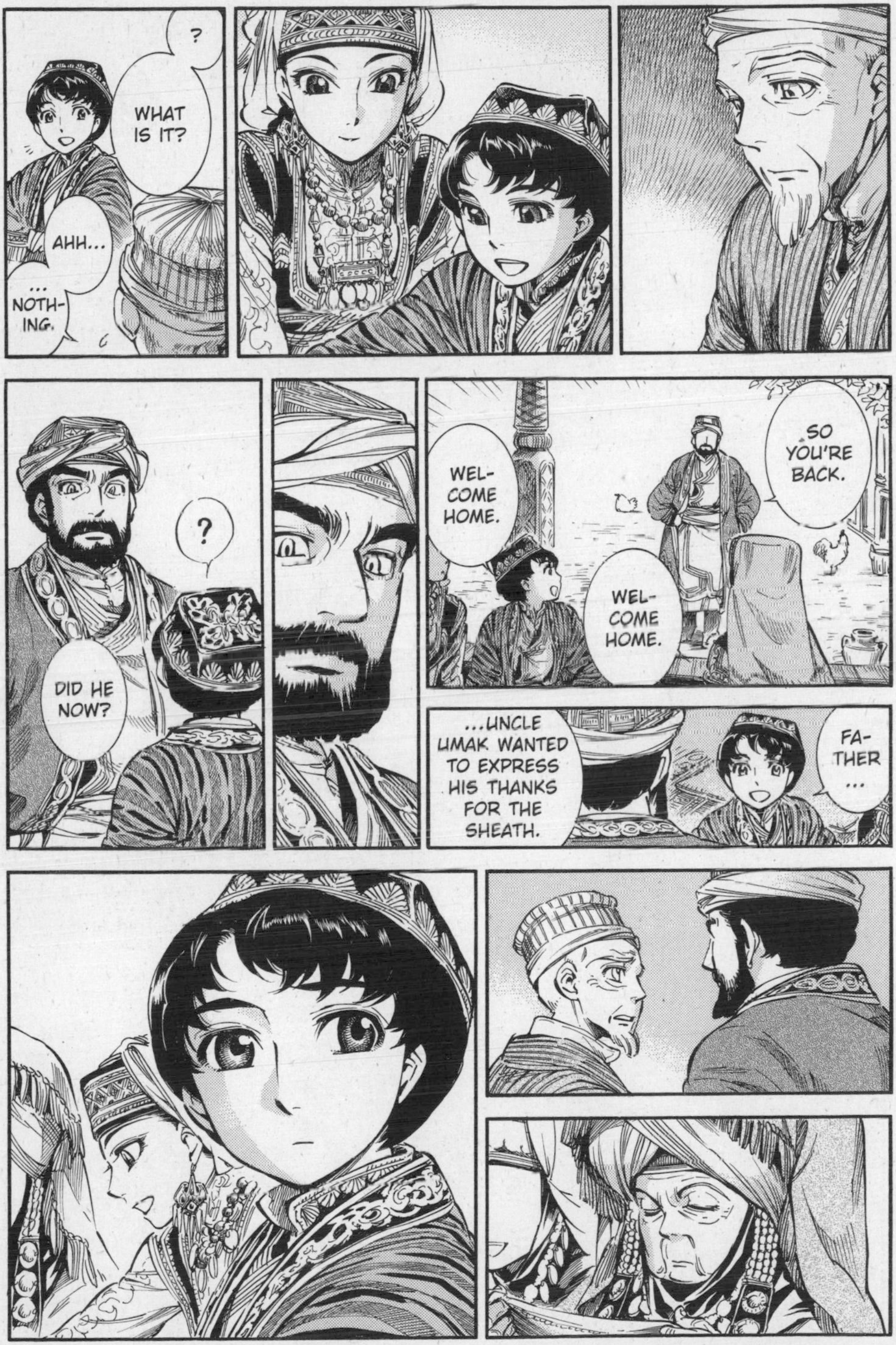
?
WHAT IS IT?
AHH...
...NOTHING.
SO YOU'RE BACK.
WEL-COME HOME.
WEL-COME HOME.
FA-THER...
...UNCLE UMAK WANTED TO EXPRESS HIS THANKS FOR THE SHEATH.
?
DID HE NOW?

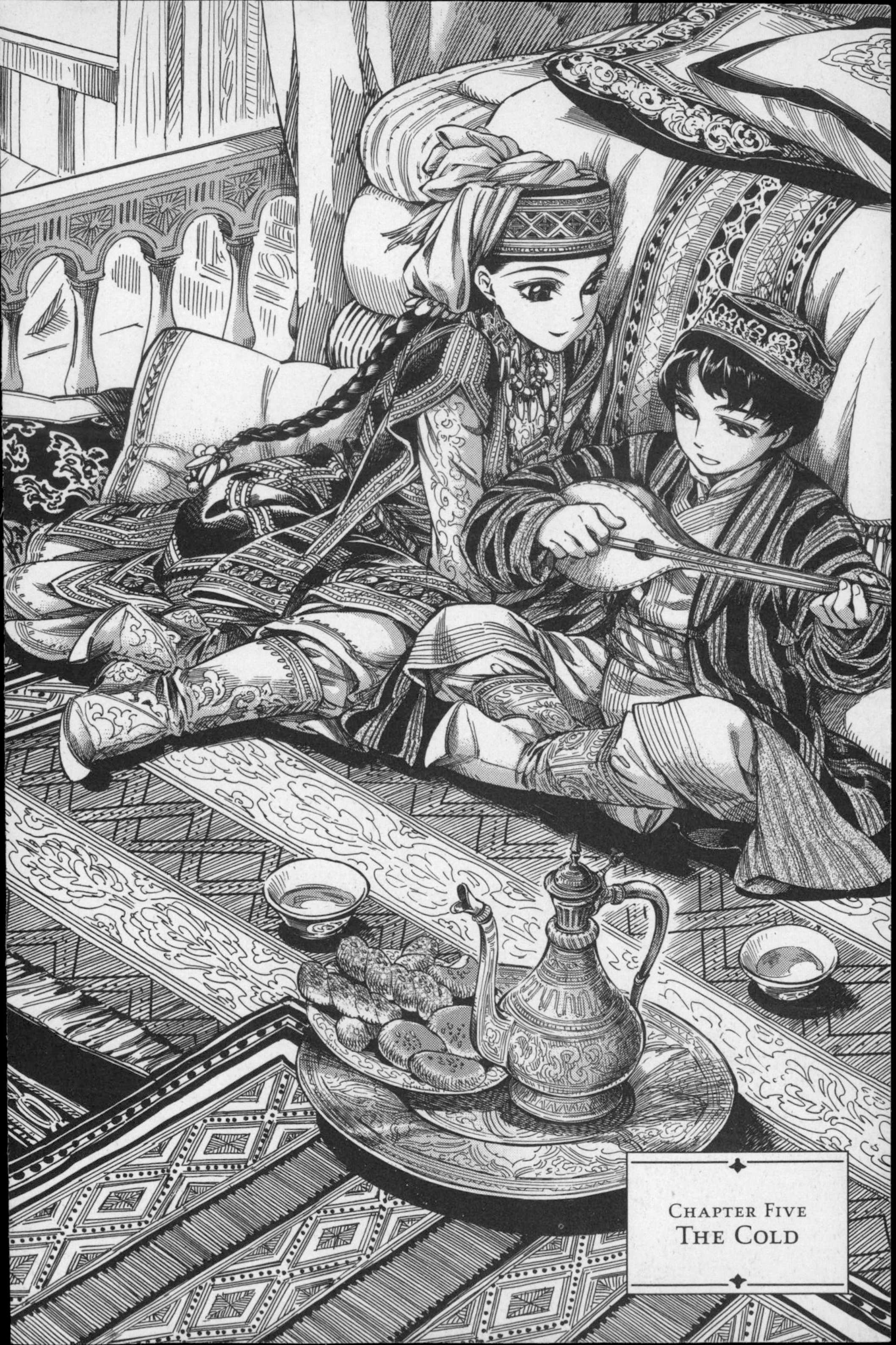

Chapter Five
The Cold

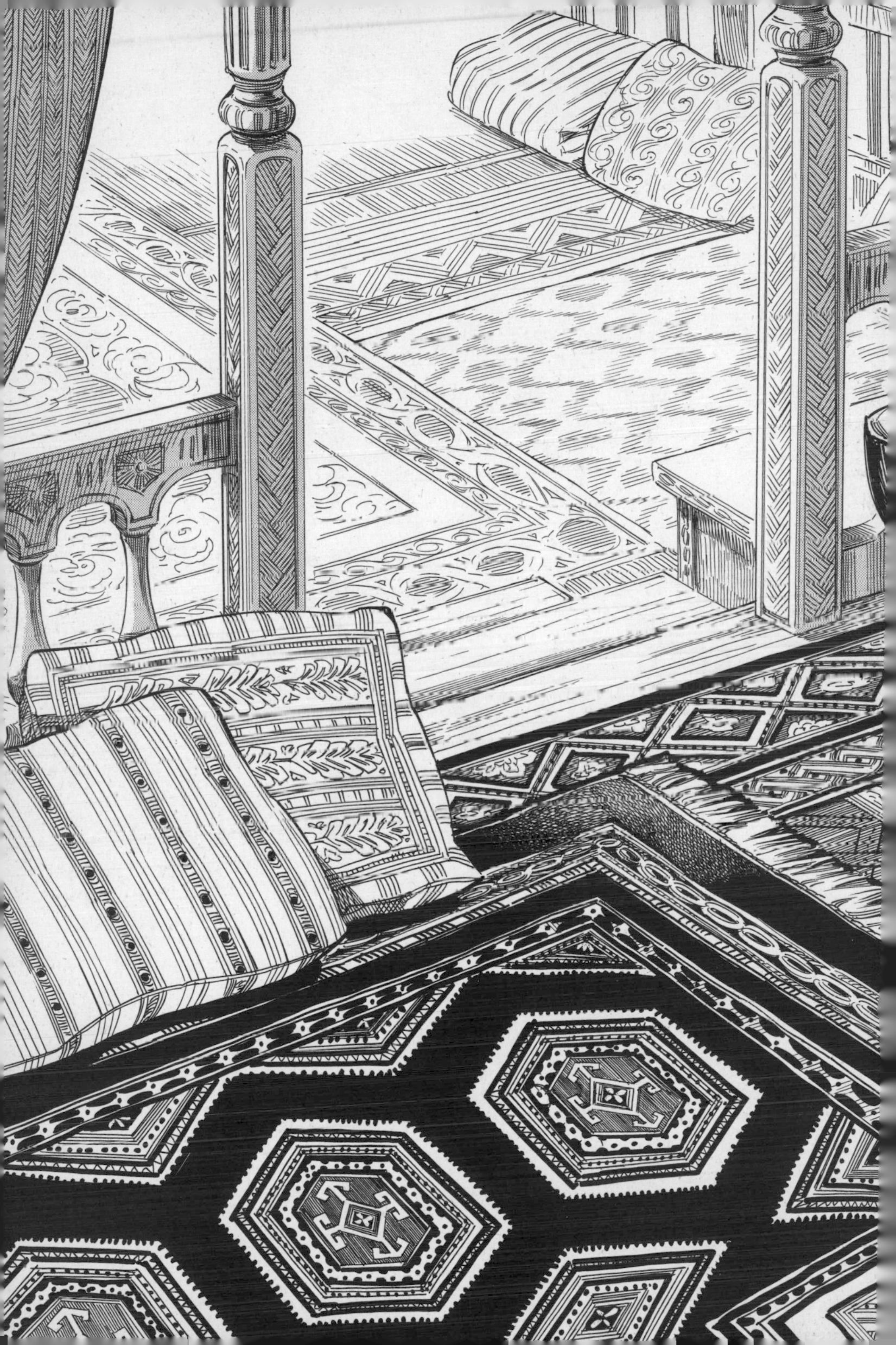

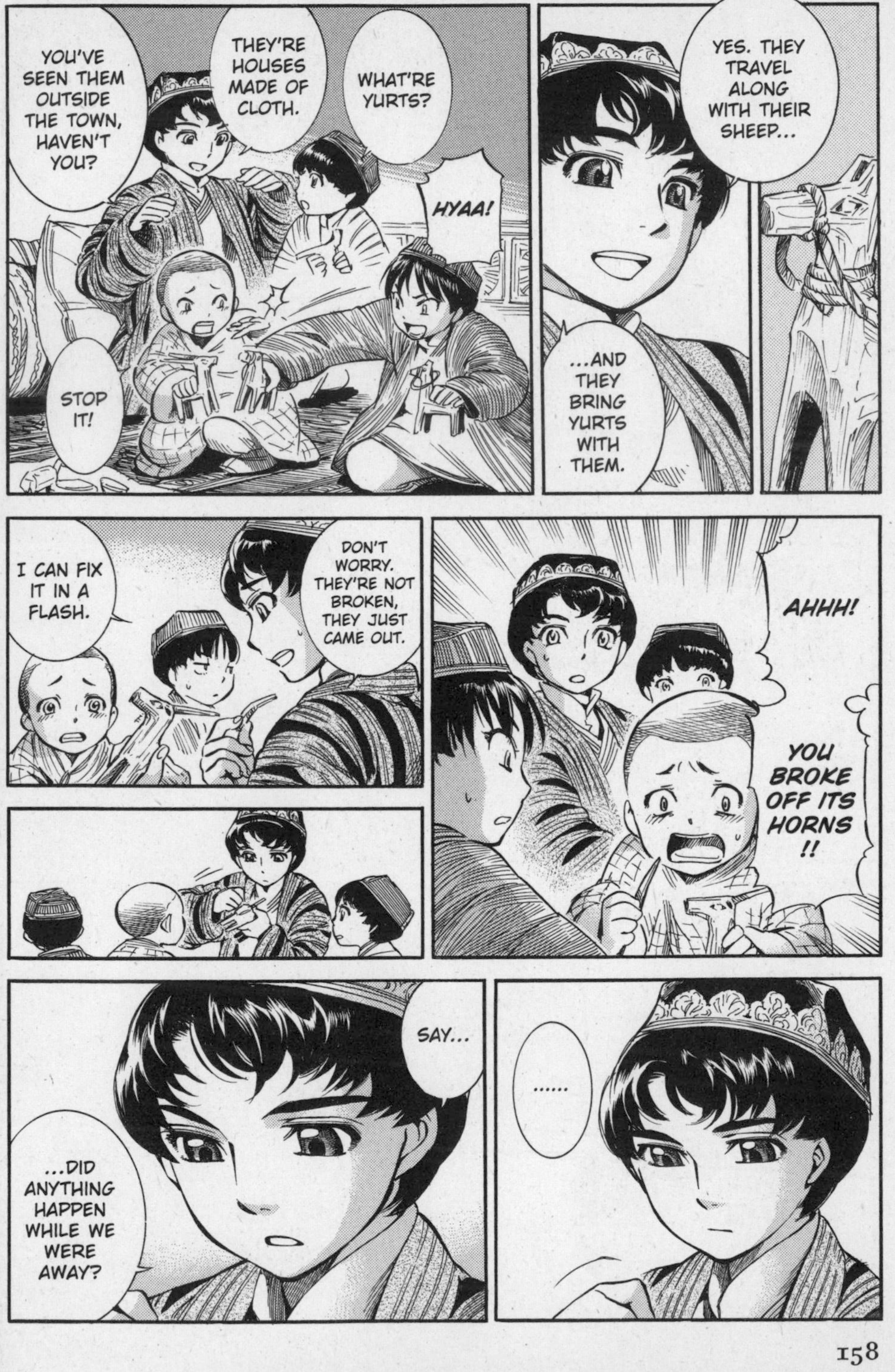
YES. THEY TRAVEL ALONG WITH THEIR SHEEP...
...AND THEY BRING YURTS WITH THEM.
WHAT'RE YURTS?
THEY'RE HOUSES MADE OF CLOTH.
YOU'VE SEEN THEM OUTSIDE THE TOWN, HAVEN'T YOU?
HYAA!
STOP IT!
AHHH!
YOU BROKE OFF ITS HORNS !!
DON'T WORRY. THEY'RE NOT BROKEN, THEY JUST CAME OUT.
I CAN FIX IT IN A FLASH.
......
SAY...
...DID ANYTHING HAPPEN WHILE WE WERE AWAY?

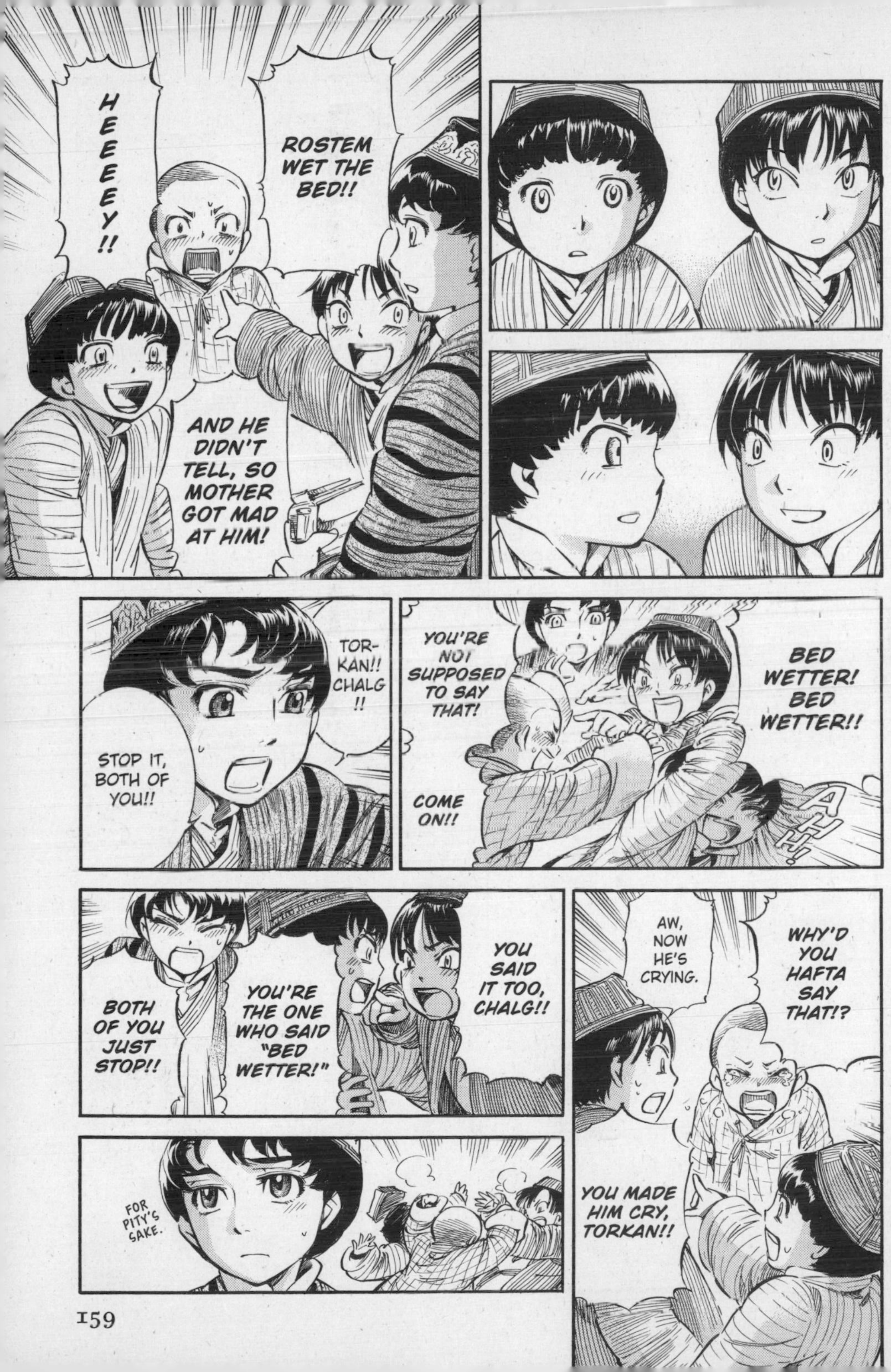

ROSTEM WET THE BED!!
HEEEEEY!!
AND HE DIDN'T TELL, SO MOTHER GOT MAD AT HIM!
BED WETTER! BED WETTER!!
YOU'RE NOT SUPPOSED TO SAY THAT!
COME ON!!
AHH!
TOR-KAN!! CHALG!!
STOP IT, BOTH OF YOU!!
WHY'D YOU HAFTA SAY THAT!?
AW, NOW HE'S CRYING.
YOU MADE HIM CRY, TORKAN!!
YOU SAID IT TOO, CHALG!!
YOU'RE THE ONE WHO SAID "BED WETTER!"
BOTH OF YOU JUST STOP!!
FOR PITY'S SAKE.

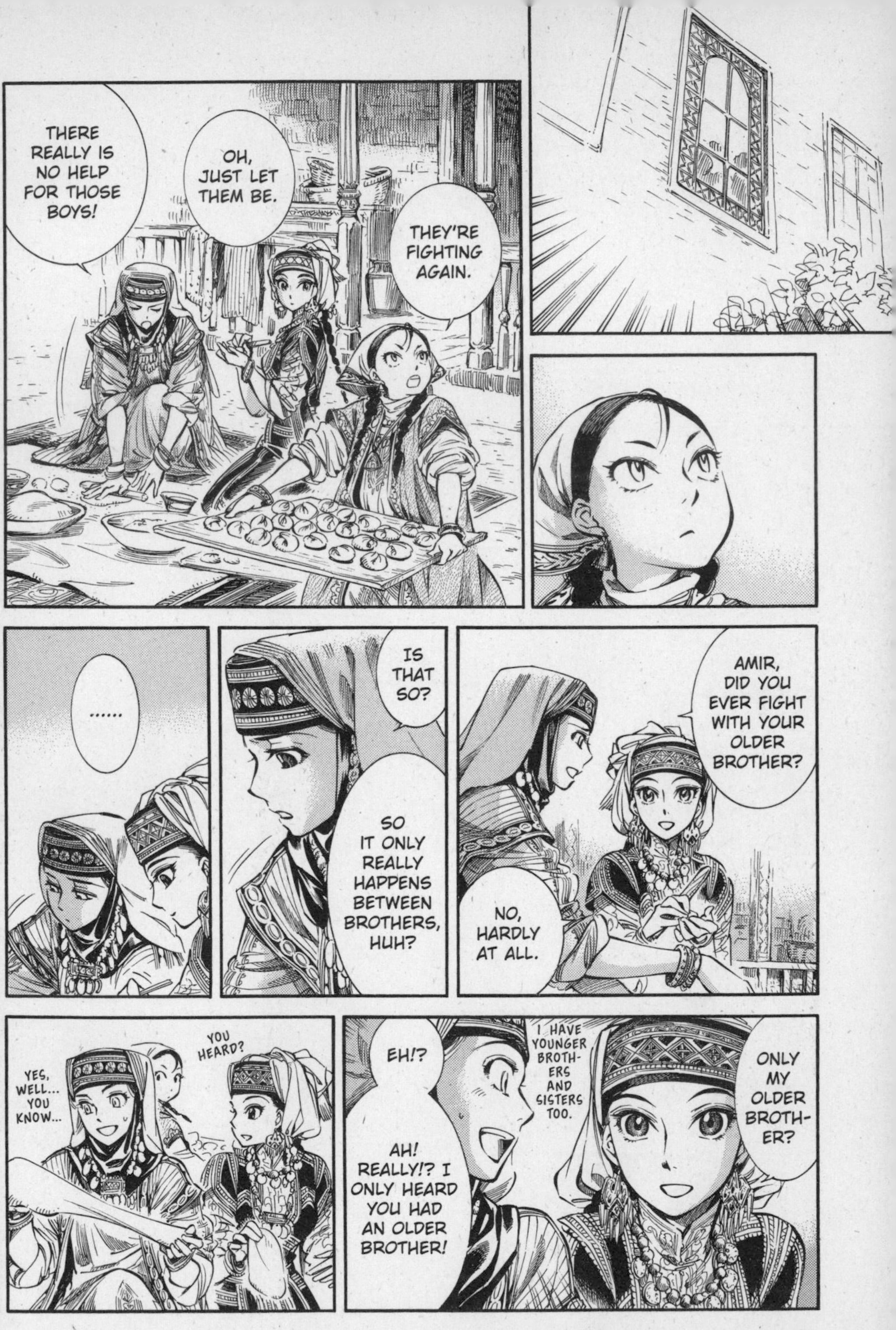
THEY'RE FIGHTING AGAIN.
OH, JUST LET THEM BE.
THERE REALLY IS NO HELP FOR THOSE BOYS!
AMIR, DID YOU EVER FIGHT WITH YOUR OLDER BROTHER?
NO, HARDLY AT ALL.
IS THAT SO?
SO IT ONLY REALLY HAPPENS BETWEEN BROTHERS, HUH?
......
ONLY MY OLDER BROTH-ER?
I HAVE YOUNGER BROTH-ERS AND SISTERS TOO.
EH!?
AH! REALLY!? I ONLY HEARD YOU HAD AN OLDER BROTHER!
YOU HEARD?
YES, WELL... YOU KNOW...

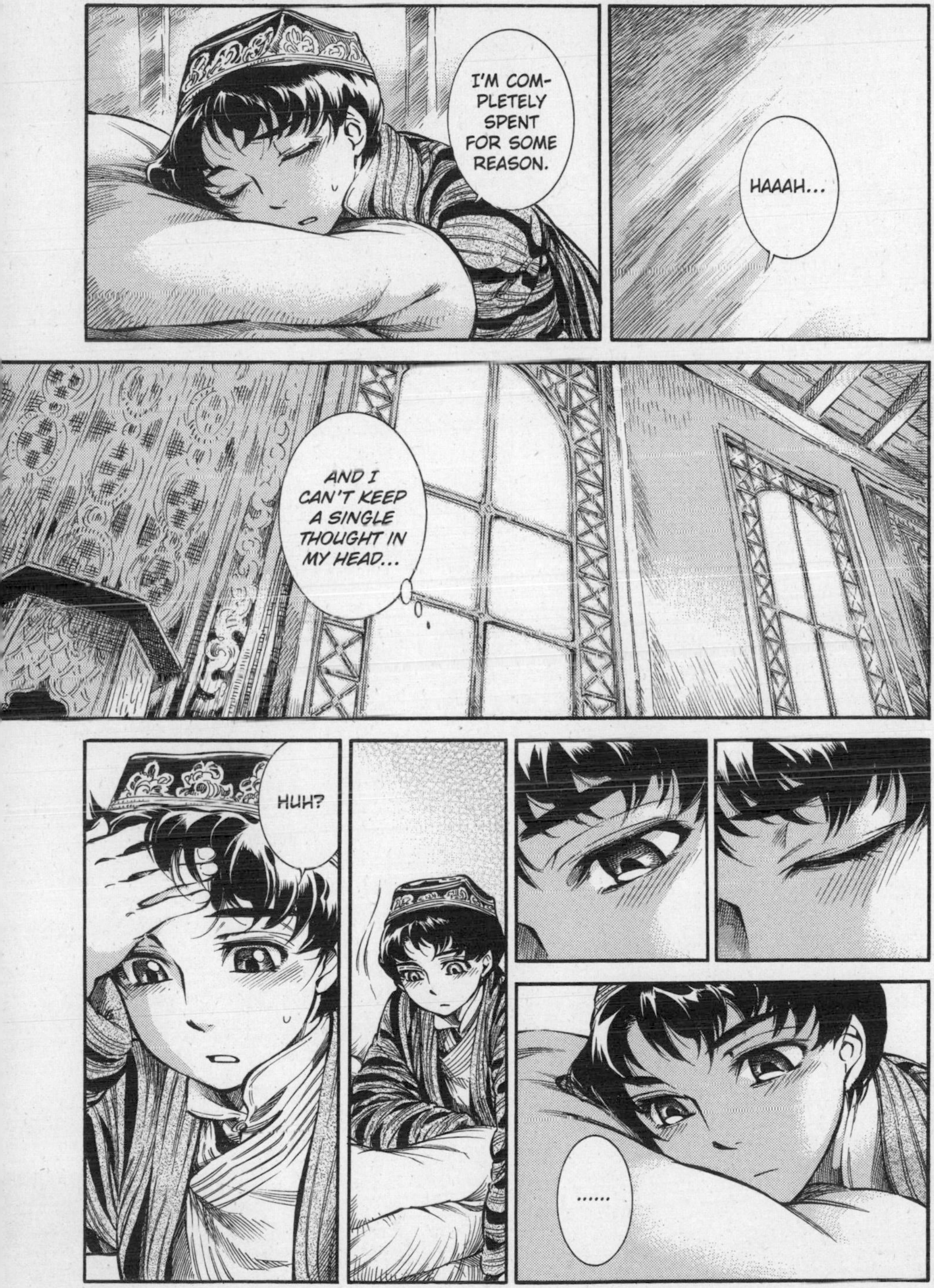
HAAAH...
I'M COM-PLETELY SPENT FOR SOME REASON.
AND I CAN'T KEEP A SINGLE THOUGHT IN MY HEAD...
......
HUH?

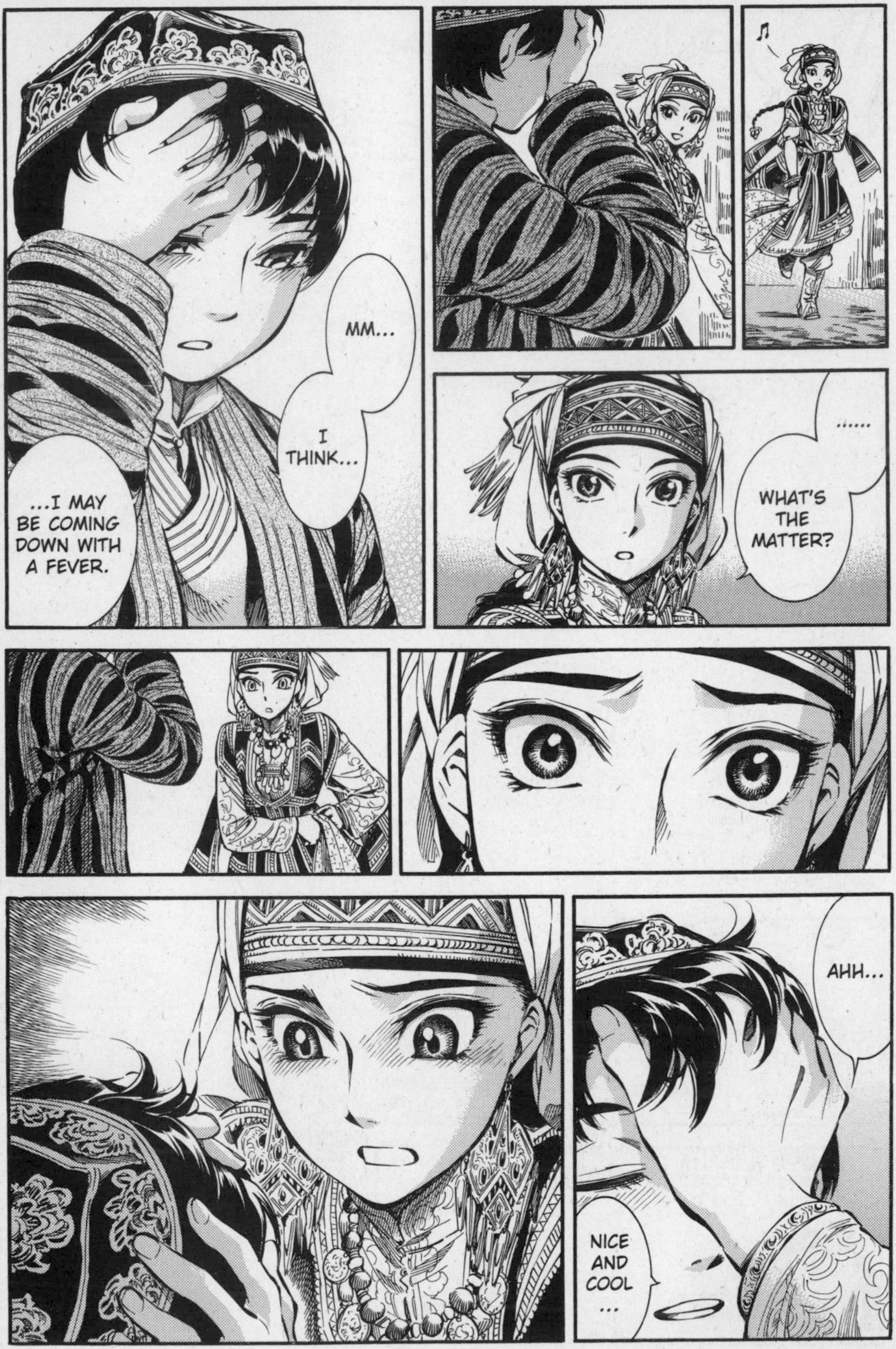
♪
......
WHAT'S THE MATTER?
MM...
I THINK...
...I MAY BE COMING DOWN WITH A FEVER.
AHH...
NICE AND COOL ...

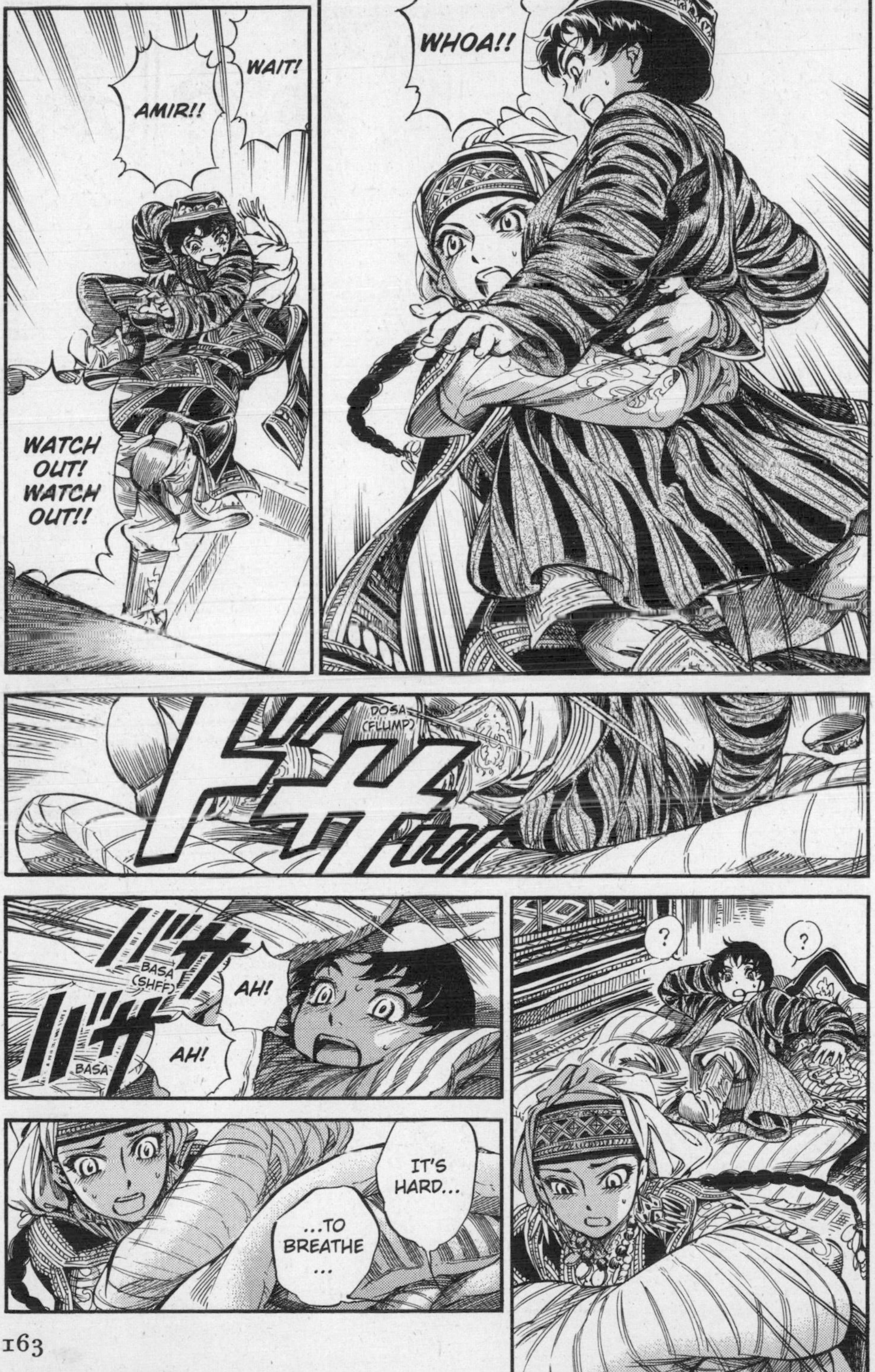
WHOA!!
WAIT!
AMIR!!
WATCH OUT! WATCH OUT!!
DOSA (FLUMP)
?
?
BASA (SHFF)
AH!
AH!
BASA
IT'S HARD...
...TO BREATHE...

PWAH!
AHH!

ZAKU
Hʼʼク
ZAKU (SWSH)
Hʼʼク

YOU MUSTN'T TRY TO GET UP!
JUST LIE THERE AND SLEEP!
...OKAY.

MOTH-ER!!
MOTH-ER!!

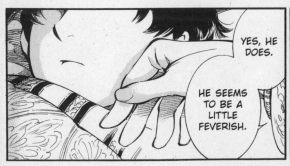
YES, HE DOES.
HE SEEMS TO BE A LITTLE FEVERISH.

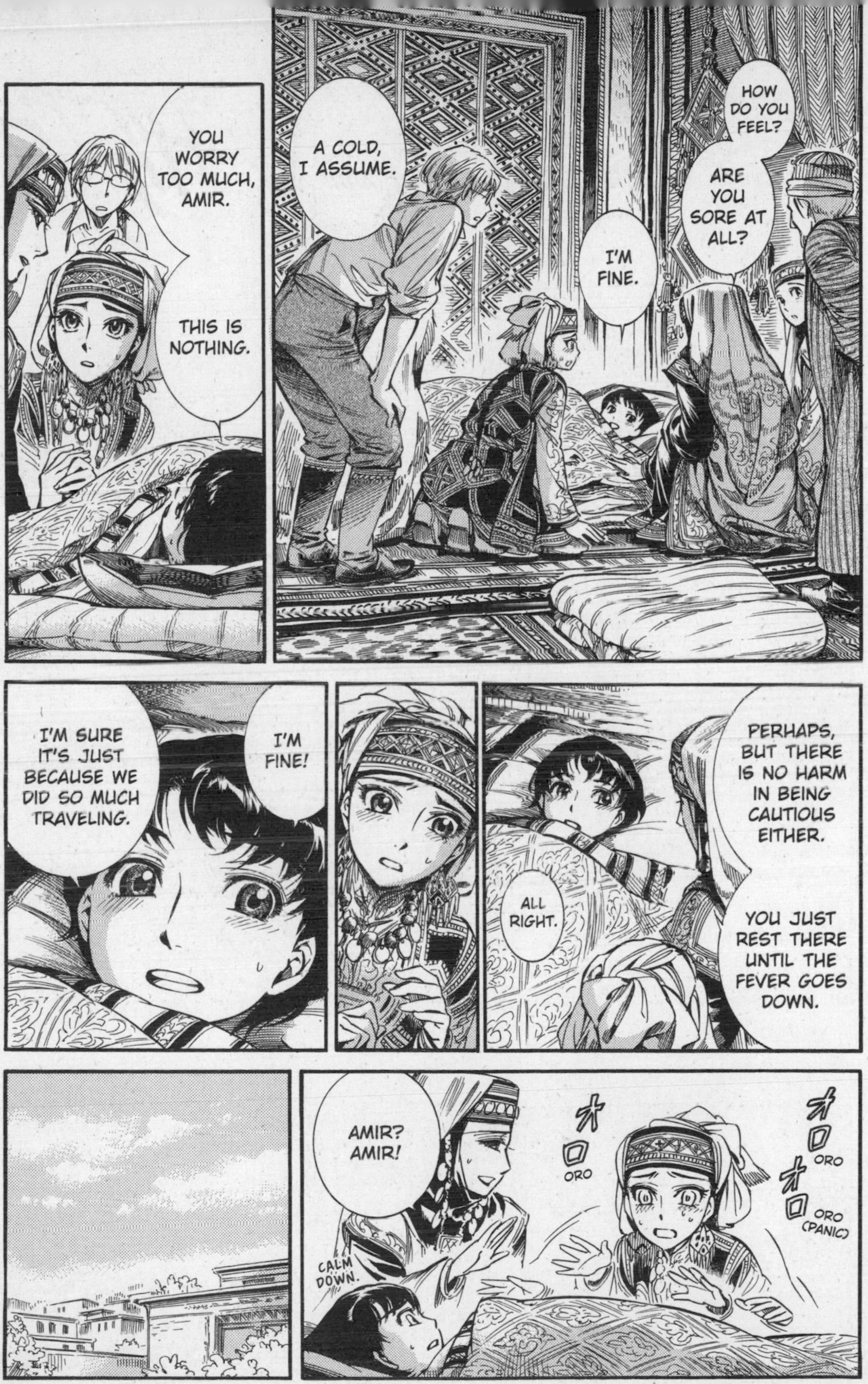
HOW DO YOU FEEL?
ARE YOU SORE AT ALL?
I'M FINE.
A COLD, I ASSUME.
YOU WORRY TOO MUCH, AMIR.
THIS IS NOTHING.
PERHAPS, BUT THERE IS NO HARM IN BEING CAUTIOUS EITHER.
YOU JUST REST THERE UNTIL THE FEVER GOES DOWN.
ALL RIGHT.
I'M FINE!
I'M SURE IT'S JUST BECAUSE WE DID SO MUCH TRAVELING.
オロ ORO
オロ ORO (PANIC)
AMIR? AMIR!
オロ ORO
CALM DOWN.

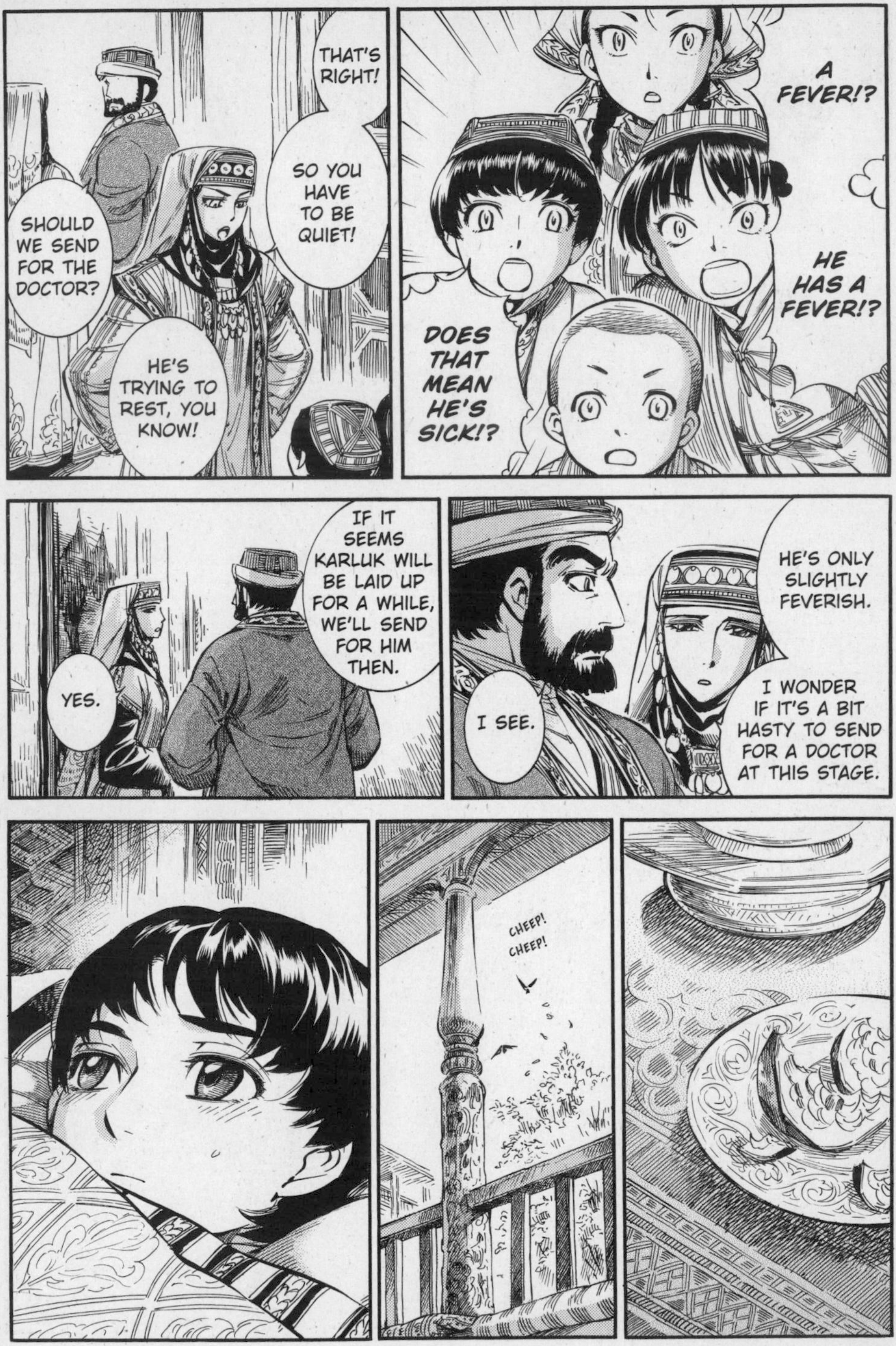
A FEVER!?
HE HAS A FEVER!?
DOES THAT MEAN HE'S SICK!?
THAT'S RIGHT!
SO YOU HAVE TO BE QUIET!
HE'S TRYING TO REST, YOU KNOW!
SHOULD WE SEND FOR THE DOCTOR?
HE'S ONLY SLIGHTLY FEVERISH.
I WONDER IF IT'S A BIT HASTY TO SEND FOR A DOCTOR AT THIS STAGE.
I SEE.
IF IT SEEMS KARLUK WILL BE LAID UP FOR A WHILE, WE'LL SEND FOR HIM THEN.
YES.
CHEEP! CHEEP!

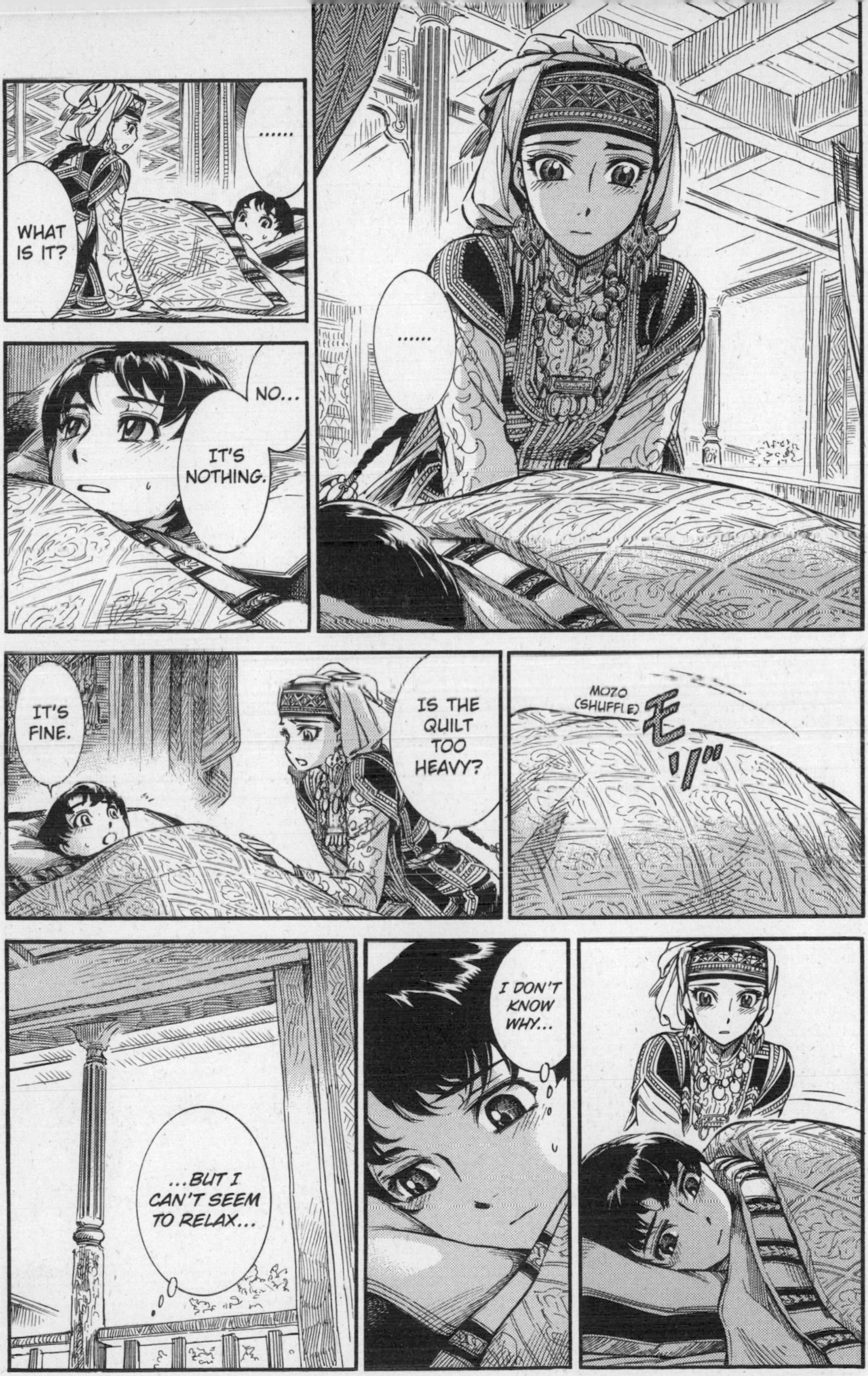
......
......
WHAT IS IT?
NO...
IT'S NOTHING.
MOZO (SHUFFLE)
モゾ
IS THE QUILT TOO HEAVY?
IT'S FINE.
I DON'T KNOW WHY...
...BUT I CAN'T SEEM TO RELAX...

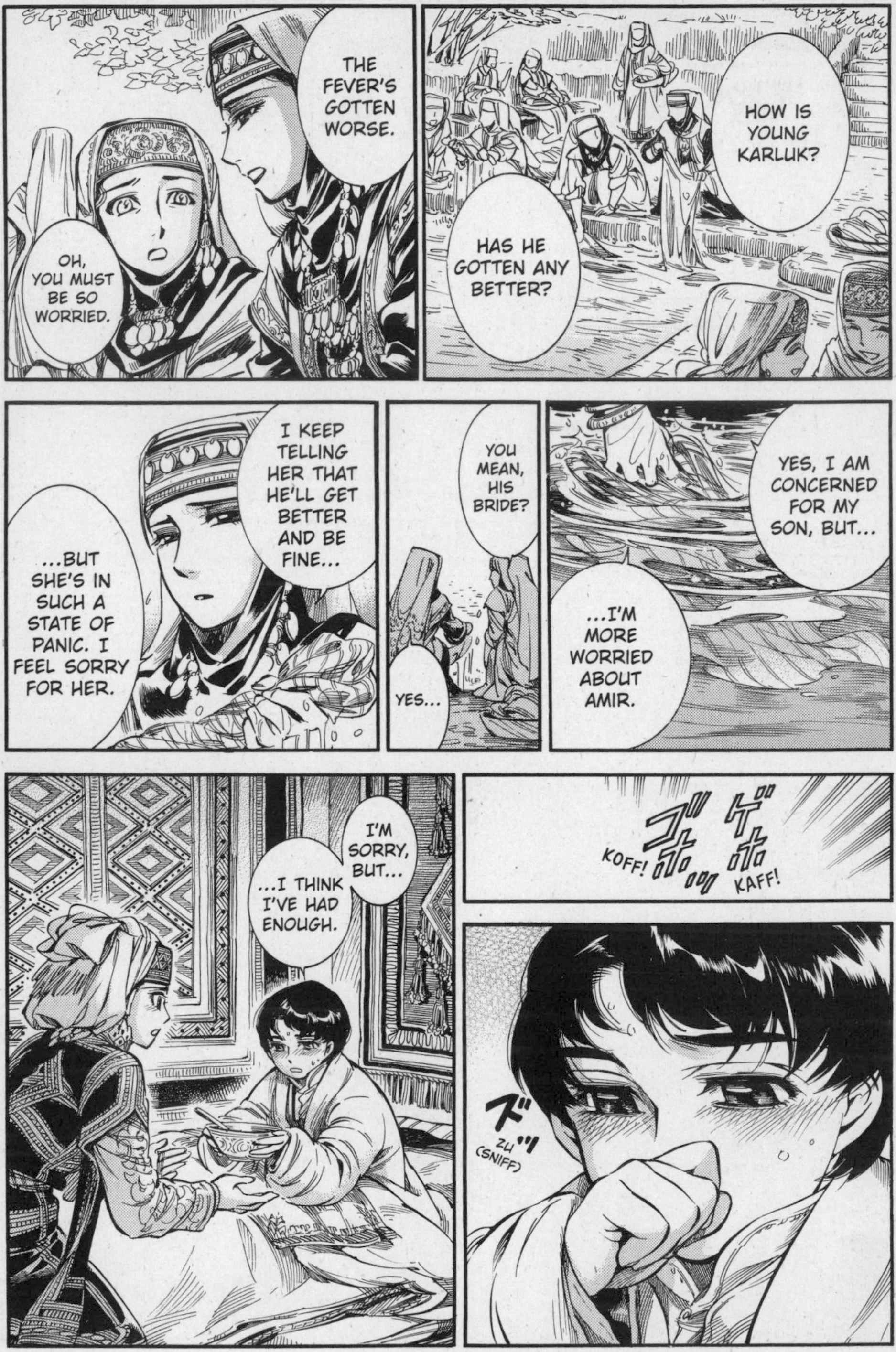
HOW IS YOUNG KARLUK?
HAS HE GOTTEN ANY BETTER?
THE FEVER'S GOTTEN WORSE.
OH, YOU MUST BE SO WORRIED.
YES, I AM CONCERNED FOR MY SON, BUT...
...I'M MORE WORRIED ABOUT AMIR.
YOU MEAN, HIS BRIDE?
YES...
I KEEP TELLING HER THAT HE'LL GET BETTER AND BE FINE...
...BUT SHE'S IN SUCH A STATE OF PANIC. I FEEL SORRY FOR HER.
ゲホ
KAFF!
ゴホ
KOFF!
ズッ
ZU (SNIFF)
I'M SORRY, BUT...
...I THINK I'VE HAD ENOUGH.

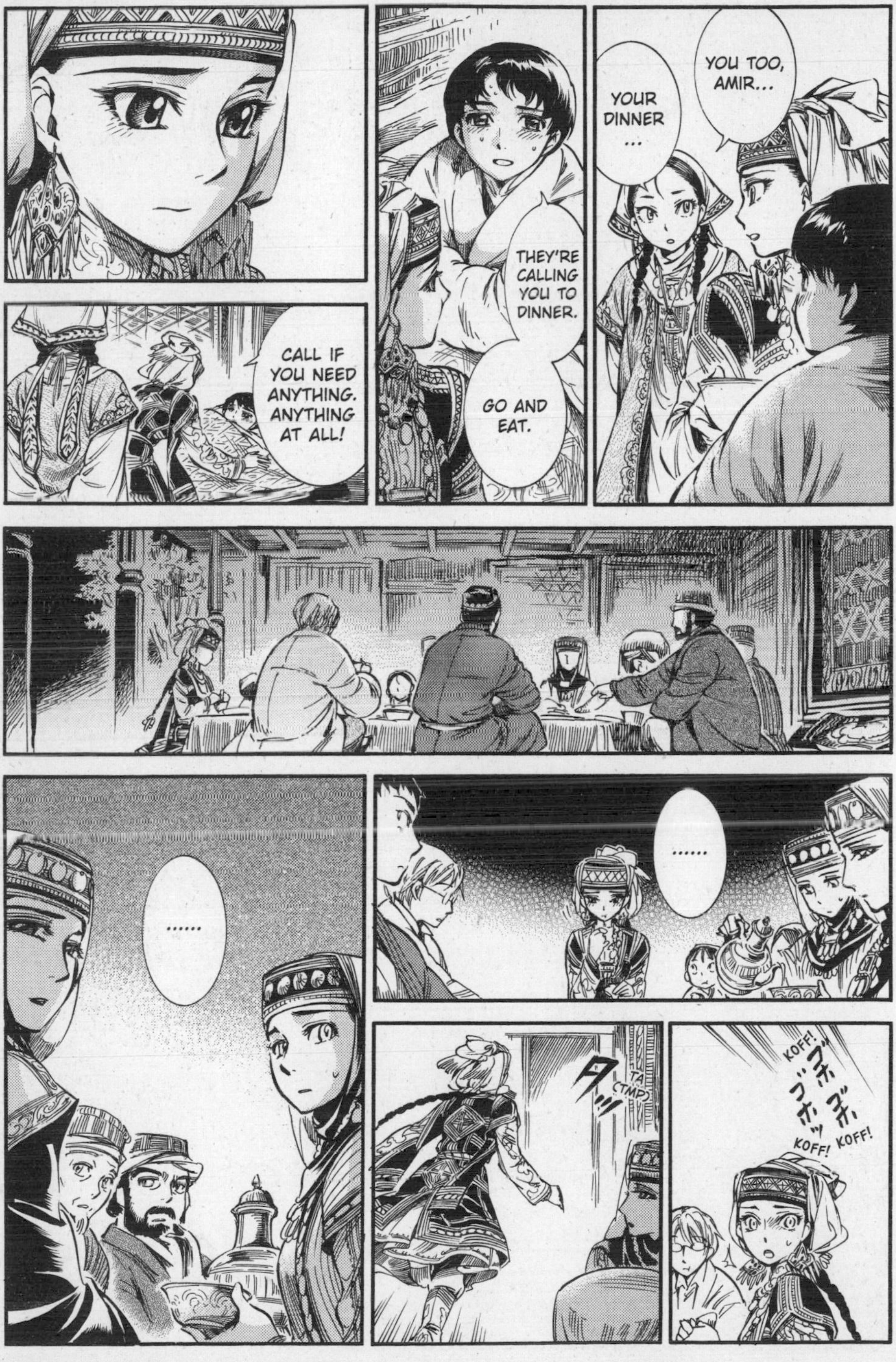
YOU TOO, AMIR...
YOUR DINNER ...
THEY'RE CALLING YOU TO DINNER.
GO AND EAT.
CALL IF YOU NEED ANYTHING. ANYTHING AT ALL!
......
ゴホ ゴホ ゴホッ
KOFF! KOFF! KOFF!
タッ
TA (TMP)
......

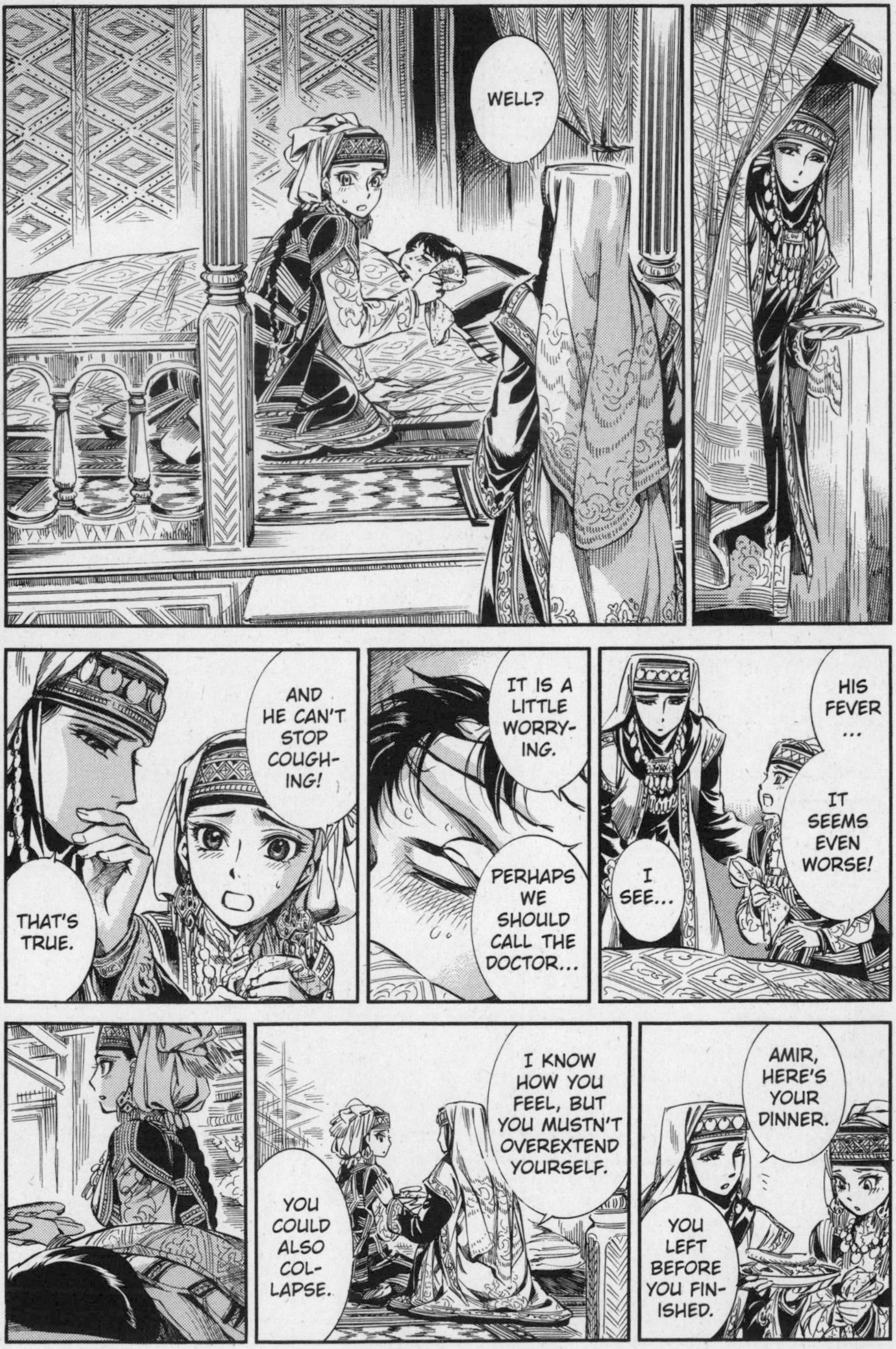
WELL?
HIS FEVER ...
IT SEEMS EVEN WORSE!
I SEE...
IT IS A LITTLE WORRYING.
PERHAPS WE SHOULD CALL THE DOCTOR...
AND HE CAN'T STOP COUGHING!
THAT'S TRUE.
AMIR, HERE'S YOUR DINNER.
YOU LEFT BEFORE YOU FINISHED.
I KNOW HOW YOU FEEL, BUT YOU MUSTN'T OVEREXTEND YOURSELF.
YOU COULD ALSO COLLAPSE.

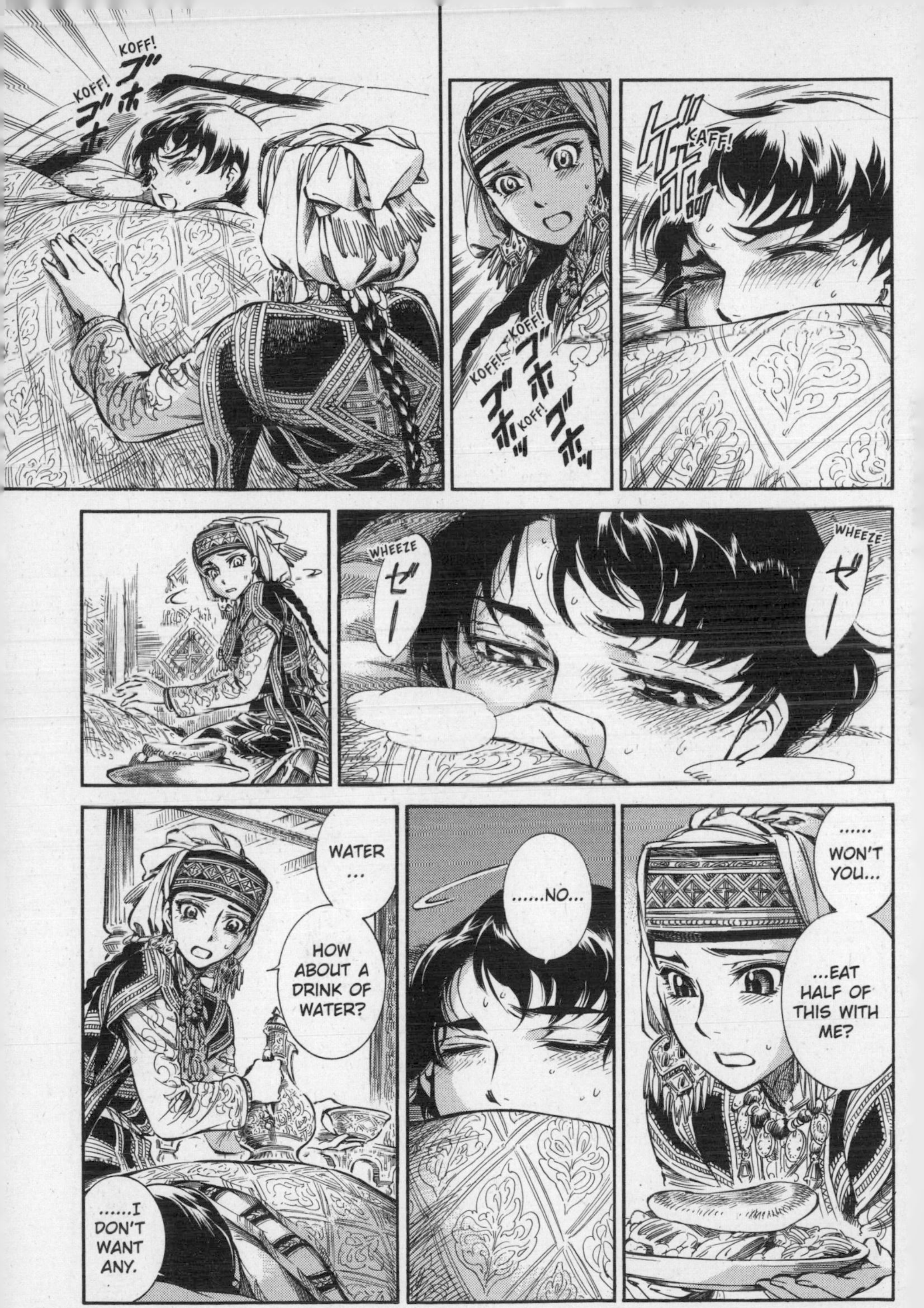
KAFF!
KOFF! KOFF! KOFF!
ゴホ ゴホッ ゴホ ゴホッ
KOFF! KOFF!
ゴホ ゴホ
WHEEZE
ゼー
WHEEZE
ゼー
......WON'T YOU...
...EAT HALF OF THIS WITH ME?
......NO...
WATER ...
HOW ABOUT A DRINK OF WATER?
......I DON'T WANT ANY.

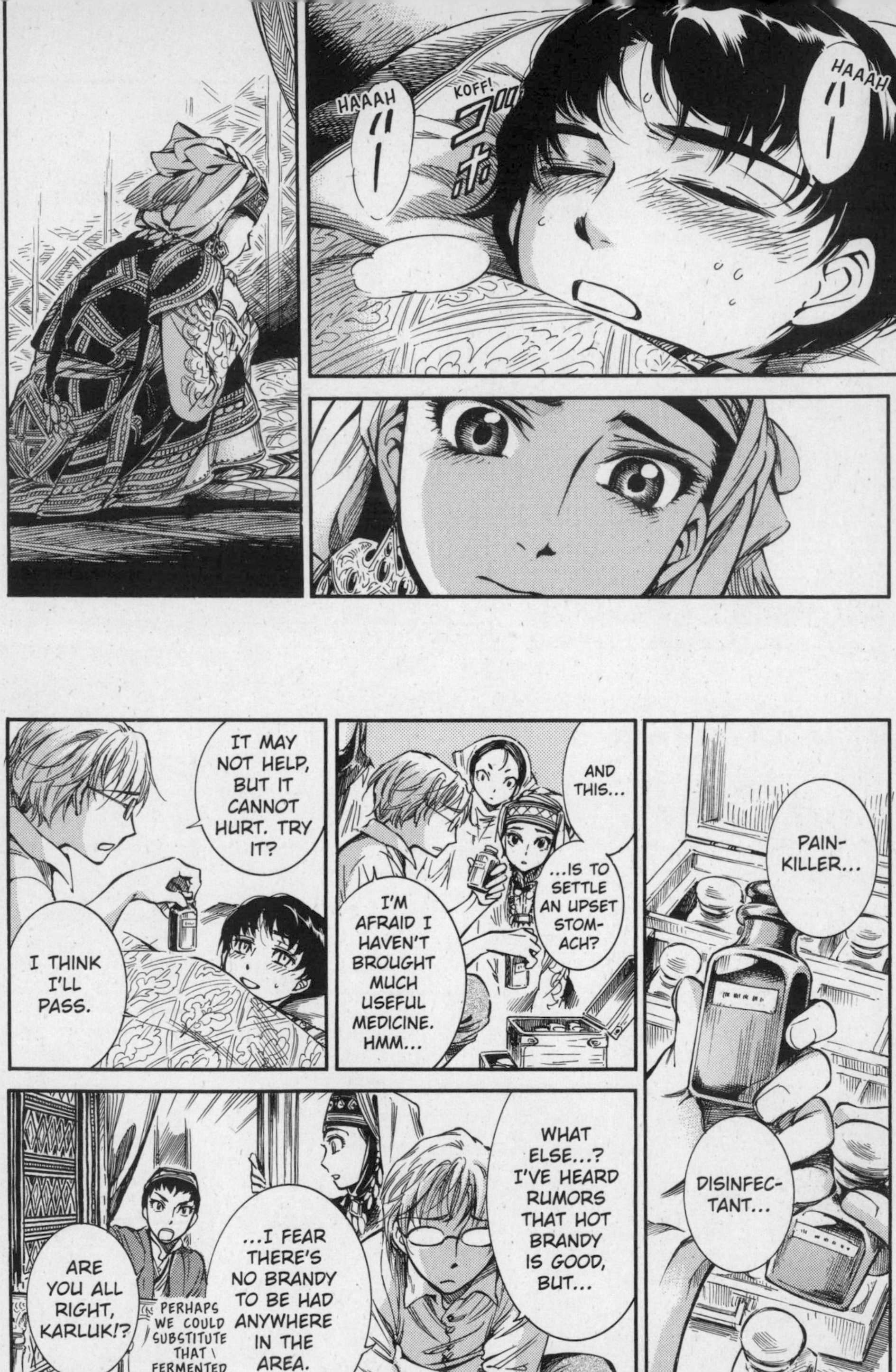
HAAAH
KOFF!
HAAAH
PAIN-KILLER...
DISINFEC-TANT...
AND THIS...
...IS TO SETTLE AN UPSET STOM-ACH?
I'M AFRAID I HAVEN'T BROUGHT MUCH USEFUL MEDICINE. HMM...
IT MAY NOT HELP, BUT IT CANNOT HURT. TRY IT?
I THINK I'LL PASS.
WHAT ELSE...? I'VE HEARD RUMORS THAT HOT BRANDY IS GOOD, BUT...
...I FEAR THERE'S NO BRANDY TO BE HAD ANYWHERE IN THE AREA.
PERHAPS WE COULD SUBSTITUTE THAT FERMENTED MARE'S MILK THEY HAVE...
ARE YOU ALL RIGHT, KARLUK!?

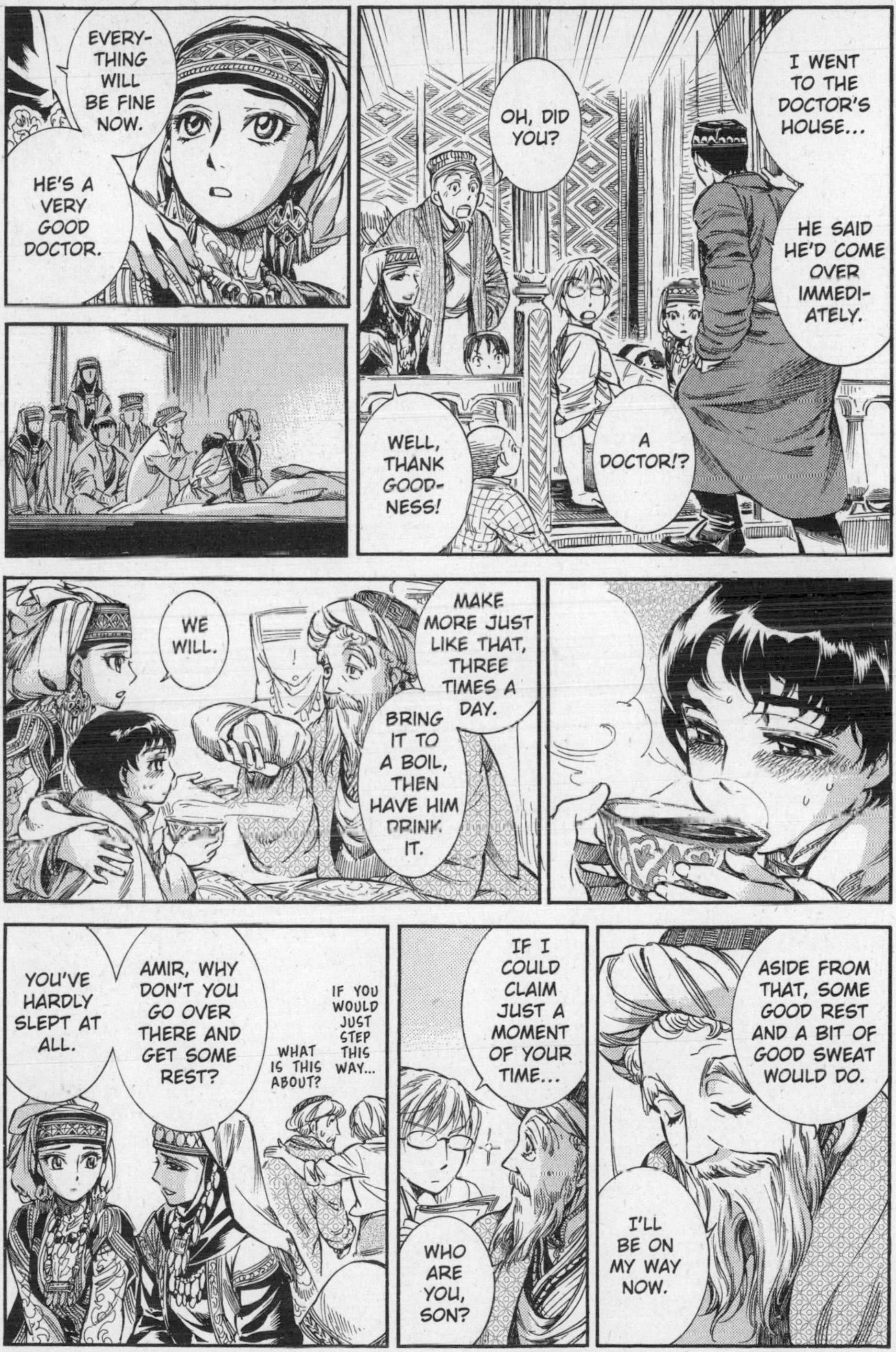
I WENT TO THE DOCTOR'S HOUSE...
HE SAID HE'D COME OVER IMMEDIATELY.
OH, DID YOU?
A DOCTOR!?
WELL, THANK GOODNESS!
EVERYTHING WILL BE FINE NOW.
HE'S A VERY GOOD DOCTOR.
MAKE MORE JUST LIKE THAT, THREE TIMES A DAY.
BRING IT TO A BOIL, THEN HAVE HIM DRINK IT.
WE WILL.
ASIDE FROM THAT, SOME GOOD REST AND A BIT OF GOOD SWEAT WOULD DO.
I'LL BE ON MY WAY NOW.
IF I COULD CLAIM JUST A MOMENT OF YOUR TIME...
WHO ARE YOU, SON?
IF YOU WOULD JUST STEP THIS WAY...
WHAT IS THIS ABOUT?
AMIR, WHY DON'T YOU GO OVER THERE AND GET SOME REST?
YOU'VE HARDLY SLEPT AT ALL.

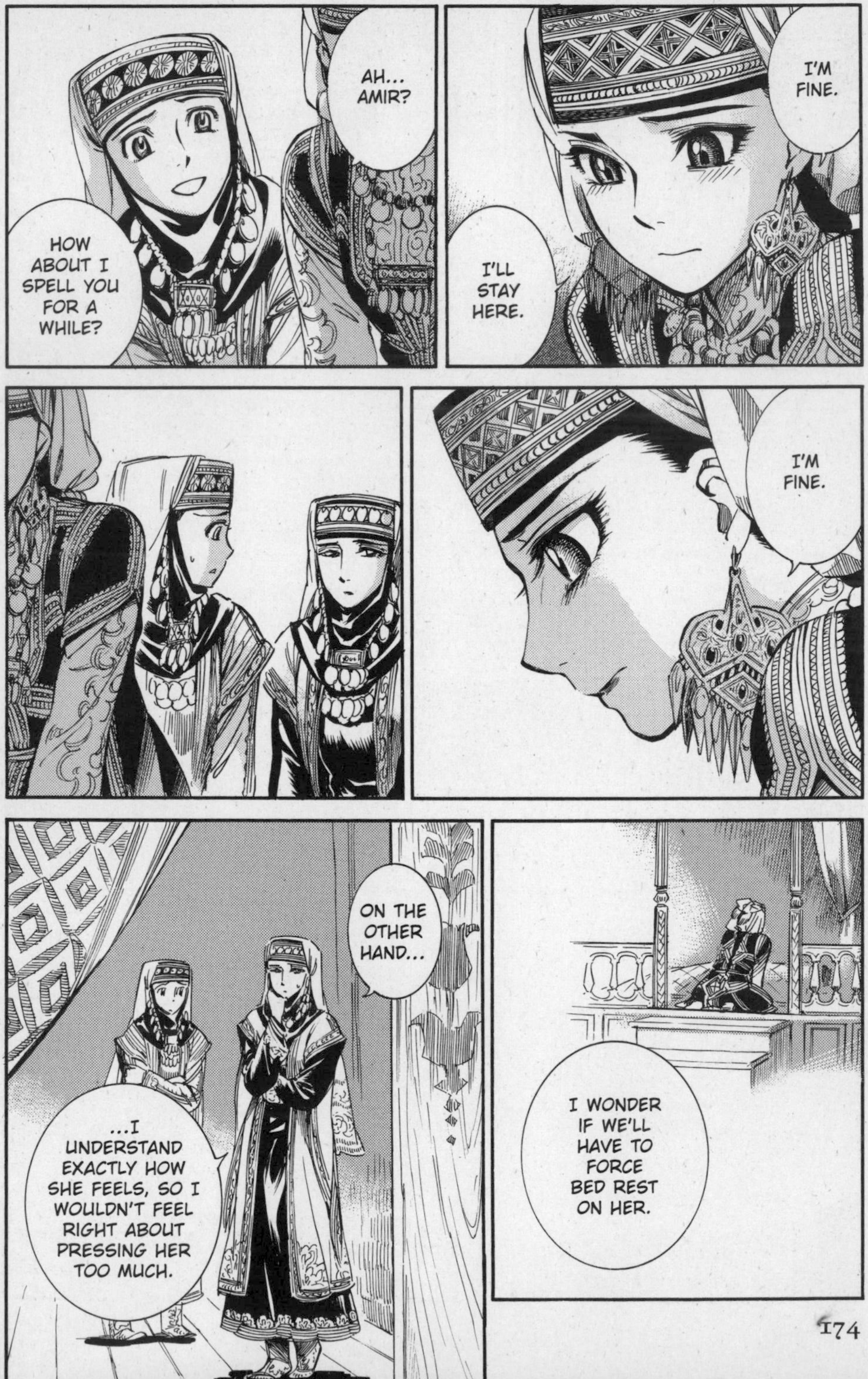
I'M FINE.
I'LL STAY HERE.
AH... AMIR?
HOW ABOUT I SPELL YOU FOR A WHILE?
I'M FINE.
I WONDER IF WE'LL HAVE TO FORCE BED REST ON HER.
ON THE OTHER HAND...
...I UNDERSTAND EXACTLY HOW SHE FEELS, SO I WOULDN'T FEEL RIGHT ABOUT PRESSING HER TOO MUCH.

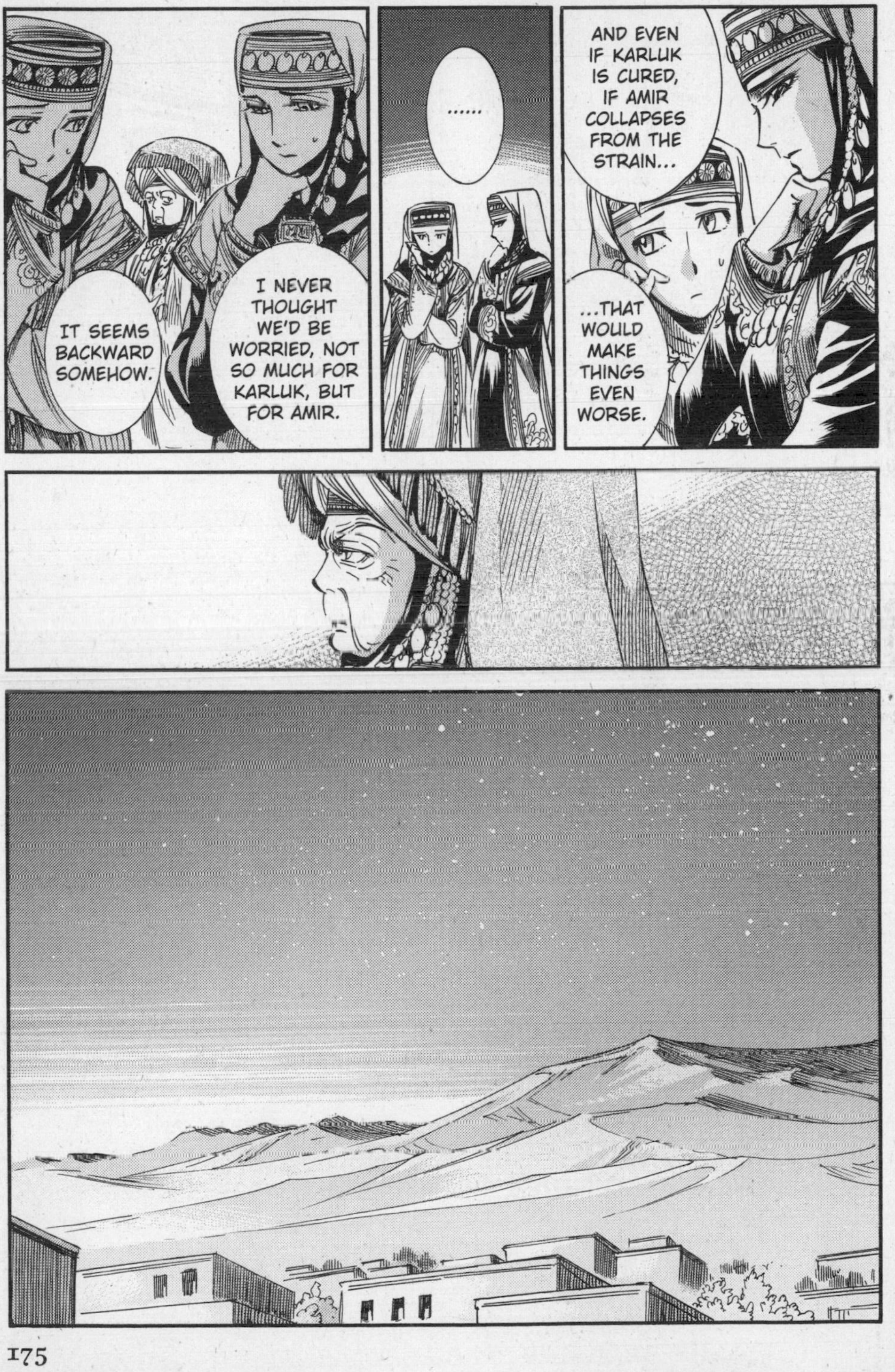
AND EVEN IF KARLUK IS CURED, IF AMIR COLLAPSES FROM THE STRAIN...
...THAT WOULD MAKE THINGS EVEN WORSE.
......
I NEVER THOUGHT WE'D BE WORRIED, NOT SO MUCH FOR KARLUK, BUT FOR AMIR.
IT SEEMS BACKWARD SOMEHOW.

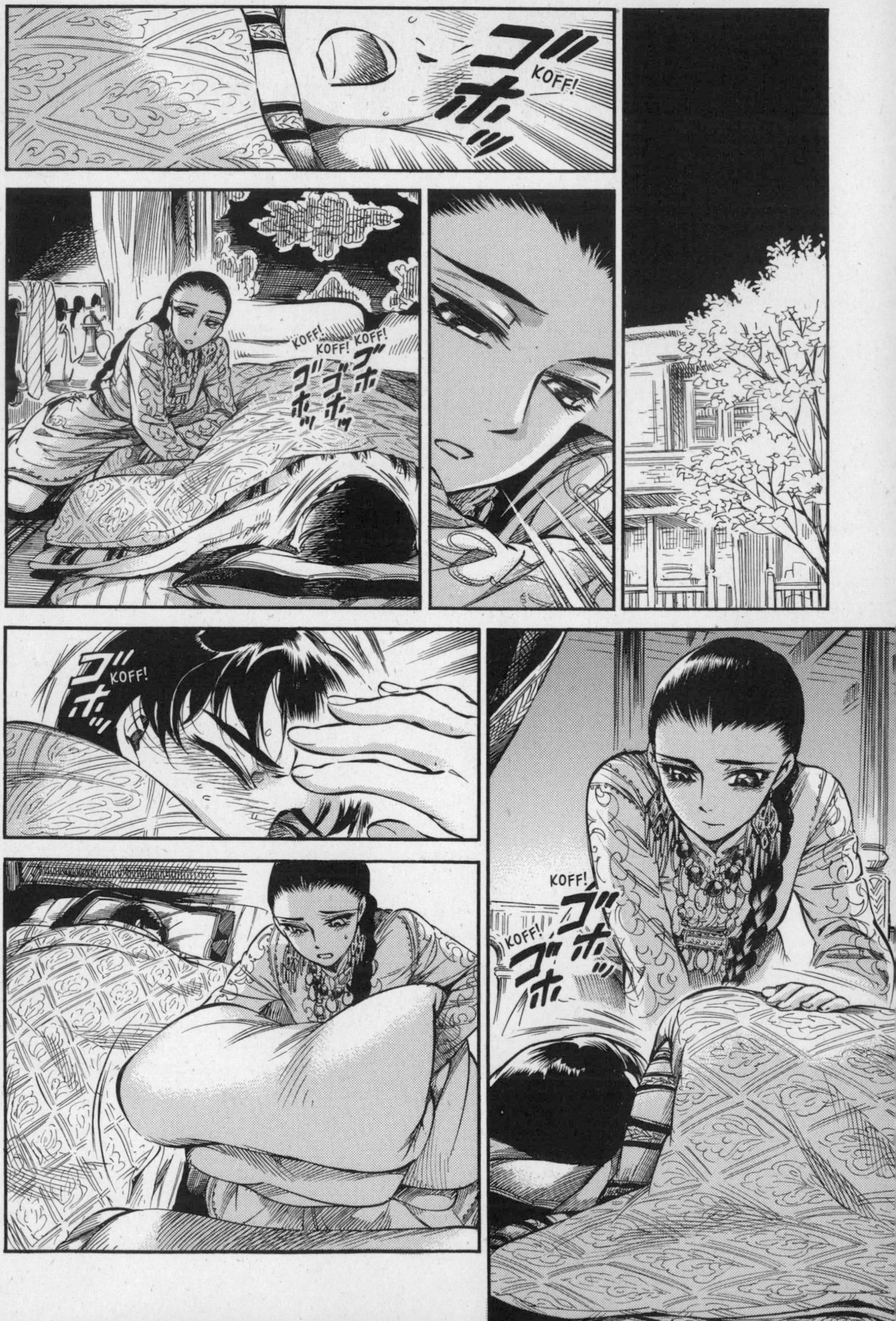
ゴホッ
KOFF!
KOFF! KOFF! KOFF!
ゴホ ゴホッ ゴホッ
KOFF!
ゴホッ
KOFF!
ゴホ
ゴホッ
KOFF!

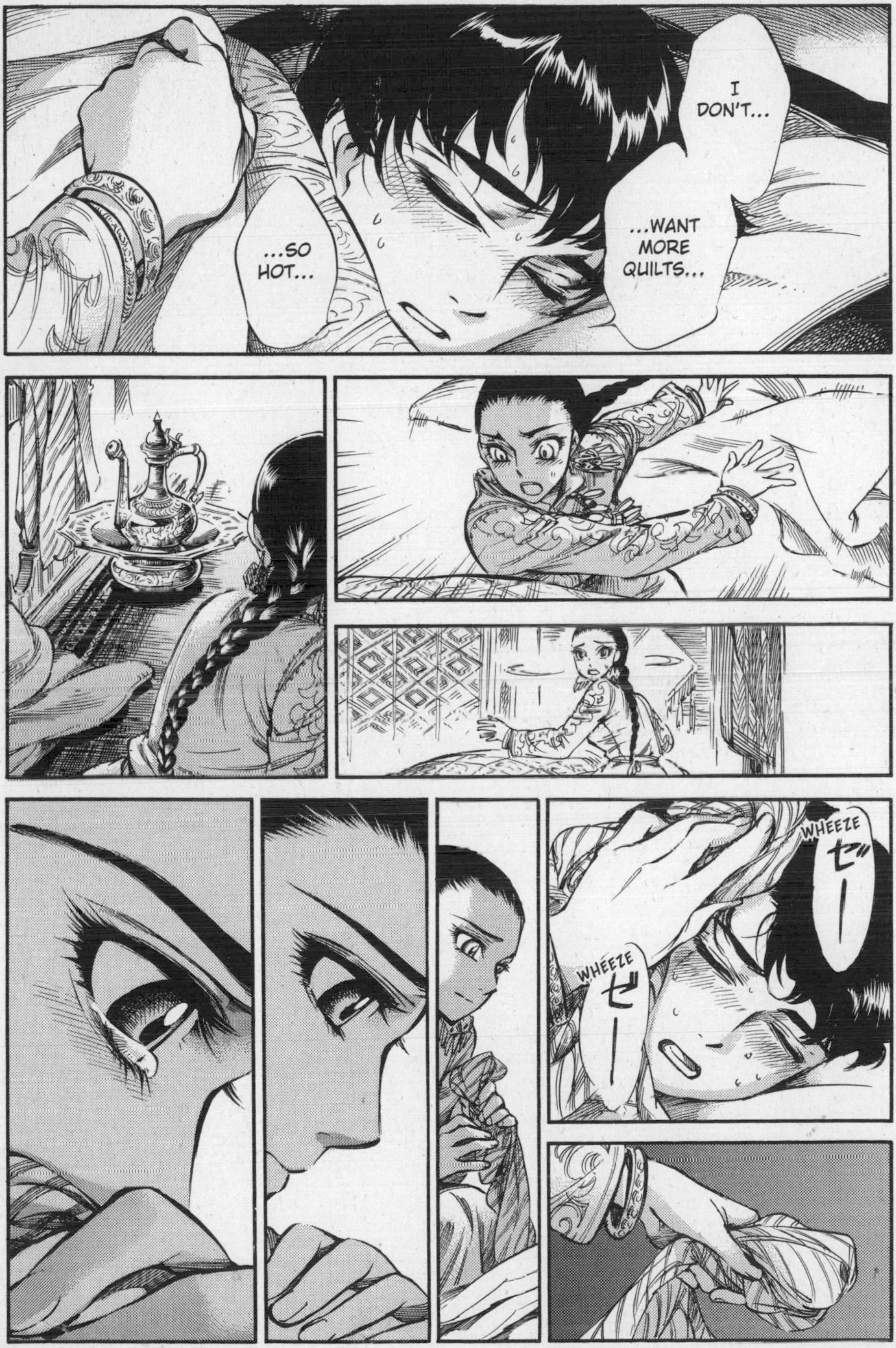
I DON'T...
...WANT MORE QUILTS...
...SO HOT...
WHEEZE
ゼー
WHEEZE
ゼー

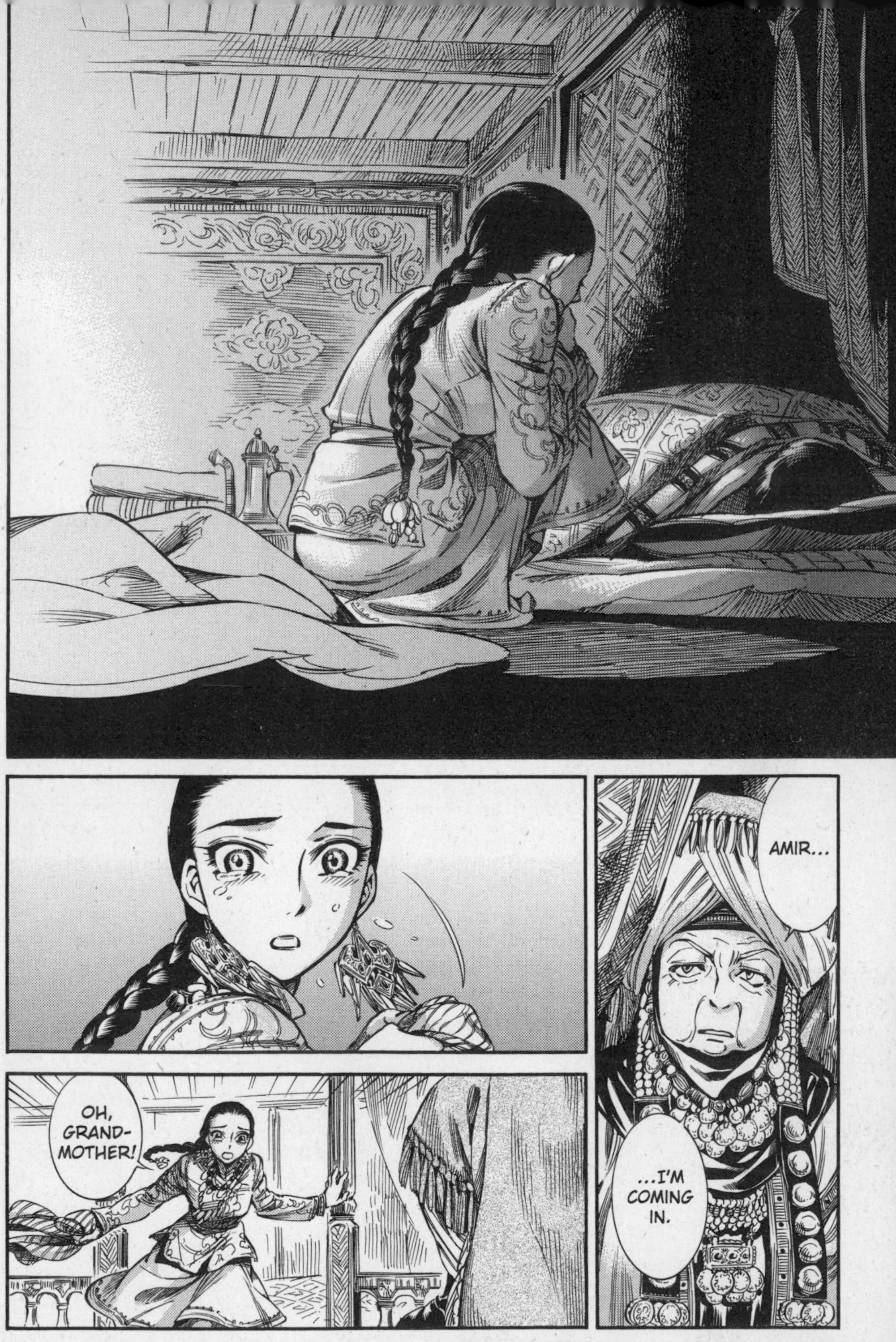
AMIR...
...I'M COMING IN.
OH, GRAND-MOTHER!

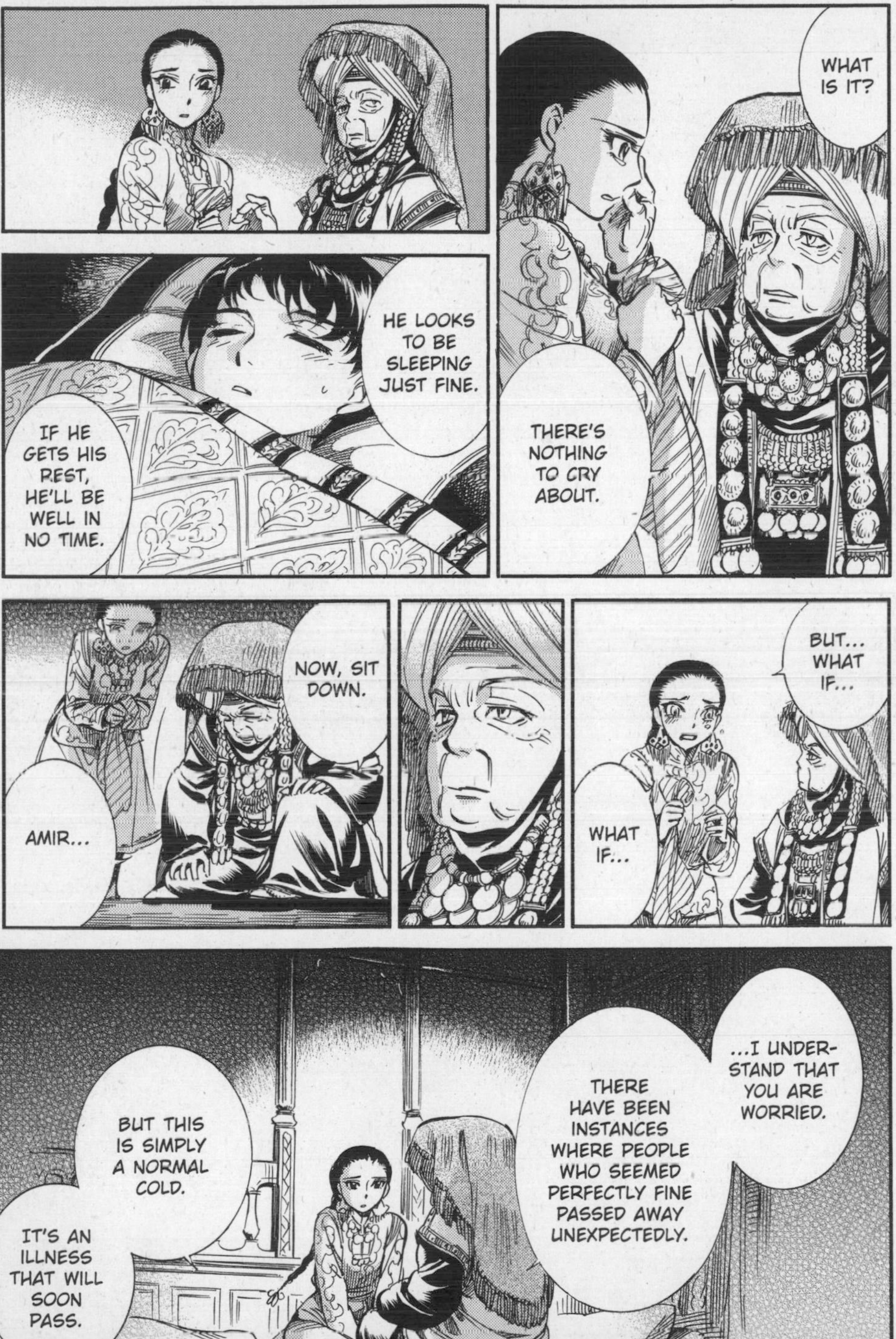
WHAT IS IT?
THERE'S NOTHING TO CRY ABOUT.
HE LOOKS TO BE SLEEPING JUST FINE.
IF HE GETS HIS REST, HE'LL BE WELL IN NO TIME.
BUT... WHAT IF...
WHAT IF...
NOW, SIT DOWN.
AMIR...
...I UNDER-STAND THAT YOU ARE WORRIED.
THERE HAVE BEEN INSTANCES WHERE PEOPLE WHO SEEMED PERFECTLY FINE PASSED AWAY UNEXPECTEDLY.
BUT THIS IS SIMPLY A NORMAL COLD.
IT'S AN ILLNESS THAT WILL SOON PASS.

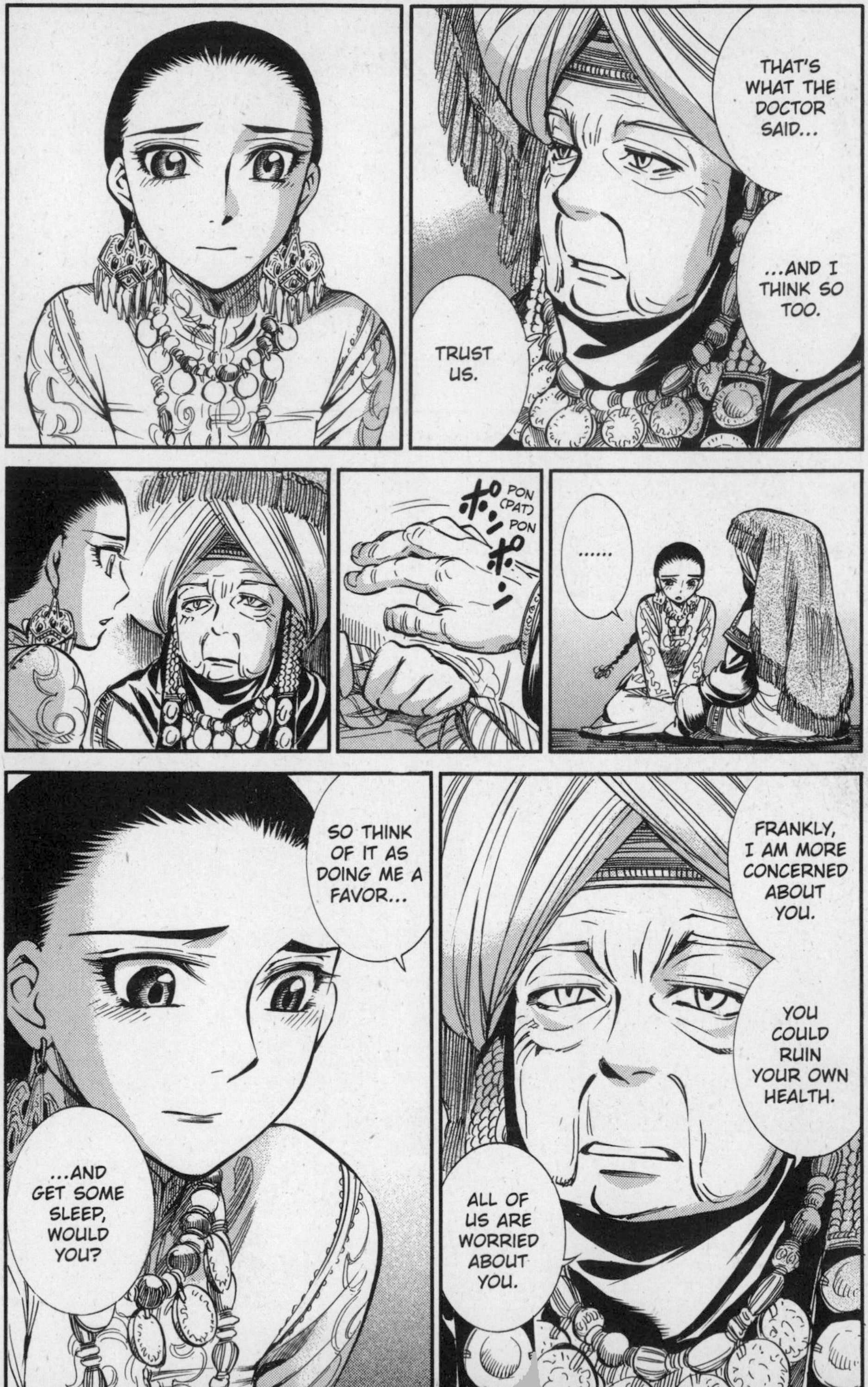
THAT'S WHAT THE DOCTOR SAID...
...AND I THINK SO TOO.
TRUST US.
......
ポンポン
PON (PAT) PON
FRANKLY, I AM MORE CONCERNED ABOUT YOU.
YOU COULD RUIN YOUR OWN HEALTH.
ALL OF US ARE WORRIED ABOUT YOU.
SO THINK OF IT AS DOING ME A FAVOR...
...AND GET SOME SLEEP, WOULD YOU?

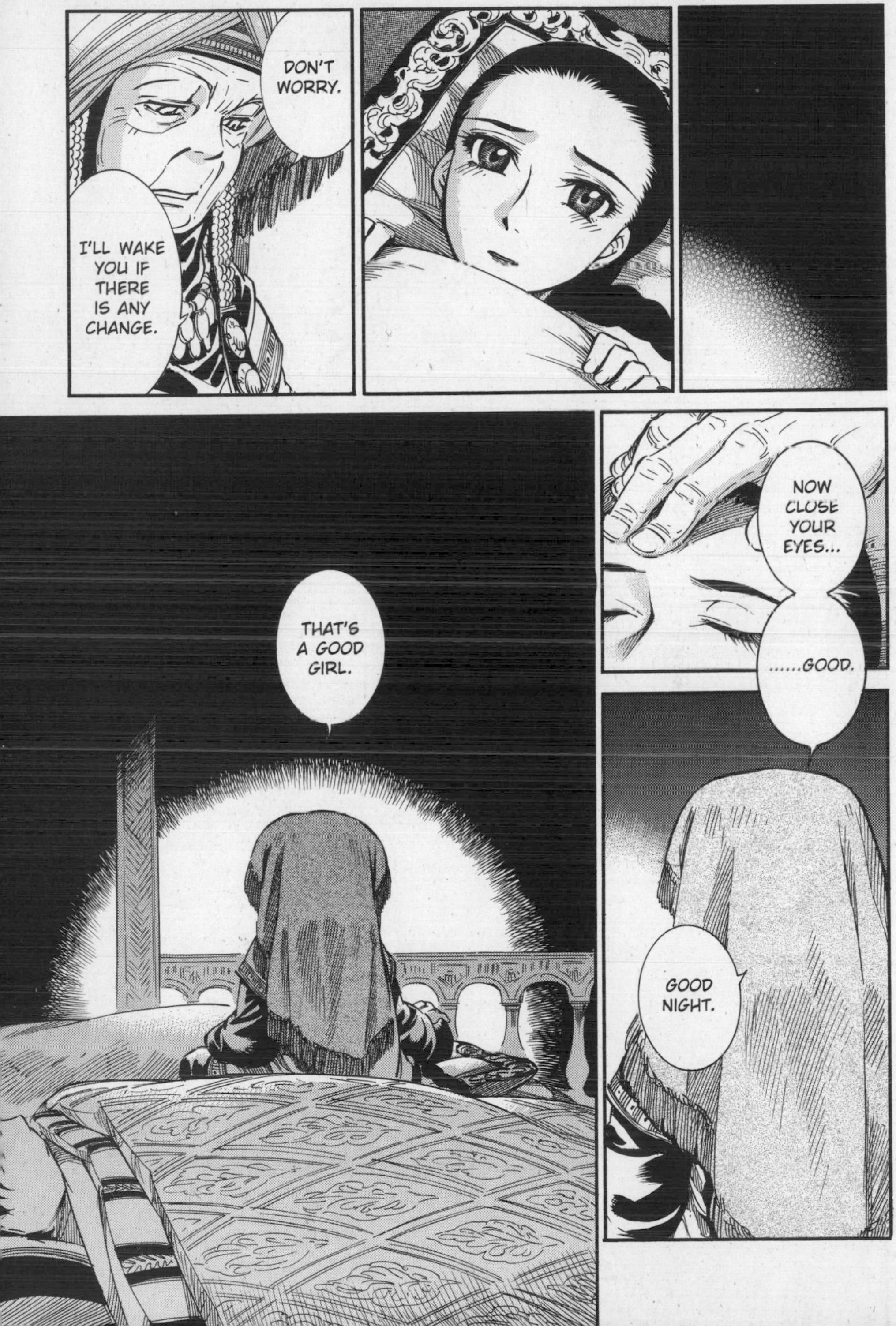
DON'T WORRY.
I'LL WAKE YOU IF THERE IS ANY CHANGE.
NOW CLOSE YOUR EYES...
......GOOD.
GOOD NIGHT.
THAT'S A GOOD GIRL.

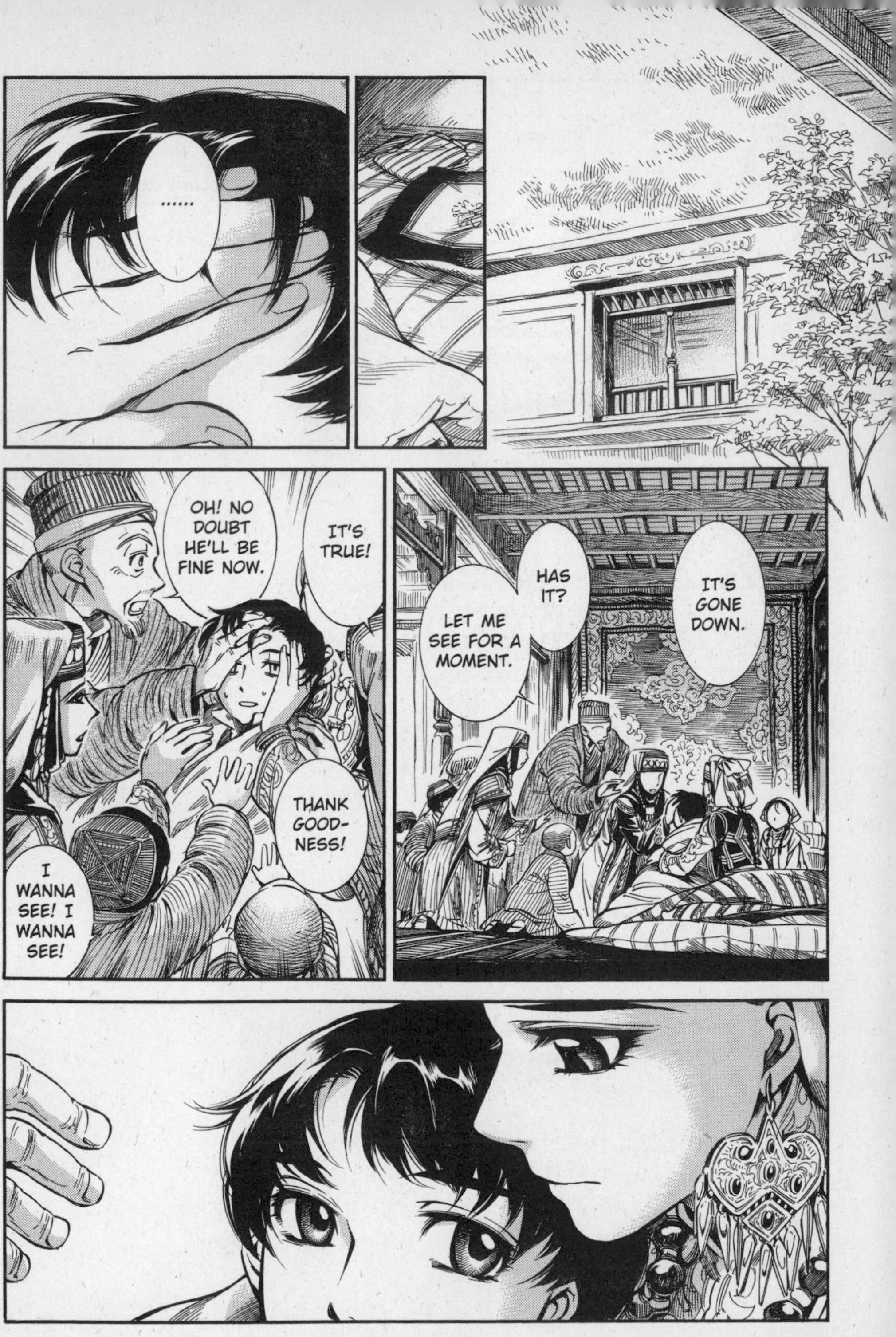
......
IT'S GONE DOWN.
HAS IT?
LET ME SEE FOR A MOMENT.
IT'S TRUE!
OH! NO DOUBT HE'LL BE FINE NOW.
THANK GOOD-NESS!
I WANNA SEE! I WANNA SEE!

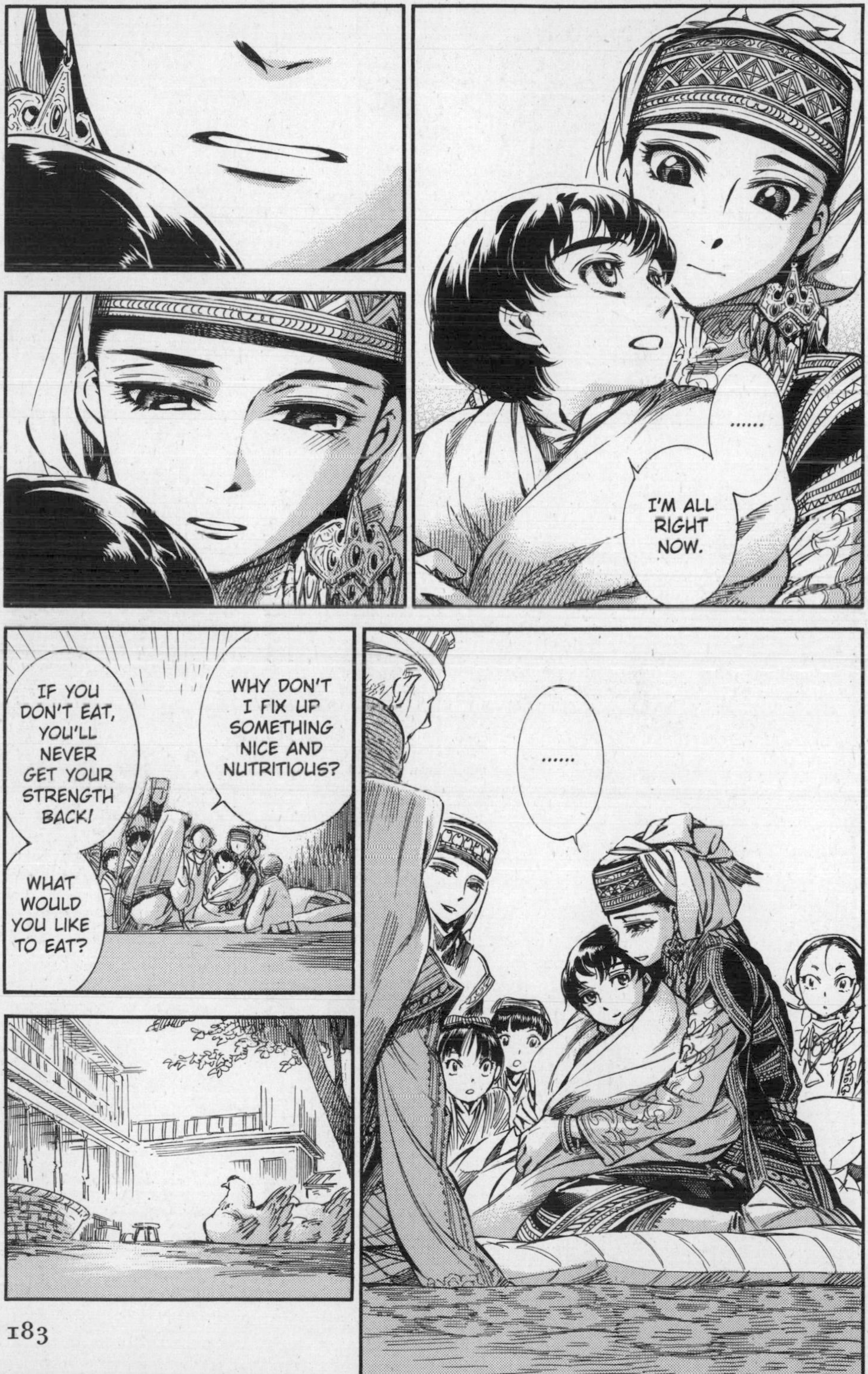
......
I'M ALL RIGHT NOW.
......
WHY DON'T I FIX UP SOMETHING NICE AND NUTRITIOUS?
IF YOU DON'T EAT, YOU'LL NEVER GET YOUR STRENGTH BACK!
WHAT WOULD YOU LIKE TO EAT?

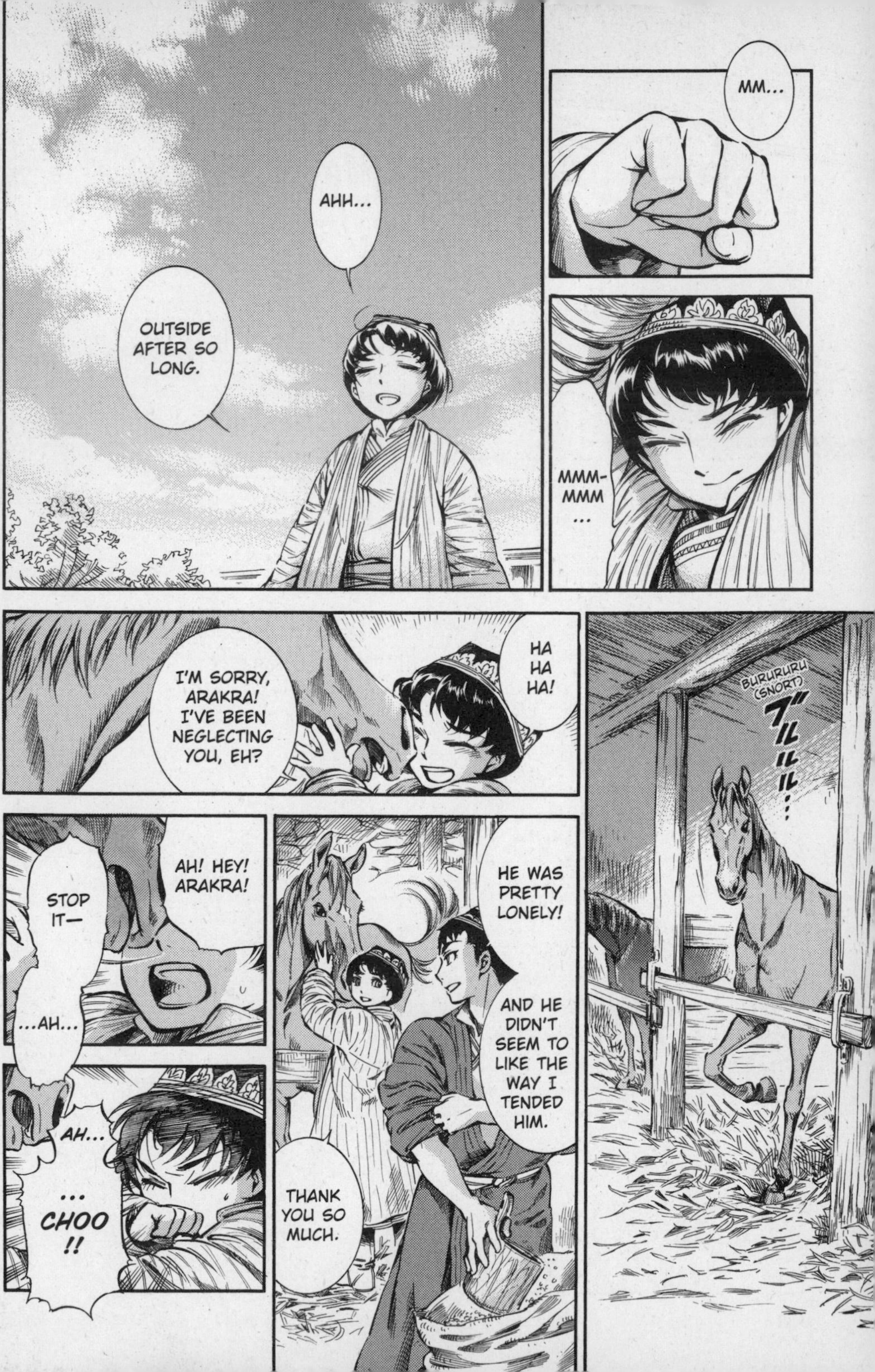
MM...
MMM-MMM ...
AHH...
OUTSIDE AFTER SO LONG.
BURURURU (SNORT)
ブルルル..!!
HA HA HA!
I'M SORRY, ARAKRA! I'VE BEEN NEGLECTING YOU, EH?
HE WAS PRETTY LONELY!
AND HE DIDN'T SEEM TO LIKE THE WAY I TENDED HIM.
THANK YOU SO MUCH.
AH! HEY! ARAKRA!
STOP IT—
...AH...
AH...
...CHOO!!

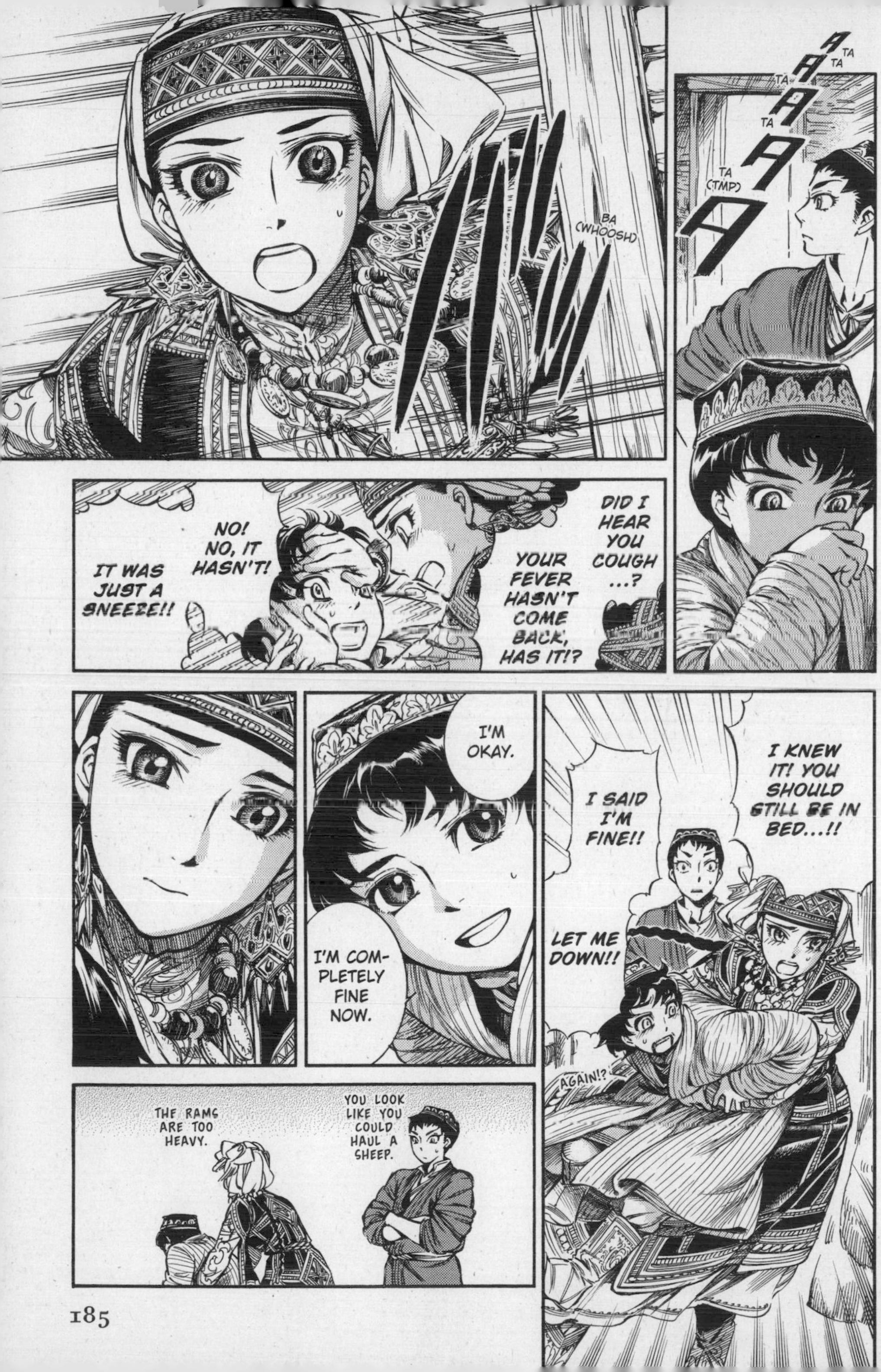
TA
TA
TA
TA
TA (TMP)
BA (WHOOSH)
DID I HEAR YOU COUGH ...?
YOUR FEVER HASN'T COME BACK, HAS IT!?
NO! NO, IT HASN'T!
IT WAS JUST A SNEEZE!!
I KNEW IT! YOU SHOULD STILL BE IN BED...!!
I SAID I'M FINE!!
LET ME DOWN!!
AGAIN!?
I'M OKAY.
I'M COMPLETELY FINE NOW.
YOU LOOK LIKE YOU COULD HAUL A SHEEP.
THE RAMS ARE TOO HEAVY.

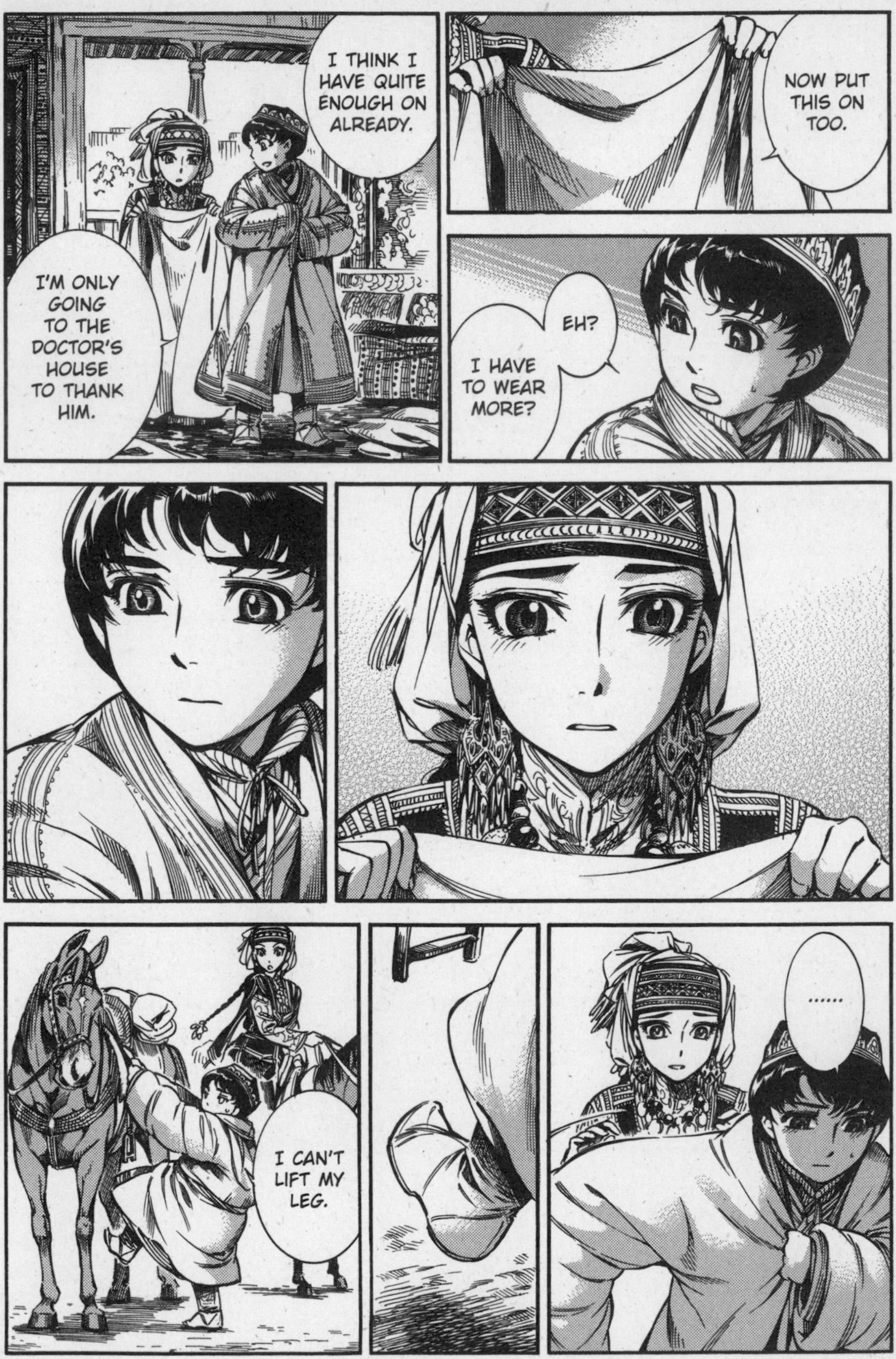
NOW PUT THIS ON TOO.
EH?
I HAVE TO WEAR MORE?
I THINK I HAVE QUITE ENOUGH ON ALREADY.
I'M ONLY GOING TO THE DOCTOR'S HOUSE TO THANK HIM.
......
I CAN'T LIFT MY LEG.

✦ CHAPTER FIVE: END ✦

AFTERWORD

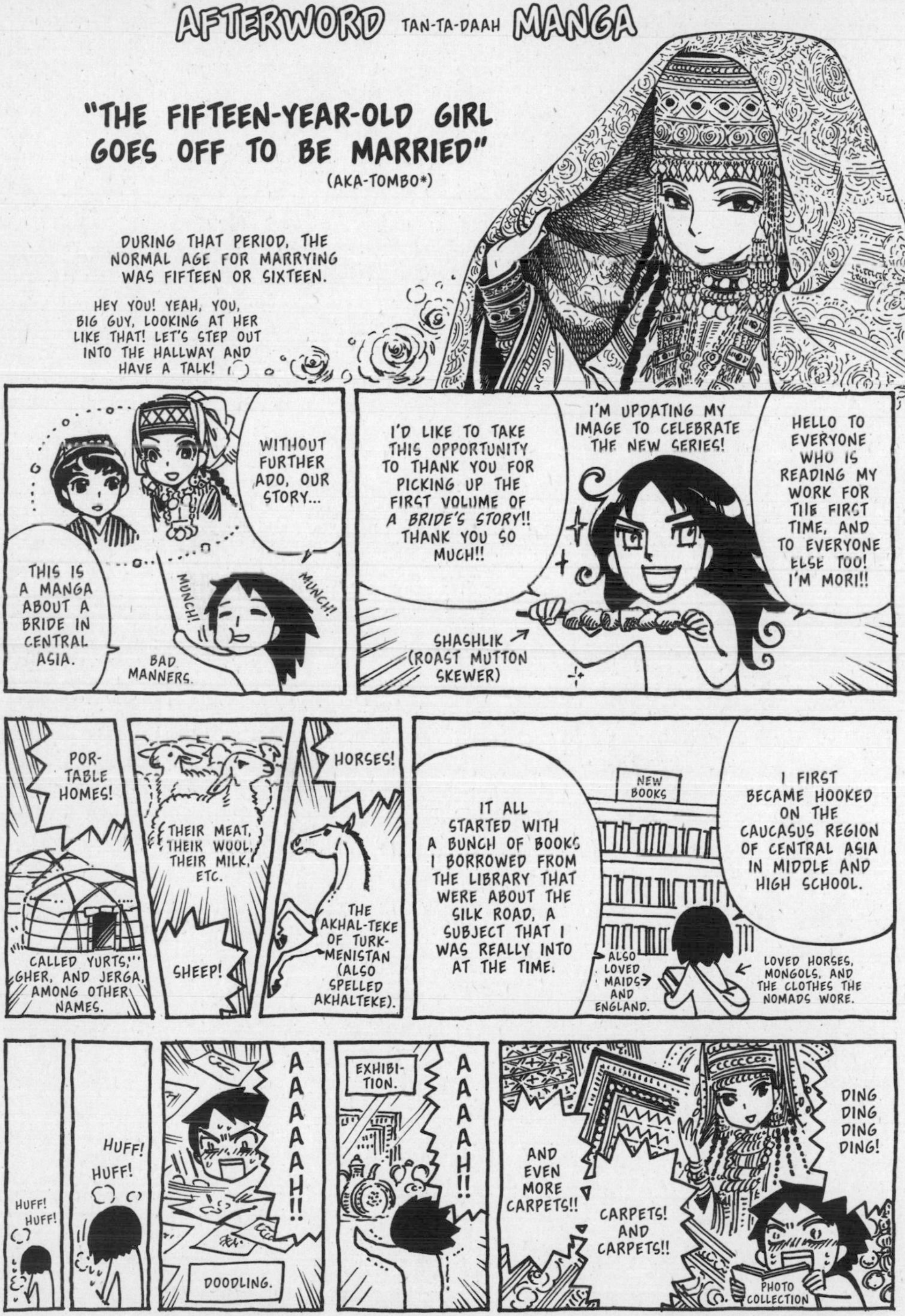

AFTERWORD TAN-TA-DAAH MANGA
"THE FIFTEEN-YEAR-OLD GIRL GOES OFF TO BE MARRIED"
(AKA-TOMBO*)
DURING THAT PERIOD, THE NORMAL AGE FOR MARRYING WAS FIFTEEN OR SIXTEEN.
HEY YOU! YEAH, YOU, BIG GUY, LOOKING AT HER LIKE THAT! LET'S STEP OUT INTO THE HALLWAY AND HAVE A TALK!
HELLO TO EVERYONE WHO IS READING MY WORK FOR THE FIRST TIME, AND TO EVERYONE ELSE TOO! I'M MORI!!
I'M UPDATING MY IMAGE TO CELEBRATE THE NEW SERIES!
I'D LIKE TO TAKE THIS OPPORTUNITY TO THANK YOU FOR PICKING UP THE FIRST VOLUME OF *A BRIDE'S STORY*!! THANK YOU SO MUCH!!
SHASHLIK (ROAST MUTTON SKEWER)
WITHOUT FURTHER ADO, OUR STORY...
MUNCH!
MUNCH!
THIS IS A MANGA ABOUT A BRIDE IN CENTRAL ASIA.
BAD MANNERS.
I FIRST BECAME HOOKED ON THE CAUCASUS REGION OF CENTRAL ASIA IN MIDDLE AND HIGH SCHOOL.
IT ALL STARTED WITH A BUNCH OF BOOKS I BORROWED FROM THE LIBRARY THAT WERE ABOUT THE SILK ROAD, A SUBJECT THAT I WAS REALLY INTO AT THE TIME.
NEW BOOKS
LOVED HORSES, MONGOLS, AND THE CLOTHES THE NOMADS WORE.
ALSO LOVED MAIDS AND ENGLAND.
HORSES!
THE AKHAL-TEKE OF TURK-MENISTAN (ALSO SPELLED AKHALTEKE).
THEIR MEAT, THEIR WOOL, THEIR MILK, ETC.
SHEEP!
POR-TABLE HOMES!
CALLED YURTS, GHER, AND JERGA, AMONG OTHER NAMES.
DING DING DING DING!
AND EVEN MORE CARPETS!!
CARPETS! AND CARPETS!!
PHOTO COLLECTION
AAAAAH!!
EXHIBI-TION.
AAAAAH!!
DOODLING.
HUFF!
HUFF!
HUFF!
HUFF!

**AKATOMBO* IS A POEM WRITTEN IN 1921, WHICH WAS SET TO MUSIC IN 1927. IT TELLS THE TALE OF A CHILD WHO SEES A RED DRAGONFLY (AKATOMBO) WHILE BEING CARRIED BY THE FIFTEEN-YEAR-OLD GIRL WHO LOOKED AFTER HIM. NOT LONG AFTER, THE GIRL IS SENT OFF TO BE MARRIED, AND HE NEVER HEARS FROM HER AGAIN. THE SONG CALLS UP IMAGES OF VERY YOUNG BRIDES IN JAPANESE LISTENERS.

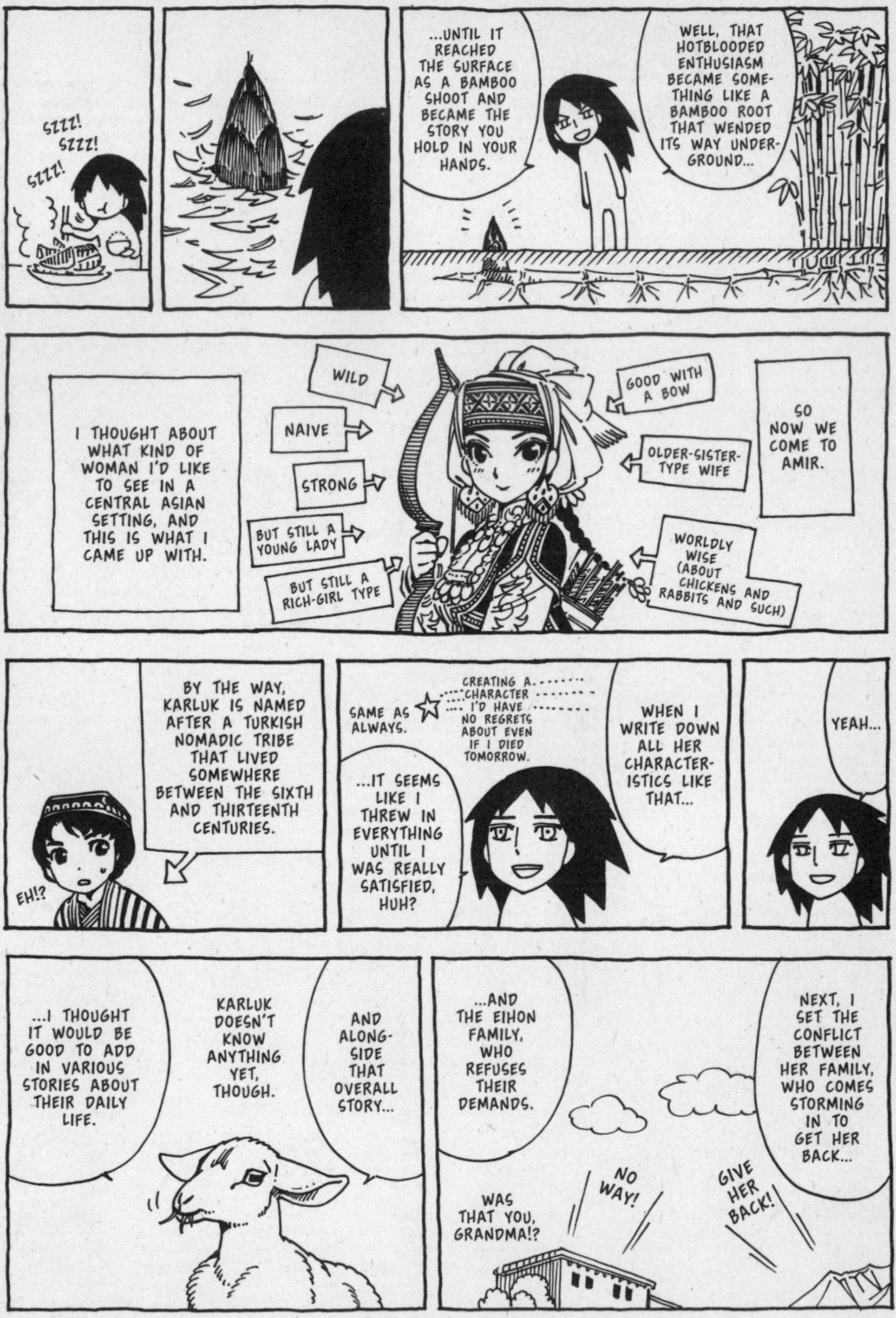
WELL, THAT HOTBLOODED ENTHUSIASM BECAME SOMETHING LIKE A BAMBOO ROOT THAT WENDED ITS WAY UNDERGROUND...
...UNTIL IT REACHED THE SURFACE AS A BAMBOO SHOOT AND BECAME THE STORY YOU HOLD IN YOUR HANDS.
SZZZ! SZZZ!
SZZZ!
SO NOW WE COME TO AMIR.
GOOD WITH A BOW
WILD
NAIVE
OLDER-SISTER-TYPE WIFE
STRONG
WORLDLY WISE (ABOUT CHICKENS AND RABBITS AND SUCH)
BUT STILL A YOUNG LADY
BUT STILL A RICH-GIRL TYPE
I THOUGHT ABOUT WHAT KIND OF WOMAN I'D LIKE TO SEE IN A CENTRAL ASIAN SETTING, AND THIS IS WHAT I CAME UP WITH.
YEAH...
WHEN I WRITE DOWN ALL HER CHARACTERISTICS LIKE THAT...
...IT SEEMS LIKE I THREW IN EVERYTHING UNTIL I WAS REALLY SATISFIED, HUH?
SAME AS ALWAYS. ☆ CREATING A CHARACTER I'D HAVE NO REGRETS ABOUT EVEN IF I DIED TOMORROW.
BY THE WAY, KARLUK IS NAMED AFTER A TURKISH NOMADIC TRIBE THAT LIVED SOMEWHERE BETWEEN THE SIXTH AND THIRTEENTH CENTURIES.
EH!?
NEXT, I SET THE CONFLICT BETWEEN HER FAMILY, WHO COMES STORMING IN TO GET HER BACK...
...AND THE EIHON FAMILY, WHO REFUSES THEIR DEMANDS.
GIVE HER BACK!
NO WAY!
WAS THAT YOU, GRANDMA!?
AND ALONGSIDE THAT OVERALL STORY...
KARLUK DOESN'T KNOW ANYTHING YET, THOUGH.
...I THOUGHT IT WOULD BE GOOD TO ADD IN VARIOUS STORIES ABOUT THEIR DAILY LIFE.

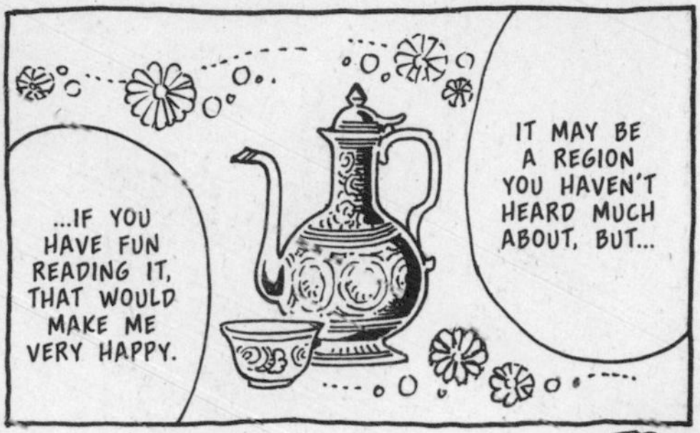
IT MAY BE A REGION YOU HAVEN'T HEARD MUCH ABOUT, BUT...
...IF YOU HAVE FUN READING IT, THAT WOULD MAKE ME VERY HAPPY.

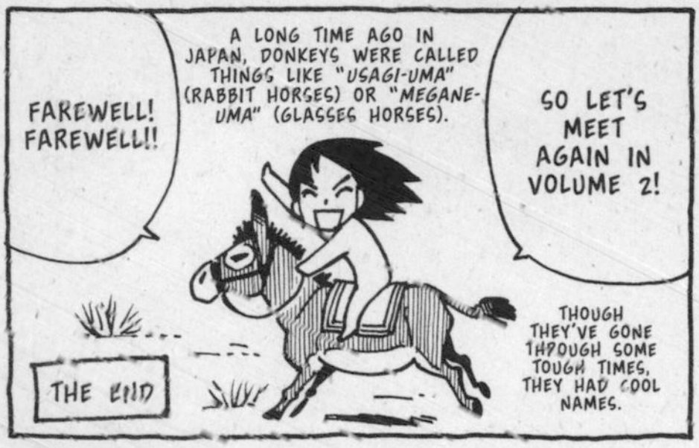
SO LET'S MEET AGAIN IN VOLUME 2!
THOUGH THEY'VE GONE THROUGH SOME TOUGH TIMES, THEY HAD COOL NAMES.
A LONG TIME AGO IN JAPAN, DONKEYS WERE CALLED THINGS LIKE "USAGI-UMA" (RABBIT HORSES) OR "MEGANE-UMA" (GLASSES HORSES).
FAREWELL! FAREWELL!!
THE END

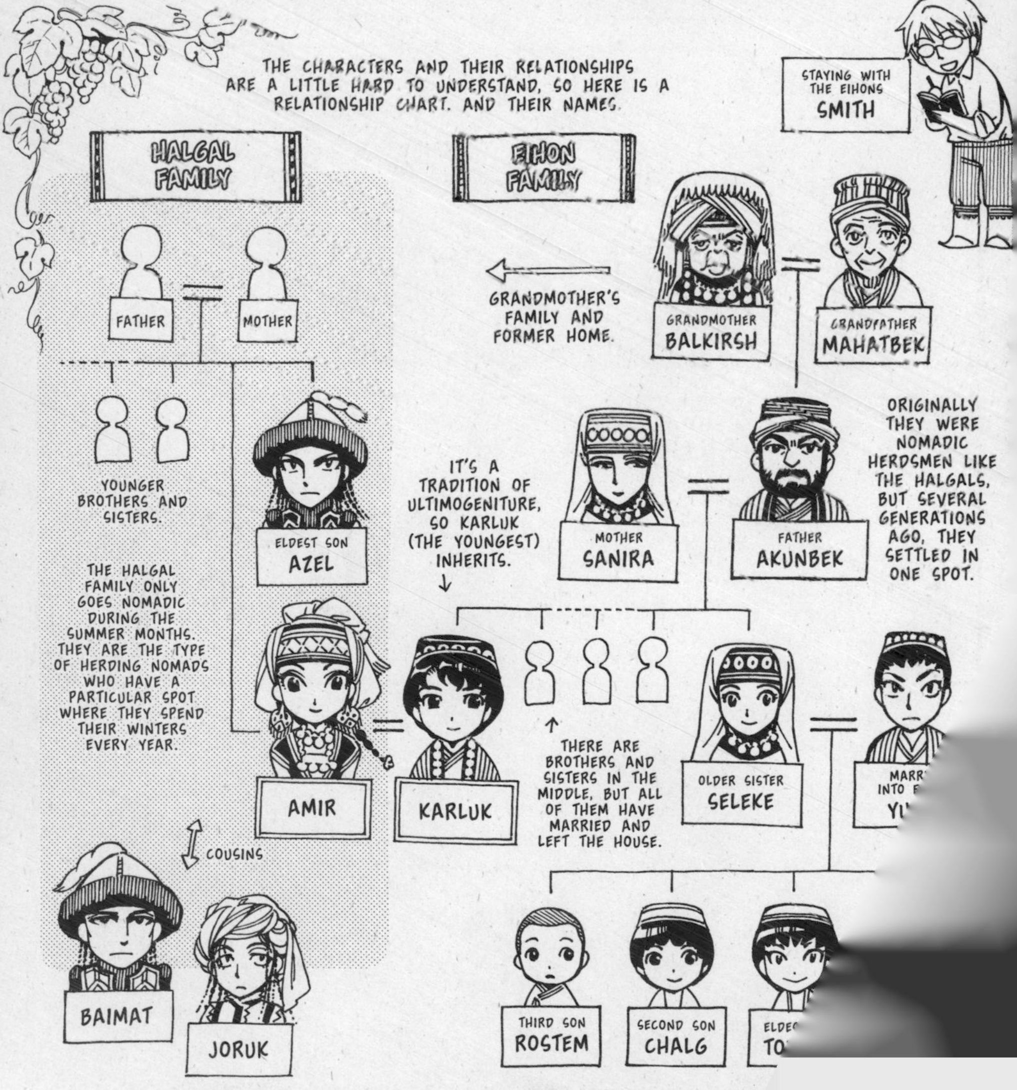
THE CHARACTERS AND THEIR RELATIONSHIPS ARE A LITTLE HARD TO UNDERSTAND, SO HERE IS A RELATIONSHIP CHART. AND THEIR NAMES.
STAYING WITH THE EIHONS
SMITH
HALGAL FAMILY
EIHON FAMILY
FATHER
MOTHER
GRANDMOTHER'S FAMILY AND FORMER HOME.
GRANDMOTHER
BALKIRSH
GRANDFATHER
MAHATBEK
YOUNGER BROTHERS AND SISTERS.
ELDEST SON
AZEL
THE HALGAL FAMILY ONLY GOES NOMADIC DURING THE SUMMER MONTHS. THEY ARE THE TYPE OF HERDING NOMADS WHO HAVE A PARTICULAR SPOT WHERE THEY SPEND THEIR WINTERS EVERY YEAR.
IT'S A TRADITION OF ULTIMOGENITURE, SO KARLUK (THE YOUNGEST) INHERITS.
MOTHER
SANIRA
FATHER
AKUNBEK
ORIGINALLY THEY WERE NOMADIC HERDSMEN LIKE THE HALGALS, BUT SEVERAL GENERATIONS AGO, THEY SETTLED IN ONE SPOT.
AMIR
KARLUK
THERE ARE BROTHERS AND SISTERS IN THE MIDDLE, BUT ALL OF THEM HAVE MARRIED AND LEFT THE HOUSE.
OLDER SISTER
SELEKE
COUSINS
BAIMAT
JORUK
THIRD SON
ROSTEM
SECOND SON
CHALG

A BRIDE'S STORY ①

KAORU MORI

TRANSLATION: WILLIAM FLANNAGAN

LETTERING: ABIGAIL BLACKMAN

First published in Japan in 2009 by ENTERBRAIN, INC., Tokyo.
English translation rights arranged with ENTERBRAIN, INC.
through Tuttle-Mori Agency, Inc., Tokyo.

The characters and events in this book are fictitious. Any similarity to real persons, living or dead, is coincidental and not intended by the author.

Yen Press
Hachette Book Group
237 Park Avenue, New York, NY 10017

www.HachetteBookGroup.com
www.YenPress.com

Yen Press is an imprint of Hachette Book Group, Inc. The Yen Press name and logo are trademarks of Hachette Book Group, Inc.

First Yen Press Edition: May 2011

ISBN: 978-0-316-18099-3

10 9 8 7 6 5 4 3 2 1

BVG

Printed in the United States of America

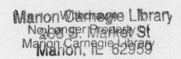

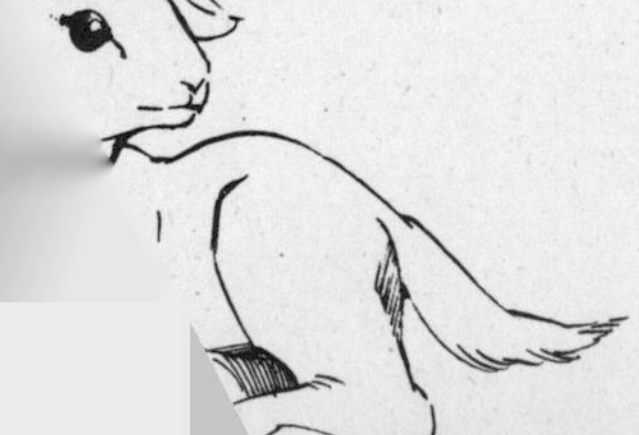

[redacted]